STAR MAGE

The Enslaved Chronicles: Book 3

R. K. Thorne

IRON ANTLER BOOKS

PITTSBURGH, PENNSYLVANIA

Edited by Elizabeth Nover, www.razorsharpediting.com
Cover design by Damonza, damonza.com
Book design by Iron Antler Books, Text set in Adobe Garamond,
Adapted from design by ©2015 BookDesignTemplates.com

For Mrs. Leonardo, who first taught me to reach down, open my heart up, and bleed on the page.

And for Joanna, who loves freedom as much as I do. Thank you for teaching me the priceless lesson of taking myself seriously.

Contents

THE GREAT
NORTHERN
KINGDOMS

SVERTI

Levapa

ISOLTE

WINOKIN

ESENGARD

Kewisali

HEPAN

Helanai

Sicat

KAVANAR

Sapana

Mage Hall

Esttore

ELAREN

AKARIA

Sobarionis

LIREN

Astennil

GILAREN

DRAMSREN

Levial

Lake
Seoseko

Smoar

TAKAR

Denerasii

SHANSAREN

Evrisal

Patnar

NUMAREN

FAEREN

Slevano

Shutnutis

GULF OF
PANAR

DETRAT

Ardenoai

Teualt

FARSA

SOUTHWESTERN
KINGDOMS

ZYGEAN
KINGDOMS

STAR MAGE

I   SEARCHING

Blackness weighed down on Thel, darker than any Estun cellar, reassuring in that he must be alive, ominous in that he wasn't sure how long that would last. His forearm had been trapped against his face by the weight, a minor blessing of protection, but angular shapes jutted into his chest, his thigh, his kidney. His everywhere, really, although the jabs from below him were warm against his back. He coughed involuntarily, then grunted as his body spasmed painfully beneath whatever was crushing him. Dust was thick on his tongue, in his throat. What the hell had happened? How had he gotten here?

It came rushing back—the voting both for and against his brother Aven, Alikar's bribing of the Assembly members, the side of the tower exploding, rubble flying.

Ah, yes. The rubble. That was the heaviness, the weight on all sides. And yet, being crushed by rock shouldn't be quite so comfortable. Something else was at play.

Yes, he could feel it now. His magic kept the rock from completely suffocating him, he could feel it now. Was the pressure lessening even now as he thought about it, or was it just his imagination?

No, indeed, he could sense more. He could feel rocks like another limb, as though he'd extended his awareness into them, could feel other rocks beyond.

Curious.

Also—just how deeply was he buried?

Panic flooded him for a moment, and it did not ease when his next breath was even thicker with dust. Gods. He fought down the panic, pressed it back and out of the forefront of his mind. Panic would get him nowhere. He had to *think*.

He was already using his magic. By all rights he should be crushed to a gooey pulp. Had he protected himself? Hmm. What had that book said? Tucked inside his jerkin, it wasn't very useful right now. It was just as crushed as he was. He hadn't gotten far learning any earth magic from it.

He'd only coaxed his mage status out of Miara a week ago. He and Teron had been the only earth mages at Estun, both untrained, so they'd searched the stronghold's library and turned up a single, palm-sized volume bound in black leather. But he hadn't had nearly enough time to study it and really learn anything.

And yet. He *should* be able to move the rock, he'd read that much. A truly untested hypothesis indeed. Reaching out around him, he sensed more rock but not an infinite amount. Above him, it ended rather quickly.

Below him, it stretched on and on... And there was something that wasn't rock.

A feminine voice groaned softly, a few inches from his ear. Well, that wasn't exactly the sound he wanted to elicit from a woman, and certainly not in this circumstance. Time to see if his magic was good for anything to get him—them?—out of here.

What had that book said to do? It had blathered on a lot about visualization. How was he supposed to visualize something he couldn't even see? And *why*? It wasn't like he needed to see the rock in order to feel it. Why couldn't there be magic words like in the old stories? Then again, his tongue was thick enough with dust that soon he might not be able to say much, so perhaps that was fortuitous.

Fine. Fine. He held an image of a pebble in his mind. Now what? A hill. Yes, a hill. And now... it's rolling down the hill.

Nothing happened. Bollocks.

The voice moaned now, and something shifted under his right kidney. Oh, by the gods, yes, the female voice was clearly crushed underneath him. Awful.

All right. Uh, a pebble... no, a boulder. He pictured himself underneath it. And some more boulders. And then gradually, in his mind, each boulder floated up into the air, into the sky, and most importantly, off of *him*.

A clatter came first, then another shudder, then a thud and a crack or two. Light fell across his closed eyelids, and warmth hit his face.

He opened his eyes but immediately regretted it as

dust went straight in. Trying to lift a hand to his face sent more rocks flying and dust swirling, but—his arm was free.

Wincing, coughing, gasping, he struggled to roll to his left, go forward, to get up in some way that hopefully didn't crush the person beneath him any further.

He shook his head, trying to clear it, and finally turned out the inside of his tunic and wiped his eyes. The room came into slow focus. A gaping hole in the tower yawned a few yards from his feet. Nearly two floors had been cut into by the bombardment, or had collapsed afterward, and rubble was everywhere. Beyond the chasm, the rest of the chamber they'd met in remained but was now empty. Something bizarrely like thunder followed by brief bouts of sharp rain fell in the distance, like a brief moment of hail that ended as soon as it had begun. Strange. Blinking to clear his eyes, he peered back at the hole he'd climbed out of.

A young woman sat in the cavity, equally bleary-eyed and coughing but clearly alive. Was that his handiwork, or was it luck? Her dress had been poor protection against the stone onslaught, its white now tinged to the pale color of bone, the thin gauze ripped in several places. Was that blood? Hair still a shade of near white fell in dramatic curls around her sharp, angular features and expressive, kohl-lined eyes.

She would be attractive if she weren't a traitor. The priestess Niat. He refused to let himself think amorously of anyone of her moral fabric; the mind was a thousand times more important than the corporeal form.

He stepped forward and held out a hand to help her up. She squinted and frowned at him but accepted, stumbling to her feet. Temple sandals were also of little practical use against the rocky terrain she now found herself in, but then again, she hadn't been planning on a hike, now had she?

She stumbled against him, and he caught her, just barely. Apparently they were both due some good luck because when Thel ran toward a falling person, the poor soul usually ended up sprawled on the floor. Years of combat training had given him little grace and only moderate reflexes. Oh, he wasn't half bad when he was paying attention. But he usually wasn't. His thoughts were often elsewhere.

That training *had* afforded him some strength, however much less than his brothers, and now he lifted her out of the depression they'd been trapped in and set her on her feet on the open floor behind him. Then he carefully stepped down and around her, hoping not to send either of them stumbling into the nearby gaping chasm by mistake.

He tried to meet her eyes, but she stared up at the sky, openmouthed. They hadn't been under there *that* long, had they? He followed her gaze.

Above them, a dozen stones of various sizes floated in air. Most were pieces of the masonry that had once been the walls of the tower, jagged and angular, not like the boulders he'd imagined, and yet it had worked. Curious.

The visualization did not have to be quite perfect, apparently. Yes, he was finally learning a little.

He glanced back at Niat, only now to find her staring wide-eyed at him. The expression was a bit crazed. What, floating stone was more terrifying than nearly being crushed to death? His eyes caught on something on the side of her hip.

"Why is your dress glowing?" he asked.

She glanced down at her hip, then back at him, narrowing her eyes. "Mage," she hissed, like an insult, an accusation.

He raised his eyebrows. "What does—" he started, hoping to ask again about her glowing hip, but in his distraction, he released some part of himself that was still connected to the stones.

He realized his error almost immediately as her gaze darted up.

Without looking—there was no time for that—he threw an arm around her and swept her a foot to the side and against him.

"Get your—" she started.

A piece of masonry crashed into the spot where she'd stood, and she gaped, eyes wide as the dust swirled up and caught in the wind, reminding him just how high up they were.

"—hands off me, *mage*," she finally finished, pushing him away.

He glared at her, then rolled his eyes. "You're the one that distracted me. A simple 'thanks' would have sufficed, but I suppose your kind words will have to do." He didn't waste time on people that stupid. Or impolite. Her merits were not exactly adding up.

He stalked past her and headed for the stairs but stopped short at the pool of blood near his feet.

A leg protruded from the nearby rubble, but judging by the amount of blood, more than one person had been crushed… unless they had been under there a long time. It didn't matter.

He swallowed, tearing his eyes away. Likely his magic had saved him and Niat, then. He didn't feel terribly happy about it at the sight of blood. Who lay fallen? Someone he knew? One of Alikar's men?

"Hey. Seer. Get down—oh, ho, what have we here." Thel glanced up. One of Alikar's men stood at the top of the stair that remained. Yes, this would be trouble. "You two better come this way. Only way down that's intact. Let's go now."

Thel glowered at him, not missing what he was trying to do. Niat marched past him, and Thel followed her down into the stair.

Just around the bend, a three-foot section of the stairway had collapsed. It was only a one-story fall through the gap, not enough to kill you, but it certainly would not feel pleasant.

Niat hesitated at the edge.

"Get goin', girl. You so much a princess I have to carry ya?"

"I'm not a princess, I'm a priestess, you dolt," she snapped.

"That's not how your da presents the facts."

She scowled at him, took a step back, then another. A running start was a good idea.

Ah, if only he'd had time to learn more. Certainly an earth mage should be able to raise up enough blocks for them to walk over, but he wasn't sure he could do such a thing while also walking over it himself. Although… he had managed to get out of the hole while maintaining the spell. He scratched his chin, imagining the fool's face as Thel tromped across blocks that flew into place to form a path at his feet.

An ominous crack was the only thing that alerted him that he'd done more than imagine it.

Niat narrowed her eyes at him over her shoulder. Beyond her, stones had risen to form a pathway. He grinned, mostly to himself, at the simple victory. Always a pleasure when learning came easily.

She looked back to the path he'd apparently now formed across the gap, but still she hesitated. He couldn't blame her for that. He had no idea if it would hold her either, really.

He pushed past her and, carefully holding his gleeful image of annoying the guard in his mind, stepped out onto the stones. They wobbled slightly but did not fall. Not wanting to push his luck, he stepped quickly across them and smirked back at her from the other side.

"Are you coming?"

She glared daggers at him.

"Get goin' or I'm gonna throw ya," the other man snapped at her.

Still frowning, she readied herself with a deep breath, then ran across the gap as quickly as she could. She was light on her feet, barely touching the stones, more like a hummingbird than a human woman.

He frowned. Whimsical, poetic thoughts like that usually meant he was taking an interest in a girl. *Foolish brain, she's a traitor and a religious zealot besides. None of that.*

The guard raced across the makeshift bridge before Thel could drop it as he had planned. *Damn.* He was often too busy thinking to remember to act. He liked to think that meant his actions were overall of better quality, but perhaps that wasn't quite true.

And he was doing it again. Both Niat and the man had begun down the stairs without him. His chances of getting away from that fool were better if he were ahead of him. *Maybe his tall legs could still overtake them.*

He headed down after them, the bridge collapsing behind him with a crash.

A thunderous boom echoed through the tower. *Odd. What could that be?* Another echoed a few moments later.

Thel managed to wedge his way past them. It annoyed the guard, but he focused on the priestess instead, grabbing her by the elbow.

"Get your hands off me, fool."

He didn't comply. At least Thel wasn't the only one getting such orders, although he tended to agree with her that nothing good was going to come from that imp's clutches.

"Shut up, seer scum."

What was that all about?

"You insult your own soul when you insult the temple," she replied, her tone even and aloof.

"I got no problem with the temple. My only issue is with liars."

She sighed bitterly, as if she'd dealt with this before. Thel frowned again. Occasionally, the temples housed priests and priestesses who claimed to be given visions and direction from the gods. He hadn't heard of any seers recently, though, and usually the discovery of one was a momentous occasion. Perhaps it was a recent discovery.

Or maybe she was a charlatan. Either fit, really.

"I am not a liar," she said quietly.

"Save it for your new husband, Priestess," he snapped, her title dripping with rancor. That seemed harsher than the actual epithets he had slung at her.

Against all reason, Thel shot a glare at the man over his shoulder. Niat was glowering at the man too, but Thel didn't miss the streak of fear in her eyes. What was that all about? More mysteries.

Of course, he didn't have much muscle to back up his glare, and Thel hated fighting with a passion, so he should really learn to keep his opinions to himself and focus on getting farther ahead of the man.

They reached the bottom, and Thel took off at a jog away from the tower. Maybe if he simply went about it with enough authority—

"Stop him!" Alikar's voice. The order was hard, voice

raw. "This city will fall in the siege to come. We need to be out of it before that happens. Grab them. Back to Gilaren."

Another stout man grabbed Thel by the left bicep now. Thel sighed and glanced around for others, but none had caught up. He couldn't see much without looking straight back, which would be too obvious. He should have taken his father's insistence on warden training more seriously and argued his way out of it a little less.

Too late to lament that now. He took a steadying breath, steeling himself for what he usually loathed to do. Then he drew his sword and spun, swinging around behind his back, catching the man near his kidney and throwing him off-balance into the street. Fortunately, the man was caught off guard enough to let go of Thel's arm. Sometimes that move ended poorly with Thel sprawled on the floor as well. Many thrusts and strikes ended that way. Gods, did he hate fighting. It came about as naturally to him as flight to a toad.

He met the next three men head-on, steel clashing as had been his goal, but when three more joined them, he knew he was outmanned. Another five appeared, riding atop a carriage.

Thel glanced around, searching for a way to out-think these brutes. The street held merchant shops that were still closed or in the process of opening—a bakery, a tailor, a butcher. Nothing that would guarantee a getaway or even a back door, nor any alleys between them to slip through.

A grate led down under the street. His best chance.

He hurled his sword—and most of himself—at the two

men between him and the grate, not intending to actually fight them but more to stave off any wounds they might land while he bowled them over and went tumbling in the direction of his real goal. Dom would have laughed at him, but his brother would try the exact same thing in this situation, he was sure of it. Dom would probably have pulled it off with more grace, though.

Thel managed to break free, scrambling toward the grate in a soldier's crawl on his elbows before a foot slammed down, crushing his hand as he grabbed for the grate.

He looked up, stifling his groan. Alikar glared down at him.

"*You're* not going anywhere. Into the carriage with both of them."

Miara did not envy Aven as the sea of people flooded in around him, cheers and raucous shouts echoing in the cellar. The room imploded around him as Samul and Elise fell back.

Crowds made her nothing but wary, and although it was almost certainly a good thing for her that Aven had just taken the crown… it didn't *feel* good. Her stomach was sinking by the minute. Why now? Why here? She'd have expected more planning, more ceremony, more grandiosity around the event.

Something was wrong.

Her eyes scanned the perimeter of the room. If spies had infiltrated Estun, this makeshift cellar turned infirmary and war room would be a stroll in the garden. And how convenient, a swarming crowd to blend into. Her right hand drifted to her dagger's hilt as she eyed each person in turn. Her left hand still clutched Luha's fingers, warm and real and safe. Hard to believe, but true.

Miara's gaze caught on Elise. The queen's face was pale as she helped Samul to a seat. Curiously, he leaned on his wife more than on any of his attendants.

Yes, something was definitely wrong. But it wasn't spies—it was Samul. Miara reluctantly let go of Luha with a squeeze and skirted the crowd. Dyon stood to the right side of the royal couple now, his brow furrowed with concern.

"What is it? What's wrong?" Miara whispered.

"I don't know," Elise replied weakly. "Everything." She sank beside Samul. *It didn't work. Well, some, but not all the way. The healing won't finish. I… I need to rest.*

The knots twisting in Miara's stomach tightened further. She reached out, sensing the lingering wounds on Samul that would not—or could not—heal. She plied the remaining tangles of chaos with bits of energy from one side, then another. Nothing influenced the wounds in the slightest. He was not fully healed, but the wounds didn't care for a moment about her magic. They were already in their natural state.

She swore under her breath, eying the crowd for danger. There were only two possible explanations for a wound that resisted healing. Neither was good.

The arrows could have been tipped with poison. Poisons were perfectly natural, and healing magic couldn't touch them. They had to be treated the old-fashioned way, with herbs and prayers. She could *create* them as a creature mage, but she would have never considered such a thing. The idea stopped her short, though. Their pursuers had had at least one creature mage among them, and a very creative one at that.

Much as the idea of Samul being poisoned worried her, the other option was even worse. One other very natural thing defied healing: death, and its harbinger, old age. While creature magic could restore wounds, fight disease, erase scars, it could not make anyone live forever. And many, many had tried.

But Samul had been fine just a few days ago. Feisty as hell. Full of energy and defiance. He'd been a better fish than she had, and she'd done it before.

It had to be poison. Had to be. Although he had given up the crown more quickly and with more ease than she would have ever expected…

His eyes were closed now. His face had not regained any color, which was understandable, considering the intense blood loss. But was there something more in those closed eyes, that pained brow? Or was it just poison doing its work? Exhaustion and pain, or the kind of exhaustion of the soul only time could relieve?

Stay strong, Samul, she ordered. *Aven needs you.*

He opened one eye to peer at her, then closed it again.

His brow softened, but she wasn't sure if that was a good sign or bad.

Where's Siliana? Miara asked Elise.

Pushed to the point of exhaustion. Collapsed on a cot in the back.

Looks like you need rest too.

Yes. But I can't leave them.

Miara scanned the room again. The crowd still ebbed and flowed around Aven. Well-wishes and congratulations and handshakes and backslapping. The pandering for favor was already beginning. Or no, it likely had begun the day he was born. She turned back to face Elise. *We need to wrap this up. The king needs a bed. And so do you.*

Yes. Tell them… Elise's voice paused, her eyes drifting shut for a moment, then snapping open again. *Can Dyon… the prince's rooms. Aven must keep the king's rooms. Don't let him argue about it—* Her thoughts fell into disorder, and Miara backed away to give the woman her privacy.

"I'll take care of it," she said quickly. "Lord Dyon, as much as I hate to interrupt—"

He nodded before she could finish. "There is work to be done. Celebration must wait."

"The king needs a bed to rest and heal. And the queen too. And he needs a healer. Tell them to check for poisons. Queen Elise said Aven should keep the king's rooms, to send them to the prince's quarters—is that all right?"

Dyon nodded crisply. "I'll see it done myself, my lady." And he turned away, summoning someone from the doorway.

Miara opened her mouth to correct him—she was no lady—but stopped. He was not wrong any longer, was he? If the title the king had granted her minutes ago hadn't given her such an honorific, surely Aven announcing to everyone he intended to marry her implied it would be hers eventually. It shouldn't surprise her; Dyon was nothing if not precise and observant.

A memory of the Mistress and her dark curls and disdainful eyes tugged at Miara. No, *no*—the Mistress was no lady. Miara had more nobility and honor in her little finger than that awful woman. She needed to find out the Mistress's real name. She'd think of her as an equal, just like Daes. Even if only in her mind.

As attendants came to help the king and queen away— or did they now carry other titles?—Miara tried to catch Aven's eye. To her relief, it didn't take long, as though he had been trying to catch her gaze himself.

I sent your parents to rest.

He nodded once approvingly.

Your father is not entirely healed. The arrows may have been poisoned.

His inward wince pained her like it was her own. *Or…?*

Or he may be just getting old. He may long to die and resist healing. But that doesn't make sense. I think it must be poison. Dyon is fetching a nonmagical healer.

Good. Thank you.

We need rest too.

Agreed. And to find Thel, and so much more. I've been trying to shoo these folks away. I'll shoo harder.

She prodded the not entirely healed wound in her leg. The ache was growing annoying, but it hadn't deserved her energy when others nearby might have been near death. Could it be poisoned too? No. It responded to her power with a furious pang, making her lurch.

But she and Samul had switched positions for the last few hundred yards so that he'd taken the brunt of the assault, believing that she could heal him but not the other way around. Perhaps, with Panar so close, the brand had urged their pursuers to do something more serious than just shoot arrows, since they had obviously been failing.

Aven worked his way through the crowd. Samul was right about one thing; he was a natural with people. The crowd circled Aven, beamed at him, fought for his attention even as he sought to rebuff them. He was in his element, as though such a danger-laden morass was where he belonged. Just watching made her nervous *for* him. How many of them had a dagger concealed? And plenty were fully and openly armed Akarian officials. If she weren't reasonably confident in her ability to heal most wounds, she wouldn't be standing idly by.

Where did she fit into this chaos? Was this the kind of moment that a queen should be standing, bleeding, arms folded, leaning against a doorway alone? Should she be more regal, graciously turning well-wishers away from his side?

She could do that. Later. Maybe not graciously, but a forbidding glare might work. She'd start when she was less bloody and not wearing Kavanarian leather. Although well loved and familiar, the leathers felt suddenly old—out of place, out of time. No longer a second skin, but now a relic of the past.

She'd get something else, after she figured out where the hell she could get a bath, a meal, and an extremely long nap. Assuming nobody catapulted or attacked anything before then. She heaved a deep sigh.

She was already exhausted, and this war had barely begun.

Thel scowled up at Alikar. "What, one charge of treason wasn't enough for you? Or was it three? Four? I lost count."

In response, Alikar ground his foot into Thel's left hand, and this time he couldn't stop himself from crying out. And—perhaps someone would hear him. He yelped louder.

Alikar withdrew his foot.

"When the storm comes, you'll turn tail and flee? Like a deer into the brush? What a mighty example of an Akarian," Thel said. He had never known when to stop, Dom had told him. This was likely one of those moments. But it was worth a gamble that his mockery might make Alikar change his plan.

Thel was rewarded for his snark with a fierce kick to the ribs.

Thel coughed through the pain. "Are your masters going to be pleased that you've failed them in unseating my brother?"

Another kick sent him onto his side, groaning. He sighed inwardly; he really was old enough and smart enough to know better than this.

Alikar's men hauled him up and shoved him into the open carriage door. Had they grabbed his sword, or did it remain in the street? He needed to leave clues that he'd been taken so Aven and his father and the others would know what had happened.

He tried to peer out the windows on the other side of the carriage, but they were boarded shut. He poked at them, then went so far as to pound a fist, but they barely shuddered. Elbowing them as hard as he could only left his elbow aching, the boards unchanged. Not that strength was his strong suit.

Hmm. Perhaps this was not an entirely impromptu plan.

Niat was shoved in next. He caught her at the last moment, her skull almost cracking on the wood of the other side of the carriage, his fingers tangling in her soft, almost white hair. "Hey, watch it!" he snapped at the empty doorway. It slammed closed in his face.

Well, at least Alikar wasn't coming with them.

"Gah, leave me *alone*," she muttered. She skittered away to the farthest corner the tiny carriage cabin would allow.

The glow near her hip remained but seemed brighter now in the dark carriage. She removed the light from her pocket; it hung like a pendant from a simple thong that she slipped over her head. The stone glowed orange, like an ember, casting a fiery light over the wood around them. Oh, now it made sense. He'd read about these stones. Elders and others used them to identify mages, but they were mostly used by…

"You're one of the *Devoted?* I thought you were a priestess."

She scowled at him and said nothing for a long moment, as if she were trying to decide if he was worthy of an answer. She *did* have the haughty demeanor of some members of royalty. What had that guard been saying about princesses? Lord Sven's position in Akaria certainly did not merit that title.

"It was a gift," she said eventually.

"Oh, *well*, then," Thel grumbled. "Lucky you." Excellent. A witty retort, Thel, very good showing. Point to you, fool. Now she probably thought him a mage *and* an idiot. He fumbled for something else to say. "Are you really a princess?"

She sighed loudly. Clearly he was an *insufferable* mage idiot, he corrected. And one who wouldn't shut up. "Are you really a prince?"

He had no idea what to make of that response. He blinked, trying to understand. "Well… yes. Of course."

Her eyes widened. "Oh."

So that hadn't been sarcasm? Did that make *her* response a no? Whatever. If she wanted to be thorny, he could shut up. He had plenty to think over—like how to get out of this carriage without the men perched all over it noticing.

He studied the carriage interior. Like many low-cost carriages, it was simple and lacked cushions—any amenities really. With the windows boarded, there were no easy or obvious routes of escape. He would have to think his way out of here. It was also black as night, except for the menacing glow of the stone. It figured that now that he could study the book, there wasn't the light for it. Unless maybe he got closer to her… No. He could just imagine her reaction. Excuse me, would you mind if I snuggled closer and read this book of magic by the light of your Devoted stone?

He glanced over. Could he ever convince her to work together? He studied the set of her jaw, the way her arms folded across her chest. They didn't leave him optimistic.

Ah, the luck he had with women. Why couldn't he be trapped in a carriage with someone attracted to bookish types or young princes or, even better, both? But no. Renala would certainly have been a better traveling companion.

His chest panged a little at the thought. She's not interested, you dolt. Let it go. He didn't believe Renala had ever picked up on his feelings for her, but she certainly hadn't wanted *him*. Or Aven. Or any man, for that matter, judging by the way her eyes followed Siliana whenever the mage moved around a room. Which made Renala's lack of interest sting a *little* less. It wasn't personal. He'd had too many women fail to notice him while their eyes had been trained on burly men with a better ability to split a log in half. Curse him for being born Akarian. How was he ever going to find a woman that appreciated him for who he actually was? Didn't the ability to quote the entire *Teminid* from memory count for anything, or was he going to have to learn to crush melons with his bare hands? Yeah, like he would ever bother. He'd just be alone forever, at this rate.

A visual inspection having turned up nothing, he returned to the boarded carriage window closest to him. He had a bad feeling Niat wouldn't want him poking around, but certainly she must want to escape as well. The wooden boards over the carriage windows were nailed in place, thick, and rather secure as he'd found out the hard way. His elbow was still throbbing. Even if he managed to remove a board, it would be massively obvious to their captors.

The carriage door was locked. He scooted across his bench and reached toward the handle of the other door, which sat about a foot or two from her knee.

The coldness of her glare swept over him like a chill wind. "Just what do you think you're doing?" she said softly.

Thel stared back, his eyes wide, unsure he even wanted to grant such a question an answer. As far as court etiquette went, it was certainly out of turn, but he had no interest in pointing that out either. He blandly tried the doorknob. It, too, was locked.

Yes, he'd just ignore her. That'd be for the best. He moved up to a partial crouch, inspecting the ceiling. She did not relax, probably because his whole body had moved closer to her and was looming over her.

That she would think he had anything but scientific examination in mind, the ridiculousness of it. How could he be any more obviously searching for an escape?

He crouched down now, awkwardly trying to position himself as far from her as possible. He flashed her a small, polite smile in the baleful light. Her face was an unmoving mask watching him, eyes dark as steel. She was… rather striking, a study in contrasts, the palest highlights and darkest shadows converging in her expression. Funny, one would think such a tiny, pale priestess would be softer, with her long curls and temple robes. But Niat was not soft. She emanated hardness, like a diamond in the blackest core of a mountain mine.

His fingers caught on something, and he gladly tore his gaze away. A panel. An emergency exit or loading panel, perhaps. It was not on the bottom as an exit should be, but on the side of the foot bed near where his calves would rest.

He twisted a latch, and a panel fell in toward him. Behind it he could see the racing wheels of the carriage and the hooves of the horses, and dirt immediately flew in. He lifted his arm to shield himself, then relented and shut it again.

Niat had not missed his discovery. Even without looking, he could feel her sour stare boring into his back. He twisted and sat down on the bench above the emergency door.

Well, that was something, but what use was it? It'd be impossible not to get hit by the carriage if they jumped out of that at full speed. Did their captors know that, and was that why it had been left unsecured? Then there were all the men that were sure to spot them, riding both above the carriage and on horseback beside it. The pounding of hooves assured him he had plenty of observers.

He mentally ran through possible uses for the panel in an escape. He worked with as much thoroughness as he could manage with her gaze occasionally on him, suspicion and judgment and wariness all wrapped in one angry look.

He didn't get very far. Her gaze was unnerving, and his options weren't numerous. He closed his eyes to try to escape her, leaning his head back against the bouncing carriage in hopes of sleep.

"Lord Beneral!" A soldier called out from the cellar side door, and the room quieted. Aven took that moment to gently shift the remaining well-wishers aside and slide through the crowd toward Miara and the newcomer.

"Yes?" Beneral made his way from the side of the room where Wunik had been working. His dark features had grown deathly serious.

"We-we can't find him, sir," the soldier said, regret staining his voice. "Prince Thel. We need more men. He's not in the streets. We need to search the houses."

As the guard spoke, Aven slipped next to Miara. "Wunik—" he whispered.

Already looking, she shot back silently. *He's following something, might be them. Thinks he's got Alikar's trail at least.*

He nodded, frowning. Every minute that passed made

his heart race a little faster, his stomach drop lower, like panic was creeping up on him very slowly. If they didn't find him soon, who knew when they were going to?

If ever.

Beneral joined them in the doorway, dark fingers curling around his ebony staff as he leaned more heavily on it than usual. The crowd returned to murmuring as it started to disperse.

"Who was the prince with last?" Miara asked.

The guard jumped, as if he hadn't even noticed her dark form blending in against the dark cellar walls. "He was on the side of the tower with Alikar and his men," the guard replied. "And Priestess Niat, Lord Sven's representative. Before the first catapult hit the tower. We never expected— It shouldn't have been able to reach so far."

"It was helped by Kavanarian mages," said Beneral.

The guard frowned harder now.

"Alikar and Niat? Isn't that the luck," she said as she shifted, leaning a little closer to Aven in a quiet gesture of support.

"Yes," Beneral grunted. "Not a fortunate group of companions—the only two who voted against the king."

Aven gritted his teeth. "If anything happens to him, Alikar will personally pay for this."

"What terms are you on with them, then?" she asked. "Did I hear some mention of treason? Also, did they know Thel is a mage?"

"I don't know if they know he's a mage," said Aven, "but I doubt it. Alikar has been charged with treason because he tried to bribe others for their votes with Kavanarian money, among other things. Lord Sven and his daughter, Niat, as his proxy haven't exactly done anything wrong, at least not that we know about yet. But they're more likely to be allied with Alikar than not. Given all that, if you were them, what kind of mood would *you* be in?"

Miara pursed her lips. "A vengeful one." She eyed the men, then added to Aven with her mind, *But I wouldn't commit treason in the first place.*

Just another of the things I admire about you. When people are asking me why I've chosen you as the next queen, I'll be sure to put "promises she won't commit treason" high on the list of your virtues.

Gods, I hope you have a few others beyond that. How can you joke at a time like this?

How can I not? Otherwise I'll go mad with worry. He smiled at her, before realizing how odd that would look since no one else was privy to their conversation. He wiped the expression off his face even as the corners of her mouth threatened to tilt up as well.

"Agreed," Beneral had muttered while they were silently speaking. He'd leaned away, taking advantage of Aven's focus on Miara, and lowered his voice so Aven could barely hear him. "Did you check the rubble?"

Aven tensed. How much rubble? Enough to crush one man at least, or he wouldn't be asking. "How many were lost?" he said, drawing the soldier and Beneral back in.

The soldier nodded, responding quietly and reluctantly in turn. "Six dead, sir, crushed by the rubble. That we've found so far. But not the prince, nor Priestess Niat. All servants of Alikar's, we believe. And there was one spot where it looked like someone had dug their way out."

Like an earth mage perhaps? Miara pointed out silently. *Don't give me false reason to hope.*

I would never. But he's been studying, hasn't he? And you were casting spells before you'd learned anything. It's possible.

Beneral nodded sharply. "All right. Head to the third barracks," he said. "There should be plenty of men available there for further searches. But don't start with the houses. Spread out beyond the city gates and work your way in. I want every gate stopping people and searching for him. Search any who enter or leave, all wagons, everything. I want Prince Thel found."

A sinking feeling in Aven's stomach told him that this was not going to be so easy. How long had it been? Forever had passed since the vote, it seemed. They'd ridden out to retrieve Miara and his father, they'd stopped the catapults, and his father had made his grand gestures before slipping into unconsciousness. Time had a way of stretching at moments like these, but the sun outside told him it wasn't quite midday. It'd only been a few hours.

Long enough for Thel to be swept out of the city and on his way to who knew where.

A wave of exhaustion hit him. The thought of searching the entirety of Kavanar and Akaria for Thel was overwhelming. He slumped against the wall.

"You all right?" Miara said quickly.

He nodded. "Those catapults, and all this... Perhaps

it took more out of me than I realized."

"You should rest, sire," Beneral said. "It will be time before the men can complete their search. The catapults are in our control now. This is the time to rest."

"What if there are more attacks?" If there were, they were sure to come during daylight.

"Wunik has checked for oncoming troops farther out. There are none before the Numaren-Kavanar border, a good day and a half's ride. They'll be reaching the southern stronghold soon, but Panar is safe for now. This morning's siege force must have been purely targeted at hitting the vote this morning and nothing else. This is as good a time for rest as any we'll get, I fear."

"He's right, Aven," Miara added. "I mean, sire. You've drained a lot of energy, both physical and magical, without any rest too."

"All right, all right," Aven relented. "Have Derk help Wunik. And will you ask Wunik to tell us if he finds any sign of my brother?"

"Of course," said Beneral, just as Miara spoke the same words into his mind.

Aven nodded and wanted to smile but couldn't bring himself to. "Thank you. Come, Miara—let's head back to Ranok." He offered her his arm and was grateful when she took it. Her warmth was solid, rejuvenating by his side. He shook his head; he'd been through half as much as she had. Miara waved to her father, her sister, Ro, and Jaena, and they gathered just outside.

They hadn't been out long before a bird's loud screech

split the air, and nearly everyone scattered back toward the wall, familiar with magic or no.

Everyone except Miara. And since Aven had been arm in arm with her, he'd stayed put too. He'd really had enough magical attacks for one day, but the king probably shouldn't flinch away if his queen didn't. His future queen, anyway.

He braced himself for incoming pain, reassuring himself that much could be healed, but then he noticed Miara was smiling.

A falcon fluttered a few feet forward, stopping at her feet and cocking its head. Feeling Aven's eyes on her, she met his gaze.

"I owe someone a meal or two for their aid. Can he come along?"

"I thought fleeing for your life and protecting the king would have kept you from having time to find a pet."

The bird leapt up toward Miara's shoulder, and as it landed, she winced, its talons digging into her. The leather was some protection, but not enough for *that*.

"And another injury to heal," she sighed. "I'm not so sure that I've taken him as a pet as much as he's taken me."

Shaking his head, he looked at the bird. "Come along, then. We're already practically a parade. Why not some animals?"

Beneral fired off a string of orders for a guard to form up around them as escort, but Aven stopped them at fetching horses. It was only a few blocks. He'd rather them use the horses to find Thel. Truth be told, he'd rather use the *men* for that too, but kings did not go strolling around cities without an escort, if not a sprawling entourage.

Although… she could transform them and they could sneak out and explore the city alone. Like they had on their first ill-fated journey, but with less death at the end. He could see what Panar was *really* like.

Maybe tomorrow. Or when the war was over. Or at least after a rest and a hot meal. Perhaps he should wait until Thel and his father were both safe and sound and healthy before he went exploring the alleys of the White City.

If they were ever safe, sound, and healthy again. War was coming, after all, with winter on its heels. A long battle lay in store if peace were to reign once again.

Jaena started from sleep with a knock on the door. She glanced at the window. Night had nearly fallen. That made sense since she no longer felt dead on her feet. But she wasn't quite ready to be disturbed yet by any visitor, well meaning or otherwise.

She peered down at Ro's face, barely containing a grin. He was asleep on her shoulder—and drooling slightly. Her right arm was completely numb, but she could just barely feel his dark hair tangled in her fingers. She let out a deep, contented sigh.

The knock sounded again, and his eyebrows rose a little. She thought he might wake, but his arm tightened around her waist, pulling her harder against him. He nuzzled his face further into her neck, beard stubble scraping softly against her skin, and stilled again.

Numb arm or no, she wasn't moving just yet.

The intrepid knocker tried once more, and then footsteps moved away down the hall. She supposed they were here at the king's grace, and perhaps she should take the summons more seriously. But it had been a long night. A long week.

A long five years.

She wasn't quite ready for this brief moment of respite to end.

Moving slowly and hoping not to wake him, she ran her left hand—the one that could still move—gently over his hair, down his braid, down his neck and broad shoulder and burly arm. To think someone who could inflict such violence on iron could also be so gentle. But that was who he was.

A fierce sense of possessiveness swelled in her, and she tightened her arms around him as best she could. This was all still a pleasant surprise, to know that someone like him wanted to be hers. At least for now.

How long would this last? Dare she hope anything beyond the present? Dare she hope—

No. It was best not to hope. Hope would only get her hurt. He had a smithy and his order. Obligations. Possessions. A life of his own that she was only a slight part of.

Perhaps when the brand was destroyed, or the winter over, or the Masters utterly defeated—if such a thing was possible—she could return to him there. But certainly he would be on his way tomorrow, if not the next day. There would be many more mages to free from Mage Hall who could use his help getting out of Kavanar. The placement of his smithy was a valuable asset. She shouldn't try to keep him all to herself. It wasn't right.

Although, as a mage, it wasn't safe to return either. Especially if the Devoted knew how the order's pendants worked, that there was a way to slip by their mage-detecting stones. But even so, his temple would have some other duty for him. Again she squeezed him against her, not wanting to think of losing him too but knowing it was coming nonetheless.

A while later, the footsteps returned, and after one more failed attempt at knocking, a note whispered under the door. Well, at least she wouldn't have to forever wonder what the knocker had wanted.

Her stomach gurgled, as if conspiring to get her out of bed, and this time Ro stirred. His hand slid smoothly from her hip to her belly to feel her stomach gurgle again. He raised his head, blinking blearily and looking faintly amused. Blood rushed into her upper arm, sending pins and needles through her weak limb.

He glanced at the window, then back to her with half-lidded eyes. She thought he might say something, possibly about the fact that her stomach was making enough noise to wake a statue, but he never did. He pressed her into the bed with a feverish kiss instead.

"Aren't you hungry?" she laughed as his mouth trailed

down her jawline to her neck. "It's night already. Who knows where and when they have food around here?"

"Only for you," he murmured softly against her shoulder.

That stole away any thoughts of food for quite some time.

Eventually she rolled out of the bed, beyond famished, and picked up the note.

Mage Jaena Eliar,
The king requests the pleasure of your and Tharomar's
company in his suite at your leisure.

It was unsigned. Well, at least they weren't late for anything. Ro swung around to sit beside her and gave her an inquisitive look. She handed him the note. The king must need something from them.

Ro looked up with a smile. "Well, now we know where to find food. Or ask for some. Shall we?"

She smiled back, nodding. "Let's. But first I have to figure out where you threw my vest."

"Ah, clothing. A tedious chore when you're around."

A silly grin slid over her face. "I don't think King Aven would appreciate otherwise, though."

"Oh, you never know. You're very lovely."

She swatted at him playfully. "You're welcome to test that theory. I, however, will wear pants."

"You're right. Pants it is. I wouldn't want to endanger our shelter for the night."

"Good thinking. I look forward to returning to it."

"I'll save the pants experiments for tomorrow."

Yet another bump on the road sent a fresh cascade of pain through Niat's already sore frame. She'd lost so much weight in the past few months that bones protruded in all the wrong places. Every jarring thud was a painful reminder of the danger looming on the horizon. Thankfully, no fever had yet taken her during these last few hours, but she didn't expect her luck to hold out forever.

The prison cell of the carriage carried her relentlessly forward. All day they'd traveled without stopping, straight toward her own personal hell. The transport even came complete with a cursed companion to escort her. Not that she had expected the ride to be comfortable, but it had been hours. She was lucky to be maintaining bladder control at this point.

She glanced at the mage. The prince, whoever he was. It didn't matter now. He wouldn't be a prince much longer. Those her father colluded with weren't far from their goals, she could tell. She had never succeeded in resisting Sven. Not for long anyway, aside from those few spare months of freedom in the temple. Oh, how high her hopes had been for life there. A life new, and bright, and free, with people who sought to serve the gods, not desecrate them.

How naïve she had been. How naïve she still was, that the hope still burned even though it'd been dashed. Even though it was doomed.

And now here she was trapped again.

Husband. That's what that guard had said. Would it be Alikar or someone else he took her to? Unsurprising that her father had finally found someone with whom to strike a deal. He'd been trying even before Peluna had gotten her into the temple. She had hoped, perhaps, that men would lose interest when word about her visions began to spread, or the fact that she'd become a priestess at all. But it was no shock that they hadn't. Her father had always negotiated well and was probably offering a very generous deal. For everyone but Niat, of course. She shuddered.

She eyed the mage again. Evil at every turn these days, it seemed. Although he hadn't shown any particularly nasty tendencies. He'd mostly been polite. Helpful, even, damn him. Part of her was tempted to let her guard down, but no. Letting her guard down never worked. No point in needlessly opening herself up to anything, even the casual betrayal of a stranger. They were both doomed, and sooner or later, his own fate would be weighed against hers, and he'd make the selfish choice. They always did.

Although…

Her visions had been slow to emerge in the early days at the temple, and many still held a hazy quality, like in a dream where she could almost but never quite see a face. The books said it should fade with time. But a blond man did sometimes feature in the flashes accosting her of late, a man that made hope flicker in her chest at the sight of him. Although why, she still didn't know. That man was tall and thin, like this mage. Could they be the same man?

She pressed her eyes shut. Dare she ask? Dare she actually call them upon her? If a fever took her here, what would the mage do? Would he help or thrust her to the other side of the carriage with his boot?

Weakening herself was a risk, but she also longed to know. For once, could her curse have some practical application that might actually help her?

Fine. She'd been sick and alone before. It often passed without terrible trauma. Most of the time. And she was likely headed for trauma anyway, in Alikar's hands.

She would try. And deal with the consequences.

Centering herself, she fell still, breathed slowly, and, when her mind found a semblance of peace, reached out for that sweet, holy connection. Up into the sky, out across the plains, deep into the stillness. So good while it lasted, so awful the moment it was gone.

Tell me, ancestors, gods, whoever you are. The priestesses insisted visions came from Nefrana, and so Niat played along, but she was not convinced they came from anyone. *Tell me. Is this man with me the one you've shown me?*

A vision slammed into her mind with the force of a brick to the head, pain radiating from her temple.

A vision she'd seen before—the city aflame. Not a city she recognized, but likely where they were going. Smoke curled up in tall columns above the city. A sense of horror, or a mistake having occurred, always flooded her at the sight. Something had gone awfully wrong.

But now there was more than just the city. She could

see more clearly around her now. She stood on a cliff, looking down over the chaos. Catapults and trebuchets thudded in the distance, some still firing on the city, some toppling suddenly out of nowhere and going over the edge.

A few feet in front of her on the cliff sat a man with straw-colored hair down to his chin. He faced the city, his back to her covered in a gray cloak. His hands were in the mud on either side of him, actually *in* the wet earth. Why?

She reached forward, maybe to tap him on the shoulder. Maybe she didn't have a plan.

As if he sensed her, he turned and met her gaze, his expression grim but different than the one she was used to. It *was* the mage who rode in the carriage with her, the blue of his eyes clear as the open sky, bright like a shining topaz.

"Well, you can give up," he said, "but I'll be damned if I do. I'm an Akarian. We don't give up. Go on, go down to them if you want. I'll think you're wrong, I'll regret you went, but I won't stop you."

He turned away.

Regret. The vision seized on the word as if it held great meaning to her, his voice echoing in her mind, but the moment in time spun around her, out of control, dizzying. Here was where the sweetness ended. Here was when the nausea came.

Here was where she paid her price.

The holy connection severed in a snap, and disappointment washed over her, both that it had been so brief and also so vague. Well, whatever or whoever lay on the other side of that connection had answered her question—this mage *was* the blond-haired man—but they hadn't given her much else.

Perhaps it was better this way. She'd often heard it was better not to know, that the visions would only drive her mad, that she would lose herself in space and time. Now that word of her visions had spread, it was amazing how many people went out of their way to assure her they did *not* envy her.

She groaned as her head spun, a wave of nausea rising. She dropped her head into her hands.

"It has been getting rougher," he said softly.

Bah, as if he cared how she felt. She said nothing.

"Do you think they'll stop soon?"

"I don't know. I think I'm going to be sick." Sweat was starting to prick her forehead. The fever rising.

"Well, that might get them to stop. Or not. They haven't showed any signs of being hospitable captors so far. Where do you think they are taking us?"

She shook her head in her hands bleakly.

"Anonil, perhaps." He had a nice voice, soft and sort of gentle, with an educated air to it, like all the syllables of all the words were worth saying and mattered to him.

But Anonil. "From what I've seen, I hope not," she muttered. She suspected the city in the visions was Anonil because it was the largest Gilaren city and one she'd never seen.

"Why?"

She only groaned. "Leave me alone."

"What have you seen?"

"If I vomit on you, will *that* get you to shut up?"

He folded his arms across his chest. "You know, this is hardly civil discourse. I don't see how I've done anything to warrant your vociferous glares all day."

"You're a mage. That's enough." An annoyingly uppity and proper mage, too. And too thin and scrawny and crooked-nosed. And a witness to her terrible moment of weakness. Several moments now, actually. That, she held against him most of all.

"Hmph. I should have left you in that hole."

"You couldn't free yourself without freeing me." Thankfully.

"A shame, really." He tried to look off into the distance, as much as you could in a tiny, dark carriage lit only by the light of his magic in the Devoted stone.

Of course, just before the boulder hit and the tower exploded, she'd seen a terrifying flash that had told her to dive behind him. Otherwise, she would have ended up just another pool of blood. He had saved her life, albeit without exactly trying, and helped her get across that gaping hole in the stair too. She was being unfair, but she felt too nauseous to muster an apology.

"How do you even know if mages are evil?" he said, apparently not content with staring into space. "How can you be so sure? Have you ever even known any?"

Her father had owned a few mage slaves in her day, repulsive as that had been. But she'd known little about them, except for Detrax, who had guarded her for a time.

She shuddered. He was as evil as mages came. It had only taken a single glimpse of that evil before Peluna had gotten her father to send him away. Soon after, Peluna had given her the Devoted stone, a way to detect the danger of mages wherever they might spring up. "In the Dark Days—"

He waved her off. "Answer the question."

She glared, then, "No, I haven't known any very well personally, but I don't—"

"Then what proof do you have?"

"Proof?" She was thrown enough by his line of reasoning to risk raising her head to stare.

"Yes, proof. Actual facts you can verify with your own five senses. Your personal experience. You know, science. Observation."

"The Dark Days are recorded in great detail."

"That's history, not science. And they're recorded from only a handful of sources that could easily have been prejudiced by time. Or knives at their throats. Other sources from barely two years earlier talk of mage priests. Every source you have could be lies. What actual proof, from your own experiences, do you have that mages are evil?"

She frowned, thinking of Detrax's sneer, then pushing the memory away. This mage's face in the vision. Did that count? No, it told her nothing morally, positive or negative. Was the vision an image of the future? A message from the gods? A hallucination caused by some further betrayal of her father's? What did 'real' even mean anymore?

Her senses were liars. She hung her head again. She was too unstuck in time and place to be considered entirely sane. "I'm not sure my five senses or my mind are any more trustworthy than those books."

She could feel the weight of his perplexed stare. "Oh, that's right, I see. You probably don't *need* proof. You have faith, right? The goddess tells you what to believe."

She just shook her head in her hands. If only. That would be so much easier.

"Or... *do* you have proof of that? What the goddess tells you?"

She met his eyes again, then gave up and dropped her gaze. She didn't want to vomit while looking straight into his face. "There's no point in arguing this."

"So that's a lie too?"

Oh, that was quite enough. Nausea be damned, she shook a fist at him. "I *wish* it was a lie. I can't point to my visions or show them to you, so I *will* not argue whether I have proof. How can I prove to you they exist? I can't. And people like you never believe me anyway." She groaned again, loudly, hoping someone outside was listening. That exertion had been too much. She wiped the sweat accumulating on her forehead with the back of her forearm. The fever was growing but not as quickly as it sometimes did. At least she had that much luck.

Silence yawned between them. Her sweat turned cold, the nausea lessening slightly. Would it really abate that quickly?

"What are your visions of? What do you see?" he said, soft again. His tone was almost gentle. She didn't trust it.

She regarded him coolly out of the side of her eyes.

She straightened a little, hoping that the worst of it might have passed. Was this a trap?

"I've seen a city—Anonil, possibly. Burning, lost to red-banded forces. Something unexpected happens there, something goes wrong." She shook her head, trying to rid herself of the swelling memory of the vision. Focus on it too long, and it would return when she least wanted it to.

He frowned. "If Anonil falls, that would be truly terrible. But it would hardly be a surprise at this point, with Alikar's betrayal."

She shrugged. "I don't pick my visions for what will be convincing to you. I don't get to pick them at all."

"What else have you seen?"

Would he understand, if she told him? Think her words were a trick? Wasn't it only fair to tell him that she had seen him before this day, that she had known the instant she'd seen him in that tower that something terrible was going to happen? That it was the sight of him, not nervousness at the vote, that had made her voice falter and shake?

"I've seen… lots of things," she said noncommittally.

"Care to elucidate?"

There he went again. "Excuse me?"

"Like what? What have you seen?"

She hesitated one moment longer, then cast caution to the wind. What did she have to lose? There was nothing left. "I've seen you."

2   HOPE

Aven stopped outside the door to his old rooms. Rooms where his father lay, hovering at death's threshold.

The dark, polished wood stood out against the white marble, magnificent and ominous, as if it concealed some grand darkness inside. He pursed his lips, trying to gather his thoughts. Servants were absent from the halls, huddled inside rooms, keeping warm with their duties. Faint echoes of far-off chores clanged and thudded in the distance, and the thin, high whistle of a cold wind moaned in the towers above.

He'd left Miara in his suite with his servants, convincing her to stay a little longer before retiring to the rooms the servants had already chosen for her. He needed to hear more of her story—and maybe have her in front of him a little longer. He needed more proof she was alive and safe and whole before he could truly rest.

Here, though, he was alone. His father lay in those

old rooms, his mother fretting at his side. Did she know the harsh words father and son had last exchanged? What had been said?

Would he have said the same things if he'd known that it might be the last complete conversation he'd have with his father? Aven couldn't regret defending Miara, especially since the vote *had* succeeded in spite of his bold announcement of his intention to marry her. If he and Miara had obediently followed Samul's instructions, his father wouldn't even be lying half-dead here in Ranok. He'd likely be all dead. Or being carted off to Kavanar.

And yet… *You're not the king I thought you were.* The cruel words floated back to him. Words said in anger, not truth. Aven understood his point of view, his desire to defend Aven and, even more, Thel. Each of them had weighed the threat of civil war versus the threat of war with Kavanar, and both had been most concerned about the conflict they were most familiar with, the one they deemed most likely.

In the end, Aven had been right, either through luck or better information, but it could have easily gone another way. Had Toyl been greedier. Had Asten resented him. Had the lightning strike hit Aven instead of his horse.

Or if Aven had thrown Alikar in the dungeon when they'd first known of his divided allegiances, his suspicious contacts with Kavanar. Regret flooded him that he hadn't done more. That he hadn't acted more decisively. With Alikar. With Evana. Even with Daes. If he'd found a way to run a sword through Daes's gut rather than simply escaping, maybe none of this would be happening. Of course he could also then be very dead.

He swallowed and shifted his weight from one foot to the other, then back. If his father was conscious, what would Aven say him? Should he apologize? No, he couldn't. But could he make amends somehow?

And if his father wasn't conscious... Well, Aven was king now. It was time to act, even if he wasn't sure of the best path forward. Even if he didn't know what he'd say if Samul was awake behind this door.

He pushed the door open and went inside.

Aven had stayed in his room in Ranok only a few times in his life. Trips away from Estun had never been long, but he remembered the room well. He remembered playing on the soft gray quilt as a child, studying drawings of training exercises they'd traveled to take part in as a young man.

The quilt lay over his father now, along with furs and skins for extra warmth. That hardly seemed necessary, as the room was sweltering. And transformed. People crowded the space, and furniture had been shoved aside. He tried to ignore his things and any memories they'd dredge up. Pangs of old memories would not be helpful at the moment. A second bed had appeared but lay empty.

His mother sat perched beside Samul, her hand clasping his. She looked toward Aven, nodding just slightly before turning her gaze back to her husband.

His father didn't stir.

Aven strode to her side. "Is he...?"

"He's fallen into a deep sleep. I'm trying to help, but…" She shook her head, and only now did he notice the dark circles under her eyes.

"You should rest," he said. "You can't help him if you don't rest."

"I know." Still, she didn't move. "Any news on Thel?"

Aven shook his head, unable to meet her eyes. "Not yet." He rounded the other side of the bed and peered down at his father, not sure what he was looking for. "Why is it so hot in here?" He was starting to sweat. Just what he needed.

A gray-haired man hastily paging through a tome in his arms stepped from the mass of attendants lining the walls, some busy, some waiting for tasks. "Because we're trying to sweat it out of him, Your Highness."

"Sweat what out of him?" said Aven.

"The possible poison." He glanced up once, then back at the book, licking a finger to page faster.

"I don't believe we've met."

"Aven, this is Nyor Hiresun," his mother put in.

"Nyor is our healer here at Ranok, Your Highness," said a refined voice from the corner. As he looked up, the head steward Telidar bowed her head. He'd heard of Telidar, but if he had met her before, he didn't remember. Her black hair was pulled back severely, highlighting sharp brown eyes. "I hired him when our last healer, Erstik, retired last spring."

"Oh, excuse me," Nyor said. "Pleasure to be of service to you, Your Highness." Nyor jerked into an overly obsequious bow and nearly dropped his book in the process.

Aven gave a small nod of thanks, although he doubted the sincerity of the healer's gesture. "Anything you can tell me about my father's condition, Nyor?"

The healer shook his head. "I'm sorry, Your Highness. There hasn't been much time. Perhaps tomorrow I will know more after additional study. I have much to reference relative to his symptoms, which are common. Weakness, cold, clammy skin, and recent wounds can be indicators of dozens of poisons and some illnesses and infections."

"They are wounds that won't heal," Elise added, a note of annoyance in her voice. "That's not common."

"That remains to be seen," Nyor replied.

"No, it doesn't. I've shown you. I've healed them, and you've watched them *reopen*. That's not normal. It has to be a poison."

"I can't scientifically rely on what is happening when you use your… abilities to heal him. I can't say I understand how they work. So I can't treat it as fact. Your Highness."

Aven frowned. Nyor's tone was decidedly less respectful to the queen. No wonder she didn't want to rest. Even now, she eyed Nyor with annoyance as the healer continued paging through his tome.

Aven stared hard at his mother, trying to catch her eye as he bent closer to Samul and pretended to be concerned with him. Finally Elise looked his way. Aven tapped his temple, hoping she would get the idea.

She blinked, glancing back at Nyor again. Then she

stilled slightly.

What is it? came her voice in his head.

Glad you figured that out. We should really have a signal for this or something.

What's wrong?

You're suspicious of Nyor. Can we trust him?

I'm not sure. He seems… overly servile at times, downright disrespectful at others. I don't think he approves of mages.

Great, another fan.

Yes.

I'll ask Telidar how he was referred to her. And I'll send down Siliana or Miara to watch him and Samul so you can rest.

Outwardly she remained poised, but inwardly, relief surged through her. *That would be a help. I don't trust this "sweating" it out. Or any of his methods. How can he know what to do if he doesn't know the poison yet? And Samul's too weak to wake and drink all that water he's sweating out.*

So tell him to stop.

What if he's right? And I say something and Samul dies? Damn this all to hell.

Aven clenched his jaw. *All right. I understand. I'll send someone as soon as I can. If he wakes, will you tell him… I'm sorry?*

Sorry for what?

Sorry we quarreled.

I'll tell him.

Aven ran a tentative hand over Samul's hair. Had his temples always had this much gray, or was that a new development? Had his forehead always held such deep wrinkles, or was it the illness? Certainly his cheeks were sunken in a little.

It hasn't been much time, he told himself. Barely hours. He'd lost a lot of blood. He'll get better. He just needs to rest.

Still… Aven wished his father were awake.

He pressed a kiss to his father's forehead, then turned toward Nyor. "I want to be informed immediately if there are any changes or developments."

"Sire, I must focus on my patient—"

"There are many in this room who can carry a message. This is not up for debate." He narrowed his eyes at Nyor, hoping his expression indicated well enough that he would brook no argument about this. Or anything else.

"Yes, sire," said Nyor, suddenly meek. Ah, yes, there it was. Servile this minute, defiant the last. Why?

Aven nodded to them all and then set off for his rooms. He caught a servant along the way to carry a message to Siliana requesting her help with the king and to summon Telidar to his suite later. He also needed to figure out to whom he could delegate things like talking to Telidar. Dyon and Asten would be busy with war planning in earnest now, and Fayton and most of his trusted staff were still back in Estun. But Aven couldn't possibly handle all this himself. Things would start to take too long, fall by the wayside.

He strode down the hall, soon lost in memories he'd hoped not to get caught up in.

How many times had they ridden away from Ranok? Each time he'd carried a certain mixture of guilt and wistfulness in his heart. Wanting to stay. Knowing they couldn't. And how had that panned out?

All those years hiding in Estun, all for naught.

He opened the door to his suite and spotted Miara asleep on the couch, still sitting up.

Well, perhaps not all for naught. Perhaps it was all the Balance at work, and he would see an order to the madness in the end. He just hoped that none of it included losing Samul. Not yet, anyway. Not like this. Not without saying goodbye.

Aven watched her sleeping for a moment. In her Kavanarian leathers, she looked much like the first day they'd met, aside from the scar gracing her cheek. Would she keep any scars from today's wounds or will them all away? Maybe they were already gone.

When they could make it to Lake Senokin, he'd find out for certain. Patience, he reminded himself. Patience. Not long now.

He headed toward her. A servant stirred in a corner, but he didn't meet their gaze, indicating he didn't need anything. It was good, though, that he and Miara weren't alone.

Carefully he cradled her, one hand behind her neck, the other behind her shoulders, and he lowered her down to the couch. She may as well sleep here. His own room was separate from this, and clearly sleep was needed. And he didn't want to let her go. Or out of his sight. Not yet.

Her hair was soft, smooth under his fingers. She sighed

briefly and stirred but didn't wake. His hand lingered against her back for a moment, then he withdrew.

He sank to the floor, not ready to leave her side. He knitted his fingers and rested his chin on them, studying her, watching the rise and fall of her breath, eerily similar to his father's.

She's fine, just tired. And so is he. They'd both be fine. Wouldn't they?

His eyelids drooped, but he tried to shake it off. He could just stay here a few moments longer, and then he'd collapse into his own bed. Lobbing fiery boulders took more out of a man than one would think.

He awoke from a heavy sleep to a crick in his neck and the gentle brush of fingertips across his jaw. The caress strayed up past his temple, combed through his hair, and pushed it back out of his face. He opened his eyes. Miara smiled down at him.

He straightened, then groaned. How had he managed to fall asleep like that?

"I'm happy to see you too."

"I'm just stiff. Didn't intend to fall asleep here."

"Nice waking up to your face again, though."

He smiled. "Agreed. Not long now."

"We should probably find your brother first, eh?"

He nodded, relieved she'd put that together on her own. But gods, how long had he been asleep? Those hours were all hours Thel was still missing. "Yes. We must also figure out how to respond to Kavanar. And my father and all. Gods." He ran a hand over his face. Where to even start?

She reclined back. "It'll be all right, Aven. We'll figure something out. We'll find what's ailing him."

He smiled, still feeling a little dreamy. "You know, my life used to be quite boring before you came around."

"I'm ever so sorry, sire." She pursed her lips, holding back a laugh.

"Oh, it wasn't a good thing. I thought we'd established that."

She grinned broadly now. "Hey, meeting you wasn't my idea."

"I'll have to thank Daes next time he tries to kill me."

"You mean, when you soundly defeat him in battle."

"Of course. Isn't that what I said?" He mock-frowned at her.

"You said when he tries to kill you." Her smile softened but was no less warm.

"Same thing, my love." What time was it? He glanced at the window as he rose to his knees, stretching. To his surprise, twilight hung glumly over the castle. His stomach gurgled in complaint. "Hungry?"

"May I be of service, sire?"

Miara started as a young man's voice came from behind them. Aven peered over her shoulder at the page who'd materialized out of nowhere. He'd forgotten about their chaperone. He should really be glad, his honor intact, but mostly he just wanted to sigh.

Maybe he could convince Miara to kidnap him again so they could just be alone for a minute or two. Of course, once they were married, they could slam the door and not come out for days. But who knew when they'd get to that?

The unfamiliar page had stepped forward and waited patiently for instructions.

"Yes, can you send for some dinner to be set up in here?"

"Of course, sire," he said quickly, bowing a little too enthusiastically and almost falling on his face.

"And your name is?"

The page looked up nervously. "Perik, sire."

"Thank you, Perik. Actually, can you just send them a message to send us dinner and then come back as swiftly as you can? We may have some other tasks for you."

"Certainly, Your Highness." Perik scampered out.

Miara breathed a sigh of relief as the door softly shut. "Alone at last, if only for a moment. But shouldn't one of us be running off as well? Your Code and all that."

"Well, it wouldn't be terribly proper to follow him down to the kitchens and back like servants ourselves either."

"I have been a servant for most of my life, you know," she muttered, a little sheepish.

"A noble occupation. But to your point, don't worry, he'll be back soon. Declaring our intention to marry should grant us some leniency. Right?"

"Leniency from whom? Does someone track whether you've kept your oath?"

"Me. My father. Lord Dyon, but I think that's mostly just a personal hobby of his. As you can see, we're all rather indisposed with other things at the moment."

"Well, I agree if we've announced our will to be... married, it shouldn't be quite the same." She smiled gently, tilting her head, but he didn't miss the hesitation.

"Are you sure about this? I shouldn't have put you on the spot earlier." He reached out on a whim and dared to squeeze her thigh just above the knee. She covered his hand with hers.

"Sure about being queen? Oh, not at all. But I have a history of rising to the occasion." She smiled again. "About *you*, I'm quite sure."

"Then why the hesitation?"

"It feels strange to say it aloud. And it's intimidating, to think we'll be at the center of such spectacle." She was right; although the ceremony itself would thankfully be intimate, much celebration would follow. "It sounds greedy, too. Overconfident. I don't want you or anyone to think I am overeager or somehow out for personal gain."

He was utterly sure that was not the case, and in fact, it was one of the reasons he'd been drawn to her from the start. But before he could assure her of that, she surprised him by leaning forward to kiss him. He leaned into her kiss, into her, reaching his arms around her hips. She rested her hands gently on either side of his face as he pressed forward eagerly. His stiff neck panged in protest, and a grunt and wince escaped.

She laughed quietly. "You must be sore, sleeping like that. Turn around."

He cocked his head in question. "What?"

"Turn around."

"We have a war to plan, don't we?"

"Just do it. Turn around and sit down too. I can help.

You'll plan better if you aren't wincing every time you turn your head."

He complied slowly as he struggled to think of why she might make such a request. He settled back onto the floor, facing the fire. She pulled him to lean back against the edge of the bench, one of her knees firmly on either side of his shoulders. He tried to ignore them.

Her fingers dug into his shoulders, working in slow circles, and his eyes drifted closed. In all the heavens, he hadn't thought of that. The thick quilting of the gambeson was far too much of a barrier between her hands and his skin. He let out a rumble in the back of his throat without intending to. "You must be… just as tired… as I am… You don't need…"

"I get the impression I slept better. Plus I have my magic to help me. I'm fine. Relax."

Her fingers worked their way up and kneaded his neck. Heat and desire swept through him. He both hoped Perik would come back soon, and that he would not come back at all. Her hands strayed into exploring his hair and the base of his scalp, kind and reaffirming and assuring in their caress.

Oh, by the gods. "That feels good," he mumbled. A slight wisp of air brushed across his face, then another. His magic playing its tricks again? He let it, this time.

She made a soft, pleased, purring sound, sending another wave of desire through him as her expert hands plied him farther down his shoulders and back now.

I missed you, she whispered softly into his mind.

Her presence blended with his. Her satisfaction at his reactions, his rumbles, the way he'd relaxed under her attentions filled his mind. She rested her chin on his head, and he let himself lean back into her, finally close, finally at least a little bit together and like the world couldn't tear them apart as easily as it always seemed to. *I missed you, too,* he remembered to say.

He was never letting her go. Or maybe even out of his sight.

She snorted softly. *I will have to bathe, you know. In fact, I need to.* The idea sent off a wave of imagery conjured by his excited imagination, and she laughed, seeing it with him to his chagrin. But her hands tightened on his shoulders and stilled as his overactive mind went further than just imagining her in the bath. Now they were together, skin to skin, his head resting on her shoulder. Hot water swirled around them, as he whispered in her ear, ran his lips in a line of kisses up her neck, took her mouth and showed her just how much he had missed her as he rose over her—

The door clicked. Aven's eyes snapped open. The fire before him whipped back and forth, the air in the room excited, teasing the flickering candles with soft caresses.

Perik entered, stopped still for a moment, then retreated to wherever he'd been hiding on the other side of the room. For a young man, he seemed rather savvy. Or perhaps he just lacked the propriety and indignation of a middle-aged mum.

Aven smirked. Who was he kidding? Nothing like

one young man to understand another.

She leaned back and returned to massaging his shoulders. *I suppose we should acknowledge the poor thing. He probably feels quite awkward.*

He nodded and scooted forward, turning onto his knees again. *At least he didn't return to find us* actually *in the bath, eh?*

She blushed in response but slowly grinned too.

"I owe you one," he said quietly, only to her. Then he slid to sit sideways beside her, addressing Perik over the back of the couch. "Any luck, Perik?" Standing would probably be inadvisable until he found something very boring to talk about. Maybe Perik could oblige.

The young man glanced up, his formerly large round eyes relaxing. "Sire, the food should be here shortly. Steward Telidar says she'll send up the tea first."

"Thank you."

"Did you have anything else you need, sire?"

Other than a chaperone? "Soon, yes. After the food arrives. I need to see if there are any updates on Thel or my father." Or any new Kavanarian troops spotted. Or, well, a hundred things. He needed to know anything that had transpired while they'd slept.

But he was glad he'd had a few moments with Miara first. She was back by his side, and he hoped that wouldn't change for a long, long time.

Thel had lost all track of time as the carriage ride wore on. The lack of any light seeping into the carriage didn't help. The road grew rougher, occasionally jolting him against the hard wooden side. Luckily, some heat remained in the carriage from their bodies; otherwise he'd have been shivering on top of it all.

The shouts of men back and forth to each other were too garbled by the raging carriage wheels to make out, but they grew louder and more frequent.

Finally, a voice shouted from outside just above them, "Getting close! Let Detrax know we're coming."

"Oh, thank the ancient ancestors," Thel muttered. He rolled his neck, trying to stretch his stiff muscles. "Maybe now they'll finally let us out." Her eyes were wide when he glanced at her. "Someone you know?"

She nodded slowly. "He was once… a mage slave of my father's."

"Your father had *slaves*? First Kavanar, and now within my own realm. By the gods. And yet I'm the one you call evil."

She glared. "I never said my father was good."

That stopped him short.

She looked deep in thought for a moment, glancing around the carriage. Then she picked up the Devoted stone and asked, her voice hushed, "Can you still open that compartment?"

He frowned. "The panel down here? Yes. Why?"

"Hurry."

He pursed his lips and considered refusing but

ultimately opened it. He shifted to the other bench beside her and jerked the panel open just slightly.

Without hesitation, she tossed the glowing stone out the panel. The cabin plunged into darkness.

"What the…" he mumbled.

"You can shut it now." He barely heard her whisper over the wheels and horse hooves.

"I don't know if that's true. We'll see if I can in the dark. What did you do that for?"

She said nothing, and he could no longer see her expression. He fumbled and got the panel back in place. He was closer to her now on this bench than he would be if he returned to his original seat. He delayed a few moments in case they needed to say more.

She must have had the same idea. A hand reached out and found his knee, and he could sense her leaning closer, even in the darkness. Her hair brushed his cheek, a soft wisp that sent a shiver through him in spite of himself.

"I promise you I won't tell them you're a mage if you don't," she whispered.

"If this Detrax is a mage, can't he see for himself?"

"He may not—"

Before she could finish, the carriage lurched to a halt. He darted back to the other bench, not wanting to indicate an association that didn't exist.

He had settled before the door opened. "Out with ya," came a voice from outside.

He stilled, waiting for Niat to go first. Dim light once again illuminated the dark carriage. Torches or lanterns?

He couldn't see much outside except a form blocking most of the view, but the sounds of an encampment echoed off the wooden interior.

Niat did not move.

"C'mon now, don't make me drag you out."

"Niat?" he said carefully. "Do you need a hand? Are you still feeling ill?"

"Oh," she muttered, as if she'd been somewhere else. Lost in thought? One of her visions? He wondered if any of their captors would believe her. She certainly hadn't expected Thel to believe her, so it mustn't be a common reaction.

He did believe her, though. Naïve of him, most likely, but in his experience the fury and indignation she'd displayed were challenging to fake. Combined with the pain in her eyes… Few could craft such a cocktail of emotion just to cover a lie, to lay claim to some kind of privilege. And what privilege did the visions even give her? It didn't seem like anyone ever believed her, or even listened.

He should really be more suspicious, given her claim that she'd seen *him* in her visions. Surely this must be some long, elaborate deception. None of the questions he'd prodded her with had retrieved any more knowledge from her on the matter. She'd fallen mostly silent, and eventually he'd given up.

Light poured in again as Niat's form moved out of the carriage and out of sight. Thel followed promptly, ready to be free from this dark cage even if it was only to be led to a new and different one.

Armed men took him by each arm. Niat was similarly

pinned, and ahead of her was a familiar brown cloak trimmed with white fur. Alikar. Before them lay a decent-sized encampment of soldiers, and Thel was willing to bet they weren't Akarian ones. In fact, he hoped they weren't, because if they were, it would mean Alikar was commanding Akarians to fight Akarians. Gods, let it not come to that.

After a brief stop to relieve themselves, Alikar led them to the largest tent, majestic and white with a sheltered entrance and an unfamiliar flag outside. Alikar ducked under the entrance flap. Niat was shoved through, and then so was Thel, narrowly stopping himself from slamming into her back. Their guards formed a line behind them, some inside the door, some outside of it. Thel couldn't see much of the interior of the large tent, but it was furnished like an ordinary living area for a field commander. He could gather nothing more from it.

"Alikar!" said a voice. The timbre of it was strangely inhuman—too low and filled with a growling decadence.

"Greetings, Detrax." Alikar stepped up to shake hands with a man rising to his feet. A man or a creature? Two ram's horns protruded a handbreadth from his forehead, and although he shook hands with Alikar, two additional arms were propped on his hips. Tattoos like those popular in Sverti covered his broad forearms in a swirling pattern, and his face, chest, and shoulders bore ridges of hair that looked more like they belonged on a wolf or moose than on a man.

Just ahead of him, Niat gasped softly. Quite right.

If Thel hadn't been staring in mild horror, he probably would have gasped too.

If *this* was what she thought of when she imagined a mage, no wonder she felt so certain he was evil.

The four-armed, horned mage turned his gaze from Alikar to Niat. "Ah, Priestess. We meet again, under better circumstances this time."

"Detrax." Her voice was paper-thin, but icy. "That's debatable."

"Congratulations on your upcoming marriage," he said with rancor.

She did not reply.

"I hear you finally made it to the temple. Which was it? The temple of tears?" He laughed languidly, darkly, as if relishing the slow mental torture before him. Thel swallowed. Whatever this man might have in store for them, it was likely not good.

Again Niat said nothing, only staring down at her hands clasped in front of her now.

"And who is this?" The beast—no, the man—took a step forward, and Alikar shied slightly to the side.

Alikar cleared his throat. "Prince Thel is the second son of King Samul. When the situation in Panar became untenable, I decided to leave. But not without acquiring a few gifts first."

Thel shot him a glare.

"Well, I'm sure the Masters will be pleased. This scrawny runt will make a valuable bargaining chip. But he's of little use to as at the moment." Detrax closed a hand around Thel's arm, and Thel glared at him and the claws that had replaced fingernails. Detrax dragged him to the right and shoved him into the corner beyond Alikar. "Our little priestess on the other hand…"

Thel didn't see the movement, it was so quick. Detrax spun and seized Niat by the hair on the back of her neck, forcing her to her knees. Then he roughly cast her aside and forward, into the center of the tent. Thel fought the instinct to lunge after her. It was stupid. He was outnumbered. There was nothing he could do at this point. Not yet. He needed some kind of advantage.

She righted herself rapidly and glared viciously at him. He laughed again, that languid, mocking growl. "Tell us what the gods say of our plans. If you are so gifted as you claim."

"Do you simply mean to mock me and toss me around? Or do you truly seek guidance?"

He laughed in her face now. "Oh, certainly I can do all of those at once. And more."

She pressed her lips into a firm line and said nothing.

"Now, Niat. We move on Anonil very soon. What awaits us there?"

She shook her head. "I don't know."

Thel blinked. She was lying to them. He supposed that made sense, but he was surprised anyway.

"Oh, I think you do." Detrax strode to a chest at the back of the tent and picked up a vial of blue liquid from a tray. "Do you know what this is?" Her wide eyes said she did well enough. A knot of concern for her tightened in Thel's belly. "Don't make me use it. Ask and tell me what you know."

She paused and closed her eyes, taking a deep breath. Was that real, or was she pretending? She opened her eyes again. "I can't. It won't come so soon. But I have seen Anonil in flames. It falls to you, I swear it."

Detrax started forward, the vial still in hand. "So you lied then," he spat.

"As if you've never," she shot back.

He raised the vial as he strode toward her, still looking determined.

"No—" she started, falling backward, trying to escape him. "I won't be able to tell you anything after that, even if I see what you want me to see. And there's no guarantee—"

"You will see what I ask, and you *will* tell me what I want to know."

"It doesn't work that way. I can't control—"

Seizing her by the hair again, he hauled her back onto her knees. Thel gritted his teeth. Was there something he could do? His eyes searched for something, anything nearby that could give him an advantage.

Detrax held the vial an inch before her nose. "You will take this," he growled, "or I will *make* you take it."

She frowned sadly at the vial, and just when Thel thought Detrax would lift his hand to uncork it, she took it from him instead. Bitterly, she whipped off the cork and downed the contents in one shot.

The four-armed mage released her. "Have the messages from the gods waiting for me in the morning, Seer," he spat. "Or we shall experiment with other methods of making you tell the truth." Detrax eyed Alikar and Thel for one appraising moment.

"We have much to discuss," Alikar said. "Not in front of them, I should think?"

Detrax nodded. "Take them to the armory tent and chain them up. We'll deal with them more thoroughly in the morning."

Daes slowed outside the generals' parlor, listening. Evening had fallen; only the light of candles danced weakly across the dark stones of the hallway. The lower floors of the palace were cold, drafty, dim when the sun went down. A dismal place.

He expected no real work to be going on inside. It'd been a day of celebration for everyone, the generals and himself included. He planned to change that, however.

The clinking of glasses, the murmur of soft voices, and then a peel of a woman's laugh reached his ears. He rolled his eyes. Had the debauchery of the court reached even into the army? A little bit of brandy was nothing out of the ordinary, but in the days he'd served under General Vusamon in the northern rebellions, he would never have imagined his former leader acting as the courtiers did upstairs. Though they had been cautious and reserved today, and rightfully so. They lived by gaining favor, and they could scent the change in the air. The disappearance of Demikin's mistress might have given them a clue.

But for whatever stupidly personal reason, Daes had somehow hoped the few standing military advisers Demikin maintained would have carried themselves with more decorum. That was probably unfair. He shouldn't be surprised. And drinking and women laughing didn't mean their was an orgy going on inside. Although if there was, he wasn't quite sure *how* he might react.

He straightened the ebony cloak on his shoulders, the one he'd worn earlier as he'd received the lords and ladies of Kavanar in recognition of his new position. Its gold trim was the only concession he'd made beyond his usual black, which Marielle had handled with a mixture of consternation and amusement. He would have expected to resent the addition, but it left him oddly moved when it surprised him in the corner of his gaze. Where that feeling came from, for whom, or what it meant, he was entirely uncertain.

He made sure that the gold circlet still rested straight and even on his brow. It wasn't the crown of the king, but it would have to do for now. He couldn't with any propriety claim the king's title so soon. To do so would be handing any near rivals an excellent excuse to challenge him. No, instead, he'd bide his time, skirt as close to propriety as they could get away with, and earn favor along the way. In a matter of three months, or perhaps six, he could seize the crown officially.

But the war didn't have months. Not after Trenedum, the loss of the brand, and the defeat in Panar of all of his carefully laid plans.

It was time to change the game.

As quietly as he could, Daes swung the door open. A dozen Kavanarian generals lounged inside, of the total eighteen. Not bad for Daes's purposes. Six sat chatting in armchairs, and three huddled around glasses of wine near the fire, all entirely respectful and proper, thank the gods.

In fact, only two caught his narrow-eyed gaze, but neither noticed. One was asleep in the corner, a glass spilled out of his hand and onto the cushion beside him. Another had his feet propped up on a map of Kavanar and a half-naked girl in his lap, the source of the laughter.

Several others stood in the back, including Vusamon, clutching brandy glasses and frowning fiercely at him. Daes recognized all but a few of them, having served with them in the rebellions and afterward, before politics and the injury to his leg had pushed him out in his prime. The fighting had been over anyway, and he'd been a rank or two too low to hope to be made a general, but it still irked him that an injury had been the undoing of so much hard work.

Mages had long ago fixed the leg, but by then he had already worked too hard to gain his position at Mage Hall. It hadn't made sense to continue to court the generals. He'd found a new army of mages, one that was his alone to command.

Now, he'd take control of this one, the one that had cast him aside not so long ago in favor of younger and fitter men.

A stillness fell across the room. Someone cleared a throat.

"Lord Cavalion, is it now?" said Vusamon, voice dangerous and stern as he swirled brandy in his glass. "Come to join us for a drink?"

The young man with the girl—whose face Daes hadn't even caught sight of—had not yet seen fit to pause his activities.

Daes stalked slowly forward, ignoring the greeting. His boots thudded loudly against the dark hardwood. He made sure of it. He stopped short of the table covered in maps and paused, his shadow looming over the girl and her lover.

She apparently was the smarter of the two and tried to jerk away, looking back over her shoulder at Daes with wary brown eyes. But the general pulled her back the few inches she'd gained.

With a swift shove, Daes thrust the man's feet off the table and sent the two of them both toppling to the floor.

"A map of our fine kingdom deserves more respect," Daes said calmly, almost casually, as he brushed the map free of imaginary grime. As if that young man had ever done enough to have dirt on his boots. He surveyed the room for reactions, his own expression blank.

Daes caught Vusamon's eye and spotted a faint smile. The girl regained her feet and bolted wisely for the door in spite of the general's protests. The youngish man, unfamiliar to Daes, levered himself into his seat and glared, but his bleary eyes looked a bit too drunk for genuine outrage.

"What brings us the honor of your presence, Lord Consort?" said another general from those seated. "Last I heard, there were no urgent matters of state concerning us."

"Indeed, when was the last time there *was* an urgent matter of state concerning any of you?" Daes mused. A few narrowed their eyes, wary of an insult. But a few more nodded and murmured their agreement.

"Your point, Lieutenant?" Vusamon said sharply. Ah, apparently he fell into the wary camp.

"I am a lieutenant no longer," Daes said, pleasantly now. "Which was a shame. I always wished there'd have been another war to fight."

"Your leg was crushed by a horse," said another, and now with the voice, Daes remembered him. Edeul, who'd been Vusamon's second at the time Daes had fought.

Daes looked down at his leg mockingly, then back up at the man. "It seems to have been fixed. And yet, I have not forgotten the long-neglected Kavanarian army."

"What are you getting at, Cavalion?" Vusamon demanded.

"Lord Cavalion."

"Of course… sir." Vusamon's eyes narrowed, but although he played the part of stern and wary adversary, Daes could sense excitement mounting.

"You've been much ignored by King Demikin," Daes mused. "You've been left without purpose or goal or mission. What use does Kavanar have for an army when there is peace?" Daes smiled, almost serenely happy.

"Indeed," muttered Edeul.

"Well, gentlemen. The situation has changed."

Chained to a tent pole. This day just got better and better. Thel kept his ears pitched for clues about the camp around them. But it was just the usual metal clangs, drunken shouts, and horse whinnies. Trunks and crates packed the dark tent around him, and the slit between the tent flap and wall revealed little but a strip of dark, dense forest.

The soldiers had deposited Niat a few minutes ago and chained her up alongside him, sitting on the dirt floor. Not even a rug. He shook his head. Brutes.

"You all right?"

She sat in a stupor, her eyes focused on nothing. Not responding. The drug—or poison?—must be doing its work.

He tried a few more times but gave up as her expression remained unaltered. She was not with him, not now. He returned to listening to the camp and trying to piece something together out of what he heard. He didn't conclude much.

A groan alerted him that something had changed. Her head had dropped into her hands, as it had in the carriage. Was that always the aftermath of whatever happened to her?

"You all right?" he tried again.

She raised her head enough to glare at him. Some light had returned to her eyes, which relieved him in spite of her glare. "Leave me alone." Her voice was hoarse and raspy.

He held up both wrists in her direction defiantly. "Trust me, I'd love to get away from you."

She glowered at him, then sank her head back into her hands.

"I definitely think I'm going to be sick this time." She groaned again.

"I don't see how, as we haven't eaten anything all day." His stomach growled loudly as if to reinforce his words.

"You say that like it changes anything." She turned away from him, or tried to. Oh. She wasn't bluffing. She was very serious about this throwing up thing.

"Hey—you out there," he called to the guards.

No one responded.

"Fevrin," he barked. The guard must have jumped, because the tent wall jerked suddenly.

"How's he know my name?" said the one soldier to the other.

"He may be a scrawny thing, but he can hear, you fool," came the reply.

Thel scowled. He was just trying to get a little help for a sick woman here. Why did the width of his shoulders or biceps have to matter to everyone so damn much? "Hey, you hear me?"

"What you want?" Fevrin grunted.

"I don't know what you store in here, but unless you think your lords want it nicely festooned with vomit, you had better fetch a bucket."

"A… what?" They didn't react for a second. "Is that some kind of fool threat?"

"You'd think a prince would have more decorum," said the other, clearly smarter one. "Although I suppose threatening to vomit on things is a creative way for a prisoner to rebel."

"Not me, you loon," he snapped. "The priestess. You have a sick priestess of Nefrana held captive in here, and you can't be stopped from your drinking to be bothered to help?"

"Now how does he know we're drinking?" said Fevrin, even more exasperated now.

"He's got ears, I told you."

"Ears like a bat, you mean."

"Yeah. A scrawny, snappish bat."

"Snappish?"

"What, that word's too big for you? He's demanding. Princes usually are."

Thel smacked a hand to his forehead and ran his hand over his face. Why did he even bother?

"Stop it," she grumbled. "They won't help. You're just going to have to turn your royal nose up in the other direction."

He rolled his eyes at her. "Your determination to think ill of me is astounding. Really. It knows no bounds. You should be proud, you've quite the knack for it."

Her only answer was another groan.

To his surprise, footsteps clomped away from the tent and returned shortly, sliding something under the tent flap. In the dim light, he groped and slid it over toward her. It was no bucket, but it was part of a broken barrel that would serve much the same purpose. If she didn't puncture herself in the process.

True to her word, she did get sick, but luckily for everyone it only lasted a few minutes before she collapsed in a shivering, feverish ball, her back against a nearby crate.

"Oh, Fevrin," he called again in a singsong.

"Gods damn you, stop calling me by my name! You're a prisoner."

"By Anara! Thanks for the reminder, I'd *completely* forgotten. How about I'll stop if you get her a blanket?"

"You're right, he is a demanding little nit."

"Come on," Thel called. "She's a mess. Shivering, sweating. Have some decency."

"Stop it," Niat whispered.

"What do you think?" Fevrin said warily to his companion.

"What can he do with a blanket?" Thel imagined the men shrugging at each other. "They're chained good and tight. And you heard her in there."

The two men grew silent, likely considering.

"What do you care?" she whispered. "The sight of normal people suffering too much for your delicate sensibilities?" Her words dripped with a dark pain, as if she were steeped in suffering, made from it.

"As Sven's daughter, a priestess, and a seer, you're hardly someone I'd classify as normal."

"Thanks for reminding me."

"Your capacity for negativity seems particularly exceptional as well. What can I say, you've got many talents."

"Go to hell." It was a hoarse, monotone whisper with exactly the same passion as everything else—very little.

He winced mockingly. "Coming from a priestess, I'm sure that's an especially powerful curse. Of course, you already think I'm going to hell, so it doesn't really make much difference."

Eventually, footsteps led away from the tent again. He eyed Niat. Her eyes were closed, arms crossed across her shoulders, knees curled in. He needed to act. Before she passed out.

He shifted onto his knees and crept closer as silently as he could. When he was just in front of her, he bent down close to her ear. "Niat," he whispered.

She jumped, smacking her temple into his forehead and groaning loudly again. Thel just barely stifled a curse as the pain shot through his already aching head.

"Please don't. Just leave me alone," she whispered. Her words were tight, maybe frightened now, but as quiet as his own.

He didn't oblige. Not yet, anyway. Now might be his only chance to try. He bent closer again, keeping his hand in front of his forehead defensively this time. "Do you know anything that could get us out of here?" he whispered. "Any weaknesses we could exploit? Habits of Detrax or Alikar or the troops?"

"Give it up, little prince," she said bleakly, and it occurred to him that she still didn't even know his name and hadn't asked. For some reason, that was even more depressing than her response. "I don't know anything."

"Think. There could be something. Detrax must have a weakness."

"It's hopeless."

He gritted his teeth, refusing to believe that. Unless… "You saw that in your visions?"

She shook her head minutely. "No. None of the visions I've gotten are about that."

"So you don't know for sure," he said triumphantly. "You could be wrong."

"I know because I've been at their mercy my whole life. I don't need to see the future. I know the past."

He said nothing for a long while, groping for some words to dissuade her from despair. None came. He eased away from her and back to the other side of the tent, intending to leave her alone. But his curiosity gnawed at him. "What are they about?" he said more casually now. "The visions."

She shook her head again, almost imperceptibly. "The bluebell is too strong. It's all a blur of light and sensation. There's lots of—stone. Boulders, florid archways, this sparkling purple tall heavy thing, white fur. Maybe a cave?" He rubbed his chin. That description could match Estun. But it didn't tell him much else. She continued, "I don't know what any of that is supposed to mean. He won't be pleased." She shrugged very slightly. "Nothing I can do about it. Bluebell is terrible for my visions. But no one listens when I try to explain how it works." Her words were pained, growing softer but edged with pain. As if she found him beyond trying. She probably did.

She was clearly ill. He should leave her alone, so he turned his thoughts to planning an escape. Of course, with her so weak, he wasn't sure escape was possible. But he had no intention of leaving her behind to be tortured with blue vials.

A lump flopped into the tent, and Thel reached out to find not one but two blankets. They were rough as burlap and stank strongly of horse, but he didn't care. He eased one over her.

Whether from the natural need for sleep or exhaustion from her illness, she had collapsed into a fitful slumber. He studied her face now that he could look without her glaring. She was paler than that morning but did not look near death. The kohl around her eyes was smudged, which made them no less dramatic, but her face was creased with lines of anguish. She was young to be so bitter.

He retreated to the other side of the tent and pulled the second blanket over himself, forcing himself to lie down and rest as best he could while chained. What did he have to work with to escape? They'd failed to search him in the tumult of leaving Panar, so he still had his boot dagger, but it wasn't going to be any help against iron manacles. If Fevrin and his smarter friend ventured close enough, he might have a chance at using it on them. Thin he might be, but he felt fairly confident he was better trained than they were. But he'd still need luck to take them both out quickly. And he felt less inclined to do so anyway, now that they'd actually had the decency to meet his demands. He'd be more likely to best them at math problems, but somehow he didn't see that knowledge helping him much in this situation.

Perhaps he could convince them she had some kind

of highly contagious disease and they were all doomed to die unless they let Niat and him go? Hmm, but if he did succeed in convincing them, he doubted Fevrin would come close enough to unchain them. The guards would more likely just let them rot where they sat.

Could he outwit them somehow? Was there something seemingly innocuous he could claim he needed to help Niat that would help liberate them? Aside from the keys to their shackles, he couldn't think of anything.

If he could start a fire somehow… but these chains were looped round the center tent pole. He and Niat would be just as likely to burn alive as escape. A bribe was perhaps a possibility, but he had a feeling he lacked the charisma for that.

He needed some advantage, something he had that they didn't. Preferably something they didn't know he had.

Magic?

Thanks to Niat, they did not seem to yet know he was a mage. Or perhaps they did and didn't care. But either way, magic was likely his best weapon.

A shame there was still too little light to peruse the book. Perhaps it was for the best, as he'd rather lose his knife than that book, so taking it out at all was foolish. No, he'd have to stick with what he'd figured out already. Which was not much.

Probably a good idea to rest anyway before staging an escape. He turned as much away from Niat and toward the door as he could, and to his surprise, he drifted off to sleep.

"I need you to take a look at this," King Aven said.

Almost before the king could unfold the slip of paper he'd removed from his pocket, Tharomar could see something strange was going on. The king held it out.

Tharomar took the sheet in his hands. It… shimmered.

Silver rays cut swaths across the thin paper. Impossible. Ro just stared, watching something like starlight snake into fine circles and lines, curls and jagged twists.

"Can you read this?" the king asked.

"I'm… not sure," was all he could manage.

The paper felt impossibly mundane in his hands, twitching like any normal map in the wind. The ordinary ink on the page looked broken, malformed. But the light was starting to put the pieces together, to fill in the blank spaces.

Serabain. It was Serabain, but mixing two known alphabets, the ancient and the modern. The broken words slowly solidified before him as new letters bloomed to life, now constructed only of pale starlight.

Yes. Yes, he could read this. With some work. The real question was *should* he?

He glanced nervously at Jaena, then the king, then back at the paper. This was strange magic indeed. What kind of information had someone chosen to encode this way? Something they didn't want easily found. Who had done it?

He had a bad feeling about this map.

"It's… like a map of Zaera's," Ro said slowly.

"I thought the same," came a voice from behind him. Ah, yes. That older mage—Wunik, was it?—was now pacing back and forth behind Ro. Jaena and Aven hovered on either side, also gazing down at the map of starlight.

"But those maps are supposed to be…" Ro hesitated.

"What?" said Jaena, looking up. Light cast a soft glow across her features, dark eyes searching his and lips slightly parted. Her body was warm against his hip, his arm.

He swallowed. "They're supposed to be cursed."

"Really?" said Wunik. "I'd never heard such a thing. Fascinating."

"What kind of curse?" said Aven.

"I'm not sure, sire. I could look into it further for you. I just remember they are supposed to be very dangerous."

He narrowed his eyes at the map. Could such a magnificent creation truly be dangerous? Evil…? His memories of the maps were a vague swirl in his mind, but he didn't think he'd read anything *good* about them. The warnings were all very dire.

And yet, it was hard to believe anything that shone with light stolen from the heavens could be truly malevolent.

He shivered. The wind picking up was frigid, yes, but it was more than that.

As the minutes passed, the map grew brighter and shimmered. Most of the words were whole now, the alphabet a perplexing and arbitrary mix. Probably designed to vex potential translators. But he *could* make out a few words.

Freedom. Was that joy? Or was it the ancient form for jumping? Huh. As wary as he was of this map, he found it a unique, fascinating challenge.

"Dangerous… how, exactly?" King Aven asked.

"Oh." Had he been waiting for Ro to elaborate all that time? Ro shook his head at himself. "I'd have to research more to tell anything for certain."

"So… can you read it? Translate it?" Aven gave him a patient smile.

Ro gritted his teeth and eyed the map again. He could definitely read it. He could probably translate it.

But whose hard work would he be undoing? Zaera's, no doubt. Were she here, would she forgive him?

He stole another quick, measuring glance at the king. He *seemed* a good man. Not the type that would abuse power or be quick to anything vile, at least based on the little Ro had seen. And without his help, Ro would still be rotting in the basement of Trenedum Palace. At the very least, he owed the king for that.

May Zaera and the goddess guide his hand. Or make him witless if this was absolutely the wrong thing to do.

"Yes, I can read this," Tharomar said finally. "Or at least, I can transliterate it into modern Serabain, and then I will be able to read it. It'll take some time, maybe a couple of days. But there's nothing unusual here."

He caught the king's crooked smile out of the corner of his eye.

"I mean, besides that we're reading it in the dark." Ro turned the paper at a sharp angle, trying to understand just how the starlight was doing that.

The king's smile broadened. "Glad to hear glowing maps made of starlight aren't an everyday occurrence for you. I was starting to feel terribly unworldly."

Ro smiled back. Aven seemed a tad young for a king. Others would probably disagree. The young man was no lanky teenager, but Tharomar probably had five or even ten years on him. He certainly wasn't going to ask the king his age and risk offending anyone. He hoped and prayed these Akarians were truly less corrupt than those who ruled Evrical, but he'd only been here a few days. The Assembly meeting had been promising. But some hid their darkness better than others under the cloak of ritual and law. The truth of these Akarians and their ways remained to be seen.

"Oh, no. Our temple never had or even discussed anything like this," said Tharomar. "I've only read the histories."

"Anything else you remember from them?"

"They mentioned maps, but never in much detail. Just that they existed. Some neglected to say even that."

"That's probably for the best. But did you say 'they?' As in, more than one map?"

Ro rubbed his forehead with one hand, trying to remember, but hastily grabbed the map again when a fresh gust of wind threatened to tear it away. He hadn't given the stories much weight at the time, thinking Zaera and her maps were myths. Or at best, relics of the past that had nothing to do with their present struggles. "I don't remember, to be honest. Maybe it was just an assumption I made."

"But your memory was of more than one."

"Yes. And, well, wouldn't you make a copy or two in case one was stolen or destroyed? I can delve into the histories and look, if you have them."

"Did you *see* those books back there?" Jaena said, jerking a thumb over her shoulder and smiling. "I'm sure they've got something." Indeed he hadn't failed to eye the books longingly as the king had dragged them straight past them and out onto this cold, dark balcony.

"I think we may have a few. If not in there, then in the library," the king said. Gods, they had a whole library of books like that? Oh, of course they did. This man was a king. Tharomar had just never been in any situation in his life where such a library might actually be his to examine. Even the order's temple in Evrical had mostly borrowed and loaned the books from other temples. He'd always had to give them right back. "And Panar has several temples with their own libraries."

"I can help with research," Wunik chimed in from behind. "And possibly even the translation a bit."

Tharomar glanced over his shoulder. He hadn't figured the older mage into his calculation of whether he should translate the map. He sighed. Too late now, plus he had so little to go on. "Of course. The sooner we translate it, the better. I wouldn't want to delay His Majesty's mission."

"Just sire is fine. Or Aven."

"Majesty is a Kavanarian title, I've come to realize," Jaena muttered.

"Should I start working now, sire?" Ro said, hoping the older mage wouldn't be game to start right away.

The king's eyebrows shot up. "Oh, no. It's not *that* urgent. We have plenty of urgent concerns, and this isn't even at the top of the list. Start tomorrow evening, if you wish."

"Yes, sire." Ro bent to inspect the glimmering characters again.

"Your brother?" Jaena asked. "Any news?"

The king's face hardened. "No. We think they've taken him out of the city."

"We can't find him with men, horses, or farsight," Wunik added, voice pained. "Derk and Siliana are still looking."

"And what of your father?" Tharomar asked. "He was ill?"

"He is stable for now, but not comfortable. The creature mages are unable to fully heal him. His wounds fester under the skin even after they are healed." The king's face darkened further. Sounded like his father had made the right choice in handing over the crown.

"Seven hells." Jaena grimaced. "That's… I'm sorry to hear that, my lord." She shivered as another gust of wind blew past them.

"Let's go inside," the king said. "That is, if your curiosity is sated."

"Yes, sire," Tharomar said quickly. "I'm not so curious that I'd like to freeze to death."

But he did hesitate a moment longer, drinking in the strange light, before handing the map back to the king.

Aven held up a palm. "No, you keep it. So you won't need me when you're ready to begin. The library is yours to work in, and any balcony you need."

"Thank you, sire." Ro gave a short bow, then followed them all back inside.

He headed straight for the hearth to warm up and tried not to care that Jae didn't join him. She did toss him a quick smile as she headed for the mages on the other side of the room. Miara sat with the little girl and older man Ro had crossed paths with at Trenedum. Her family? They were deep into a rooks and pawns game.

Ro watched as they spoke, marveling at the sight. Here were *four* mages, all free from Devoted clutches and Kavanarian corruption. Four who had done the impossible. Four more than a month ago. A small victory, but a victory nonetheless.

He let the warmth seep into him, both from the fire and the view. He hadn't had time to pray yet today, so he sent up an invocation of gratitude to the goddess for a day like this.

All his days were suddenly sweeter, and more precious, thanks to her. Jae caught him staring, and he averted his eyes, grinning wider. Her laughing eyes bored into him as he sought another place to rest his gaze.

The king and Wunik joined him by the fire. "Did you find accommodations?" the king asked. "In all the chaos, I lost track."

Tharomar grinned wider in spite of himself. "I... Yes, I found some, sire."

"And were they acceptable? Comfortable?"

"Well, the bed is a wee bit small for two, but I have no complaints," he said. "My lord," he tacked on hastily, clearing his throat.

Both men's eyebrows rose now, and they glanced at each other. "I... see," the king managed. He glanced over his shoulder at Miara, then back at the fire.

"With your approval of course, my lord," Ro added.

"My what? Oh, of course. No approval is needed." Aven's eyes were distant now, lost in thought.

Perhaps this was his chance to ask a favor. "I should also send word back to my order soon," Ro said. "They may be in danger from the Devoted. I hate to impose, but do you have some simple means to send a message to Evrical?"

"My journeyman Siliana can send a bird for you," Wunik said. "Write a scroll, and she can send it tomorrow."

"Thank you," Tharomar replied. "I'll do it first chance I have."

Ro joined the king staring into the fire. What he was going to say to the temple, he wasn't sure. Of course, he'd tell them about the Devoted's discovery of the pendants and their purpose. But why hadn't *he* been informed of their purpose?

And what he really wanted to know—had his order known he was a mage?

He glanced over at Jaena again. She was heading over to join him. A certainty bubbled up inside him, a determination to stick with her as long as she'd have him, no matter the cost. By Nefrana, how had she grown to mean so much to him?

He tried to put the message out of his mind. It might get him answers, but it wasn't going to change anything. Nothing that mattered, anyway. He hoped.

Aven was still dwelling on the discussion with Tharomar when the suite's door was flung abruptly open. He shoved the irrational bout of jealousy down. Not everyone was born to swear knightly oaths or bear royal progeny. What did it matter if some people had freedoms he didn't? He'd certainly gotten plenty in exchange. Besides, he'd been born to be king and had never wanted to be anything else. A few weeks of impatience were nothing in the grand scheme of things, right? And he certainly shouldn't envy Jaena or Tharomar their happiness. They'd been through quite enough.

Perik made a hasty but ultimately doomed attempt to slow someone down. Derk burst past the poor young man. Siliana hovered fast on his heels.

"We saw something," he said, panting as though he'd run the whole way there.

Siliana added from behind him, "It may be nothing, but—"

"It's something, all right." Derk cast a dark glare at her.

"You didn't spot the *prince*, you just spotted a scrap of fabric, you dolt."

"Stop pissing on my campfire."

"By the gods, must you be so crude?"

Derk ignored her. "He's there, I swear it. Aven, you want to see or not?"

"And don't be so familiar," Siliana chided him.

Aven stepped forward, giving Siliana a thankful nod. He didn't particularly care, especially when it came to Derk, but he did appreciate her efforts at decorum. "What did you find?"

Derk spread his hands, and the air between them ripped open, revealing a view of a forest and a military encampment, all from the twilit sky. "Here. This is a short ride outside of Anonil."

All eyes were on Derk, and Aven gestured for the others to come closer. He trusted every one of them—except for possibly Perik, but only because of their short acquaintance. Miara, Jaena, and Ro took him up on the invitation, crowding around. Wunik and Miara's family held back.

"This is inside Gilaren Territory?" Aven said.

"Of course. Where else? See that flag on the large tent?" said Derk.

A red flag waved. "That's the flag of Evrical," Tharomar put in.

"And the one next to it—that's Gilaren Territory, right?" Derk said quickly, gesturing with his chin. He couldn't move his hands without disrupting the spell.

"Alikar," Aven growled, gritting his teeth for a moment before he spoke again. "Yes. Look, can you move over there? That's his carriage. You can even see that cloak of his, right there."

"Any sign of Thel in particular?" Miara asked.

"No," Derk said. "But I wondered if maybe somebody shouldn't stop by and ask. Loudly. With weapons."

"And arrest that traitor," Aven added. "The chances that Thel is with Alikar are good. My brother wouldn't just run off on his own, and Alikar's just as missing as Thel is. All right, let's—"

Miara laid a gentle hand on his arm. "There's work to be done *here*, Aven. And you still need to rest."

"The others need to rest too."

"True, but you're the king. And your father needs you here."

"That line of reasoning has failed me before, I'll warn you," called Wunik from the hearth.

"As I've said before, people rarely listen to reason." Miara smiled slightly, but it faded fast. "You have many who would be willing to help by going. And there's a war to plan, I believe?"

Aven only frowned.

We've barely been reunited for barely half a day, she said silently. *Surely others can help.*

Who can I trust with my brother's life? He eyed the tents of the encampment, hoping for some glimpse or confirmation that Thel was truly there.

You're going to have to trust a few people. We can't fight a whole war with Kavanar alone.

He sighed. That was quite true. "All right. Perik?"

"Yes, sire?"

"Get me Warden Asten."

The group of them studied the scene as they waited. "Those look like Kavanarian troops to me," Ro said into the silence.

"Agreed," said Aven. "The traitor has already let the enemy onto our lands. I shouldn't be surprised."

A few more minutes passed in silence before Asten appeared in the doorway. She still wore the same armor over a silver quilted gambeson she'd had on this morning. "Yes, my lord?" she said briskly.

Aven explained the situation so far. Miara was right. He did have allies he could trust, and he was going to need every bit of help they could give. "I want you to take whatever men you need and get me my brother back. Think you can do that, old friend?"

"It would be my pleasure, sire. If you approve, after Prince Thel is recovered, I'd like to head over to the Dramsren stronghold. Our troops from Shansaren should be arriving there, and I'd like to meet General Inoin. Even then, we may be too late for them to reach Anonil in time."

Aven scowled. "Given Alikar's treachery, the city may already be lost. But we must do what we can. Do as you've planned. Are the plans my father asked you to put together complete?"

She nodded. "Of course, sire. They were finished with four copies before we left Estun. Dyon has several sets of drawings for you."

"We'll dig into them in the morning."

"Excellent, sire. I, for one, have been ready for this fight for some time." She gave him a small, wolfish smile.

"With your leave, I'll go rouse the troops. I'd like to leave before midnight, if possible."

Aven opened his mouth to bid her goodbye.

"Wait," Miara said, starting from a daze. She'd been staring at the encampment during the exchange with Asten. "They'll have mages. You should take some of us with you."

"If they're smart, they'll have air mages," Jaena added.

Derk sighed dramatically. "She's right. Fine, fine. If you insist, I'll go."

Aven raised an eyebrow. "You've been searching for hours. You've got to be exhausted."

Derk jutted out his chin. "I'm perfectly fine. Siliana's been helping, and I've got the whole sky to drain dry."

"Don't even joke about that," Wunik snapped.

Derk dropped the view of the encampment to wave off Wunik's comment. "Jaena's right—they'll have air mages. An air mage needs to go. You need to plan this war. And you need Wunik's knowledge, not him riding off into battle. And other than that, we haven't got much to choose from, do we? Not anyone trained, anyway. I'm the only option."

Aven winced. "Well, I've never liked admitting you're right, but I especially don't like admitting it over this."

Derk grinned. "And the ladies are backing me up. Aren't you?"

"Don't get used to it." Miara scrunched her nose at him.

Aven hid his gratification at her expression. "All right, you're right this time. Damn, we're so unprepared. But there's no changing that now. Thank you for volunteering, Derk. Does that suit you, Asten?"

She nodded brusquely. "As long as he can be ready to ride within the hour."

"Course I can. I can be ready right now, for you." He winked at Asten.

The warden shot a glare at Aven. "And as long as he stops winking at me."

"No winking at your commanding officer, Derk," Aven said sternly.

"Aw, you're no fun."

"I mean it. You're in her service until I let you out of it, and that means you follow every order she gives you. To the letter. You're a soldier now as far as I'm concerned. Got it?"

Derk's eyes widened, but he didn't look put out by the intensity of Aven's words. "Got it. Sire."

"Wait, wait," Miara said. "Don't just rush off. One more moment. Let's think. Tactics." She glanced hopefully at Jaena. "You shouldn't go charging in. Some should stay back from the group maybe? Find out who they have and what's going on first."

"If the air mages attack, you don't want to be bunched up together," Jaena added. "Treat it like… like they have catapults. Very fiery catapults."

"Good ideas," said Aven. "You know how to handle artillery, right, Asten?"

"I'll treat it as such, sire."

"They'll be faster, though," Jaena added hastily. "It's

not really artillery. They're adaptable. They've got no need to reload. And you can't be sure of their range; it depends on the mage's talents."

Asten nodded. "Harder to spot at first than a catapult, too, I'd wager. Any foot soldier could wield that power."

"Promise me you'll hang back and let a scout or greeting party go in first," Aven said, stepping closer to her. "And you'll keep Derk with you."

She scowled now, casting a sidelong glance at Derk. "You know I prefer to be out front, Your Highness."

"Hence why I'm asking specifically for you *not* to be." He leaned forward, trying to drive the point home.

She raised her chin. "I'm not the kind of leader who cowers."

"You won't be cowering. You're observing their tactics and developing a strategy instead of throwing yourself into a lit bonfire and artlessly risking your life. I want all of you coming back, Thel included. We cannot afford to lose any of you." He clapped a hand on her shoulder above the pauldron. "Even Derk."

"I'm right here, you know," said Derk.

Asten frowned, not quite swayed.

"Consider this information gathering, if you must. The objective cannot be to just destroy the encampment. We need Thel back, but also the more we know about what we're facing, the better."

She sighed. "Understood. You're right, sire. I'll do my best to bring him back to you and learn what we can."

He nodded now, dropping his hand. "And... thank you.

For everything you did with Alikar at the vote this morning."

Asten waved him off. "Proved himself a desperate fool even to approach us. I don't need to be your friend—or respect you—to give traitors no quarter. But I am your friend, and he could easily have known it."

"I still appreciate it."

She bowed more graciously now.

"May the Balance protect you," he said. "And the gods speed your horses."

And with that, Asten turned and was gone, Derk on her heels.

Aven sighed and sank back beside the fire, but it wasn't long before he felt Wunik's presence beside him. "Yes?"

Wunik looked as tired as Aven felt, with rings under his eyes and his brow more haggard than Aven ever remembered seeing it. But he straightened and said, "Do you think we should look for more mages to free, sire?"

Aven rubbed his forehead. "After the day we've had, it's admirable you remembered that."

Wunik shrugged. "Naps work wonders."

"So I've heard. Yes, let's try."

Without saying anything to the others, he and Wunik quietly absconded out to the balcony. The elder must have understood on some level what Aven was thinking, because he didn't bring out his usual setup with the water. No, instead he drifted to the side of the balcony with Aven, out of sight of the others, and opened up a simple window of light in the air. If they were really going to free any mages, they'd need Miara's help to talk to them.

But Aven had a very bad feeling that no help would be necessary.

Wunik's shimmering portal glided across pines and roads and wheat fields until it came to Mage Hall. The older man let out a slow breath.

Aven's hopes fell at what he saw, though he wasn't surprised.

Not a human in sight, mage or no. Not even the towers were manned, though they had been before by mages in physical chains. Fires lit the windows of the long, low dormitories, but fewer now.

"They've been sent off to war," Aven said quietly. "Not all of them, but many."

Wunik nodded, collapsing the window as he clasped his hands.

"Sent after us." Aven looked out over the city, *his* city, his fists closing against all reason. The majestic towers of white stone stretched up in a seemingly random pattern, like stalks of graceful flowers reaching up toward the sun. To stare down at the black, hollow shell of Mage Hall and know that those who'd labored there traveled toward this beauty, likely on a mission to destroy it—against their will at that… Something in him hardened like the red-yellow of steel cooling to bitter, angry gray at the injustice of it.

Wunik hung his head. "Let's not tell the others."

"Only if they ask." Aven was already nodding.

"Yes. I'll keep checking nightly. Something might change. But I wouldn't count on it."

"I don't intend to."

Wunik hurried back inside, but Aven stopped and

stared out at the rooftops. He gripped the marble balustrade and tried to calm the anger roiling inside him.

Thel had vanished into thin air. His father's life was teetering on an edge no one could make any sense of. And now this. What if he never freed another mage? His father never recovered? Never saw his baby brother again?

And here he'd thought his life would get easier after the vote. Simpler. In truth, the complications were only beginning.

3   Maps & Messages

"Wake up, runt."

Thel was hauled to his feet. Shaking himself awake, he struggled to focus on the blurry monstrosity in front of him. The only thought that successfully formed was that he was way too tall to have ever been called "runt" by anyone. He blinked the grit out of his eyes, and the events of the day before rushed back.

Detrax.

The beastly mage was hauling him up by his jerkin, out of the tent he'd shared with Niat, and toward the larger one. The tiny mage book slipped slightly in the spot he'd tucked it into, threatening to fall out. Thel clamped an arm to his side to pin it down, hoping he didn't give anything away.

He stumbled and hit his knees as he was lobbed through the front tent flap. The scent of porridge and honey made his mouth water in spite of himself.

Detrax loomed over him, frowning. Thel returned the expression.

"I hear you're a prince," Detrax growled. "Lot of good that'll do you now."

Thel said nothing.

Detrax clapped twice. A man stepped in from outside, fidgeting and obsequious. "Porridge. And paper and charcoal."

To his surprise, Detrax crossed his legs and sat down on the carpet-covered ground, gesturing for Thel to sit as well with all four arms in unison. Thel complied and tried not to stare at the extra appendages.

The servant returned and handed him a bowl, and Thel dug into it without ceremony. The requested paper and charcoal were placed on the carpet between him and the beast mage.

Detrax watched him silently for a while, then narrowed his eyes before he began to speak. "War's coming." He paused. His voice had such a low, slow growl. Had it been altered with magic too? "Certainly you know that by now."

Thel faked hesitation and then nodded slowly, buying himself as much time as possible to inhale the food.

"The Masters want your lands. They'll not be stopping before they're satisfied."

Detrax stopped and seemed to want some response. Thel weighed his options and chose a moderate path of slight objection. Complacency would only seem like a ploy. "You know Akarians won't go without a fight."

"Aye, I do. But not sure the Masters know that. Or care. But no matter. I've got three dozen mages with me, and more followin'. There'll be naught they can do about all that. Hopeless. Truly, I tell you."

Thel took another large bite to buy another moment before responding. "I'd have to be a fool to simply take your word for that when nothing has happened yet."

"Aye, you might." Detrax inclined his head at the servant again, who now brought them both a dark liquid in small mugs that Thel prayed was tea. This was a lot of hospitality for a prisoner. Detrax must want something, likely to do with the empty vellum before them. What did Thel possibly have that Detrax wanted? He waited until Detrax had taken a drink, then took one himself. He didn't have the luxury of abstaining in this situation, but after that blue vial, he couldn't help but be wary.

"Thanks for this," Thel said, raising the mug slightly. It might earn him nothing, but gratitude couldn't hurt.

"Well, can't have you dying like the damn seer. Least not yet."

Thel choked midswallow. "Like the seer?"

"Aye, gift's killing the girl. Didn't you notice? A shame, not that I'll tell her that to her face. Mere mortals can never handle the gods in their heads. There's a reason the gift's rare."

"So you think it's real?" Thel said, stalling whatever Detrax's request would be. More information about Niat couldn't hurt.

Detrax chuckled, and Thel struggled not to gawk at the horns looming above the mage's head. "Aye, it's real all right. She'd ditch the gift if she could, I bet. But there's no denying the gods."

No, indeed, there wasn't. Something about the proclamation saddened him, however.

"And there's no denying me either, boy. Now down to business. Here's my offer. You'll get it without consequence but once. Then the cutting starts."

Thel's chewing slowed to a stop. Cutting…? That did not sound pleasant. He forced himself to down another huge bite, lest it be his last chance.

"The Masters want your lands, as I said. But I'm fixing to get my own share of this before the fighting ends. And you're a Lanuken."

Thel nodded slowly.

"So the Lanukens have mines. You know where they be. Draw me a map of where they lie, and we won't have no cutting."

Thel froze, only staring. Of all the things, he hadn't expected that.

"Anonil, my lord?" The servant prompted softly from near the door.

"Oh, and you'll be telling me the defenses of Anonil, as we crush it on the morrow. Or mayhap the next day."

Thel's eyes widened. "I don't know the defenses of Anonil." Inwardly, he winced. Shit. That phrasing implied that he *did* know the mine locations. He knew both, of course, at least generally. But he was less willing to give up the city. Men would lose their lives over that information. Whether anyone would die if Detrax knew the locations of the mines was possible but less certain.

Detrax scowled and jabbed a finger from one of his four hands at the blank vellum.

Thel stared at it. Dare he give him the information? Many Akarians stood between the beast and those mines. Could he rely on them to keep Detrax from getting there? He could lie—draw a false map. But he was unsure what means Detrax might have to verify his claims. But was outright refusal any better? What would that accomplish, besides… cutting?

Thel took a sip of tea, frowning. Moving as slowly as possible, he picked up the charcoal and drew the mountains, the roads, all of it as slowly and meticulously as humanly possible. These were the things Detrax could already know, things that could be easily verified.

He added two dots in the middle of the toughest passes he knew. Not remotely near any mines. Then he dropped the charcoal to the carpet and dusted off his hands.

Detrax squinted at the vellum. "There be more than two. And add labels."

Thel shook his head. As Detrax's eyes widened in rage, Thel said, "Dinner."

"What?"

"I'd like to live to see dinner. Tomorrow, perhaps, I'll give you the information, but not all at once."

Scowling, Detrax's face slowly turned red, veins in his neck straining. "You… little…"

Thel crossed his arms and scowled back at him.

"I could beat it out of your thick skull."

"You could," Thel acknowledged. "Or you could try."

"Aye, time for that at the fortress, eh?" Detrax said to his servant, who snickered darkly behind him. Detrax paused. "Aye, but that's no fun."

In a blink, a dagger bit into Thel's thigh, Detrax's thick fingers curled around the blade. The beast mage released the hilt and leaned back, chuckling as Thel gaped at the blade hilt in his leg. His blood welled up around it. He forced his eyes to Detrax.

The vicious glee burning in the mage's eyes sent a shock of pure fear through Thel. This was not just a man who used pain to achieve his ends. Fierce, bloody rapture emanated from Detrax, sadistic ecstasy, his hand still gripping the blade hilt.

The mage squeezed a bit harder and twisted.

Thel's shock wore off at the new flash of pain, and he couldn't stifle a cry this time. His hands automatically reached for the dagger, fighting to remove it. To his surprise, Detrax withdrew, letting Thel cast the dagger aside on the carpet. Blood only rushed out faster, and Thel cursed himself. Shit. He should have known better, remembered his training, thought longer. He was going to die here, bleeding out on this beast mage's floor.

Detrax loomed closer, laughing slowly, savage and perverse. "You feel that life draining out, my boy?" He chuckled darkly again. "You remember that, that feeling when you see this face. Got it?"

Thel nodded, probably too vigorously.

"I'll tear you in twain, no worries about it, if I don't get what I ask. Let that be a lesson not to lie to me."

Thel nodded again, and suddenly, to his relief, the wound began to close. Right—creature mage. Thel gritted his teeth, this agony almost greater than when the blade had entered and twisted—but he was determined not to give that bastard any more satisfaction than necessary.

Before the wound had fully healed, the agony abruptly stopped. Detrax leered at him, radiating pleasure. "I can keep you from dying. And I will. 'Cause that's just more I can wring out of you."

Detrax stood and put both sets of his hands on his hips, looming over Thel, surveying his handiwork.

"Is this—cutting?" Thel managed, glaring.

Detrax chuckled again, eyes twinkling. "Aye, a taste."

"That all?" Thel shot back through gritted teeth.

The beastly mage scowled. "The cutting is just beginning for you, little prince."

Ro lay awake that morning, listening to the rumbles of the city waking up, the whispering early winter winds, and Jaena's soft breaths beside him. In spite of the larger bed someone had seen fit to arrange for them—the king?—he still couldn't sleep.

Before they'd retired the night before, he'd jotted down a warning to his order and handed it to the creature mage

Wunik had mentioned. Siljana had sent her crow off a few minutes later. Just like that, the message had been on its way through the dark night sky.

Ever since, dread had been brewing within, the intuitive feeling that he'd made some kind of mistake, not foreseen something he should have. Certainly he had needed to send word as soon as possible. Members of the order would be marked by the pendants they wore, and the Devoted could find them, as long as the knight he'd encountered had shared her news. And why wouldn't she? For all that knight knew, those golden sheaves of wheat might indicate a mage every time.

Then again, for all Tharomar knew, that might be true.

Why had they lied? Could they have not known? But why the enchantments then?

The sick feeling of dread in his stomach was not eased by the hope that his order had been ignorant. What kind of mage protectors could the order be if they couldn't identify and protect one right under their noses? They were either terrible at their mission or lying about it. Or they had believed hiding his true nature from him was the right way to fulfill their mission.

Which possibility was scariest, he wasn't sure. All of them pissed him off.

Outside, a tree's branches tapped against the glass of the balcony doors, swayed by the wind, as if beckoning him.

He turned on his side, away from the tapping tree and toward Jaena, moving his eyes along the lush curve of her shoulder, her skin dark against the gray quilt. Her sweet grin drifted through his mind, the way she asked more questions than she ever answered, her shy ambition. The merchant story might have been a cover, but there had been truth to it too. A future she longed for. That he longed to see with her, to help her reach.

He lingered but couldn't fall back asleep, so he eased out of bed, moving slowly and smoothly so as not to wake her. He slipped quietly toward the fire, intending to pray if he couldn't rest.

The tapping on the balcony door returned, different this time. He stepped closer. A crow fidgeted on the railing, wings flapping.

A crow with a message box tied to his leg.

Tharomar carefully cracked open the balcony door and stepped out into the icy morning air, shutting it behind him. Quickly as he could, he extracted the message, gave the crow a little pat, and stepped back inside. The bird flew off, presumably returning to Siliana for its reward. He'd have to inquire later.

Shutting the door with a soft thud as he returned inside, he glanced at Jaena. Still sleeping peacefully. Good.

He unrolled the message.

Tharomar Revendel,

Thanks be to Nefrana for your message and your service. I was glad to hear you are safe, as word had reached us that the smithy had been vacated when the Devoted were searching near the town.

I've sent Inoril to tend to the smithy in your absence. Does this mean you found what the Devoted sought? We hope that you and any companions are safe and free of the Devoted as this reaches you.

We will send word through the order of this new danger from the Devoted blight. The loss of the pendants is unfortunate, but I am unclear on what additional abilities of the pendant you are referring to. The ability to recognize the sign of our order has served many in troubled times. Has something else transpired that you do not name? I look forward to the full story upon your return.

Things have worsened here in Evrical, and indeed everywhere. We've seen mages hunted down and captured in the streets, and not just in Evrical. The Devoted have been reaching farther, as far as Detrat and even into Farsa. Here, we fear they suspect the true purpose of the temple. We cannot risk the discovery of the order, not before we are ready to fight them. I'm sure you will agree this is of the utmost importance to our cause. As one of our most capable warriors, your return will be much anticipated as a boon to defending us.

In Nefrana's Name,
High Priestess Danal Shian

He stifled a groan. They wanted him to return? Not only that, but they *expected* it. His hand drifted down of its own accord, weakly dropping the missive on the desk.

The future he'd just caught the scent of seemed to go up in smoke before him. He had duties. Commitments. An oath to obey their orders. And Jae was safe now. He gazed at her sleeping form. She didn't *feel* safe. What was he going to do?

He shook his head. He knew exactly what he was going to do.

Nothing. Not a damn thing. Oath or no oath, he wasn't going back.

That had been the dread pooling in his stomach, that had been the apprehension. He hadn't feared what the letter would say. He had feared what he was going to do when the time came.

Staying was the only option. Nefrana had never given him so much. How could he turn his back on these gifts?

On his magical gifts, sure. Going back to the temple would have meant abstaining. But he wasn't entirely sure where he stood on that point, anyway. Magic was a minor gift compared to the others. Jaena was a gift. And Akaria itself was a gift—a land where mages could be free.

Both of them needed him, didn't they? Or was he the one that needed them?

It wouldn't be long before the star map was translated. And Jaena… If it hadn't been for her injury so close to her pursuers, she would have been fine escaping Kavanar without him. Now in Akaria, with all the support of a free kingdom at her back? He was fooling himself if he thought she needed his protection or his help.

So then, perhaps it was selfish to stay. Could he do

the most good elsewhere? Perhaps it truly was the temple that needed him most.

Even so, he couldn't bring himself to change his mind. He wasn't going anywhere.

He pulled on some clothes and stoked the fire, adding a log as quietly as he could. How odd that he could still learn things about himself at this age. He'd never thought he'd had a selfish streak. But then again, he'd never had anything worth hanging onto, nothing he cared much about losing. Yada, the smithy, even the weapons and books, he'd given them all up easily.

For her. For the mission, too, but if he was honest, it was mostly her.

Fire raging again, he slipped out of their rooms, heading down toward the library. As usual, he greeted the guards he passed along the way, asking their names, inquiring about the weather. He had learned a few things from his childhood, and one of them was that knowing a guard's name—or his wife's—was a powerful thing when your luck went awry.

Maybe he'd head outside. He needed… something. Something to distract himself from this new, disturbing facet of himself. Maybe some fresh air.

He definitely wasn't going far.

Stone columns and wide windows bathed Aven in pools of cheery morning sunlight and cold, dewy shadow as he strode down the corridor toward the war room, barracks, and training yard. Ah, Ranok wasn't home, but it sure was nice. Maybe it could be home, someday. It certainly had more light. Did Miara have a preference between mountain holds and city fortresses?

The sounds of troop muster echoed off the stone, like it had the few times he'd visited Panar as a young man for training maneuvers. Not far away, the town market was in full swing, the sounds of haggling peppering the brisk air. No snow yet, but it would be on them soon, even this far south. Another thing he needed to discuss with Dyon.

But first, he had to find Miara.

Thuds from the training ground reached him before he could see the wide, dusty square. Rounding the corner slowly, he leaned against the stone in the shadows, folded his arms, and watched.

A sword flashed in the sunlight as Miara assaulted a wood-and-straw practice dummy. The slashes and jabs had an air of thoughtful experimentation rather than true aggression, but she was quick and decisive, clad in new leathers this time in the midnight blue of the royal guard.

She paused for a moment, resting the sword tip in the dirt and her hand on the pommel as she wiped her brow with the back of her other hand. Wisps of red had escaped from her bun and danced in the feisty wind.

Are you trying *to hide in the shadows or just waiting for an opening to say hello?* Her mind's voice was growing to be a familiar presence in his thoughts, and now he caught a hint of a smile in her tone.

He grinned. *A little of both. Come speak with Dyon and the war planners with me.*

I'm sweaty.

So are they.

She snorted, then her gaze flicked to him. *Care to give me a few pointers? I'm without my tutor, with Dev still in Estun.*

He'll be here soon. Dom can't stay away for long, and Devol will come with him. Especially when they hear about Thel.

He could sense her spirits fall at that, her light a candle in danger of flickering out for a moment. *It would be nice to have a few more friendly faces around here. I miss Fayton and Camil.* She turned and strode toward the weapons rack.

Me too.

Does your mother usually take part in war planning?

What my mother did doesn't have anything to do with what you do. You're not her.

So that's a no?

She didn't join us often, but she also wasn't recently defected from the enemy.

Is that a positive or a negative in my favor?

Both, probably.

I may not be her, but people will have expectations based on what she's done.

And we can change them. There also haven't been any significant wars in my father's reign for her to sit out of planning.

A fair point, I suppose. Weapon returned, she strode toward him, frowning at the sky and looking every bit the woman who'd kidnapped him, just garbed in a new color now.

"Wasn't it the short sword last time?" He switched to speaking aloud.

"And hand ax. But I couldn't find that. Your brutes probably prefer more sizable weapons."

He smiled. "They're your brutes, too."

"Not yet."

"Soon."

"All right, *our* brutes probably prefer large, hefty weapons. Good for smashing."

"How did you find the long sword?"

"Lighter than I'd thought. Having both arms to wield it seemed easier than two smaller weapons, actually."

"It's not a bad choice. I know you're accustomed to clawing at eyes, but the longer range is an advantage. If they can't reach you, they can't hurt you."

"And I'm getting a few pointers after all. Thanks." She smiled as she found her cloak on a peg, swung it over her shoulders, and lifted the hood—her old black Kavanarian one, hopefully not a detail that Dyon or any lieutenants would notice. Clearly not everything had been replaced yet. She smiled brightly, her cheeks flushed with the activity. "Ready to plan a war?"

"Never a good time for that, but we haven't much choice." Aven smiled back and held out an arm, guiding her back toward the war room.

"I'd think with all your military prowess, you Akarians would be chomping at the bit for war."

He sobered a little. "Only those who don't know much about war anticipate it." And he didn't have much direct experience, but he could read. Not that there wasn't a rush to battle itself, but the truth of the matter was that war was inherently dark and bloody and everybody lost something in the end.

The small, plain room where Dyon, a few wardens, and the regiment lieutenants waited sat along the corridor that led from Ranok proper to the attached barracks. It had more in common with the drafty soldiers' quarters than the palace, with its dusty dirt floor and its wooden walls hung with maps.

Aven swung wide the heavy oak door. Just for a thrill, he shut it with a gust behind them. He wasn't going to get any better if he didn't practice, right? The corner of Miara's mouth ticked up as she noticed his extravagance. Or laziness. A handful of lieutenants, wardens, and arms masters waited around the outside of the room, taking notes and making drawings. One young, brown-haired warden raised her eyebrows and eyed the door.

"Drafty in here, eh?" Aven said to the warden with a smile. She smiled nervously and nodded back.

You don't need to hide your magic anymore, Aven. Miara's silent tone had a surprising edge.

Force of habit.

If we don't show them magic, how will we get them to accept it? They have to see it can be harmless. Or even helpful.

Even sarcastic comments referring to my magic at all feel very bold, trust me.

We'll work on it.

A stone hearth to their right fought off the morning chill. One stone arch led out to the grounds and the market, as well as unhelpfully letting in a river of frigid air. Wunik and his glowing water sat under it on a pair of rough-hewn logs, bathed and enlivened in light. Could Aven convince them to take this outside? One glance at the table told him definitely not; too much was already carefully positioned there.

"Take a look, Aven. Miara." Lord Dyon jabbed a finger at the table before him as one of his lieutenants— Jenec?—scowled and placed another small brown stone inside charcoal lines that marked off Gilaren territory.

Miara smiled. "Good morning to you to you too, my lord."

Dyon grunted a hasty greeting without looking at them. "We've got these bastards staked out across the map. The talents of your mage friend are making an enormous difference in our planning."

Aven smiled at that, but his expression faded as he surveyed the scene they'd set. More than a dozen smooth stones were arrayed inside Kavanar and Gilaren, with several poised on the edge of Numaren. Some represented Akarian forces, but most indicated the enemy. He pointed at the two closest markers, perhaps intended for assaulting Panar itself. "That's barely a day's ride away."

Dyon nodded. "Indeed it is."

"Well, you've all been busy." Aven ran a hand absently through his hair, taking it all in.

"And so have they. But this knowledge is a huge help. We won't be riding out blind, guessing at everything. We can respond faster. The Kavanarian forces may move, but Wunik's efforts enable us to make much more informed plans."

Aven nodded numbly. "Glad there's a positive to this situation." He paused, then remembered Miara's comment. "I think you'll find there are many spells that can be helpful to us in war. However, we must keep in mind Kavanar can do this just as well as we can. If not better. They'll be able to see our movements easily too, as long as they bother to look."

"How many men do those stones represent?" Miara asked.

"It varies," Dyon replied. "Around one thousand each. Their force isn't as uniform as I'd prefer if they were mine." He sniffed at the stones in distaste and leaned his elbows onto the table. Akarian companies were always as close to one hundred soldiers as possible, although the mix of horsemen and footmen was not always the same, and every regiment had as close to ten companies as they could manage. "Look, I know it's a lot of pebbles, but we are better trained, better armed, better armored. I daresay it may be a stroll in the garden, kicking over urns, if we're lucky."

"If it were only soldiers, I'd agree with you," said Aven. "Can you discern how many mages they have on the move?"

"No," Wunik called from where he sat. "Haven't

noticed any differences in armor to give us any clues. Well, not exactly."

"What do you mean 'not exactly'?" Aven asked.

"Some are cavalry, some infantry, of course. Some of each don't have armor," Dyon said. "But that could mean they just don't have enough armor to go around."

"Or they don't need it," Miara put in.

Dyon gave her an indecipherable look. "I would expect that Kavanar doesn't have enough equipment, whether the unarmored are mages or not. They haven't been serious about this war for long. In fact, it's surprising they have suddenly become so aggressive."

Aven rubbed his freshly shaved chin. "Well, their Alikar plot failed. And then there's Trenedum Palace."

Dyon squinted at the map, frowning. "What about it?"

"We attacked it. Demikin was caught up in some kind of coup—dead by the end of it."

"Dead? Well, that might explain a few things. When did you have time for all that? And how?" Dyon managed.

"With a bit of help from our mage friends, we made a last-ditch rescue effort. Two nights ago? I think that's right. Spiraled into an outright attack. Stealth has never been my strong suit."

That's what you have me for, Miara said silently.

If only you hadn't been stuck somewhere in the woods with my father at the time.

"Can't argue with that," Dyon grumbled. "But why were you there in the first place?"

"We rescued Miara's family and Tharomar from the

dungeon there; Kavanar was trying to use them as leverage against us."

"'Bout time somebody struck back at those bastards," Dyon said. "If you ask me, we've been at war since they kidnapped you, sire."

"What's this about a coup?" Miara said. "I missed that in Jaena's recap, I think."

"Daes seemed to be arranging something, and we walked into the middle of it. Ultimately, Demikin fell to his death accidentally, but nobody—including his personal guard—helped him. Last I saw him, he was facedown in a fountain." Aven filled in a few more details of the attack that he'd glossed over. "Daes has likely used our attack to cover it up, so he can pin the blame on us."

Miara swore under her breath.

"Demikin didn't leave an heir," said Dyon. "So if he's dead, who's in power?"

"And these troops must have already been in motion before this coup took place," added Jenec, scratching his head.

"The coup wasn't an act of opportunity. Daes is the careful, planning type." Aven paused, remembering seeing Daes arriving at Trenedum in the water and Shanse's words in Anonil. "Kavanar's crown can descend to the queen, who appeared to be a close ally of Daes's. A spy also reported that troops had started to move on the queen's orders specifically. Hmm."

"King Demikin wouldn't need the queen's help," said Dyon.

"Exactly. But Daes would."

"One of those Masters?"

"Yes. The leader. He started all this." And it would end with him, too, Aven was certain. He rubbed his shoulder absently.

"He'll have more power than ever," Miara said, voice sharp and angry as a knife's edge.

Aven nodded. "When were the last reports received from our spies in Evrical's court? We need news from there."

"I'll inquire. Given that Evrical's a four-day ride around the gulf, their reports likely predate any action you took."

"We should look into getting them help to send news faster. Mages could do it, if we had enough of them. I wonder if anyone at that temple of Tharomar's could aid us." Even as he said it, Aven knew they were far from having enough mages for that.

Jenec shifted uncomfortably. Not comfortable with all this magic about, eh? But afraid to say so in front of the new king?

Well, whether Jenec liked it or not, they were quickly going to be outmanned with the Kavanarian troops this spread out. If all of them had come for Panar, Aven could have clustered all the Akarian mages and sent all available troops against his enemy. Maybe they still would. As it was, he would have to choose where to engage them—and potentially what to risk losing. Kavanarian troops might be spread thin, but then the Akarians would be too. Should he try to cover each city with a unit of mages or keep them all together to better their chances? As if they had that many. Already he'd sent Derk away. And what if he didn't come back? They should have sent a creature mage with Derk in case of injuries—Siliana being the only option. But then she'd be unable to assist his mother. No, covering every city with mage forces wasn't an option. They couldn't even cover Panar at this rate.

"Can we recruit more mages?" said Miara. "Surely there must be some in hiding or practicing secretly. They may not be well trained, but they could be taught to draw energy for those that are."

"We should try. But it may be a delicate matter." Aven massaged his forehead, trying to think.

"It would certainly need to be carefully worded," Dyon said sternly.

"Not everyone will support the use of magic in war," said Jenec.

"We have no choice," said Aven. "It's being used against us. We can defend ourselves or die."

Jenec's eyes widened. "There must be some conventional way to win. Certainly it can't be that serious."

"Oh, it is," Miara said. "If enslaved mages have the orders to do so, they can be very deadly."

Jenec opened his mouth to say something else, but Aven spoke first. "It was King Samul's guidance that we should know at least enough to defend ourselves and our people from a mage threat, and I agree with him. And if Kavanar is flinging all they have at us, we're going to need more on our side. It's not clear how well a conventional army can stand up to magic."

"If it can at all," Miara said. Jenec narrowed his eyes

at her.

Aven wanted to slam a fist on the table but forced himself to take a slow, steadying breath and only grip the table edge a little too hard. They'd all been *so* concerned about sharing the news of his magic with leaders in power, within the insular world of Estun and the Assembly, but no one had given one whit of thought to selling the idea to the people. News was likely already spreading. How many reactions would be tainted by unfounded fear? Or skewed by those preaching hate? Right now, no one's reactions were being guided. He needed to do something, and soon. They should have started recruiting mages the day he'd arrived back in Estun.

Dyon's voice cut into his thoughts. "I agree more mages will be needed. What else? You said Warden Asten will be heading to Dramsren to meet her troops?"

"Yes. The regiment from Shansaren should arrive by then. Assuming everything with Thel goes smoothly." Assuming she survives, Aven thought. Assuming any altercation would go smoothly would be horribly naïve, of course. Thel's easy return was, in fact, the least likely thing to happen.

"I saw them on the road," Wunik called. "They should get there as planned tomorrow."

"Good." Aven eyed the table. Four of the twelve stones were clustered within northern Gilaren. Maybe three to five thousand men. Anonil had barely more than a thousand armed men, but there *was* the stronghold nearby to help. "Think those are heading for Anonil? Does it still stand?"

"For now," Dyon said. "But the outlook is grim. The regiment stationed in the southern Gilaren stronghold has yet to encounter any Kavanarian troops, and there's at least one Kavanarian unit between them and Anonil now. Worse, the Kavanarians marched right past the northern stronghold and its regiment without incident." He pressed his lips together into a thin line.

"By the gods," Aven muttered. Alikar had ordered them not to engage. What general had he bribed to pull that off? Alikar *would* be in their existing chain of command, though, but letting Kavanarians pass freely couldn't have sat well with the troops. He hoped. "I wonder if Anonil will offer any resistance."

"I almost hope it doesn't," Dyon said. "Let them come beyond the city, and we'll crush them all the easier."

"We don't want to have to fight our own fortifications, sir," Jenec said bleakly. "We should send support there now. It'd be better if they don't take the city."

"Of course," Dyon said. "But if they must, I'd rather them not damage it. Or kill too many. And exactly who would you send? The regiment at the northern stronghold who let them walk by? That's who we'd have sent, if anyone. That's who *should* have stopped them." Dyon's hand slowly closed to a fist at the table's edge.

Jenec rubbed the back of his neck, brow furrowing.

"Kavanarian troops may still kill many even if Anonil offers no resistance," said Aven. "We'll see how well they're led. All right, so the northern stronghold has been compromised. Have you received news from the southern regiment?"

"The last report came yesterday. They haven't encountered any Kavanarians. The catapults we dealt with yesterday appear to have taken a wide berth, some disguised as wagons, and assembled in Gilaren forests, closer to Panar."

"Did word come by horse or bird?" Aven asked.

"By horse," Dyon said. "So the news is at least two days old. And we observed something amiss at the stronghold via Elder Wunik's spell. It appeared under siege, everyone shut up in the innermost heart of the keep, gates barred and closed."

"Except there was no sign of any enemy," Jenec added.

"Nothing?" Miara frowned.

"Nothing. No one outside," Wunik added from his perch. He looked warm over there. Glowing. Aven itched to join him.

"Do you think it could be Kavanarian mages at work, Wunik?" said Miara.

"Perhaps," he said, but his tone implied yes.

Hmm. Aven scratched his head. They could send a bird, but a bird couldn't stroll inside and ask questions. Or knock. "So you're thinking someone should head there. See what's afoot?"

Dyon smiled slightly. "You read my mind. That magic of yours is coming in handy."

Aven shook his head and didn't miss the return of Jenec's scowl. "I'm an air mage. Like Wunik. We can't do that."

"Old man sure seems like he can read minds,"

Jenec grumbled.

Aven laughed. "Maybe he can, but not with his magic."

"Who *can* do that then?" Dyon asked.

"Creature mages. Like Miara." Aven didn't add that his mother could too, and had been able to as long as Dyon had known her. Miara flushed and smiled slightly.

Jenec now looked taken aback. "Wait, you're not joking? They really *can* read minds?"

"Only some mages," Miara added gently. "And we very much prefer not to. It can be—"

"—uncomfortable and hazardous to their health," Aven cut in. That sounded better than it could drive them mad. He didn't need anyone envisioning mages as crazed lunatics. Reality was hard enough to accept without people trying to accept something much worse and extremely unlikely.

Jenec did not look terribly relieved.

"We can also heal mortal wounds," Miara added, smiling as sweetly as she could.

Dyon chuckled at that. "I've seen it myself done by this fair maiden right here, Jenec. Any woman who can gut herself, sew herself back together, and walk away like nothing's happened... Well, let's just say I know quite a few men without the stomach for that."

"Uh—did I hear that correctly?" Jenec blurted, eyes wide.

Miara turned bright red now.

"I'll explain more later," Dyon said. "Let's use the king's time wisely, eh, Lieutenant?"

His own cheeks coloring slightly, Jenec nodded.

Aven decided not to react to any of it. Just another inconsequential observation. "Do you have any proposals on handling this situation, Dyon? How does all this square with the plans you and Asten worked on?"

"And our lieutenants worked on, of course," Dyon said, nodding to Jenec and several others busy taking notes behind them. "This is one of the three routes we expected, although we had assumed they'd meet *some* resistance from the northern Gilaren regiment. As a result, we'd estimated them to be further behind than this in the north, traveling slower. I'm glad they aren't coming straight en masse for Panar, but I'd expect it fairly soon. Either that or they'll cut across and meet up in Dramsren, at Lenial. Cut the south off from the north."

"Or they'll do both." Jenec folded his arms across his chest.

Dyon's brow furrowed. "And divide their forces?"

Jenec shrugged. "Moving into Dramsren is not particularly smart either. A front to both the north, where they must anticipate Liren and Elaren troops, and the south, with all our leadership here? We could easily find a way to flank them."

"We're not *that* divided. Even with three regiments in Panar, we can at best spare one with all the pieces they have in play. We can't abandon Panar."

"Why not?" Miara said slowly.

Every eye in the room seemed to focus on her.

Jenec opened his mouth, frowning, but Aven quickly cut him off. "Because the White City, in addition to being the capital, is by far the largest city in Akaria. Almost a third of our people live here. The civilian devastation could be massive."

"All right, but maybe she has a point," said Jenec. "What if we could move the king and all our leadership deeper into the interior—say, into Shansaren's forests? That would stretch their supply line. We could wear them down, especially with winter on their heels."

Aven raised an eyebrow. "And just give up Panar?" Those around him shifted uncomfortably at the idea.

"Maybe they'd march right past. Or go through Dramsren."

"I'm sure Lady Toyl would be pleased to know you'd prefer to sacrifice Lenial instead," Dyon said, smiling crookedly.

Aven shook his head. "I appreciate the thought, but they're not going to waltz right past Panar. We can't draw them out without facing civilian casualties and the loss of cities we would first give up freely and then need to reclaim. We should pool our eastern forces here instead, make our stand in Panar."

"It has the best fortifications of any of our cities as well," Dyon added.

"Our relations with the Takarans are also good; they'd stand to lose a lot if they tried to take advantage of this situation. Though Shansaren is keeping one regiment just in case." Aven pointed at the eastern border.

Jenec rubbed his chin. "All of that makes sense. However, just because something doesn't seem like the smartest decision to us doesn't mean they won't do it. If I were them, I'd have already pooled my forces and headed to Panar at full strength. It's likely their only chance to be able to take the city, and with our access to the sea, I think it's doubtful they can do it. If they take losses in these smaller cities, will they have enough left?"

"You're not accounting for the mages as part of the force, though," Miara pointed out. "Even a few with the right orders can do a lot of damage."

Jenec didn't seem to know what to make of that. He stared for a moment, then continued on. "The way they have their forces divided will tempt us to do the same."

"Perhaps that's what they're hoping for," Aven said softly.

"Hmm," Dyon said. "Keeping their largest possible force together and attacking our less defended areas allows them to make progress. They can draw troops away from Panar and have a much easier target if they've taken control of Gilaren and Dramsren. And who knows, maybe Faeren too. If Alikar's a traitor, maybe Sven took his bribe and will be sending more defectors at us from the east, by land or even by sea in ships coming into the gulf."

"We can afford to divide our troops to a point," said Aven slowly. "They cannot afford it as easily. But *we* can't afford to divide our mages. Maybe they are building the campaign around that."

Dyon grimaced. "It's possible."

"And we've already divided ourselves even by sending Derk off," Miara said, shaking her head, her voice hard. "At least one other is down now too." Her eyes told him she was referring to his mother, without wanting to say it out loud. Aven had lost track of who knew his mother was a mage and who didn't. "How many does that leave us?"

Aven shook his head. "Six? No, wait, should I count your sister?"

"Might as well," she said, then sighed.

"Eight? Nine, when Derk returns?" Ten if he counted Beneral, but he wasn't sure if he should. Teron had stayed in Estun with Dom. Perhaps he should send word for the Takaran to come to Panar along with Dom and Devol. They'd need all the help they could get. And what the hell had ever happened to that last Elder his mother had sent for? Was Wunik really the only one left?

Dyon scowled, and for the first time Jenec also looked concerned on a mage-related point. "That's practically nothing," Dyon said.

"Against mages trained for war?" Miara said. "It *is* nothing. We're not even all trained at *anything*. Jaena's had a year or two of war training. I've been a healer. The only thing working in our favor is that as slaves, they may not *want* to fight. So they'll likely only do what they specifically have orders to do. If their orders are narrow, they'll take less initiative than if they were fighting of their own accord."

"Let's hope," said Aven. Miara had certainly found ways to undercut her mission orders. They'd have to pray that other Kavanarian mages were inclined to do the same. "If I had my druthers, we'd send at least four creature mages with each force. Their capacity to heal wounds would be invaluable, and furthermore, the Kavanarian troops are likely to have the same."

"That could get... strange." Dyon frowned.

Aven nodded. "Yes, it could. But we have only three. Total."

"My father's a creature mage. Luha too."

"Great—five then. Still meaningless in terms of dividing us up. Ideally, we'd match Kavanar mage for mage. But considering they have at least five hundred or more, that's definitely not happening."

"Five *hundred*?" Jenec whispered.

"Yes," said Miara. "Although we can hope they left some at Mage Hall to defend the place."

"And we have... nine?" Jenec asked. His discomfort with magic seemed rapidly diminishing.

Miara nodded once. "Yes. Beyond the training issue, others aren't going to be marching out with the troops anytime soon." Wunik harrumphed, but Aven guessed she'd been thinking more of his mother. Jenec's mouth hung open in dismay. At Aven's gaze, he snapped it shut. Dyon looked grim.

Aven pressed his lips together. "If you're feeling like we're unprepared, it's because we are." Jenec swore, and Dyon's jaw tightened. "So perhaps they are trying to divide us up. Miara, any idea how much Daes knows about war?"

"He was born a minor noble, but fought in the past, until he injured his leg. That was how he came to be at Mage Hall. I was probably twelve when he arrived. He quickly took over. I don't know what he did or in what conflict, but the missions he gave me were always carefully planned. They rarely went awry." *Except for yours, happily,* she added silently. He stifled a smile.

"The nobility of Kavanar gave *you* missions?" Jenec blurted. "And we have you here why—"

Aven winced. He opened his mouth, but Miara jumped in first. "He gave me missions because I was his slave. One who found a way to be very inefficient in my mission and, in doing so, saved your king's life." A stunned silence fell across the room. "Aven gave me my freedom," Miara said, slower now. Her voice was as hard and demanding as the stone of Ranok. A thrill went through him at the glimpse of the queen within her. "I have already fought bravely for Akaria. I brought Aven back from Kavanar, and I rescued King Samul from three mage slaves determined to kill him. Tell me, what have *you* done to prove your loyalty to Akaria, Lieutenant?"

Jenec stared, completely caught off guard. The room remained silent, but the texture of it was different now, more anticipatory than tense. "I beg your pardon, my lady."

Dyon cleared his throat. "Arms Master."

"What?" said Jenec.

"She outranks you. King Samul granted her the title."

"Your pardon, Arms Master," said Jenec, bowing slightly. Grudgingly, perhaps.

Miara let the silence stretch on a moment longer, then nodded. "Back to the matter at hand. Daes is smart. He plans well. He should not to be underestimated."

Aven nodded curtly. "We need to investigate this southern stronghold. And soon we'll need to decide. Do we send mages north with Asten? Do we cluster all the mages here to hold the capital at all costs? What do we think the Kavanarians will do next?"

Jenec's face hardened, this time in determination. "The northern Kavanarian force seems to have acted independently of the southern force. I think one is tasked with Anonil, and the other Panar."

Dyon shook his head. "Surely the fools would join their forces before attacking the capital."

"They ought to. But what does it look like they're doing?" Aven asked.

"As much as I hate to admit it, I think Jenec's right." Dyon scowled. "They seem to be taking a two-pronged approach. They've little experience actually working together. Or in strategy. Even if this Daes is a master planner and is indeed pushing for war, they still might not follow his plans if he's not on the battlefield."

"He will be," said Aven.

"How do you know?" said Miara. "He's cautious; I don't think he'll risk it."

"But he's also savvy enough to realize this is his chance. He can't afford to lose it."

"Hmm." She pressed her lips together, annoyed. At him?

Dyon nodded grudgingly. "Dramsren is closer. If they want to rack up wins to take to whatever king has replaced Demikin, perhaps they'll rush to the easier target."

Aven blinked at the wording. *Whatever king has replaced Demikin.* Of course. The news wouldn't come until tomorrow, or maybe even three days out. But he knew exactly who the king's replacement would be.

Daes.

Daes had run for the queen instead of Aven back on that fateful day in Trenedum. *Daes* had traveled to Trenedum in the first place. Of course, it all made sense now. He wasn't just allied with the queen. She was his path to real, direct power.

Conniving bastard.

Aven raised his chin. "All right. Asten and General Inoin will be ready with one Shansaren regiment if the enemy heads there. We have three Numaren regiments garrisoned here. Who's heading to the southern hold, and what are those troops doing once we've solved their issue? Heading north to Anonil or reinforcing Panar?"

"I think you and I should head to the southern stronghold personally, my lord," Dyon said soberly. "We should be on the front line to direct and respond. Beneral and the others can handle this city. It's a blessing from Anara to be able to see what's happening right now, but we're still one, two days' ride away. We can't adjust course, even if we know what's happening."

"Creature mages could get us to the front faster," Aven mused. "It would still take a few hours, and there's a limit as to how many they can carry. Not a whole regiment."

"With time, soldiers could be transformed and learn to fly themselves rather than be carried," Miara put in. "But we don't have time."

Dyon shrugged. "And also we don't have many creature mages to go around, do we?" He sighed.

Aven pointed back at the map. "At least two Numaren

regiments will stay here to defend the people and the capital. But we need to see what's gone wrong at the southern stronghold. We may have to use the third for that, or at least detach several companies for the mission."

"Could the southern regiment just have been bought out?" Miara asked. "Bribed to all go home?"

Dyon frowned. "By the gods, I hope they're not that disloyal. The whole regiment? You'd think at least *some* of them would not want to ruin their lives, and it can't have been much of a bribe to spread across a thousand men, *plus* another thousand in the northern regiment. Alikar doesn't have that kind of money."

"But does Kavanar?" Jenec muttered.

"They'd never. Sell out to their sworn enemy? I'll flay each and every member of that regiment myself if we find that's the case."

Aven gritted his teeth. "They may not need to bribe the whole regiment. Perhaps just a general or a few lieutenants, with the right orders. Wunik, can you show Miara and me the hold?"

"Working my way there; call you in a moment."

"And once we address their issue?" Aven asked. "North to Anonil? Back to Panar? Into Kavanar, even?"

"We should see what's happened to Anonil, where the troops have moved, update our understanding," Dyon said. "If Anonil is in trouble, we can move there. If it's been lost, we may want to keep the southern stronghold well fortified. Or we may want to follow Kavanarian troops if they're on their way to Dramsren and come in from behind and flank them. Falling back to reinforce Panar is a good default, though." He shrugged. "We've got plans for each contingency."

Aven smiled. "Getting used to this farsight thing, Dyon? What if we don't have it?"

"Well, *you'll* always have it, right?" Dyon arched an eyebrow and smiled.

Off in his corner, Wunik snorted. "I assume I'm staying here. Which is as I'd prefer it, although you could have asked."

"Assuming I'm conscious, that's a fair bet." Aven chose not to mention how frequently magic and unconsciousness went hand in hand in his experience. "You *are* always keeping me on my toes, though, aren't you?"

"That's my job." Dyon smiled slightly.

"I thought your job is Assemblyman of Liren."

"That too. I'm very talented."

"And humble."

"What about the mages?" Miara asked. "Should we divide them?"

"No. We'll avoid it as much as we can. Keep the main force stationed here in Ranok. Miara, I want you to focus on organizing them and using their talents to defend the city."

"Got it," she said.

Dyon cleared his throat. "My regiment is on the march from Liren, but it will take another week and three days before they make it around the deep forests and arrive in southern Elaren. Once there, we can evaluate taking back Anonil if it's been lost."

"Good. Dyon, talk to Beneral about readying one of the regiments for the march within the week. I've got other urgent matters to wrap up before we leave, and another day or two will allow us to get a better glimpse into what Kavanar's strategy is. Keep an eye on them and keep this map updated. But the rest of the day, we'll review your plans for each contingency. Let's take a short break and meet up again in an hour."

"Yes, sire," Jenec added, and Dyon gave a slight bow. The group dispersed somewhat, but Aven hung onto the table a moment longer, glaring at the pebbles.

And what are these urgent matters you need to attend to? Miara continued.

We have some priestesses who are going to be delighted to meet you. They've been demanding an audience with the king quite fervently.

Oh, by the gods.

"Ready for you now, Miara, Aven," Wunik called.

Striding to a seat next to Wunik, Aven sighed too loudly as the light enveloped him. The corners of Wunik's mouth pricked up a bit in understanding. The sunlight was no less intoxicating than it had been back on the balcony in Estun. That felt like a lifetime ago. Miara hovered beside Wunik, not sitting down.

"Here. The hold." Wunik lowered the view.

Aven leaned forward, studying it. "Looks deserted."

"It does. But there are horses in the stables. Or there were, yesterday."

Aven frowned. Why, by all the gods and ancestors? "The main gates are barred and shut."

Wunik nodded, solemn.

"If they're anywhere inside, they must all be holed up inside the main hold barracks. But why?"

"Indeed. Why? And if your troops are *not* there—what happened to them?"

Aven frowned. "There's no sign of battle."

"No signs of the destruction air mages would have certainly brought about either," Miara added. "No char marks, burns, craters."

Wunik's face darkened. "If you go, you should take Siliana with you."

"What?" Aven looked up. "What are you thinking?"

"Why not me?" Miara said, an edge to her voice.

"Creature mages have ways of killing large numbers of people too, you know. Slower ways, mostly. Don't they, Miara?"

She winced. "I try not to think about it. And I never, ever do it if it can possibly be avoided."

"Many are quite unpleasant. Siliana is just as capable as Miara." Wunik's eyes were dark with a meaning Aven struggled to decipher.

Aven lowered his voice. "Just what do you think happened here?"

"Could be nothing."

"Or?"

"A creature mage—or a dozen of them—could charm a pack of wolves into rampaging the place. Or any number of powerful carnivores. But as you said, there's no blood."

"Out with it, Wunik," Aven said, trying not to sound harsh. Miara was glaring at Wunik too, no doubt disliking the idea of not coming with them and Siliana replacing her. And he didn't like it much either. He'd sworn not to let her leave his side. She was no stranger to battle.

"Disease is my concern, Aven. What if they've made them all deathly ill? Frankly, I'm not sure *any* of you should go. But someone does need to figure out what has happened, lest it happen again. If they have mages willing and able to infect us with these things, we need to know. Be watching for them. Likely they would only work in a confined area like this, not the entire city here, but—"

"By the gods, Wunik." Aven lowered his voice further. "You're that sure they're all dead?"

"No. I don't know. They could naturally be sick. But they are clearly under siege from an enemy we can't see. How many options does that leave us?"

Aven swore under his breath. "I'll stay back from the fray if I go."

"If it's a disease," Miara said harshly, "you shouldn't go. The *king* should not ride willingly into a quarantine zone." As her voice grew above a hush, some eyes glanced over toward them. Aven held up a hand, she pressed her lips together again, and they waited awkwardly for the two lieutenants and one warden to look back at their drawings and plans.

Wunik was the first to speak. "*Something* forced them inside. Siliana should be able to offer some protection, but who knows how many might need her help? She has worked with curing disease some. Local villagers near my cabin."

Miara sighed. "I don't like this."

"Neither do I," said Wunik quietly.

"If you don't like war, then you're paying attention. There's nothing at all to like about it. Keep an eye on that hold, will you?"

"I'll check back often."

Aven nodded. "Good."

Their new room was empty when Jaena awoke. She sat up, blinking blearily, and listened for Ro nearby. Only the crackling of the fire burning low met her ears. She fell back into the impossibly soft bed—where did they get beds like this anyway?—and shut her eyes again for a moment, hoping he'd return now that she'd stirred and curl back against her in the warmth of the bed.

Minutes passed. He didn't return.

She sighed. The light outside the balcony doors brightened from a dull twilight to the full-fledged light of morning. He'd probably gone to start his duties, eager to look at that enchanted map. Which figured; it was incredible. Not something you ran across every day.

She, however, had nothing to rush off to. She didn't exactly have a task, a role to play. They were all concerned about the elder king, the missing prince, how to decode the map. The brand…? Well, it was in Akaria, in Jaena's hands and not the Masters', and that was better than before. Good enough for now.

She was likely the only one still thinking about destroying the cursed thing.

Just as well. She also didn't want to lose it. This was *her* revenge. Her prize she'd stolen from them. If anyone wanted her to give it up, she wouldn't be doing that easily, as Aven had seen. She should get on with it. Time to don her vest and trousers and start the search. There had to be some way to ruin the thing and take its power away from the world—permanently.

Rising, she splashed water on her face, dressed, and strode back to the bed. She was reaching for the knapsack tucked between her and the wall when she noticed a curled sheet of parchment on the desk.

Had that been there last night?

She strode to it instead and picked it up. Her stomach dropped as she read it.

I look forward to the full story upon your return…

. . . your return will be much anticipated…

Damn.

She'd known. She'd expected it. Still, reading the actual words hurt like all seven hells burning her at once. Angered her too. The insolence of it—why should they assume he had nothing else to do? No one who still needed him? No more pressing mission? His work here wasn't done. She had the *brand* to destroy, damn it. How dare they assume all their efforts were more important, that his loyalty belonged to them, first and foremost?

It did, of course. It must. They were probably right.

He couldn't be expected to turn away from those who raised him, who'd cared for him, who'd given him his livelihood and his purpose. But it still pissed her off that they took it for granted. Took *him* for granted.

And they'd lied to him, by the gods. They couldn't be trusted any farther than she could throw this sheet of parchment toward the fire. She scowled at it bitterly. They hadn't even acknowledged that the pendant hid magic or that they must have known he was a mage. Perhaps they were loath to admit any of that in writing.

Or maybe they wanted him back so they could turn him into the Devoted themselves. Or to pressure him into never using any of his magic, never returning to her.

She frowned even harder and threw the paper back onto the table with disgust. No, this couldn't stand. She couldn't let him just go back there and put himself in their hands.

She'd convince him to stay. Or she'd go with him. That might be best, because he needed answers. Yes. She would go with him.

But first—the brand must be dealt with.

She snatched the knapsack and headed out of their rooms quickly, heading to the library, hoping she would find him there simply hard at work already.

Let her not find him in the stables, saddling up Yada and preparing for the trip back. Without her.

The bright marble halls of Ranok bustled with the

morning, servants carrying food, linens, baskets, and all sorts of other things to their destinations. She stopped one friendly looking woman for directions to the library. She thought she had it, but no point in wasting time wandering the halls of this fortress-palace-thing. Who knew how far it went on. And on and on.

She eased open the door, unsure if she needed to knock and whether it was a private or public space. Her eye caught on a familiar shock of white hair woven into a black braid down a neck that was growing terribly dear. She instantly longed to run her fingers down it, feel it, memorize it in case— No, she couldn't lose him now.

He sat on a high oak stool, hunched over a tall cabinet filled with scrolls, inks, and other writing supplies. No one else lurked nearby, so she slipped inside and closed the door behind her. Woven rugs of a serene, rich blue warmed the stone floor. Shelves heavy with leather spines in black, forest green, brown, and aubergine rose up on every wall and loomed over her, threatening to bury her in tomes.

He turned and smiled brightly when their eyes met. She smiled back and strode to his side, craning her head at the grandness of this place as she went.

"So many books. Have you gotten to look at any of them?" A moment late, it occurred to her that no greeting had truly seemed necessary. Why? And what, if anything, did that mean?

He shook his head. "No, just went straight to work on this thing. I'd like to get done what I can before the stars come out."

"How early were you up?"

He smiled broader, but he continued his work, his finger tracing glyphs. "Not *that* early."

She circled the cabinet while he worked, wondering if there were any answers to her own quest in these texts. "Any clues on how to destroy a certain burden we carry?" she mused idly.

"We?" He looked up abruptly, as if her wording had surprised him.

"Yes, we," she said more firmly, raising an eyebrow. Oh, of course. He would be leaving. He would be thinking of the damn thing as hers now. "I mean, no. You don't have to worry about it, it's mine to—"

"Oh, no, no, no. I didn't mean that." He stared back down at the star map, not saying more, shoulders tense. But he wasn't reading anything. Just staring.

He didn't want to tell her what was in the note.

She couldn't blame him for that, of course. Embarrassment flushed her cheeks as she realized she should have asked for permission to read it. Too late.

"So… see anything about it?" she said into the awkward silence.

"Oh. Uh, no." He didn't look up.

"My, you're jumpy." She smiled and stepped closer, trying to put him at ease.

"I just didn't sleep well." He released his determined stare at the map and met her gaze, looking a little relieved. His arm snaked out and pulled her closer. He nuzzled his head against her neck and shoulder.

She laid her arm across his back and took a deep breath, breathing him in. Might not be many more moments like this one if she couldn't convince him to take her with him.

"Some answers are likely here," he continued, "but nothing specific. It's all symbols, types of power. Doesn't tell you much about how to use them, and even then the guidance is very slight. No room on the map. I think that may have been wise."

She nodded but said nothing, pressing her face into his hair.

"It shouldn't take too long to decode this. Then we can start figuring out how to get rid of it. We'll figure it out, I promise."

His breath whispered across her chest as he spoke. She frowned. He talked like he hadn't received that note. Like he wasn't going anywhere. He couldn't be thinking of lying about it, could he? About leaving without telling her or something?

And yet, he hadn't been terribly forthcoming about the whole I'm-on-a-secret-mission-to-help-you thing. She'd have to confront him about it sooner rather than later and tell him she was definitely coming with him.

But not before breakfast. There was at least that much time.

"Are you hungry?" she said softly, running a hand over his braid and down his strong arm, tucking the memory of those sensations away for later. "I am."

He nodded against her. "I was planning on coming

back up to find you. Didn't think you'd be up yet."

She glanced at the fully bright day outside and snorted.

"Well… maybe I got lost in my work." He pulled away, grinning.

"I'll get you something," she said, squeezing his shoulder. "And me too. If we're allowed to have food in here?"

"I think so, yes."

"Watch this heavy thing for me, will you?" She held out the knapsack and the cursed brand. No one else would get such trust, and when he was gone, she'd have to keep it with her always, at least as long as they let her. She'd take advantage of having a trusted ally while she still could.

She shook her head at herself. As if he were just an "ally."

"Of course." He accepted the pack and placed it by his feet before turning back to his work, smiling now.

She hesitated, suddenly not eager to rush off. She leaned forward and kissed his ear quickly, earning a laugh before scampering off into the hall. She thought she could feel him staring after her as she escaped, but she didn't look back. She had no desire to know if that feeling was only wishful thinking.

Miara knocked on the exquisitely polished dark walnut door. A moment later, the door opened to reveal—a servant. Answering her father's door? Did she have the wrong room? A kind-faced, blue-eyed older woman smiled, seemed to recognize Miara, and swung the door wider.

Her father had risen from a table set for breakfast and was striding toward her, smiling. "Meesha, lovely morning. Have you eaten?"

"Good morning, Father," she said, smiling. "Not yet."

"Always forgetting to eat. Come, sit with us. Thank you, Teulan." He nodded at the servant warmly and led Miara to a table bathed with light from a glorious sunset beyond the leaded windows. Luha was cheerily munching away on an inordinately large pile of rolls, cheeks puffed out like a chipmunk. He gestured back to Teulan. "Apparently, someone decided we needed an… attendant."

"Feels strange, doesn't it?" Miara said, relieved she wasn't alone in the feeling.

He nodded. "I can't imagine why anyone thought we merited such a thing." His words were heavy with meaning, and he leaned forward and studied her with laughter in his dark eyes.

Miara sank slowly into a walnut chair with an elegantly patterned back. A thick cushion the color of blueberries was soft beneath her. She couldn't bring herself to answer his implication—the whole scene before her just seemed so strange. Placid and wholesome to the point of impossibility. The pleasant morning sun cast a gauzy, otherworldly glow over it all. This must be from some dream. Soon she would wake up and discover this was all a fantasy.

No. No, the Masters were still out there. Many mages were still enslaved. She and her family were simply the very, *very* lucky ones. None of this affluence would feel comfortable to her until they'd stopped the Masters and brought it all to an end. Maybe it wouldn't feel comfortable even then.

Her father poured her a cup of tea, although Teulan fought valiantly to make herself useful by filling Miara's plate with something of everything.

"Oh, you don't need to do that," Miara muttered at Teulan's elbow.

Finishing her ministrations, Teulan surprised her by laying a hand on Miara's forearm and giving her a knowing smile. "Beg your pardon, my lady. But yes, I do."

Miara almost let her drift away, but at the last second, she admitted what she was really thinking. "Why? Why must you?" The idea that anyone felt required or obligated to serve her, that literally they *must*, turned Miara's stomach.

Teulan spun gracefully and said, "Because your station requires it. You have much to concern yourself with and worry over. I am honored to do my part to make those a few less." Teulan curtsied and headed back toward the door.

Huh. Well, if she thought about it that way… At least she'd feel less like the Mistress when these women tried to fawn over her and more like… like… Aven. The obviousness of the revelation that she must think of herself as more like an Akarian royal than a Kavanarian one made her feel silly for not having adjusted her thinking already. But she'd known the latter for perhaps a month and Kavanarians her whole life, so perhaps it wasn't so silly.

Her father was eying her hard, as if waiting for her to

say something. What had he been saying again?

"Aren't you going to tell us more about this 'friend' of yours?" Luha asked finally, mouth full and gooey.

"Gross. Get done chewing first, will you?"

"She's dodging the question, isn't she, Da?"

"No, I'm not." Miara frowned down at her now-full plate. Was she blushing? "What about him?"

"What happened after you left us, meesha? I take it you found your prince." Her father's eyes crinkled with laughter, twinkling as he sat.

She snorted. "Well, yes. I did."

"Your plan clearly worked to free him. And then?"

"We went back to Estun—where the royal family had been living. Had to tell them all what had happened."

"And...?" Luha said, grinning.

"And what?"

Her father glanced at Luha. "Like pulling teeth, isn't it?"

Miara snatched a hunk of cheese and took a huge bite, saving herself from responding immediately. What was he getting at?

Swallowing, Luha sobered, set down her roll, and leaned closer to the table. "Miara, is it true you're going to be *queen*?"

Miara nearly choked on the overly ambitious bite as she tried to swallow too soon. She groped for her tea.

"I know you said he fell in love with you," her father mused. "But I had no idea... I mean. Well, if you're not going to come out and tell us, is it true you're going to be married?"

Miara flushed further now, but a grin threatened. She had never anticipated having this conversation with her family at all. Ever. But if she had, she was pretty sure she wouldn't have dreamed this up. She took a steadying breath, letting her grin break free.

"Yes, it's true. He's asked me to marry him."

"That's wonderful!" her father exclaimed.

"And you accepted. *Didn't* you?" Luha demanded, as if concerned Miara might have done something terribly stupid.

Miara smiled and folded her arms across her chest at her sister. "And if I didn't? You going to go beat down his door and make him ask me again?"

Luha narrowed her eyes and frowned playfully. "Don't tease me!"

"Yes, I accepted. Yes, it means I am to become queen." This time, to her surprise, the phrase came out more naturally, without faltering.

Luha clapped her hands together in delight, eyes shining. "Can you believe it?"

"Honestly, no." She shook her head. But I'm working on believing it, she thought to herself. It was hard work, too.

"When will you marry?" her father asked.

Miara frowned. "I am not sure exactly. Our plan was to go soon after this vote was completed, but with war so close on the horizon, it will likely have to wait. We thought there'd be more time before... everything fell apart. But can we really celebrate while we should be fighting?" She shrugged. "I don't know that I'd enjoy it as much, with so many trapped back at home. No, not home. At Mage Hall."

Her father nodded. "Looks like we'll be making a new home. Perhaps here?"

"Here or Estun. I have no idea, really. Wherever he wants to go is fine with me. What is one city versus another? I haven't seen any of them or grown roots here, so…" She shrugged. "What about you two? I know you said there wasn't much to tell, but perhaps that was just because there were too many people around."

Her father shook his head. "No. We were locked in our rooms nearly the whole time, until the Dark Master—"

"Daes," Miara cut in harshly.

"Daes?"

"His name is Daes." She was surprised at the edge of force in her words. Surprising or not, it felt damn good. "He's not your master anymore, Father."

His expression faded from surprise to a new amusement. "I suppose you're right. Eventually *Daes* took us with him to Trenedum. They were bringing new slaves there for some reason. The dungeons at Mage Hall were full, but they weren't bringing them out to the dormitories. Just keeping them in there. Strange, no?"

Miara's eyebrows shot up. "Oh—we never mentioned." She lowered her voice, but Teulan had wandered from the room. Hopefully she could speak quietly enough so that no one else would hear. "When Jaena escaped, she managed to steal the brand and bring it with her. They *can't* bring them out to the dormitories, because they can't brand them. Although we do believe they are trying to make a new one."

"Aven said something like that during our rescue. But I thought it must be a bluff."

She shook her head. "No. No bluff. It's real. We have to figure out how to destroy it. More easily said than done, I'm afraid. But let's not speak of it anymore." She forced herself to select a sausage from the plate and take a bite. She was talking too much; she'd sit here and forget to eat again before something else came up.

Her father shook his head, staring down at his plate. "We'll keep mum about it. Right, Luha? But if they can't make mages... The Devoted were bringing them in greater numbers than I've ever seen. That can't be good."

"Why?"

"How can they be keeping so many in *dungeons*? Air mages, maybe—but how are they keeping them all from transforming or breaking out? Surely some are unaware of their abilities, but not all."

Miara frowned. She hadn't considered that before. "Drugs? That'd be the only way for them to be sure. Keep them unconscious."

Her father nodded curtly. "And that's dangerous. And possibly deadly."

"If the Devoted are bringing them there instead of killing them, they must want them alive. As slaves. Or otherwise why bring them?" She took a ragged breath. "They couldn't just…"

"I'm sure they want them alive. I'm just not sure they're

all going to stay that way. We have to keep helping them."

"Agreed. We've quite had our hands full, but I haven't forgotten."

He leaned forward and ran his hand over hers. "Sorry. I didn't mean to diminish your victory. This is astonishing, meesha. Can you believe all this?"

"No, no, don't be sorry. It's important we think through these things." She shrugged. "It is more than I could have ever hoped for. And yet, less than we need."

"Was anyone else freed?"

"Yes, you'll be delighted to hear we did break the enchantment on Brother Sefim, Menaha, and a young man named Kae, although it is unclear if any of them have actually escaped from Mage Hall. The reins tightened considerably once the brand disappeared."

"I'll die a happy man if I can see Sefim alive and free on this side of the border." He smiled.

Miara returned his smile. "I hope we all live to see that. But hopefully you have a few other reasons to live happily. And wait a long time for any death to come knocking."

"Like a daughter's betrothal? And marriage? And *grandchildren*?" He grinned wider now.

Miara froze, her mouth open, but she had no idea how to respond. Before she could even form words, a knock at the door saved her. Her father nodded to Teulan's inquisitive glance.

"My lady Miara," said Perik, stepping inside and bowing deeply. "Our lord the king requests your presence in the planning room to review the next set of maps."

"Guess we'll have to talk about that later, Da!" She jumped from her chair and cheerfully pushed it back under the table.

He chuckled, then looked at Luha. "When did she turn into such a secretive creature?"

"What? Don't criticize. She's clearly good at it. One of her strengths." Luha popped another bite of bread into her mouth.

Her father clucked his tongue, shaking his head at her, but his eyes were playful.

"Since my secrecy has made you potential relations of a king, I don't think you should be complaining." Miara gave him an impish scowl.

He let out a bark of laughter. "You've got me there, meesha. Congratulations again."

Through a combination of determined questioning, wandering, and pure luck, Jaena found the kitchens in the far lower levels of Ranok and convinced the head cook to part with enough breakfast for the two of them and a tray to carry it all.

As her feet carried her back to the library, she pondered their options for the brand. How could they destroy it so that it could never be stolen back, so that it could never harm anyone ever again? If they had a smithy, would that be a start?

She slipped back into the library, and Tharomar

glanced up at her with a smile. Many of the characters must have been translatable without starlight, because he refocused quickly, caught up in his work. She set the tray down on a nearby cabinet but away from the map. They had enough problems. They didn't need to add spilling tea on ancient artifacts to the list.

His strong hands looked like they would snap the quill he held so carefully. Perpetually a little dirty where the earth rubbed into roughened calluses and cuts, his fingers held more gentleness and dexterity than one might initially assume. A flush crept into her cheeks at the thought. Then again, smiths bragged that their craft was not just about power, but accuracy. Precision and control. Power coupled with accuracy was a far greater achievement, and necessary for quality work. That was not so at odds with the precision of scratching tiny symbols on vellum. One bathed in fire, the other in ink, but were they really so different?

Absently, she poured herself some tea before he could catch her staring.

A moment or two later, he scribbled something down, set down his quill, and stood up, stretching his arms to the sky and groaning mightily.

"I want to melt it down," she said, now that she had his attention.

Tharomar straightened, dropped his arms, and stared for a second, blinking bleary eyes. "What now?"

"If I can find us a smithy, can we melt it down? You know." She tilted her head toward the knapsack.

"Oh. Maybe. Depends on the smithy. We might need a smelter. A castle like this ought to have both somewhere. But what are you going to do with it once it's melted?"

"What do you mean?"

"What are you going to recast it into?"

"I'd rather not recast it into anything."

"I wish it were that simple. But if you melt it, then you'll have liquid iron." He shrugged. "At the very least, it'll harden and cool into a lump. We can't just leave it in their smelter. We could pour a new ingot. No one would know what the ingot once was. Or we could heat it up in the hearth and hammer it into something else entirely. Or both."

She rubbed her chin. She didn't want it just turned into a slightly different shape. She wanted it obliterated. Gone. Up in smoke. Nonexistent. "Hmm. Let me think about it."

"You found breakfast, I see."

She nodded and extended a teacup. He dragged the knapsack over and sank onto a new stool beside her. "Nice to provide *you* with something for a change. Even if it's just living off our host's hospitality." She smiled up at him.

"We're doing valuable work for the Akarians. I'm sure they won't begrudge us tea. Or whatever this is." He pointed at a small, impressively fragile-looking white bowl full of doughy lumps.

"Some kind of dumpling? Let's find out."

He took a bite and frowned. "Is that apple?"

"I think so. It's not that I think they'd begrudge us

anything, but you know, I'd like to pull my own weight. You're doing the work, not me."

"Perhaps I'm doing it for both of us?" He raised an eyebrow, smiling.

She ignored the sudden flush of heat at those words. "Hmm, well, I'm not planning to live off their hospitality forever."

"I'm sure they'll be glad to hear that. But you certainly have earned some rewards for your past deeds, I think." He tilted his head at the knapsack.

She waved it off. "Hence my obsession with melting things today."

"Ah." He took a long swallow of tea.

"You're all doing things, fighting battles. I'm just sitting around and napping."

"You're recuperating from battles barely two days ago. That stone monstrosity didn't make itself."

"Well, I've recuperated. Now I need a job."

"We've barely had a few hours to spare."

"I believe we slept—and did—other things—for more than a few hours."

He chuckled. "Those were also quite necessary, I assure you. Seriously, Jae, there's plenty of time. Relax."

She stared at him, trying hard not to make some kind of swooning, moon-eyed expression. It was difficult, but he thankfully stayed focused on his dumplings. Still, a nickname, even a simple one… Her mother had often called her that. A man who was planning to run off and never talk to her again wouldn't be inventing nicknames, right?

"I have high expectations for myself, I guess," she managed finally. "Every minute is another we risk losing this damn thing without so much as denting it."

"I should be finished with the daylight portions of this by the end of the day. I'll have more to do at night, which should be nice and awkward. Writing in the dark and all. I may need your help."

"Of course, whatever you need."

"But after that…" He hesitated, stroking his beard for a moment.

Why? Why was he hesitating? Because after that he'd be riding back to Evrical?

"Think you can find a smelter today? And a smithy?"

"I probably can. If I can get the king's help, I'm sure I can figure something out."

"Then we could probably try some metal arts tomorrow morning, if you're so inclined." He smiled at her, leaning closer, like he hoped it would please her. Oh, he knew it did.

She leaned over too and pressed a quick kiss to his mouth. Before she could lean back, though, his arm caught her shoulders, and his lips snatched her back for more. Smothering laughter, she gave in to him as his other hand ran softly along the line of her jaw and curled around her neck. There was a warmth to this, a joy, a freedom that seemed even more precious than before. She had kissed him in desperation, in passion, in the solemnity of the dark of night. But this was something more.

It struck her as odd that a casual, spontaneous kiss

would seem so meaningful, like such a pinnacle. But the others had been stolen, in limited supply, her last chance. Possibly her only chance.

This morning, in spite of the note, his lips promised many, many more, days and weeks and years of them, and for the first time in a long time, her heart was free to make that promise back.

4 FIRE

Every one of the candles in the war room had burned low before they were finally done. Or as close to done as they were going to get. Feet aching, eyes blurry, and just about asleep on his feet, Aven finally called the meeting to a close.

"Hungry?" he asked Miara as he rubbed a hand over his face.

She leaned an elbow on the map table as the last of the wardens filed out. "Most definitely."

"C'mon," he said, ushering her after him.

They fell in step, her hand taking his elbow. They walked arm in arm more easily than he'd have expected. Like they'd been walking like this together for years. Like his parents always seemed to. He slipped his hand over her cold fingers and frowned.

While Miara had been with her family, he'd been checking on his. While Samul showed no real change, his mother looked more fatigued every time he saw her. She insisted she wasn't healing Samul or trying anything, but Aven didn't believe that. There was no other reason he could think of for her to be getting paler every time he saw her.

As they neared the main, and much warmer, part of the fortress, he flagged down a servant and ordered food to be sent up to his rooms. A meal was a glad excuse for some time alone, or as alone as they could be, and he needed it right about now. Hours of quieting his instincts and acting the calm and collected leader had left him dog-tired.

Because his instincts said they were screwed. Of course, even if they were screwed, this was still the right thing to do. The war, freeing the mages, admitting his magic, all of it. But he was suddenly in need of a small reminder.

Instead of sharing any of that darkness, he asked, "Did your father have anything to say?"

"We talked about the status of Mage Hall, but you know most of that," said Miara. "He thought maybe they were keeping the new mages drugged so they couldn't escape, since they can't brand them. But mostly I just answered his questions. They're still finding this all a bit hard to believe."

"Are you?" he said softly.

"Less and less."

"But still a little."

She shrugged, then shook her head at him. "If I think too hard about it, I dread waking up from the dream. If I think about all the work we have to do—and how uncertain victory is, and how many mages are still enslaved—I just want to get started."

He squeezed her hand beneath his. "Let's focus on all the things we need to do then, shall we?"

They walked for a while in silence, but she was frowning now. He waited to see if she'd say what she was thinking, but she didn't, only frowned down at her feet. They made it all the way up the stairs and into his rooms in silence.

"What is it? What's bothering you?" he said, flopping down on the couch and feeling more glad than he should that she immediately settled beside him. Of course, the food that was arriving alongside them might have helped. Telidar ran a speedy hold.

"I think there's even more we need to do than what we talked about today. More we're forgetting." She continued to frown, into the hearth fire now. Along with the food, someone had built up the fire into a pleasant, crackling blaze.

"More? Like what?" He tried to sound enthusiastic, but his voice must have betrayed his exhaustion.

"We can talk about it later." She met his eyes and forced a smile.

"No, you thought we needed to talk about it now. What is it?"

"Do you ever think about Galen?"

Whatever he'd thought she might say, he hadn't expected that. He blinked, the image springing to mind very clearly. "The boy we saved? In Regin's camp?"

She nodded.

"I hadn't in a while, no."

"Or Emie?"

He smiled. "Not since we got back to Estun. We've had so much going on. Why do you ask?"

"I see now why you were so eager to get away. It's easy to get caught up and shut off. And out of touch. And not help people."

He winced. "And not help anyone but *yourself*, even." Wasn't that what they'd been doing? He was completely focused on his father, his brother, his war. This war felt far more personal now than he'd ever thought a war could. In training exercises and lessons as a boy, he'd been through these situations in low stakes, in miniature. But those had felt like puzzles to solve. This felt much more like a wolf at the door.

A wolf he was going to fight to the death, if he had to.

"I didn't mean it critically," she said softly, bringing him back into the moment.

"I did."

Her frown changed, incredulous now. "Don't be so hard on yourself. It's barely been two days. But you *are* king now. If you want to help people, you can do it."

"As soon as we've settled this war and then—"

"No," she said sharply. "With this war coming, I think now is exactly when we need to do it."

He was frowning nearly as hard as she was now. "Go on. I know you have more you're thinking."

"Think about all we talked about today," she said, the words coming out fast and urgent now. "It's horrifying what this war could bring on. This could be worse than the Dark Days."

"But we'll be defending people this time."

"Maybe. Maybe they were defending people in the Dark Days too. I think we're going to lose in the long run if all Akarians see are mages wreaking death and destruction."

"Even if it's on their behalf?"

"Maybe? I don't know. There's only a handful of us. Who will they remember, us or them? Will they even be able to see a difference?"

He frowned. She was right. Since they would likely be outnumbered twenty-five to one, if not fifty to one, the chances the average Akarian would see and remember an attacking mage slave over a helpful freemage were pretty good. He ran a hand over his face, the feeling of defeat he'd fought off all day looming larger. "You're probably right. But we have to figure out how we're going to *win* before we can even worry about who they remember."

She eyed him. "You're thinking something. What is it? You weren't telling Dyon everything, were you?"

"No."

"Tell me what were you holding back."

He regarded her carefully for a moment. But if there was anyone he wasn't going to scare the pants off of, it was Miara. She was the one person he could tell the truth.

He sighed deeply. Then, as quietly as he could keep his voice over the fire crackling, "Honestly? I don't think we can win."

Perhaps he'd been wrong about telling her the truth,

because her eyes went wide and her mouth fell open. "How can you say that?"

"Well, we have to try. We'll do our damnedest. But they have too many mages. It's not looking good, as is. Maybe if we figure out a way to recruit more mages, we'll have more of a shot." He kept his voice low.

"Why didn't you tell that to Dyon?"

"He may be thinking the same thing. But I don't want the lieutenants and wardens thinking things are hopeless, or they'll *make* things hopeless."

"What do you mean?"

"If our soldiers can find any hole, any weakness to exploit, we may find a way to win. We may get lucky. But that all requires hope and determination and showing up ready to fight. Having me tell them I think it's a losing battle and we're all dead this far in advance doesn't exactly engender confidence. Which would be especially tragic if I'm wrong. Maybe when we're facing down the enemy, but not yet."

She frowned down at her lap. "Do you think you could be wrong? We can't be beaten already. We can't be. How can the Balance—" She cut off the words as her voice turned bitter.

"I certainly could be wrong. I'm trying to think it through, look for some weakness in their armor, some other weapon we can wield to neutralize so many mages." All he could think of was the star map, and he didn't really know if it'd say *anything* useful when Tharomar was done with it.

They sat in silence for a long moment.

She took a long, deep breath. "Gods, I hope you're wrong."

"I know. Me too."

"Well, listen. I was thinking about something before the battle. When the battle is joined, all we can do is our best. Right?"

"Right."

"The battle will come. People will see mages rain fire and hurl rock and wreak destruction. If that's all they see, we're going to have trouble getting people to accept us, or actually let mages live out in the open and free. Even if we win."

"What other option do we have?"

"In battle, none. But before then, we can do something. We need to people to see mages helping people too."

He raised his eyebrows. "Helping people?"

"I'm talking about showing people that mages can be something other than an evil nightmare from the Dark Days, deviant abominations who'll corrupt all in their midst. We should do what you wanted to do all along: help people. Akarians need to see mages doing good work as well as bad."

"But how, exactly?"

"Healing, for a start? Like Galen? Too bad it's not summer, or we could do so much more in the fields."

His mind was racing, trying to fit this piece into the overall plan. "If we shape the people's opinion around mages, that may help us recruit mages, too."

"You think?"

"Definitely. Mages won't come forward if they think it means people will hate them. We need to give people reasons to not hate mages. That's your point."

"Yes. They need reasons to admire them, even. Other than that their handsome king is one of them."

He snorted and then shook his head. He glanced at the darkness outside just as he caught Perik's quiet yawn. "That's a really good point. Have I told you how wise you are?"

She smiled widely. "Not enough."

"You're very wise. And I'm very exhausted. Let's get started on that tomorrow, first thing."

"Not right now?"

He grinned at her enthusiasm. "It's midnight, you know. The whole city's asleep."

"Except fools like us."

"Basically. People may not take kindly to you barging in, waking them up, and demanding to know if anyone is injured."

She stifled a laugh. "All right, all right," she said grudgingly. "But can't we at least make a list? I'm full of ideas here."

He rose to get a quill. "Anything for you, my love."

Detrax forgot about Thel for the rest of that day and into the next, presumably busy with Niat. She was not in the tent for most of the time that Thel was. The hours were long and dull and would have been frigidly cold without the blanket. He'd thought through just about every angle he could on how to escape. He'd listened to hours of guards talking about beer, their superior officers, their women back home, their women more recent than that. The chatter was just barely less tedious than staring blankly at the tent flap. When the sun reached its zenith, a bit more light filtered into the tent, and Thel would risk reading a bit of the tiny book, clutched so he could hide it at the first footstep or rustle.

He peppered them with requests to be moved to a different, more pleasant tent, but unsurprisingly, nothing came of it.

About midday of the third full day of his capture, someone remembered he existed and stumbled in via the tent flap. The soldier unlocked Thel's manacles, led him out of the utterly desecrated tent, and clamped on a new set of chains.

A dozen or so people in plain clothes milled around a campfire in front of him. As they approached, the soldier shoved Thel's shoulder down, forcing him to sitting on a log.

"Watch him," the soldier snapped.

The nearest woman narrowed her eyes at him and didn't acknowledge the order. The guard stalked away.

Thel glared after him, noting the short sword, the stripe of red on his shoulder. Kavanarians. Not that he was surprised, but it still stung a bit. Alikar had been suspected of working with Kavanar, but this was worse than Thel had expected. He would bet they were still inside

Gilaren. This coup must have been underway long before anyone had suspected; the encampment was hardly new. The enemy troops must have crossed into Gilaren before the vote on Aven as heir had even happened.

The people fidgeting around Thel were not soldiers, but what were they then? The air was tight with tension—knees jumping, hands whittling or polishing or prying or mending, eyes darting at the horizon or the woods. The woman ordered to watch him stayed near his side. Upon closer inspection, she wore leathers like those Miara had shown up to Estun in. Several others did as well. Not something that made him feel at all optimistic.

Shouts behind him drew his attention. She eyed him as he turned. A tent had collapsed down in a heap. An accident? No, the encampment was packing up. He scanned his surroundings as casually as he could. The carriage, horses, and wagons were being packed and readied. The gathering point was just behind them on the other side of a low, wide-branching tree.

Everyone in the entire camp could see this central point from where they were packing. Ah, so they weren't depending on only this woman watching him. More than a few suspicious glares came his way as his gaze slid by.

He shivered and bounced his knee, blowing breath into his hands. The campfire cast some heat in his direction but not nearly enough. It was far too late in the year to be sitting still outside without a cloak.

He groped for ideas to use his magic to get out of this, especially now that he could see the whole encampment and what he had to work with. But people swarmed the place—Kavanarians in particular. He could try to split the earth or lob a boulder. But how far could he get? If he could even find a boulder or rip it out of the ground, how many could he really take out? Surely as soon as it started, someone would be at him with a dagger to the throat or worse. At the very luckiest, Detrax would still figure it out. Maybe there was a way he could cause a distraction instead.

He eyed the chains. Even if he managed to kill or distract enough to free himself, he'd still have these unfortunate companions.

A crack rang out behind him. He glanced back sharply, spotting where an arrow had connected with a tent pole. Several dozen more arrows rained down suddenly on the first row of tents, then the second.

Thel ducked automatically, hitting his knees and shrinking down as best he could. Another volley of arrows fell, all aimed at the tents behind him. A distant rumbling caught his ears over the shouts and grunts of the encampment rising.

The odd folks around him didn't hunker down as he had. Several perked up, others rising to their feet. His guard glared down at him.

The rumbling grew louder—the thundering of hooves against the earth.

"Incoming!" shouted a man to her right.

"A wall, Ridan," the woman beside him barked. "We need defenses *now*."

"You heard her. Form it up!" the man—Ridan?—responded.

Out of the trees raced a dozen riders screaming a war cry Thel knew all too well. Another volley of arrows accompanied them, one piercing a man a few feet in front of Thel this time. Others riddled tents with holes, hitting who knew what inside.

The noise rose around him—cries, shouts, groans, horses neighing, swords drawing from scabbards. Thel knelt and scanned the camp behind him. Two men down behind him, three tents collapsed, one with a roiling monster of bodies writhing inside. Detrax stepped out of his tent, dragging Niat with him.

Flame erupted from the ground just before the riders. Thel gasped. The blaze curved up and over the campfire area.

Thel stared in horror, recoiling against the log as the flames thickened until he almost couldn't see through them.

The riders. It was sweeping toward them *fast*. Barely enough time to change course.

Or none. The first rider and his mount plunged through the flames and into view. Screams of horse and man rang out, and Thel threw up a forearm to block his view of the horror.

The fiery barrier wasted no time, pushing outward to engulf more of the riders. Even those who struggled to turn couldn't escape their fate. The barrier faltered at one spot, and one rider stormed through, his lowered sword catching a man in the throat before he, too, was engulfed in flames.

Mages, Thel realized. The people crowded around the

campfire were mages. Killing Akarians.

Akarians here to save him? To capture Alikar?

It didn't matter. They weren't saving or capturing anyone.

"There—on the far hill under that oak!" shouted Ridan, who seemed to be their leader.

"I see them," answered his companion. Her hands were braced in front of her as if she held off the Akarian onslaught with them directly. Her face and brow were creased with effort, and sweat beaded at her temples. Was there a touch of the same horror he felt in her voice? "Are those their leaders?"

"Commanders, I'd wager, a mage among them—take them out! We can hold the wall."

She winced, before grunting, "Fine." Her hands relaxed and then she raised them higher, fingers splayed out. She eyed a hill in the distance. Thel followed her gaze. Four horses stood in shadow on a slight slope three hundred yards back. They *should* have been hard to spot and out of arrow range.

Could Aven be among them? Any number of friends, family, and comrades could be waiting there, doomed on that hilltop. He had to help them.

The mage's fingers began to curl slowly into fists.

Thel didn't wait to discover what that gesture portended. He launched himself at her, shoulder first, and collided with her ribs. She toppled immediately, sprawling off the log and onto the ground.

"Gods!" she swore as she went down.

The man barreled toward him now, and Thel ducked,

catching his assailant in the stomach. Grabbing Ridan's knees wasn't too hard even with manacles, and he easily sent the man flying over his shoulder.

Thel straightened to see the blaze sweep forward through the trees toward the Akarians and catching on them too. By the gods, they'd burn the whole forest at this rate.

The woman straightened and renewed her focus on the hilltop group, ignoring Thel. He staggered forward, but hesitated when he realized Ridan had recovered and refocused too. He couldn't stop them both, so he opted to tackle the girl again, the two of them sprawling into the dirt as she dug up a new string of curses at him.

A sharp crack split the air behind them, silencing them both. The mage leader had fallen flat on his back, the skin on the side of his face red and black as though burned and eyes gazing emptily at the sky.

Thel staggered to his feet and squinted just in time to see the four far-off riders turn and pick up speed. Good—he wasn't going to have to keep launching himself shoulder-first at mages and hoping for the best.

Footsteps to his left caught his attention just in time for him to lean back, a third mage's punch missing his jaw by an inch. Thel reeled back, tripping over one of the logs. The woman and the new mage closed in on him and hauled him to his feet, calling out for help.

They dug their fingers into his arms like talons, but Thel didn't struggle. Knowing they could make a wall of flame that obliterated any hope of rescue didn't make him inclined to try to break away.

Instead, he looked out at the devastation.

Steaming, reeking black mounds before him had once been living Akarians, both human and equine. Steeds loyal and brave. Men and women who'd had children, lovers, homes to return to.

All of them, no more.

Thel realized his mouth had fallen open and snapped it shut. He gritted his teeth as that horror teetered on the edge of a mad rage.

Dead. All of them. And what had Kavanar lost? A few tents?

Thel didn't know how long he stared. Detrax snapped him out of his shock by responding to the calls of his captors, a sullen and pale Niat in tow.

"Hey—you there." Detrax snapped his fingers at a soldier behind them, frozen and staring. "Get these two into the carriage. No reason to be delayin'. This place reeks enough as it is."

Numbness setting in, Thel let himself be dragged to the carriage, Niat now by his side.

"Hopeless," he muttered. "I see."

"I told you," she whispered.

Soldiers shoved them into the dark wooden cage, and the two of them fell silent. The image of charred bodies and the sound of their cries echoed long after they'd left the carnage behind.

Golden curls appeared in the doorway of Miara's room, followed by Elise in one of her sapphire dresses. Intimidatingly elegant as usual. Her skin was paler now, though, and her smile weak and tired. Two attendants followed Elise, both middle-aged women, one with a high chin and proud shoulders in a black robe, and another more matronly looking woman with freckles.

"Ah, there you are, Miara," Elise said, clasping her hands in front of her. Miara made a note of the poised gesture. She needed all the poise she could get. "I have something to show you. That is, if you don't mind taking a break from your studies?"

Miara had been poring over the list they'd made last night and a map of Panar, trying to decide what good they could do with the most visible impact. A bit of a crazy idea was stirring in her mind, but she was looking for something better and more of a sure win. But she wasn't really getting anywhere.

"Of course, my lady," Miara said. "Is Samul doing all right?"

"Siliana just stopped by to give me a rest."

Miara wasn't entirely sure why they were taking shifts when the old king had so many servants and healers around him, but she got the vague impression that Elise and Siliana were guarding him. That they dare not leave the old king alone. "My father is a creature mage, and I'm sure he would be happy to assist you if you need it," she offered as she stood and put the papers and map away.

"That is good to know. I think Aven may have been concerned about burdening him so soon after his recent ordeals."

"Oh, he gets just as bored as the rest of us."

Joining the queen, she nodded at the door and followed them out of her room. Elise led them down the hall and up the grand staircase that led to the king's rooms. Miara hadn't thought there was anything up on that level of Ranok *other* than the king's rooms, but surely Elise would have mentioned if that was their destination.

"I haven't told Aven about this yet," Elise said softly as they walked. "I wanted to speak with you first."

Miara blinked and stayed quiet, unsure how to respond. They reached the top of the grand staircase and turned right down a corridor Miara hadn't noticed before. Through an elegant archway and another turn, she came to a set of closed double doors similar to the king's, except that the great oaken double doors were painted with a viciously roaring brown bear with eyes of sparkling emerald green.

The freckled woman scampered ahead of them and opened the door, the bear parting to reveal a giant room bathed in sunlight.

"Thank you, Kalan," the queen murmured.

The only rooms Miara had seen that were nearly this large—outside of Kavanar—were Aven's rooms, the king's rooms. The wide foyer was graciously covered by a large, thick cobalt rug. A small, white marble table sat in the center, topped by a broad planter filled decadently with cut white roses, lilies, and a dozen other flowers she didn't even recognize. The light shining over it all seemed oddly colored, and she stared at a vast and glorious masterpiece of azure and emerald leaded glass, pieced together to form the shape of the continent. By the gods, the work that must have taken, the expense…

Tearing her eyes away, she spied other areas beyond—sitting areas, a broad oak desk, a bed with posts nearly half again as tall as she was. To her left, a dressing room opened up that was bigger than the room Miara had just left. It alone might have been bigger than her whole family's rooms in Mage Hall.

A blue velvet chaise lounge sat serenely in the dressing room, and an immense row of closets lined the far wall, their walnut wood starkly elegant. On the lounge lay three or four familiar-looking sapphire dresses.

Oh. It hit her. She knew where she was.

"These are *your* rooms," Miara breathed.

Elise smiled. "Yes and no. They are the queen's rooms. I'd like them to become your rooms sooner rather than later. Right now, in fact."

Miara raised her eyebrows. "Now? But we—"

Elise held up a hand. "I know we haven't formalized anything. But Aven *has* announced his intentions, and as far as I know you're still amenable to the arrangement?"

At first, she could only stare at the queen like she'd gone mad. Who could take a poor slave girl to a room like this and say, are you certain you still want it? But Miara recovered quickly and nodded. "Yes. Yes, of course.

But I fear there won't be time to formalize anything for a while now anyway. War fast approaches, based on what we discussed yesterday. Won't that be a problem?"

"Winter has a way of slowing wars. And also weddings. At least in Akaria, fewer tend to declare their love when the lakes freeze over. But no, I don't think it need be a problem. We all know you are to be queen; the rest is more ceremonial than anything else. The Assembly voted their support of Aven—mostly—with full knowledge of his intentions, so I am not concerned."

Miara swallowed, unnerved by Elise's certainty. She didn't feel certain of any of it. She wasn't even certain they'd survive the war, not after their talk yesterday. There were too few mages on Akaria's side. That she'd become queen was even less certain. What if something happened? What if Aven found some reason to change his mind? Unlikely, but… Before she could figure out how to voice her concern without offending, Elise moved on.

"Good. I see you are with me. Now, there are certain duties that fall to the queen, both in peace and in wartime. And I am not the wife of the king anymore."

"But neither am I."

"Exactly our problem. There is no queen, or there are two."

"No, no, I'm just… an Arms Master, if that. Certainly, no one would fault you for continuing the queen's duties at a time like this."

"Indeed they would likely prefer I did continue them." Worry lines deepened in her face. "But *I* don't prefer it."

"I don't understand."

"I need to care for Samul. I *want* to care for him. I want to devote all my attention to saving him. The rest… It is time to let the rest of it go. My husband needs me, and that means I need you, just as Samul needed Aven."

"I don't understand, my lady."

"I want you to start taking on the duties of the queen."

Miara froze. Then she opened her mouth, but what was she even intending to say? Of course, she'd assumed this would happen eventually, but so soon? The only thought that swirled in her head was one she was desperate not to voice—but am I ready?

"I'm sorry we haven't treated you better. I'm sorry we haven't always trusted you as much as we could—"

"You were just looking out for Aven."

Elise seemed to have been planning to apologize at much greater length, but her eyes held a world of relief at Miara's words. And now she regarded Miara evenly, patiently. "Can you do this for me?"

"Am I allowed to?" Miara said quietly.

"I can instruct others that I am choosing to share my authority with you. And there's this, which will offer proof." Elise touched gentle fingers to the emerald at her throat and then looked to a prim attendant who came forward and unclasped the necklace. "Thank you, Opia."

Then Opia turned and approached Miara, as inevitable as a storm on the horizon, holding the necklace like she planned to collar a dog.

Miara's eyes widened, and her blood was suddenly

pounding in her ears. Before she could even think to protest, the attendant was sweeping her hair aside and clasping the necklace around her throat.

She forced herself to take a deep breath. This is not enslavement. This is a gift. This is not imprisonment. It's power. Another deep breath. She hoped all those words were true and not a hopeless fantasy.

Opia stepped back, and Miara just stared at the pendant in a mirror on the far wall, shocked and a little frightened, struggling to calm her body. The same pendant Miara had admired the effortless grace of so many days ago in Estun glittered at her, as if winking. Was the panic coursing through her trying to tell her something or merely the echoes of past suffering? She had been a slave for over twenty years and free for barely twenty days. Perhaps even the similarity to enslavement, however untrue, was enough to set her on edge.

"Thank you, my lady," she said, frowning when her voice faltered and bowing deeply to hide it. "What is expected of me?"

"Now, not so low, dear," said Elise. "From now on, everyone bows lower than you, if you choose to bow at all. *Everyone*." Lowering her chin, Elise leaned forward to drive home her point. "Understand?"

Miara's eyes widened as she straightened. She nodded hastily. "What about the king?"

"Samul and I bowed to each other when the occasion arose, but I suppose you should ask Aven. I for one am fairly certain that he's never been looking for a queen who knew how to bow. That was his problem all along, really."

Miara fought the urge to bow again. "I… understand."

"It does take some getting used to, but the honor of the office demands it."

Her shoulders loosened just a little to know that Elise had also found it initially difficult and unnatural to refuse to bow to anyone. "It's… hard to stomach that I deserve such honor," she admitted.

"Think not of that. Think of Akaria. Does *it* not deserve such honor? The ruler of a great nation is worthy of respect, is she not?"

Miara inclined her head. "I suppose so."

"You are now Akaria's representative, one of her most powerful. You are her steward. Her caretaker. You must demand respect on her behalf."

"I will, my lady," she said, more firmly now.

"Now, no more 'my ladies' either. Not that *I* mind, but you will need to break the habit. The one getting the honorifics is you now, my queen." Elise smiled, although deep sadness still lurked in her eyes. She emphasized her words with a small bow that made Miara feel like she should fling herself lower as quickly as she could.

She braced herself bolt upright and only nodded.

"Good work. It gets easier." Elise smiled more broadly. "Now, when people come to me with issues, I'm going to send them to you as much as I can. At first it will likely be small things—what to eat for a feast, matters of stewardship of Ranok that Telidar cannot handle alone. But as time goes, harder things will pop up. Audiences of subjects with complaints that are perhaps important but not important enough to see the king. Also, a great deal of time is taken up by simply attending to people. Showing up, letting them be heard, socializing, arguing on behalf of Akarian desires and agendas."

That sounded awful and possibly painful too, but Miara said nothing.

"Not that it's unimportant work. Those relationships will matter when times like these come upon us. For instance, Takar could take this opportunity to attack us, with Kavanar on the move. And perhaps they will. But our trade agreements make that highly unlikely. They'd rather not."

"What's covered in the trade agreements?"

"We offer them coal, diamonds, emeralds, stone, and wood. They offer us fabric, spices, iron, fish, wheat, and their good gold coin. There are some limits and guarantees of amounts and costs, but those are the general details."

Miara nodded. Gods, let that be enough to keep them. They did *not* need an additional problem on their hands.

"Now, these rooms—they will be yours now. I haven't been in them anyway. I'll be at Samul's side. And my attendants as well. Please meet Opia. And also Kalan." She gestured gracefully at each, who bowed in turn. "Etral will also attend you, but she's fetching us some tea. They are very talented women."

The two women gave her slight curtsies. Perhaps it was good that Miara didn't have to bow or curtsy because she still wasn't entirely sure which she ought to be doing.

"Thank you, my—" She cut herself off before the title could come out. This was definitely going to take practice. She took a deep breath. 'Thank you, Elise," she said more deliberately. There, that wasn't so hard. That felt good. Dignified, even.

Aven's mother smiled more broadly now. "Excellent. Better already." She gestured at the room around her. "Feel free to make of this what you will. Now, let me show you around."

Heat bathed Jaena's front as the charcoal grew red, then yellow, surrounding the brand. The master smith hadn't stopped giving them odd looks, and Ro hadn't stopped valiantly pretending nothing out of the ordinary was going on.

"Where's your ore?" he asked.

"Oh, the king has something special he'd like melted down," Ro said. That was not entirely a lie either.

The smith raised an eyebrow. "Into a lump?"

"Yes," Ro said confidently, while Jaena struggled not to wince. This part was her idea—and, now she was seeing, the weakest part of their story. "He's not very particular about its future form as long as it's not in its current one."

"Something 'special'?" He narrowed his eyes at Tharomar.

Ro shrugged and looked bored enough to yawn. "I don't interrogate kings on their requests, sir. I don't know about you, though. Maybe you should go ask him yourself."

Jaena smiled as brightly as she could manage. "Just doing as we're told. Very sorry to put you out of use of your smelter for a while, but the king demands secrecy." She again offered up the signed and wax-stamped letter Aven had provided them with. The smith didn't more than glance at it. Either the stamp was proof enough for him, or he didn't believe them for a second.

Ultimately, after more glares, several more questions, and finally a thorough letter perusal, he relented and left them to the smelter by themselves. But he continued to eye Ro from around the corner from time to time.

"I'm using my magic to heat the furnace faster," she said softly to Ro, hoping the sounds of the blaze and the smithy muffled it all easily. She probably wasn't helping matters by doing that, but she didn't want to be standing there for eight hours either.

"You can do that?"

"You can do it too. You already were doing it."

"And here I thought I was skilled. Or lucky. Goddess blessed, even."

She smiled. "Maybe you are."

He snorted. "Which one?"

"Blessed."

"Oh, I know I am." He snaked an arm toward her waist, but she batted it away, grinning.

"He's already suspicious of us enough as it is."

"So you don't think I'm skilled?"

"You think I'd have a plan to make money off your work if I didn't?"

"You were somewhat under duress at the time. I thought you might have just been being nice."

She scoffed. "You know you're skilled, you don't need me to tell you."

"But I still like to hear it," he said, grinning.

"Skilled at deception too," she muttered under her breath. She tried not to worry that he was lying or neglecting to tell something to *her*, but she had to admit that for a religious man, he sure was quick with a fabricated story.

He folded his arms, a smile still wide on his face. "It's a handy skill I use happily at the goddess's direction."

"They teach you that in temple? They seem good at lies. Or omissions." She winced inwardly at the edge of bitterness to her voice.

"No," he said, expression darkening. "I learned how to lie long before that."

She cursed under her breath. "Sorry," she muttered. She should change the subject. "You want me to show you how? To heat the charcoal?"

He shifted his weight uneasily. "Is that where mages usually start?"

"Sort of. Feeling the energy move is the first step. Absorbing, losing, expending energies. A heating spell is a good place to start expending energy."

"Hmm," he hesitated. "Maybe let's start tomorrow."

She quickly tucked her disappointment away, nodding and forcing a smile. "Sure." Damn, her voice sounded far from the casual she'd been going for.

"We shouldn't get distracted," he added.

"Of course," she muttered.

The time passed slowly, but as the hour wore on, Ro's nonchalant shell started to crack. As bells in the city rang in the beginning of the second hour, he was outright frowning.

"What is it?" she said slowly.

"It's... still black."

"What? Is that not normal?"

"It's just a thin rod of iron. I don't know how much faster you're hearing that furnace, but... it seems a great deal hotter than it should be." He paused, rubbing his chin. "I have a bad feeling about this."

She raised an eyebrow. "About what?"

"Let's give it a little longer."

After another hour inside the heat and more charcoal shoveled in, the furnace was raging. Sweat dripped from both of them even after backing away as far as they dared.

Still the brand sat, quietly and defiantly black, stoic amid the hell of charcoal surrounding it.

She reached out with her senses. She'd hesitated to since the very first time she'd felt the writhing horror locked in its branding end, but there was no bypassing it now. And there it was—twisting agony locked into the metal. Who could have created such a thing? That bit was blazing and ready to sear its mark into innocent flesh. But it was far from hot enough to change shape. And the rest was barely warm. In fact, she could almost feel the evil thing pushing the heat away, defending itself from the onslaught.

"It's not going to work, is it?" she said softly.

"No. I don't understand how it's possible, but it's not acting like iron should."

"By the gods. This must be part of its spell somehow." She swore under her breath. "Let's give it a little longer."

He nodded. "What else do we have to do?"

"I can think of *one* thing." She barely stifled a laugh.

He elbowed her. "How can you think of that at a time like this?"

She sobered. "It's…" Emotion welled up unexpectedly, stealing the words from her throat. It—he—was all she had to remind her that this world wasn't as terrible as it seemed to be. Whatever tenuous connection they had, however long it lasted, she would cling to it, *especially* in the face of defeats like these.

In spite of the heat, he pulled her closer. If only she could read him as well as he seemed to be able to read her. She rested her head on his shoulder, and it was enough. The wave of emotion subsided, and her determination to destroy the brand took its place. If this didn't work, they would find some other way, even if she had to carry the brand with them all the way to Evrical and back. It had to be destroyed.

It *had* to.

Still, three hours later, they returned to Ranok, sweaty and exhausted. The now-cool brand sat once again in her stolen knapsack, very much intact.

Miara clung to Aven's arm as they followed his escort through the bustling streets, on foot as the temple wasn't far. Arm clinging was convenient for gawking—or maybe gawking gave her an excellent excuse to cling closer. As it was, she didn't have to watch her step across the uneven cobblestones. She could catch herself from the inevitable trip and simply take in the beauty of the White City. She had been to Evrical, of course, and several of Demikin's palaces, but this was something different. At the very least it was not quite so filthy as the Kavanarian capital.

Dappled sunlight caressed red slate roofs, brown awnings, and flower boxes bare with dark earth for the winter. On many a door hung a slender sheaf of wheat, others a vial of water swaying in a cool wind, a few a nail suspended from rough twine. The wheat must honor Nefrana, and such offerings had appeared in Mage Hall often, but of the others she wasn't so sure. Many a door and wall were pale yellowed bricks or white stucco, ricocheting the sunlight around the streets.

The temple of Anara awaited them near the city center, sitting low and squat across from a wide cobblestoned market with a long and slender pool in its center. Or was it some kind of watering trough? No horses loomed about, even amid their small party.

Blue paint adorned the temple walls, and a white door beckoned to them beneath a black slate roof. Balls of evergreen adorned benches outside that would be more inviting were it not growing chillier by the hour, by the day. Nothing hung on the door of the temple, but the faint tinkling of bells and the sweet, spicy smell of incense reached her.

The lead of Aven's escort—well, also her escort—approached the door and knocked three times.

The door revealed a dark-haired woman dressed in a black robe trimmed in bright cerulean. Her eyes grew alarmed. "Can I help you, sirs?"

"May I present King Aven Lanuken and his betrothed, Arms Master Miara Floren."

The guards parted neatly as their leader bowed off to the left, leaving a wide berth between the woman and the two of them.

Miara tightened her hand around his elbow but tried to smile.

"Your Highness, may the goddess keep you and the Balance protect you," said the woman, curtsying deeply, and again Miara wondered if she had ever breached that protocol at some point. She really ought to remember to inquire about it further, but they'd had so many other things to worry about.

"Greetings, my lady," said Aven smoothly. "And who might you be?"

"Priestess Kawe, Your Highness. Is there some way our humble Sapphire Temple can be of service to you? We regularly receive noble worshippers at the Emerald Temple to the south. As I'm sure you already know, sire."

She added the last bit hastily, as if worried she might have caused offense.

"Yes, of course, and I'm sure our visits will take us there eventually. But for today, we are here. Priestess, we've heard there is an infirmary here. Is that correct?"

"Indeed, sire. This temple does not serve open worship but houses those in need, in particular the ill and injured. Not a place for someone such as yourself." She had braced herself in the doorway a touch protectively, Miara realized.

"Ah, but I've brought a great healer with me, and she'd like to see if there's any good she can do your patients." She elbowed him in the back, moving as slightly as she could. His polite smile only grew to a grin. "That is, if you don't mind a mage doing the healing."

For a moment, the whole entry was frozen still, as if waiting to see how this bit would turn, how their luck would play out. How deep did the fear—and hatred—of mages go? Kawe's dark eyes flicked from Aven to her and back again repeatedly, almost panicked. She hated mages, certainly, or she'd have answered quickly. But she had either gotten word of the new king's mage powers or was starkly tempted to accept help, hatred or no.

"You can heal people?" Kawe said slowly.

"Some people," Miara answered. "Injuries, especially. If you show me, I can tell you for certain." Hopefully she could avoid explaining all her weaknesses to this priestess who likely hated her.

A long moment passed, and Kawe took a step back.

"All right. Come in."

"Is your high priestess here today, Priestess Kawe?" said Aven as they followed the woman into a white tiled entry.

The priestess smiled sweetly for him. Just like Renala had. He had a way of getting women to do what he wanted, didn't he? It had certainly worked on her, now that she thought about it. Come to think of it, the only woman Miara could remember not quickly striving to please Aven was Lady Toyl—and perhaps herself, at least outwardly. Inwardly had been another matter, and even then she'd caved to teaching him. Funny how it took seeing him around others before she really understood this about him—and about herself.

"Yes," the priestess said, attention fully on him now. "Shall I fetch her for you?"

"If you can see us to your patients first, we'll look around and then I will speak to her about further work we can do for you when she's ready."

"Of course." Kawe turned to Miara with a slight bow, her smile noticeably fading. "If you'll follow me, my lord and lady."

They followed Kawe, and to Miara's surprise, two of the guards followed on their heels.

The infirmary was down a long, dim hall filled again with the sound of bells tinkling, louder this time. Kawe opened the door, and Miara peered inside. Two rows of cots, one on each side, holding maybe thirty. Not many, really. Blankets of faded and assorted colors covered each small cot, and cheerful plants sprung up between each patient. A few faces turned toward the door, but most slept. Natural light filled the room from a row of high windows, giving it the feel of an atrium.

"These are some of our ill," the priestess murmured. "What is it that you can and can't do?"

"Injuries. Cuts, breaks. Abscesses." Wait, did humans get abscesses, or only horses? "I can't heal things that occur naturally. Like aging. Getting old isn't something anyone can heal."

Now Kawe did smile slightly. "If only. I'll return with the high priestess and to help if need be."

"Yes, thank you," said Miara. Aven had fallen quiet, studying the room carefully. "That will do fine."

Two others in black robes trimmed with azure were bringing water. A boy and a girl. They bent over patients, murmuring to them and tending to basic needs.

She approached the first cot quietly. Aven stayed back, leaning in the wide doorway and studying the room. She examined the first woman as she slept. No visible injuries plagued her, and reaching out, Miara could sense nothing in particular either. Not a promising start. She glanced at the plant at the bedside, lively and green. A small purple bud peeked out on the right side, ready to bloom.

This late in the year? Hmm.

She glanced around at the other plants. All were lively. Unnaturally full and lush. Several held forth small pink and orange blooms, some as grand as springtime.

Miara cautiously let her senses sweep the room. Her eyes locked on the girl, who was keeping herself busy at the far end of the room, head down, fixed on the water basin she was refilling. A sandy-brown braid fell down her back, and her face was smudged with dirt here and there. Much dirtier than Miara would have expected a girl with her job should be.

"There's already a mage here," she said softly, glancing at Aven. He looked up.

The girl froze, then turned to peer over her shoulder. Her dark eyes were wide as if she were a mouse caught in a trap.

In a blink, she bolted. The pitcher she'd been pouring from crashed to the ground as she raced out. Several patients started in surprise from their sleep.

"Wait!" Miara rushed after her, jumping over the shattered pieces and darting into the far doorway. But it was too late. The girl had vanished.

Miara turned back, frowning. Aven had raced after her, and now he looked out the doorway too. Just empty street and alley back there, no fleeing girl.

The boy was staring at her, stunned. "How did you know?"

"Because I'm a mage too. Do you know where she lives? Where she might have gone?"

He mutely shook his head. Miara probed cautiously but sensed no spark of magic in him.

"If you're done creating a ruckus, you could look at my leg," grumbled an old man who'd eyed her from the first.

She glanced over her shoulder at Aven. He shrugged, as if to say, what's done is done. They'd lost the girl. For now.

"I can take a look," she told the man. He had a long,

bushy gray-and-black beard and lively eyes. "But I can't promise anything. Any injury resulting from age won't be something I can help."

He frowned. "Hey! My leg's not old just because I am. It broke and didn't heal up right, years ago. Aches every damn day. See for yourself."

She took a step closer to the man but hated to admit defeat. She eyed the boy a moment longer. "What's your name?"

"Reed," he said simply.

"And hers?" She jerked a thumb over her shoulder at the alley.

"Wessa."

"You see Wessa, you tell her I'm looking for mages. They can train to be healers too if they want. Got it?"

The boy nodded, but his face was pale, as if the mission she'd charged him with scared him.

Grudgingly, she stepped forward to examine the old man's leg. "Gods, was this even set by a healer?"

"No. Long story. Skirmish on the Takar-Shansaren border, pretty far out."

"I could heal it, but we'd have to rebreak it first," she said, wincing. "I'm sure you don't want to do that. It will hurt a great deal. And then it'll hurt even more when I repair it. The healing works, but it's immense agony while it lasts. Are you sure you're up for that?"

He frowned. "I asked, didn't I?"

"Does it hurt right now?"

"Damn thing comes and goes."

"Your choice."

"I can stand a few minutes of pain to make the nag go away for a while." He locked his gaze, as if daring her to admit she couldn't really grant him that.

Miara took a deep breath, hoping she was right in her analysis. She glanced at her two guards. "Which one of you wants to help me break his leg?" she said with a smile.

Their eyes widened, terrified. "We dare not touch a citizen like that, my lady."

She frowned.

"Guess that leaves me," said Aven, stepping up to her side.

She picked up a stool and pantomimed cracking him in the leg with it.

"Ah," he said smoothly, taking the nearby stool from her hands and eying it speculatively. Then he looked to the man. "You ever have your leg broken by a king?"

"Can't say I have, sire."

"Not many can claim that, so cling to it, my good man." Aven grinned.

Kawe had returned and was eying them warily from the doorway.

"Do you have something you do for pain?" Miara called to her.

Kawe fetched a round peg of wood bound with leather and handed it to the old man, who propped it between his teeth. "Ready when you are," he said, muffled but still managing a grin. He grasped Kawe's hand.

Grimacing slightly, Aven positioned the side edge of the stool's base along the break, then backed up, holding out a hand to one guard. "Your truncheon? Unless you'd rather part with your sword?"

"Here you go, sire."

Without warning, Aven swung the short club overhead and brought it down hard on top of the small stool.

The bone broke with a sickening crunch.

Barely realizing he'd already swung the truncheon, Miara hastily poured energy into the leg, inundating it with power. She snatched a bit from Aven along the way; the practice would be good for him.

"Hey, stop that. Isn't there a chipmunk you can rob?" Aven grumbled.

"Try and stop me." She grinned wickedly at him, but sobered quickly. Possibly not the best expression to have shortly after willfully breaking someone's leg.

The old man, to his credit, didn't scream. He hardly let out a shout. His face contorted, he dug his teeth into the leather and wood, but he didn't attempt to knock Miara across the room.

A good sign.

Finally, the bone snapped back into place, nerve and muscle weaving themselves around it once again. The need lessened, then lessened again. She inspected the rest of him, shooing away a festering heat near his lungs. Otherwise, he now appeared in fine shape.

She took another apprehensive breath and inspected the wound. "It should be healed now," she said calmly. "There may be some bruising, but the bone should be mended."

The old man stared at his leg, rapt. He rotated his foot

around his ankle, then bent it at the knee. "It seems… good as new."

Miara nodded. "Yes, it should be. Well, close to it anyway." Now did not seem the appropriate time to point out that *he* was not exactly new.

A cry came from the far room. Miara turned and rushed toward it instinctively.

At one end of the room, in a closet full of basins and other tools, Reed stood clutching his hand as blood oozed through his fingers.

She knelt and studied the boy's hand, brows knitted. Odd. The shard looked as though it had been directly jammed into his hand on purpose. His eyes studied her, calm and intent. Then they flicked warily to Kawe.

Ah. He wanted a chance to speak with her quietly, alone, and was willing to stab himself with a shard of pitcher over it.

"Ah, Kawe, can you get me some towels for the bleeding, please?"

"Of course, my lady." She hurried away.

As Miara closed her eyes and channeled energy into his little fingers, his cheek brushed hers.

"Wessa knows others. Mage friends. They meet sometimes. They keep hidden. The Third Temple will send Devoted after them if they know. They can't reveal—" The words came out in a torrent and stopped abruptly.

It was just as well that Kawe had returned because the spell took hold. Reed gritted his teeth with admirable stoicism and watched eagerly as the wound healed up.

Miara accepted the towels from Kawe and began mopping up the blood.

"Allow me, my lady. I'll not have it said that a future queen was forced to servant's duty on my watch."

Miara stood and faced her, returning the bloody towels. "I have been a servant my whole life. It won't be the first time. But you can get rid of these for me while I look to more patients."

Kawe raised her eyebrows and, after a moment's slight hesitation, hurried away without a word.

Miara bent down to Reed's ear. "If you see Wessa, tell her that everything is going to change. And take this." She pulled two of the handkerchiefs out of her pouch. "If you need to see me, or she would like to be taught, come to the castle with that cloth, and they will bring you to me. Understood?"

He nodded, surprise and wariness darkening his eyes. Miara patted his head and headed back around the corner to her patient.

The old man was hopping around on the healed leg in the center of the room, grinning. "Well, I'll be," he kept muttering.

She caught Aven's eyes and smiled. "One more," she murmured. "Then we'll have to come back another day."

"Anyone else up for having limbs broken by the king?" He grinned. "No one?"

Miara, shaking her head, approached a nearby woman and began her inspection.

"Well, well. I had to see it for myself to believe it."

Daes groaned inwardly. Seulka. He turned at her approach. Same as always, same perfectly constructed exterior with dark hair and satin gown. He forced a smile, giving her the slightest bow. Much slighter than he would have at Mage Hall, and even there it had only been a courtesy. They'd been equivalent in rank then.

Now, he surpassed her.

"Seulka. How fares Mage Hall?" he said as politely as he could muster. Marielle was right; there was power to be gained in friends, even if his natural style leaned more toward making himself useful rather than making himself liked.

"Crammed full of unenslaved slaves," Seulka replied. "We can't handle much more, you know."

"I've told you, you can ship them off to—"

"Trenedum Palace is full too. Shall I start sending them here?"

"There's probably somewhere closer. I'll see what I can do." Gods, couldn't the Fat Master figure out *anything* on his own? He was probably too busy counting his coins.

She smiled sweetly. "You just don't want *your* home ravaged by enraged, magic-wielding prisoners who are not interested in staying imprisoned."

He frowned. "Since when is Mage Hall not my home? We plan to travel back within the week. And are you using the stones the Devoted sent or not? The potions?"

"We're doing our best," she said politely. "Which is enough. Most of the time. Have you made any progress in finding our brand, dear Daes?"

It might have been his imagination, but he thought Marielle's gaze shifted toward them at those words. As if Daes could ever take an interest in anyone as ridiculous as Seulka when he had a queen like Marielle. What kind of fool would he have to be? One like Demikin, probably.

"We have excellent spies at high levels working diligently on finding its location. Have your mages found any further trace in the libraries?"

Her brow furrowed. "No. There are hundreds of volumes to search, though. They may still find something... Eventually."

"Well, if all goes according to plan, we'll flatten Akaria and track down the brand amid the ashes, eh?" He grinned at her, and to his surprise, she grinned back. What, no lecturing censure? No lengthy explanations about why he might be right but he might also be wrong and he should be very careful?

Of course, he *had* been right. Demikin had proven to all of Kavanar what a fool he was, even if he'd had a little helping from Daes. The star magic did exist, and the Akarian royal family wielded it happily. Everything he'd predicted and feared had come true, in some cases worse.

Still, the grin felt out of place, and when Marielle appeared at his elbow and oh-so-gracefully slipped her hand into the crook of his elbow, he was glad of her presence.

"Lady Seulka," Marielle said politely. "Glad to see your

health has improved enough for the journey."

Seulka's smile took on a bit of mirth. "It has indeed. I regret I couldn't be hear to see my old friend crowned consort, but I am so glad to see that he is happy in his companions." She kept her gaze trained carefully on the queen, ignoring Daes's eyes.

"And we are lucky to have him," said Marielle.

"I hear you all have much to do, with the attack on Trenedum by those warlike Akarians. Kavanar must defend itself." Seulka clasped her hands in front of her mildly.

"I have already sent troops to the border." To her credit, Marielle owned the words and didn't parrot them, even if sending the troops had been his idea.

"I am glad to hear it. Mage Hall is not far from Akaria, you know."

"Yes, it was a lovely trip when I was last there." Marielle's eyes twinkled.

Some of the amusement drained from Seulka's face, her smile suddenly forced. "Yes, I recall. The late fall really is the last good time to travel. Do you think you will be traveling for the war? Winter seems a bad time for it."

Daes opened his mouth to say definitely not, but Marielle beat him to an answer. "Yes, of course I'll be going with Daes."

His eyes widened. It took every bit of control he had to force a smile.

This was not the time or the place to confront her on the matter. But they would talk *after*. For the first time it occurred to him that he couldn't make her stay. She was the one person in the world he *couldn't* try to force to obey him. All his power depended on her granting it to him. And yet, he cared more that she be safe than… Well, he couldn't think of anyone else he particularly cared for the safety of, other than himself.

This was terrible indeed. A risk he had not anticipated.

"That's very brave of you," said Seulka, her amusement returning. Was it Daes's imagination or did she seem delighted at the prospect of the queen traveling into a war? Oh, *now* who was wishing for the death of their monarch? Of course Seulka would care about her cousin's welfare, but not that cousin's wife. That was a woman entirely unrelated to Seulka now, apparently. Self-serving fool. "You know we are hard-pressed without Daes at Mage Hall. We miss his assistance greatly."

That was just because they were all utterly incompetent. Except for the Tall Master perhaps, and it was *he* who'd left the brand unattended. So no, all incompetent.

Marielle's fingers tightened slightly around his elbow. "I'm sure Daes can still aid you from afar. I know he traveled widely and was rarely in Mage Hall anyway."

Daes smiled at that. Well played, my queen, well played.

"Still, we are wondering when you will appoint a new Master, if he is to be indisposed at your side."

"Now, wait a minute—" Daes started.

"He certainly will be very occupied by his new duties," said Marielle, her sweet, courtly voice subtly biting. "I shall think on the matter."

Daes gritted his teeth. "Now, that's really not necessary.

I can be as much a part of Mage Hall as I ever was. As you said, I traveled all the time anyway. Were you not just asking for my help as to where to house new slaves?"

"I wasn't asking for help." Seulka blinked, her face innocently blank. "You merely offered it."

Was she *mocking* him? He scowled. Fool. Or had she only been playing stupid all along? Trying to make him underestimate her? Mage Hall was *his*, and they were *not* taking it away from him.

"Oh, look, Daes," Marielle said sweetly as if suddenly distracted by a butterfly. "Priestess Siata has arrived. We must greet her, Lady Seulka, if you'll forgive us."

"Of course," Seulka cooed, bowing with appropriate deference.

"I promise you I will think on your concerns, never fear," Marielle said, and she led him away, like a horse to the stables.

He stayed as quiet as he could manage for the rest of the affair. Small talk had never been his strength anyway, and his concerns over that discussion burbled just under the surface of his thoughts. He didn't want them escaping accidentally in front of someone inopportune.

He downed brandy instead, which tended to make him more quiet and brooding, not less, and let her lead him about. Like a pet. Like a damn trained monkey for everyone to see. He considered pointing out to her that he was not just another of her accessories to be shown off to her friends—at which point he put the brandy down and decided to stop drinking.

Later, when the gathering had ended, they retired to her rooms, nearly alone. He'd been granted his own rooms nearby—not the king's but close enough—but if he was going to be someone's pet, he wasn't leaving until he'd said his piece. And he might have also wanted to be around her, the real her, after the parade of fools he'd just endured.

Daes admired the efficient way her swarm of attendants removed the accoutrement of her royalty. Over the last few days, they'd given up on objecting to his presence, although several still cast uneasy glares at him as they peeled away the layers of feminine show and left the real Marielle behind. He tried not to roll his eyes. It wasn't as if he hadn't seen all that before, and underneath, as his title clearly proclaimed.

Hair down and clad in a pale-golden robe that fell gracefully around her feet, she sent the servants away before turning to him expectantly.

"What?" he said, still surprised by her perceptiveness. Had she wanted rid of them or sensed that that was what *he'd* wanted?

"You have something you want to say. What is it?" Her voice was sweet, but she didn't smile as she drifted to the lounge across from his newly added black armchair. She was closer to the fire than he, the wavering firelight dancing across her curves, her feet bare even though the marble floors of the palace were almost never warm.

She caught him looking. "Old habit. Reilin is much warmer than here, you know."

"Yes. Yes, I was there once. In the Southern Kingdoms." Why didn't he just spit out what had been pecking at him all evening?

She smiled slightly at him. "But that is not what you wanted to say."

"No. I—" He faltered and cleared his throat. "What do you mean, you'll think on her concerns?"

"What do you think I mean?"

"You can't appoint another Master in my place. Mage Hall is mine, Marielle. I made it what it is. I built it. Those people, those armies—none of it would exist without me, not in a form that can actually do anything for Kavanar. You can't hand it off to some ass-kissing young fop. They'll ruin it. And those three might manage to do it on their own, without me."

She snorted delicately, probably at his foul language. "Have I ever told you how much I appreciate that you are always honest and straightforward with me?" She smiled slightly now, but it seemed courtly. Calculated, although possibly still sincere.

He blinked. He supposed it was true. It was always easier to be straightforward than to manage a lie, but he hadn't realized he'd been so transparent. He hadn't realized that she *knew*. The growing uneasiness in his gut twisted further. "Don't change the subject," he said, remembering the topic suddenly.

She smiled more broadly, almost amused. "I'm not."

"What is there to be laughing about?"

"I'm not laughing." But her smile only grew into a grin.

"Marielle, this is serious. Mage Hall is my life's work, it's my—"

"Daes," she said gently. He gritted his teeth at being cut off, but he let her. He'd already granted her many things he'd give no other, what was one more? "I didn't say I would appoint anyone in your place."

"You said you would think on it, you assured her—"

"Exactly," she said, sharper this time, still grinning. "Explain."

"I simply plan to think about it very, *very* carefully for an exceedingly long time."

He rolled his eyes at himself. "You're a very convincing actress, you know that? You even had me fooled." He scratched his head. Did he truly believe her? But she had no incentive to help Seulka. It was he who'd gotten her out of her mess, hadn't it been? Was that enough for her loyalty? "That's... not very straightforward or honest of you."

She sat forward, a bit of laughter burbling out. "I know." Proud. She was proud, wasn't she? That was it. Proud that there was something she did better than he did.

But that reminded him of the other thing he'd needed to bring up, something she did *not* do better than him. "You told her you were going with me," he said tentatively, waiting to see if that was a subtle misdirection as well before launching into objections this time.

"Yes," she said, serious now as she leaned back on the lounge. "I am."

He frowned. "Marielle, it's very dangerous. You can't."

"You can't stop me," she said quickly, as if she'd considered it. Her eyes threatened, as if to say, don't make me show you that you can't.

Gritting his teeth, he stared her down. She was a puzzle. Someone he needed to convince, not coerce. Not command. He needed new means of making her do what he wanted her to do, and he hadn't much in the toolbox, as she'd just so delicately illustrated. "I know," he said carefully.

She relaxed. Good.

"I don't want you to get hurt. Or worse," he murmured. Perhaps honest and straightforward truly was the best tactic with her. *Painfully* honest. "There's no telling what will happen in war. Commanders are often targeted, and they'll be no hiding who you are from the enemy. You could very well die. It will not be safe for you there."

"We are all dying," she said mildly. "What's one way or another?"

His eyes widened. "I don't think you understand me. It will be truly dangerous. The Akarians are formidable warriors—"

She narrowed her eyes at him. "But you already know that and have a plan to defeat them."

"I do."

"Do you think me simple, Daes?"

"Of course not—"

"Do you truly think it will be less dangerous for me here? Without you?"

He stopped cold. Focused on the war, he hadn't given that part of his plan much thought.

"I have my allies," she said. "But I've made my enemies too. Demikin's mistress was popular enough, even if *he* wasn't. She had many friends who hoped she'd depose me. Together, you and I have more allies, and I have someone who would avenge my death, which is likely disincentive enough on its own for most."

He thought of his annoyance at being trotted around like her pet. It *had* been like that, but it had also been like... a bodyguard. So he had not been imagining it; she had been showing him off not as a new toy but as a weapon. That *did* make him feel a little better about it.

"Without both our allegiances," she continued, "my position is much more precarious. And when you're off and can prove nothing of what might have happened to me? And most importantly, what happens when I die and you do not yet have any claim to the throne?"

His expression hardened and his grip on the arm of the chair tightened. "You will not die on my watch. And that's not what's most important." It was more important that she *live* than who was on the throne. Something about the thought struck him as extremely unusual, but he brushed the reaction aside for now.

"But it *is* the most important. To your plans. If I were to die without leaving an heir and with you days away at war, many would have a claim to the throne much greater than yours."

"Without you, I haven't any claim at all." In many of their eyes, he barely had a claim to nobility.

"I know. A challenger might cement their claim before

you can even return. Now that is actually a very good incentive to slice my throat, don't you think?" She smiled sweetly now, and it terrified him a little.

"I'll kill them before they can do that to you," he vowed. His brain was suddenly racing. Such challengers with a competing claim could be easily identified. In truth, he'd already been watching several. Perhaps they needed a clear demonstration of just who was king—in truth and in practice, if not in title. Or perhaps they might even need to meet the mistress's bitter end. He made a mental note to isolate as many upstarts as possible and find some weak spot, an arm he could twist if needed.

"You'll kill them if you are here by my side. But how will you kill them from days away at war?"

He scowled at her for a long time, and she met his eyes with the calm certainty of someone sure she was right. Finally, he sighed. "You win. But I still don't like it. And if they try to make a play for the throne while we're both gone from Evrical?"

She smiled. "Well, if we die, we won't care. And if we win, we'll return with a seasoned army at our backs."

"And scores of mages at my command. Assuming you're sincere about not replacing me."

She pouted. "What would ever make you think I wouldn't tell you the absolute truth?" And then she grinned.

And to his surprise, he found himself grinning right back.

5   CONTROL

Miara lay on a dark, nearly black couch in her rooms and held the map of Panar above her. Its fine brown and black lines were scrawled in charcoal and ink, then sealed. Some careful hand had drawn in some lovely details. Each of the north, west, and east gates were illustrated in stony gray. The harbor was filled with tiny blue waves and a great sailing ship. Temples and markets and barracks were all marked. None of them sparked any further ideas beyond the one that was itching in her brain, wanting to get out.

Near the door, Kalan cleared her throat as the door whispered open. "King Aven to see you, my lady."

She sat up to find Aven already halfway to her couch, smiling. She scooted over to make room for him.

"So, about recruiting more mages," he said, holding out a sheet of fine vellum.

"Yes?" She raised an eyebrow and took the offered sheet.

"It's an announcement I've been working on."

The sheet before her was covered with text written in a fine, elaborate hand. The beautiful words detailed the attack on the city, Aven's ascension to king, and the start of the war with Kavanar. It ended with a call for more mages, instructing them to come to Ranok.

And to find her. *Seek out Arms Master Floren for further instructions.*

She stared wide-eyed for a moment, uncomprehending. For a moment, she felt like twelve dozen eyes were all looking at her, and memories of the vast expanse of the city sweeping out around her and the sheer number of people in it made her balk. And then the practical part of her caught up with her instincts.

What *else* were they going to do? Who else could they send mages to?

She looked up at him, crushing the fear down and nodding resolutely. "Good. I'll be ready."

He smiled, but he looked relieved too. "Anything you think we should add?"

"What do I know about royal proclamations?"

He slanted a dubious look at her. "I think you know plenty. But you know about being a commoner, don't you? What would you think if you read this?"

She tried not to let those words sting. He didn't mean them in a cutting way. What would she think if she'd read this on an average day? "Let's see. It might be… a little frightening. What does this all mean to the average shopkeeper? Maybe you should state more clearly what Akaria is doing in response, other than calling for more mages to help."

His eyebrows rose just slightly. "Great point. Anything else?"

"Hmm." She rubbed her chin. "Maybe…" No, no. That was a silly idea. She was getting overambitious.

"What is it?"

"Well, what did you think about the visit to the temple yesterday?"

He shrugged. "It's a start. A good show that's definitely helpful and not harmful. But it is heavy work. Personal. And in that environment, few people saw it. They'll talk. The old man will show people his leg and tell stories. But it's still limited."

"I agree. We need something with a bigger impact. Something the whole city can see. Something public. Even if it's setting up the healing in the square outside the temple, that would make a bigger impression."

"True. Like what?"

"If it were summer, we could enrich the fields. All manner of things. But with winter almost here…"

"You *did* comment on the number of flower boxes."

She eyed him. "Am I getting predictable, or are you starting to read thoughts now?"

"What?" He snorted. "Since I have no idea what you're talking about, I'm going to lean toward predictable."

"I keep thinking, what if I put something in those flower boxes? Something useful and practical, like something you could eat. My father's got carrots, beans, and peas growing in his room already."

"In his room? Is the food not to his liking?"

She waved him off. "He just likes growing things. Practical things, not like me."

"The things you grow are beautiful. That's not without its use." He smiled at her, but she dodged his eyes, not wanting to blush. Or get distracted from her bold plan.

She bit her lip, then caught his gaze. "Here's a wild idea. Announce our betrothal as well, refer to me as the queen, and tell them the new plants in all the window boxes are from us? Like a betrothal gift. Isn't that the sort of thing nobles do?"

His eyes went wide, and she wasn't sure if it was from horror, shock, or fear.

"What?"

"That's…" He finally recovered. "That's a great idea. Can you do it tonight? For the morning? Do you need help?"

She took a deep breath. It wasn't like she was doing much else around here. "With my father's help, I think I can. I'll get Siliana if I need to. Might need a guard escort, but I can just ask Telidar for that, can't I?"

He nodded. "The guards at the queen's door would be even better. Eventually, you'll have a full guard dedicated to your security. Right now, half the queen's guard is still sticking to my mother, but as I've stolen some of my father's away, that's necessary to cover them both. This isn't Estun, you know."

"I noticed. I guess I should get started, then."

"And I'll get to revising this and hand it off to the scribes."

"I was wondering, I didn't think I'd ever seen your handwriting that fine."

He smirked. "It's nowhere close. I was too busy chasing and hitting things as a boy to get very good at that."

"Oh, wait—before you go. One other thing I forgot to mention. The boy from the Sapphire Temple said one of the other temples works with the Devoted to capture local mages."

His face went stormy. "Even in Panar. By the gods. Did he say which one?"

"The Third Temple. One of the Nefrana ones."

"I know the one." He glared off into the distance a moment before returning a calmer gaze to her. "That must definitely be stopped. The priestesses have been clamoring for an audience, so maybe that's the perfect time. Some prominent business officials and diplomats as well. I've granted them an audience tomorrow. At the very least, we can confront the high priestess about it there. Her name's Ediama."

Miara nodded. "Got it. Guess it's time to go work my magic?" She grinned.

To her surprise, he leaned forward and gave her a chaste peck on the cheek and then returned her grin. "Happy growing."

She flushed and glanced at her attendants. "Fetch my father, please."

The youngest nodded and ducked out. Gods, she hoped she wouldn't regret this whole wildly ambitious, quite possibly ill-advised scheme.

Tomorrow would tell, and until then, she had work to do.

"Princess Evana Paranelin has arrived. She says she is here to see you, Lord Consort," the guard announced.

Daes sat forward in his armchair, setting the map of southern Akaria aside. Had Marielle stiffened in her seat next to him, or was it his imagination? They were alone in the sitting room of the royal chamber. The richly appointed room had far too much red velvet and brown leather for his taste, but it radiated warmth. And more importantly, it was to Marielle's taste, and that made him like it more than he would have guessed. After barely five days at her side, the room was already starting to feel like home. He certainly didn't miss Seulka or competing and sniping with the other Masters in Mage Hall. Although he should return there soon and make sure they weren't screwing up everything he'd worked so hard to build. And that Seulka wasn't up to something.

"I'll receive her here," Daes told the guard. No reason Marielle should not hear anything they had to discuss.

The queen rose as he sank back in his chair. "Give me a moment. I should freshen up."

He certainly saw no need for that, but he wasn't going to complain either. His eyes followed her swaying hips from the room.

Evana arrived moments later, her usual full, black skirts cutting a broad and swirling path. She greeted Daes with a raised eyebrow and more of an amused smile on her face than ever. Her mouth barely curved upward in both corners, but given the light in her eyes, she was mightily entertained at the recent turns of events.

"So what do you I call you now? Lord Daes? Your Majesty King Daes? Great Lord of the Rolling Hills and Red Skies—" She swept out an arm grandly.

He rose and waved her off, then bowed sarcastically. "Law doesn't permit that *quite* yet. Royal Consort Daes will have to do. You may address me as Lord Consort. But you know," he flashed her a quick grin, "I'm working on it."

"I should have known you'd figure out something like this."

He shrugged. "More luck than conniving. This time."

"Of course. It couldn't be the careful machinations that you're so famous for." She didn't look like she believed him in the slightest.

"I'm not famous for anything. And it serves the king right for leaving a beautiful and intelligent woman so unattended," he said brusquely, irritated for no reason he could discern.

Both her eyebrows rose now. "My, I'm almost persuaded you actually feel something for her."

"I *believe* that's exactly what the title of Royal Consort is supposed to mean."

"Hmm. Or perhaps it means you're simply the most convincing at that act. Please, Daes. As if you even had a heart to give."

He glared, speechlessness surprising himself again.

"At any rate, we have business to discuss."

He winced inwardly. He would much rather dwell on these recent victories than the complete picture at the moment. While his partnership with Marielle was a boon, the news was not so good on other fronts.

"Please, have a seat." He held out a hand toward the seat across from him, careful she not take Marielle's place.

"The brand," Evana demanded. "Have you made progress in replacing it?"

"Queen Marielle," an attendant behind them announced.

Marielle swept back into the room, looking the same to him. Ah, no. The front portion of her hair was swept up and pinned back under the softly glimmering three-ruby crown. Did she feel the need to assert her rank because of Evana's nobility? Whatever necessitated the choice, he would ask her of it later. Perhaps there was something more here he did not yet understand. Her assertion seemed random, but he trusted her judgment enough to know there would be good reason behind it.

Evana rose and curtsied, and Marielle returned a regal nod before both women sank simultaneously back into their seats with the perfect poise of two cobras eying each other.

"I apologize for interrupting, my lord," Marielle said only to him.

"Not at all, Your Majesty. The princess here was simply inquiring as to our progress in replacing the mage brand. Unfortunately, the news is grim. Our mages have found nothing yet." He scowled down at the elaborately woven red carpet. He would not mention the disappearance of one of the three mages who had been doing the research; he couldn't afford to fly into a rage at this particular moment, and it boiled in him at even the thought of that talkative, out-of-turn fool.

"Should we slow our efforts to capture more mages?" said Evana, all business. "Do you even have anywhere to put them now?"

"No. And no. But we'll figure something out."

"Would you care for some tea?" Marielle asked politely.

Evana leveled a cold stare at her, somewhere between resentment and condescension. "No, thank you, my lady. I plan to return to the road soon. Perhaps immediately."

He squirmed inwardly at the strange tension between them. He owed much to Marielle, but even with his newfound power, Evana's alliance had always been one of the few that had actually borne fruit. What was this sudden frigidity between them? "The good news is, now that I am consort, we shall be able to do much more to get the original brand back in the first place."

"Such as?" Evana retrained her icy gaze on him, which was strangely relieving. He was used to her glaring at *him*.

"We must determine where the brand is, first. I expect this shall not be particularly difficult, since the Akarians have been easily and repeatedly infiltrated." And since he had plenty of high-ranking spies also in Panar, although none of them had been able to find anything yet. As far as he could tell, the prince—king—and his pet creature mage didn't seem to have the brand. But *someone* had to. "Once we know the brand's location, we will simply attack there with the full force of our army. Eight of our best should have reached our encampment in Gilaren by now. General Vusamon is simply overjoyed at actually having something to do." While Marielle had been keeping her eyes trained on Evana, her gaze flicked to him now.

"Easily and repeatedly infiltrated?" Evana repeated. "So your spies have been successful, then?"

Of course she'd ignore the bit about an army at their back. "Well, yes and no. Of course, if the prince were dead, that would have been the first thing I'd have told you."

"What, then?"

"Infiltrating their inner circle has not been difficult, especially with the use of creature magic. But the actions our mages and assassins attempted beyond that have been less successful. We did do serious damage to parts of Estun."

"Parts. I see. Larger parts than the pieces of Trenedum Palace that have gone mysteriously missing?"

He cleared his throat. "Let's call it even. But we know much more about their inner circle than before."

"And yet, the prince lives."

Daes pursed his lips. "Indeed. Slippery little snake. Unfortunately, our spies are better at sneaking than swordplay, and they're not facing inept warriors, as you well know. And, well…" He hesitated. "The news worsens. It appears he is no longer just prince, but king. At least for some period."

Evana's eyes widened and her nostrils flared with barely contained rage. "King? Tell me you're joking."

"We received word this morning. It is both a victory and a defeat. We succeeded in driving them from Estun. My mages ambushed the Akarian caravan going from Estun to Panar according to plan. They attempted to strike the prince, but he managed to survive. The king, however, was gravely injured and briefly captive."

"Briefly? Gods, *someone* needs a lashing." Evana looked as if she wished to administer the punishment herself, and he didn't doubt it.

Marielle's eyebrows rose.

He cleared his throat again. "They *would* if they had survived the mission. Only one has yet to report back. The other two were killed when the Akarians mounted a valiant attack to rescue their king."

"Why was it so brief? What kind of valiant attack?"

Daes gritted his teeth. She knew how to scent out the details he didn't really want to tell her, didn't she? "That damned escaped creature mage rescued him."

Evana scowled. "Akarians, eh? Hmm." She took a deep breath, thinking. "She has been a thorn in our side indeed." He was glad to hear her say *our*. He'd started to wonder if he'd stacked up enough failures to make her question their allegiance. Then again, what other allies did she have?

He sensed Marielle watching him again, and he met her gaze. Her eyes were closed off, though, unreadable. Strange, they weren't normally like that. He frowned.

Enough admitting defeats. He didn't want Marielle *or* Evana considering their cause lost. At the very least, he needed to distract them from the situation, and *now.*

"One piece of news our spies reported might be of particular interest to you. We have it on good authority that the creature mage is actually now betrothed to the prince." It hadn't come as a surprise to him, as he'd seen how she'd fought to free the prince. There'd been something between them, something dangerous he had not counted on. But he didn't think Evana had taken it seriously, if she had noticed. Nobility mattered to her sort; Daes knew how arbitrary it really was. He kept his expression as casual as he could, studying her eyes.

Evana almost did not react, except in that she sat perfectly, unnaturally still. Did he detect a twitch of her eyelid, her lip, her fingers, or was it his imagination? Although she was fighting to contain it, her frozen stiffness told him the woman was on the knife-edge of rage.

He cleared his throat. "I mean—she is *indeed* a thorn. Perhaps we can use her as leverage against the prince somehow." He had not meant to goad Evana on, or insult her, or bring up past wounds. No, of course, he wouldn't do *that.* He smiled with satisfaction as she relaxed at his words. At the smile, Marielle shifted in her seat, something she normally didn't do.

Her eyes flicked from him to the queen and back. "Hmm. Leverage. You *are* good at gaining leverage on people, Daes. Getting them to do what you want."

He didn't know that he'd done anything to earn that impression, so he simply shrugged.

"I do have some news from my elders."

"Oh?"

"Although they denied my request to assassinate the prince a long time ago, they did recently send word of *some* help. I found it… intriguing. They've located another Great Stone, split in two halves, similar to the one in Estun but smaller. It is only the height of one man, but it is complete enough for a person to fit inside. It's in their control in the monastery in Faeren territory in Akaria."

"Oh. Uh, interesting." He had no idea why. "But how did they imagine this would help us?"

"It can be used as a prison. For mages. Especially the creature and earth ones, who can escape conventional imprisonment."

Seulka would be jealous. He raised his eyebrows. "A prison for whom?"

At this, she smiled broadly, her lip curling in wolfish, predatory glee. It was an expression that cooled even Daes to his very core, and Marielle leaned back ever so slightly in her chair.

"Perhaps it is time we put that renegade creature mage of yours back under our control."

Miara stroked the neck of her lovely horse as she fed energy into the nearest fallow pot. The mare's hair was so silken and snowy Miara couldn't keep her glove on. Her dramatic black mane hung over the graceful white arch of her neck, three braids intermixed with the free-flowing strands. Her name was Ataeralia, a surprisingly elaborate name for a horse who didn't appear to have a specific owner to care for her aside from Ranok collectively, and Miara couldn't help wondering who'd bothered to braid her hair.

She was surprised they hadn't given her Lukor, the horse that had carried her from Estun with Samul, but she hadn't requested him either, figuring he deserved a break after all that work. Ata, as Miara was hoping to call her for short, wasn't terribly talkative, but her presence beneath Miara was strong and reassuring as Miara's group lumbered through the streets of the White City, greenery curling up in their wake. A brisk wind blew in off the ocean cliffs, tasting of the salty sea and late-evening meals cooking over smoky hearth fires.

The falcon that seemed to have adopted her soared overhead too. He hadn't taken much interest in coming inside her rooms, but when she went outside, he always visited. And hoped for some duck. As if sensing her thoughts of duck, he swooped down and perched on her shoulder briefly, today's thick cloak protecting her for once.

Life burst from the soil where Miara had been focusing. Beanstalks twisted up, twining to the trellis that leaned against the gray stone of the wall behind the pot. Beans had grown here this year, and they'd grow again in the spring. Miara was just adding another harvest, hopefully one that someone would pay attention to.

"Did you ever name that bird you've picked up, Miara?" her father asked.

She shook her head. The falcon took back to the sky,

letting out a loud screech that spooked Ata—but only slightly.

"You should call him Scri—that's the sound he makes," said Luha, smiling. "And it's the Melbaric rune for bird."

"Well, aren't you learning your foreign languages," Miara laughed. "Scri it is." Not that she suspected he cared about having a name.

Ata strode on, confident and certain in her continuous pace whether Miara was quite done or not, matching the pace of the soldier's mount in front of her. She could guess why the stable master had selected the fine creature. Ata had a presence to go along with her fancy name, a confidence verging on arrogance. The horse deserved more of an honorific than Miara did. A royal horse, at least in manners. A queenly one.

Miara spotted an apple tree that had lost its leaves up ahead and smiled. Before she'd even neared it, she sent out energy to the short, broad tree, a joyful outpouring of life. Flowers burst into bloom along the branches.

"Oh, that's nice," Siliana murmured from behind her. The mage was hardly prone to niceties and compliments, which was probably a long-ingrained habit from spending most of her time with Derk. Miara smiled a little wider.

Her father also looked pleased, breathing in the air deeply. A contented peace radiated off of him like the sun's heat in spring, and that warmed her heart more than any hearth could have. In truth, it was far from spring. Clouds blanketed the darkening sky with a fluffy layer that blocked what was left of the sun for the day. Everyone was bundled in scarves and gloves and cloaks, except for her one hand entwined in Ata's mane, and there was a feeling in the air an air mage might have been able to tell her meant snow.

In the end, Siliana and Jaena had joined Miara, her father, Luha, and the four guards Aven had ended up ordering with them. Jaena and Luha—and Siliana to some extent—had mostly just wanted to see the city, and Miara was glad for the company. Guards were nice, if she knew she could trust them. Which she didn't. These mages were her people.

If no one had noticed the beans just yet, the apple tree was a different story. Miara had focused on it because she'd thought Ata would appreciate an apple—and perhaps the other horses too—but the glory of spring blooms amid the desolateness of late fall was hard for anyone to ignore.

Men and women opened their doors, gaping, and a few people stumbled out of a local tavern, looking both amazed and then concerned they'd drunk more than they'd thought they had.

Miara took a deep breath. Time to make an impression. Hopefully it'd be a good one.

She pressed Ata forward, using her mind rather than heel or rein, and circled around the guards to ride up to the tree alone. She stopped short in front of it.

One of the sharper-eyed guards caught up with her quickly, looking irritated, but his expression softened when she gave him a thankful nod. She needed a way for people to know this was her doing. *Someone's* doing, and not the gods', except as they acted through her hands.

Feeling a bit ridiculous, she raised her arms up as if embracing the tree. Of course, she needed no such ridiculous gestures. She could bring the tree to fruit without even looking at it from around the block, if she was close enough. But then no one would understand that magic had been the cause. And that *she* had been the cause.

Magic could be something beautiful. And useful. And she was going to prove it to them.

The flowers were so beautiful, it was sad to push past them into the leaves of summer, but it'd hurt the tree to leave it so unbalanced. She had to take it nearly this far into the cycle, perhaps to its state a month ago, so that its thinnest branches would be ready for the coming snow. She could feel a strain in the tree, a tiredness—it was old and had grown there for many years.

Jaena, can you take a look at the soil? she asked silently. *Seems worn out of something.*

Not my specialty, but I'll do my best. Jaena's horse rode up to join them, and the mage dismounted, approaching the tree, taking her staff with her from its strap on the horse's side. They'd had to press the stable master for that, but Miara didn't blame her. Neither of them had been free long enough to take that freedom for granted. Miara dropped her hands and paused to take a breath and regain some small amount of energy. Jaena's tall, dark form paced around the tree, bending down to brush the soil that escaped above the cobblestones near the center. She closed her eyes briefly, and then opened them again, nodding.

As Jaena mounted up again, Miara returned her hands to the sky, trying for calm and dignified, even though the silly feeling wouldn't fade. And it was easier now, the tree reinvigorated as she pushed it from spring toward summer.

Apple-blossom petals rained around her, the cold wind whipping them in small whirlwinds, and the fruit began to grow and ripen. Buds became berries, which became apples that went from green to yellow to blushing full red in places. Oh, a lovely variety. So much beauty locked in the dormant states of winter.

One apple fell, then another, and then she slowed the flow, lowering her hands and hanging her head for a moment. Perhaps she looked tired. Truth be told, she was whispering a silent prayer in her mind, an almost wordless plea: let this interference be for the good and not the bad. Let this walk in line with the Way of Things. She only wanted to help. And she had no other ideas, short of walking around healing people one by one. Certainly none as grand as this one.

The tree's owner opened a door to the left of the cobblestoned area around the tree and stopped short. A warm orange glow vibrated out of the bustling tavern behind her dull blue dress. She put a hand over her mouth and stared.

"Is this your tree?" Miara called, just barely cutting off a "my lady" at the end. Not including it almost physically hurt.

The woman nodded mutely.

"A gift. Enjoy them," Miara said simply, keeping her

face serious. Regal, or as close as she could get. It didn't matter, the woman wasn't looking; she was still staring at the tree. Miara steered Ata back and urged the group on to the next block. If they were going to cover most or all of the White City, they couldn't dally.

She'd leave the apples for the citizens, she decided. For... her subjects. Surely the stable master had some apples on hand. Now that the moment was upon her, she realized that taking any of the fruit—even to give to the majestic Ataeralia—would have made the whole gesture self-serving. And that would entirely defeat its purpose.

Her father caught up with her as her more attentive guard overtook her. Pointing to a small sign along the road up ahead, her father met her gaze. "I think I see a garden patch beside that temple. Look. A small one, but just the same."

Miara raised an eyebrow. "Really?" She glanced back over her shoulder. The apple-tree woman had walked out, picked up a fallen apple, and now stood staring at it in her hand.

He nodded. "It's, uh, ripe with opportunity. If you'll pardon the pun."

Behind them, Luha snorted.

"Let's go."

Leaving the garden patch, they moved on. Flower boxes brimmed with wheat and roses, carrots and lavender, beets and daisies. At times, they drew a crowd, gazes suspicious, apprehensive, curious, wary. After the apple tree, the feeling of being watched didn't go away whether there was a crowd joining them or not. So many eyes had her on edge—and vowing to bring more than four guards next time. And more daggers. And maybe a bow. Massive magical work that could push her to the edge of her abilities and risk unconsciousness was not ideally done with a large audience.

Definitely not an audience of... the entire city.

She gulped down her fear and brought another rose to bloom, trying to ground herself. A white blossom for the White City. She hoped someone would notice such a thing, but the crowds were mostly silent, save whispered murmurs containing phrases like "the king," "mages," and oaths to the gods. She was glad for the guards, though, and their short black capes bearing the sword-and-shield insignia. The procession was clearly royal, and no one started any trouble that Miara would have to regret. Luha was with them, and her father. She wouldn't have let any fight go on for more than a few moments, if she could help it.

By the time they returned to Ranok's stables, every one of them was dragging, even the guards. That *might* have been because near the end, she'd started stealing meager amounts of energy from them. Nothing to harm them, just enough to finish the job so everyone could go home, though it left them exhausted. She wouldn't make a habit of such a thing, but then again, she had no plans to regularly douse the entire city with ripe plants with not even five mages to help.

The horses were the only ones who seemed happily

invigorated by the exercise. Miara rode Ata to her stable, attempting to shoo away the stable hand with little success. But even if she was supposed to be a noble now, she still loved horses, and Ata was a fine creature. It'd be a joy to brush her down and feel the horse's enjoyment. She was not letting that fellow steal such simple pleasures.

"If you want to help, go get her an apple," she said to the young man, who looked at her like she'd lost her mind, but to her surprise, he obeyed and trotted off.

She had dismounted and begun with the saddle when Wunik's voice rang out in the stable, alarmed.

"Siliana? Siliana, come quick."

Running a calming hand over Ata's side and flank, Miara forced herself to move slowly to get around the horse. She might be able to communicate with Ata, but they barely knew each other, and she didn't need to be healing a kick to the ribs after all the work they'd just done.

Miara's eyes caught on Siliana's red tunic just as she reached Wunik. The elder's expression was grim. Whatever news he brought couldn't be good. "What is it?" Siliana said, panting.

"Derk has returned. He's hurt. Come, quickly now."

Miara thrust what energy she had remaining to spare at Siliana as she jogged after Wunik. The woman couldn't have much left. By the time Miara had even blinked, they were gone. For an old man, he sure could run when he cared to.

Thanks, Siliana said silently, gratitude coming with the thought like a warm blanket falling over her.

Miara turned and started to step back to start again with Ata, but she stumbled, weakness overwhelming her for a moment. Maybe she'd have to let the stable boy do his job after all.

She trudged to her rooms—the queen's rooms—and collapsed onto the bed without even undressing. She was lucky she'd gotten her cloak off and managed to down the warm tea one of her attendants offered.

Unfamiliar voices floated through her dreams, and she fought to wake, to identify them, to be sure she was safe. But each time she tried to wake up, she got lost along the way, twisting her way through a dream where she forgot what she'd been fighting so hard to reach for.

Sleep had her hard, harder than it seemed like it should, but she hadn't much choice. She slept and dreamed of darkness.

"My lord! My lord!" Perik came running up the stairs and into the king's suite. Aven cocked his head to the side, surprised by the young man's urgency.

"What is it, Perik?"

"Telidar told me to send word straight away. A rider returns from the group sent to find your brother, sire."

"Just one?" Aven's blood went still, frozen in his veins.

"Yes, sire. A man. Alone. He'll be here shortly."

Aven waited, pulse pounding, afraid to hear what was to come and equally afraid not to hear it.

Finally footsteps came up the stairs, uneven and heavy.

Concerned voices murmured around them.

Derk slumped in the doorway. Blood soaked one leg of his trousers. Out of breath, filthy from riding—he looked like hell.

Aven stood and strode toward him. "What happened?"

Derk's usual irreverence was gone, only darkness in his eyes now. He pressed his lips together in a thin line. He opened his mouth, eyes dropping down to the floor, but then he shut it again.

He didn't know what to say.

"You return alone," Aven said softly.

"Asten is alive," Derk said quickly. "She deemed it best she head straight for Dramsren, after the... after what happened. They have even less information on the mages than we do."

"And the others?"

"Asten ordered Feri and Geulin to stay, monitor the situation. The camp looked like they were picking up and about to move."

Aven swallowed. "And... the rest? And Thel?"

"We saw Thel," Derk said slowly. "He was alive."

The two men only stared at each other for a long, somber silence.

"They're all dead, aren't they?" Aven said softly.

Derk winced, his jaw a grim line. His gaze dropped down now, contorted in pain. Finally he nodded. This man was no soldier. Not that any of them were particularly war-hardened.

"What happened?" Aven made sure to keep judgment

from his voice.

"Air mages. Like us." Derk's voice faltered near the end.

"Not like us. We're not kidnapping people or killing anyone with magic."

Derk looked up and caught his eye. "I killed one of them. But then we just turned and ran. I can catch fire from one, maybe two. But I could have never handled them all. And the soldiers were all dead by then anyway. At least I got one."

"What else can you tell me about the battle?"

Derk took a deep breath. "We decided to charge in, take them by surprise. It didn't help. About twenty mages reacted before the riders could even reach the encampment. Burned up the whole force in a matter of seconds." He winced again and rubbed the bridge of his nose. "I'm not sure any of them even drew swords. Maybe a few. The mages also spotted the group of us in the distance. I was watching with farsight, that's how I saw your brother among them. Thel launched himself at one of them, then another. Disrupted their casting and caused a ruckus. He saved our lives, I think."

"I realized after you left that hanging back might have made you a target in its own way."

"Maybe it did, but we were a hard-to-reach target. Being in the group charging in wouldn't have been any better. They were ready to torch the whole forest. We were far outmatched." He glanced down at his leg. "In hindsight, maybe a healer with us would have been a good idea. But… gods, Aven. It was horrible. I can't believe they're all dead."

Aven laid a hand on his shoulder, his expression dark. "They fought bravely and died in pursuit of justice, which is all any of us can really ask. We'll work to stop this, to make sure their sacrifice was not in vain."

Derk gave him a somber nod.

"That's enough for now. You've had a long ride. Let's get someone for your leg."

Even as they were turning back to the stairs, Siliana appeared at the bottom landing. Her brown eyes widened, and her mouth fell open as she dashed up the stairs to take Derk's arm. Aven had never seen her show any emotion toward Derk other than mild annoyance and barely constrained irritation, but now she looked sincerely concerned.

Aven stared down at the marble floor, listening to Derk's uneven gait and her murmured questions as he shut the door. He'd never thought he would miss Derk's cocky, snide remarks, and yet he'd have given anything for a sarcastic quip just now. Something to tell him things weren't so serious.

But they were. Deathly serious, in fact.

Two dozen men had been lost. His brother was still Alikar's prisoner. His father was no better. And this catastrophe didn't bode well for what a normal military force would do against an equivalent force supported by mages. Or even a weaker one.

When he was sure Derk and Siliana were out of hearing range, Aven slammed a palm against the doorframe.

Inside, he heard Perik jump and drop something, and the guard beside him turned to look, but Aven ignored them and stalked back to the desk. They were so unprepared.

They were going to need a miracle.

Three more days passed before Thel saw Detrax—or anyone—again. The new fortress had a proper dungeon that he'd been thrown into, one where he could be chained at wrist and ankle and left for days, save the occasional scrap he had to scare away the vermin to get. As if he weren't skinny enough already.

He had some range of motion with his short chains, but not many positions in a dungeon could be comfortable. Sleeping mostly occurred when he passed out, and he dreaded waking and having to deal with it all again. The place was mostly silent, although occasionally he thought he could hear Niat—either groaning or sick again. Poor thing. Whatever she thought of him, nobody deserved all that. Of course, the sounds were far off and faint. It could be someone else or his imagination. She could have been swept off to her waiting betrothed by now.

As painfully uncomfortable as his new accommodations were, they did bring one boon. Light filtered through an arrow slit in the wall—it seemed this fortress hadn't always had a dungeon, and this dungeon was oddly not underground. Perhaps it was more accurately termed a prison? At any rate, while the arrow slit also brought a frigid wind that was beginning to make him constantly shake, it also allowed him just enough light to read.

And read he did. He tucked his knees up to his chest for warmth—and for privacy—and he nestled the little book against his thighs, hidden from any who cared to glance inside. He studied diligently and then studied some more.

What else did he have to do? But of course, he would have been studying this book had he been at home, in a nice armchair in the library with some hot cider in one hand. And it'd have been nice to have his choice of books to read, rather than just this tedious volume. Oh, and a fire. And some pumpkin pie. His stomach gurgled. Okay, perhaps this fantasizing wasn't helping.

By the third chapter, he'd encountered descriptions of spells for warmth, and he was glad to practice them. One other boon—the prison-dungeon was made nearly entirely of stone. Except his chains, of course.

A few hours of practice and he was able to draw the heat from the stone around him, and even heat the floor and walls as well. His accommodations instantly became more tolerable.

He was reading anxiously on how to reshape soil when the heavy locks on his door began to groan and clank open. Swiftly, he tucked the book back into his jerkin and forced his face into a more bored expression.

Of course, it was Detrax.

"Aye, there's the runt. Ready to finish yer map?"

A guard unlocked the manacles, and Thel stood

gingerly, grunting.

"No games. I may feel like leaving you loose, *if* you play nice, boy."

Thel nodded, feigning beaten cooperation. Of course, the day they'd arrived, the images of the burnt Akarians still fresh in his memory, that would have been a fairly accurate description of his mental state. But his new-found knowledge from the last few hours and days had reinvigorated him. Cooperation would likely get him no further with an enemy than resistance would anyway. Detrax had relished that stab wound in his thigh enough that Thel doubted anything would stop the beast from "cutting" if it was on his mind.

"All right, then. This way."

Detrax led Thel—flanked by eight guards, which seemed a little overkill—to another room, where a table and two benches awaited them but not much else. An interrogation room. But for this interrogation, the map of Akaria lay on the table, with the two points Thel had marked.

As a hand shoved Thel into one low bench, he considered whether lying, cooperation, or outright defiance would be best. It probably didn't matter; he was in for a tough time either way. Detrax of course eschewed the chair and slowly began pacing around him.

"All right. Have it out. The rest of the locations of the mines."

Thel didn't move.

"I don't exactly want to slice you in twain, but maybe just a finger…"

"How exactly would that help? Hard to hold a charcoal with sliced-off fingers," said Thel. Apparently outright defiance was his doom of choice for today.

Detrax continued as if Thel had said nothing. "I could just break your fingers, but I favor blades. There's just something beautiful about steel. The way it slices through and opens a dog up. You see the insides of people. What they're really made of." He stopped straight in front of Thel and leaned on the table, a grin showing off wolfish teeth. For the first time, Thel wondered if the request for the mine locations was even sincere. Maybe it was just an excuse to justify whatever truly dark urges lurked behind the mage's eyes.

Thel was probably going to find out. He swallowed, in spite of himself.

"Or I could break your legs," he mused, continuing his pacing in a circle around Thel. "That'd be a mite inconvenient for you, I think. Don't know as I'd like to deal with the stench that follows."

"You already have Niat for that, if my experience is any indicator."

To his surprise, Detrax chuckled, and Thel felt a little dirty. "Aye, I do." He stopped in front of Thel again. "I also could just rip it all from yer mind, ya know."

Thel froze.

Right. Creature mage. Shit. Could they really do that? If so, there were a *lot* of things Detrax could rip from his mind, beyond Anonil's fortifications and mine locations. What options did he have? His mind was only a blank slate of fear, though, shocked still by the unknown.

Detrax drew a dagger, bringing Thel back to reality. He resumed his slow pace, chuckling softly to himself.

Thel picked up the charcoal but couldn't bring himself to move his hand. If he marked the wrong locations, certainly Detrax would know. Would he dip into his mind to check anyway?

If there was *any* way to keep him from doing so, Thel needed to try. If Detrax knew about his magic… Thel pushed the thought from his mind. He wouldn't think it, lest that be the moment Detrax chose to dig into him.

Detrax's footsteps stopped directly behind him. Thel held his breath, shoulders tensing as the silence stretched on.

Two strong arms seized Thel's, while a third snarled into his hair and pulled his head slowly to the right side, exposing his throat. Thel forced a deep, ragged breath, straining to pull his head upright again.

The cold, hard point of the dagger slid along the skin of his neck, almost sensual, not breaking the skin. Yet.

"Course, there're some wounds that bleed out so fast they can't rightly be healed. Or I may not be motivated to try."

Thel swallowed, unsure if the threat had any teeth.

"Think your precious family will miss ya, boy?"

Thel spoke cautiously, careful not to move against the blade. "How will you get information out of me if I'm dead?"

Detrax chuckled softly again. "A smart one, eh? Maybe I don't need your information." He lowered his face and his voice so the next words were a whisper in Thel's ear. "Maybe I can rip it from your flailing mind while you writhe down into hell."

Thel did his best to shrug without cutting himself. "That tickles."

Detrax guffawed now, and all three hands shoved Thel toward the table, slamming his ribs into the table edge. The charcoal dropped from his hand, but he slowly picked it back up, gritting his teeth against the pain.

"Mark the map, and mayhap you'll get dinner again tonight. Finish it." Detrax's voice was soft and not soaked in its usual rancor. Had to be a trap. But what difference did it make if he could pull the information from Thel's mind? It was only a matter of time now before the beast would reach in, at the very *least* to verify that information.

Grudgingly, flattening his lips together in defeat, he marked three more spots on the map, these accurate, and labeled them all.

"Aye, that's a good runt." Detrax cuffed him on the back of the head, sending Thel's hair flying into his face, but not hard enough that it hurt for more than a moment. The creature mage circled the table and sank down on the bench before Thel.

"What, no cutting today?"

Detrax shrugged. "I haven't decided as yet. There's always the seer."

Thel glared at him. "I can't imagine that helps her visions."

Chuckling again, Detrax said, "You're mighty concerned about that seer, no? She is a pretty slip of a thing."

His glare hardened into a scowl. "She's a traitor. Just like you."

"I'm Kavanarian, I'm no traitor to you. Which is not to say that I wouldn't betray the Masters, if I had much of a choice in the matter." Detrax grinned, showing off his teeth again. Were they unnaturally pointy? "Still irks you the seer's not on your side? How can you justify gettin' in those holy robes if she's a traitor?"

"She could look like a goddess, and I wouldn't care one whit about her." Thel let his face go bored in hopes that the subject would drop. "And she's not on *your* side either."

Detrax grinned even wider. "You're a hoot, runt. Too proud to admit you've got it hard for her?"

"I'd have the same concern for any of Akaria's subjects."

"Suit yourself with whatever lies you like. You can't hide from me."

Detrax lowered his head, and Thel had only a split second to realize just what that meant and why Detrax had finally sat down.

A deluge hit him, and everything went black. Who needed eyes? Who had a body? What even existed anyway? He gasped for air, unsure he even had lungs to breathe, and groped blindly around him, searching for something, anything, of the world he'd been in a moment ago. He tried to shout, to scream, but if he succeeded, there was no sound. He thrashed violently now, searching for the table, the map, lunging toward where Detrax should be. Anything.

There was nothing. Everything was gone, and he was beyond alone.

He sank into the utter blackness of empty space.

The smelter was barely warm today, but thankfully, even this part of the smithy was warmer than it was outside. Tharomar took a deep breath of the familiar coal-smoke smell in the air. A tinge of burnt honey floated in there. Someone was working with beeswax.

He and Jaena had something much more unpleasant to toy with today.

Jaena pointed to the cloudy glass of the bowl that sat on the floor of the king's smithy. Tharomar had talked the smith into giving them the smelting area again and getting out of the way. He hoped they weren't going to do anything to make the smith regret relenting to his charms. But if the brand was finally destroyed, so be it.

No larger than a washbasin, it had steep sides, and the clear liquid inside had a slight yellowish cast. Tharomar shook his head. How were they going to destroy the brand in *that*?

"I know," she said. "This is all I could get my hands on. I've been all over the city and bought up everything I could find." A dozen different glass bottles of different shapes and sizes lay uncorked and empty on the nearby table.

"We're lucky Aven gave us a generous stipend then." He couldn't tell how much acid was in the bowl, but it'd take forever to dissolve a whole rod of metal in that. Or would disintegrate be a better term?

"Yes, I'd say so. Also, the alchemists warned that putting iron into this could be very unstable. We should stay back as far as we can."

Well, he knew a thing or two about staying back from dangerous things. "Let me get some tongs."

It'd taken two days to find this stuff. While acid was sometimes used for etching swords, that wasn't done terribly often by most smiths, and the amount they'd need to destroy something the size of the brand? It was ludicrous. Maybe just the bottom would suffice.

Tharomar had spent the intervening days bent over the star map, and much of his nights too, occasionally answering a question or fifty from Wunik on the Serabain alphabet. Working by starlight each night, he'd transcribe some ancient Serabain to its modern version, and by daylight, he'd translate it. It was meticulous work and, sadly, not something he really needed help with, so he'd spent it mostly alone.

With some instructions, though, Jaena had been able to canvas the city healers, apothecaries, and smiths, gathering up as much acid as she could. The idea of getting it from so many different sources made him nervous about combining it all, but she'd done it already, apparently without issue. And what else could they do? Say a prayer and have a healer on hand?

His labors over the star map also bought him time to think. The temple's message weighed on his mind, but as each hour and day passed, he was able to convince himself the translation was more important; he would reply and break the news to them soon. Just a bit later.

He had tucked the missive in a drawer in the desk in their room and hadn't mentioned it further. Not to Jaena, not to anyone. What was the point? He wasn't going to act on it. He wasn't going anywhere. And explaining the message meant admitting… a lot of things he wasn't too keen on talking about. Jaena still thought of him as a man of honor, and integrity, and morality, and while he didn't expect such an idealistic, romantic vision to last, he had no interest in hurrying her toward the truth.

So he had focused on the scroll, and when his work was done for the day, they'd headed back to the suspicious royal smith and his smelting room to have another go at destroying the cursed thing.

"Let's see this thing done," he said, returning with long tongs, apron, and gloves that stretched up his arms. They were made for heat, not acid. A leather apron wouldn't do much of anything, but he gave Jaena one too. He eyed the bowl for a long moment. He didn't have a good feeling about this.

Jaena pulled the brand from the pack and held it out. He took it in the tongs and moved forward. She backed toward the far wall, slipping the apron over her head and pulling her braid of braids out and over the shoulder strap.

Leaning his head back as far as he could from the bowl and the brand, he sank to one knee and lowered the iron into the yellowish liquid.

He listened, not sure he even wanted to turn his head at first. Iron scraped against glass from the slight shaking of his hand. He smelled nothing new. The tings of the smiths' hammers in the background and the wind whipping outside met his ears, but there was no sound out of the ordinary.

Finally he looked. The iron might as well have been sitting in water.

"Did they say how long it should take?" he said. But his heart was already sinking.

"What's it doing?"

"Nothing."

"They didn't say."

"Any chance this isn't acid, and those alchemists lied?"

"Several took a dropper and showed me some reactions. Not that I knew what to look for. They were... fairly happy to have an audience."

Ro smiled crookedly at that. A pretty young woman as an audience probably hadn't hurt. "Think you could run back and ask how long it should take? Any of them close by?"

"Yes—hold on."

He wasn't sure how long he waited, but he'd devised in his head an elaborate system of tongs, barrels, crates, and a bellows to hold this damn thing for him indefinitely when the door finally opened. He considered himself fairly strong, he could hammer with the best of them, but even his arms were starting to shake, holding the thing without a break. Just a little, but still.

She strode right up beside him.

"Bad news, huh?" He could sense it in the air.

"He said five minutes, maybe. He agreed I added enough water. That we should see some bubbling. Fizzing. Something. He wanted to come back and help us, so I spent half the time talking him out of that."

Ro scowled at the thing. A faint line beside the edge of the circular brand caught his eye. He squinted—a reaction? Maybe one of the samples had been weaker or not quite right, and it was just taking a little longer.

No. As he looked closer, he could see it now.

"Is there a… bubble around the metal?" he said slowly.

"You mean it's starting?" she said excitedly.

"No, I mean, I think it's not touching the acid even. It's pushing the acid away."

"What?" she took a step even closer. "Gods, I see it."

"Go out and ask our best, most loyal friend the royal smith for just a regular piece of scrap iron he doesn't need back."

"Got it."

As she left, he slowly raised the brand from the liquid. There was no submersion line, no darker wet portion. No drips. No nothing. He carefully set it aside in the dirt, several feet away, near the smelter. Nothing bubbled or fizzed near the end that had been inside the acid—or supposedly had been.

Returning, Jaena held out another piece of iron, not even the size of his hand, and he took it and plopped it in with much less caution this time, dropping it fully into the deep bowl.

It was a good thing he didn't need to hold it, because clouds of something sprang up from bubbles that frothed and hissed angrily to life. He staggered back, Jaena with him.

"Well, donkey balls. *That's* more what I was expecting," she said softly.

He smothered a laugh. "Donkey balls? Some diplomat you would have been."

She waved him off, sobering, and he followed suit. "This isn't going to work, is it."

"I don't think so." He backed away another foot as the piece let out another bout of bitter bubbling and hissing.

"Maybe it *can't* be destroyed," she said, voice faltering. "Maybe it's hopeless."

He gritted his teeth. Normally he was optimistic. Normally he'd say, we'll keep trying, we'll find a way.

Normally iron and acid did not peacefully mix.

Rock jutting into his cheekbone was the first sensation Thel regained. He groaned.

The memory of the blackness returned to him, and he shuddered, forcing his eyes open. How long had he spent adrift in the nothingness, searching for... for what? For anything and everything. It was as if someone had seized his senses and ripped them away.

Not someone. Detrax.

A chill went through him, and his whole body shook

again, something between a shiver and a shudder. He was back in his cell, and the air was icy around him. But he also shook at the realization that... creature mages could do *that*. Whatever that was.

Horrifying. No wonder people were afraid of mages. No wonder Niat thought Thel was evil.

They were all terribly, horribly right.

Thel forced himself to sitting, every joint screaming in protest. How long had he lain there? How much time had passed? In spite of the ache, he ran his fingers over the stone beneath him, delighting in the rough scrape of rock against his skin. The light of dusk or dawn filtered through the arrow slit faintly, but even that and the chilling wind were reassuring, grounding. Detrax might have the power to steal away the world from him, but it had all returned. For now.

What had Detrax discovered?

If he had discovered Thel's magic, there was no sign of it. The cell was very much the same. He either hadn't discovered it or had deemed Thel not to be a threat. Which, well, might be true. He sank into the stones, warming them, and he leaned back against the wall, pleased to connect to the rock around him, to feel the solid, quiet hum of it, to smile at its silent acceptance of his request. Rock didn't mind if it was warm or cold. It might even prefer warm, or he might be having a fit of overactive imagination.

He hadn't noticed closing his eyes, but they shot open as a thought hit him. The book. He reached for it in his jerkin pocket.

It was still there. He heaved a sigh of relief.

He spent a while sinking into the stone, tired in a deep way he couldn't remember having ever been before. He let his mind glide through the crevices and seams in the masonry around him, a join, a hunk of limestone here, a slab of sandstone there. A seam, a weakness.

A crack.

Opening his eyes, he leaned his weary form toward the spot in the outer wall he'd sensed... Had it been a glimmer of hope, a flash of intuition? Or was it possible he was merely mad from exhaustion?

Focusing his attention hard on the spot, he gave it the slightest push.

Stone scraped against stone. Barely half a finger's width, but it had *moved*. He'd made it move with his will alone. Well, and his magic.

Leaning back again, he stared at the slight change in the wall. How far was it down? If he could break the wall open, what would he do next? If he could get out of the fortress, could he survive out in the increasingly wintry forest? And was there a way he could rescue Niat at the same time? He couldn't wait forever—Detrax had shown him he likely didn't have that long—but he also couldn't see leaving her to their blue vials either. And that meant *two* of them escaping and surviving in the dead, cold woods.

He needed a plan.

6   CRACKS

The raging fire was crackling away cheerfully, and Daes found himself in something of a good mood as he moved about his Evrical rooms, choosing what to pack into his trunk for tomorrow's trip. The generals he'd sent were of course already in Gilaren, most likely. He took a deep breath and straightened, imagining the clangs of steel in smoky air, the shouting of men, the brisk, cold wind that would carry the smell of blood from the battlefield.

He missed it, he had to admit. And if only Marielle weren't coming with him, he'd feel downright upbeat about the journey. Of course, she was right. Politically it was the only smart move. But that didn't mean he had to be happy about it.

Suddenly, the door flung open without announcement or ceremony and slammed loudly against the opposite wall. Marielle stormed in, a swarm of women following her in a hasty, alarmed cloud. Her striking red dress was gathered in all the right places and fell in straight and clean lines toward the unfeeling marble.

"Was all of this just so you could someday be king?"

He sat down the leather-bound book he'd been holding and straightened, frowning at her as his heart sped up. "What?"

"Is that the only reason you even spoke to me?"

Daes frowned harder now. As if he would concoct such a foolish, dangerous, stupid plan. Only luck—was it that?—could have taken him this far. "I could say the same to you. Was it all about getting rid of the king? And his mistress?"

To their credit, the women behind her shrank back but showed little reaction beyond concern at either his or her words.

She glowered back as she strode toward him. "You used me so you could fight your war how you wanted."

"I did not. I would not."

"The first thing I did for you was send out troops."

"Because it needed to be done. Time was of the essence. If you think *that* was what I was thinking of when I approached you in the gardens, you do not know me." Certainly he had been hoping some gratitude might come from the encounter, but he would have been utterly mad to believe she would someday grant him as much power as she had. It was all luck.

She folded her arms, clearly skeptical. "How can I know you? It's not been long enough to know each other, truly. Your friends speak of you as a master manipulator.

Would you tell me they're wrong?"

He gritted his teeth. He was certainly better at political machinations than most, but he had never tried to manipulate *her.* "Friends? Neither Lady Seulka nor Princess Paranelin are friends."

"They know you well."

He shook his head in disgust. "No, they don't." He resumed packing, picking up another book as he dropped another into his trunk, not looking at her, willing her to drop this. The crowd of women staring at him wide-eyed was making him uncomfortable, and it was hardly proper.

"Daes. Look at me, Daes."

He paused and glanced over at her. "Go." He flicked his fingers at the archway where one of her attendants hovered. "Your ladies are waiting for you."

"I'm the queen and the one giving the orders here."

He pursed his lips, trying not to glower at her. "Why are you bringing this up now? Clearly you have social activities to attend to."

She waved angrily at the woman to be gone. Frowning, her attendants backed out of the doorway, one of them shutting the door behind them. Silence stretched out between them, as if she waited for the women to move farther away.

"You don't even care one coin's toss about me, do you?" she said bitterly as she turned back to him, now that they were alone.

Rage shot through him, the intensity of it terrifying him. Why did he care so much what she thought, what she said? A strong desire to backhand someone flooded him, but he stayed still, setting down the new book carefully. As he did so, she charged the rest of the way toward him, stopping barely a foot away. His body went tense, vibrating with hard, pent-up anger. "Why are you even talking about this?"

"Why are you even fighting this war?"

"To protect all I've built. Because *I* don't turn a blind eye to obvious threats, unlike your former lord." He hesitated, more words on the tip of his tongue, words that were very unlike him to say. The truth, but could he admit it? That it was also to protect her, too? No. Not in those words, at least. "The Akarians hold the power to undo all I've built. We risk losing our only advantage against them. Our position has only worsened. We must crush them while we still can. I'm simply trying to protect what we have."

We. There. That was close, wasn't it? It wasn't the same as telling her that it was all for her now, that everything had changed, but it was the best he could do.

Her expression softened, and she looked away, not meeting his eyes. "Some say you are power-mad. That I am just a foolish pawn, a cog in the wheel of a machine that you would destroy as readily as any mage."

His scowl returned. "Tell me who said that."

"No."

"Tell me." He clenched his jaw and forced himself to take a deep breath through his nose. "I would kill anyone who would dare call you, their queen, a pawn.

You are far from that. They should be struck down for their disrespect."

"Am I not a pawn? I am not so sure. You don't trust my motivations. You don't want me to come with you. I know little of your plans, for this or for the war."

"You are *not* a pawn. Damn it, I had no plans for this. I have no particular lust for power, Marielle. I am only concerned with security, and I'm willing to take the initiative to keep it. It's not my fault everyone else is so damn lazy and blind that they fail to act."

She gazed back at him, still uneasy, eyes narrowing. "How can I know you aren't using me?"

"You can't. How can *I* know you're not using me?"

"I would never."

"And I would never have moved against the king if you hadn't needed it." If you hadn't asked, so sweetly. If you hadn't drawn me into your bed.

"How can I believe you? This has all served your purpose mightily well."

"We are to be married eventually, after all. Aren't we? Shouldn't you simply believe me? Shouldn't I simply believe you?"

She pursed her lips. "Only if we are fools."

"Perhaps I should take a mistress to test your motives, then—"

Almost before he got the words out, she stepped a few inches closer and slapped him across the face. "I'd rather you cleave me in two," she said, her voice breaking.

He reeled for a second in shock, partly at the slap, but

even more at his own reaction. Any other woman—or man, for that matter—he would have backhanded so hard, they'd be sprawled on the fine Corovan marble.

But not her.

And in fact, no anger coursed through him, and instead in its place was an inexplicable sense of immense satisfaction, of amusement even. At *what*? It made no sense. At having goaded her into losing her composure? Yes, but not out of spite. There was something deeper. He brought his hand to his face, rubbing at the sting, mystified. His eyes locked with hers. In their blue depths was a mixture of hurt and fear that in the silence was slowly melting to terror. "My lord, I—"

He kissed her then, hard, almost violently, crushing her with the force of it, gripping her neck and holding her to him. But he didn't need to. She didn't shrink. Indeed, the press of her mouth against his was nearly as ferocious. The pounding of his heart went from double to triple time.

He heaved her up, gathering her in his arms and setting her atop the nearby desk, hauling up her skirts and daring her to stop him. He broke away to measure her eyes, her face, for any trace of fear, any measure of cunning, any sign he should stop and walk away from her in disgust.

He saw only a kind of intensity that grew familiar, an intensity he had seen now more than a few times. Patient, if fiery desire, even… trust. He captured her mouth with his again and didn't release her this time.

He did not understand this. He did not understand

her, or what was motivating this sudden outburst, or why he deserved her, or if either of them actually cared about each other the way he was beginning to hope—and believe—they might.

He was filled only with a desire to remind her she was his and no one else's. And to make her see the opposite was also true.

Gods, he was a naïve fool. He'd likely end up beheaded or quartered for his foolhardy sincerity. It was entirely unlike him. He didn't understand any of this.

He fell back on the one thing between them he did understand, and her soft gasps told him she understood this part at least too. The damned meddling ladies-in-waiting could do just that. They could *wait*.

Although they hadn't found the right words at all—in fact, they'd mostly found the wrong ones—he had a feeling they understood each other.

Miara awoke with a pounding headache. Emerald and sapphire light lanced into her rooms, dappling the queen's bed with moving blobs of color. She sat up with a groan. Pain sliced around her skull like someone was trying to crush it, and she lifted a hand to block the cheery light, feeling more out of place than ever.

The sea of fabric around her was smooth as a lamb's ear. Camil had always said Elise cared for fine cloth because she hailed from Dramsren, but Miara had had no idea.

She'd had no idea cloth like this even existed. She felt like she was getting such extravagance dirty. How many meals could this pure sea of soft white buy?

The door opened. The groan had been a mistake, alerting her watchers—her attendants—that she'd risen. The three of them bustled in now, arms full and looking like they meant business. Miara put both hands over her eyes and then rubbed her scalp, trying to ease the pain away.

She hadn't had a headache last night when their work had finished. She'd had the whole night to sleep and recover her strength. And yet, she felt more tired than ever. Very strange. But there was no time for worrying about it now. She downed more tea from an elegant wooden tray as her new attendants swarmed her with details of arrivals of notable guests later in the day. Her belly warm, the ache in her head immediately started to lessen.

"You're to be prepared to receive them royally," said Opia—the proper one, using a tone more appropriate for addressing an unruly schoolgirl. Although perhaps "unruly girl" was exactly how the woman saw her. "I will do my best to inform you of each of the illustrious personages, but there are *quite* a number who may attend. Up, up. We have work to do."

If Miara hadn't already missed Fayton and Camil, she would now. Who would have thought that she'd come to miss Estun and its heavy darkness and its merciless, oppressive Great Stone? It meant a lot more to her now, and she found herself wishing that someday they would go back. But she shut the thought away. They had a war to fight first, at the very least.

Her heart panged in particular for Camil's steady, calm, faintly amused smile now, though. Nothing ruffled Camil, and Miara was pretty sure the young woman would *never* use the phrase "illustrious personages."

Still, pretentious or not, Opia was right that they had work to do. It was time to give this queen thing a serious shot. Miara hauled herself out of bed and devoured a plate full of dumplings and asked for more. She was of course twice or three times as starving as any normal person would be because of last night's exertions, but her ladies eyed her, and she could tell they were thinking—oh, we have so much work to do. Or perhaps they were thinking, she eats like a horse.

Probably right on both counts.

Who would have thought cabinets full of fine fabric would prove such regular adversaries? Miara scowled at the colored silks and regretted that her hasty departure from Estun had left behind what little progress they'd made toward clothing that didn't horrify her.

"Now, this is a fine wardrobe Queen Elise has provided for you," said Opia, chin high. "I'm sure it will be quite hard to choose from all of these glorious options."

Miara eyed the woman. Did Miara's fear show on her face, or could her attendants just smell it?

No. She shook her head. No, she *would* conquer this ridiculousness. There were more important things to do than worry about what to wear.

She imagined herself in Elise's place, the way Elise

emanated a quietly welcoming energy, beaming a friendly warmth and placid confidence. But imagining herself in the same mode sent the image up in smoke.

She sighed. If Renala were here, *she* would know what to wear, what to choose. But none of the gowns would magically bequeath her grace or friendliness or any of their well-bred, noble-born qualities.

Her mind drifted back to sitting around that campfire with Samul. Hmm, Aven did indeed have enough friendliness for the both of them—for the right audience. She imagined herself glowering icily from his shoulder instead, daggers close at hand.

Yes. That was an image she could almost see. She wouldn't be Elise—or Renala. Or any of the flighty, giggling ladies she'd observed in the Kavanarian court. The problem was not the dress, was it? The dresses didn't matter. What mattered was how she wore them, and she'd wear them like herself, and no one else. Nothing else was an option.

Challenging herself, she seized one purely by color—a stormy, grayish blue. There was no more Akarian color than that, in her estimation. Elise wore it frequently, and Renala had already shown her the power of color to make an impression. The gauzy thing whipped in a chilly draft that swept by. It was little more than a bundle of fabric. She had no idea where a body went into it or how to put it on.

Not that her new attendants were going to let her dress herself anyway.

She held it out to the nearest, the freckle-faced woman with warm, dark eyes. Kalan? Yes, that was it. "What do you think of this one?"

Kalan's eyes lit with delight. "You'll be a dream. Not that you wouldn't be a dream in all of them, my lady."

Miara shook her head as she cut at the air with the knife-edge of her hand. "You've no need to flatter me. I need the truth."

Wincing, the woman looked at her warily. "I would never lie to you, my lady."

"No, I mean it. Sincerely. Your name is Kalan, is that right?"

Calming slightly, but still wary, the woman nodded.

Miara glanced at the other women. Oh, no—there were four now, even though the proper one was briefly gone. Gods, the servants were multiplying like rabbits in the clover. This is fitting, she chided herself. This isn't about you. It's about Akaria. It's about freeing your people and then some. It's about a land that's worth living in, a land many people believed was worth dying for. And if she wanted power, well, pomp and circumstance came with it. She wasn't just herself, but also one who stood for all of them, and in that light, humility did no one any good.

She softened her voice, warmed it. "Truthfully, my dear Kalan, I want nothing but honesty from all of you. It is all that will be rewarded. I am no noble—certainly you've heard that much."

Grudgingly, they all nodded. Their expressions ranged from worried to guarded, though.

"Is it—" started the youngest before Kalan shushed her.

"No, what is it?" Miara said, trying to sound welcoming and friendly. Not something she had much practice at.

"Is it true you were the one?" When she stopped and didn't explain further, Kalan elbowed her. "The one who grew the plants last night?"

"Oh. Yes. Did you see them? What did you think?"

The air went still, the fear almost palpable.

"I thought… well, it does seem quite unnatural, my lady," the girl—Etral?—whispered.

Miara hid a wince. Had it all backfired? Instead, she forced a smile and nodded. "It is a bit unnatural, but all the plants are back to their late fall cycle. None will be harmed by it, and I thought the harvest might help some through the winter."

"I thought it was beautiful," said one of the new-comers, whom Kalan glared at slightly. She seemed to be speaking out of turn. "Woke up to fresh roses in my window box." She glared back at Kalan, whose expression softened quickly.

As if realizing the implications of her expression, Kalan straightened up. "It will help some through the winter. My brother's little garden brought in a whole second yield."

"Tell me what you've heard," Miara said as gently as she could. "Both the good and the bad. Honesty only, remember?"

They all glanced nervously at each other. Miara was glad the proper one hadn't returned just yet. She had a feeling she knew which side that attendant would be on: any side quick to pronounce judgment.

"I think that about sums it up, my lady," said Kalan.

"I heard a man outside the temple crying evil and corruption, but to be honest I'm not sure many were taking him too seriously."

"Why not?" said Miara.

A sly grin snuck onto Etral's face. "I think it's hard to buy something as corruption when it's as beautiful as roses and daisies and fresh apples, my lady. I mean, really. If that's vile pestilence, I'd like some more please."

Kalan elbowed her again but relaxed as Miara's snort of laughter registered as actual amusement and not offense.

"Thank you for your honesty." Miara was surprised at how gracious that had come out. She almost sounded like she knew what she was doing. "I am new to all this. I'll need your advice, and I trust it greatly. But I am also no Queen Elise. I must cut my own path. I fought my way here, and I'll not be setting aside my dagger or my magic. So…" She hesitated, wondering if admitting weakness would help her or hurt her in their estimation. She decided to risk it. "If you would, I want you to make me look like the queen I will become. But it must be the sort of queen who carries a dagger. Or ten. Will you help me?"

Kalan raised an eyebrow but stepped out from beside the girl and very carefully took the dress. "We can make you look like a queen, my lady." She glanced uneasily at the others. She was clearly making no dagger-related promises.

Etral stepped forward to examine the dress too and then gave Miara a long look. Wondering if Miara would be true to her word about honesty? If her lady was truly a plague of corruption? "Aye, we can do that, and we will.

You, uh, may have to help us with the dagger bit, my lady."

Miara snorted again. "That I can do."

The women set to work. The dress truly was little more than a gauzy collection of fabric. That, in fact, was the magic of it, Miara discovered as it took shape around her. Soft, thin silks and fabrics she couldn't name concealed nearly all of her, but seemed to risk covering a little less at any moment. An illusion, but a powerful one.

But the dress was only a portion of their ministrations. The youngest presented Miara with ten different hair ribbons, eight sets of beads, and three different jewelry cases. The hair ribbons were easier to select than the dresses; a brilliant cobalt ribbon and silver beads were drawn from their box, although quite a lot of braiding took place before she could see them in action. To the women's credit, the elaborateness of the braids woven with ribbon and beads and wrapped carefully in a suggestion of a simple crown around her brow did not scream of as much effort as they actually put in. The effect was rather understated. Hmm, Elise's effortlessness might take more work than Miara had thought. Was that a good thing or a bad thing?

Eventually, Kalan pushed her in front of the looking glass to evaluate their handiwork.

Miara caught her breath. The woman in the glass was indeed regal, and at the same time familiar. The dress seemed like it was out of a bizarre dream, some other reality, and it didn't feel like it belonged against her skin. The lightness of it compared to leather riding gear made her feel uncomfortably naked. It certainly wouldn't protect her from anything. But she'd be able to move just fine. It would have to do. She'd try out this particular tool, and if it didn't suit her, she'd try another one. She took a steadying breath, smoothing damp palms down the sides of the dress and watching it shift and settle around her.

"My, you ladies do know what you're doing," she said quietly.

"Your daggers, my lady?" The youngest held out her boot sheath with a grand sweep, like it might be a fine vintage, or a box of a dozen colored ribbons. Good. The girl was trying to go along with Miara's bizarre requests.

"Thank you, Etral." Studying herself in the mirror, the dress revealed her calves at times, and they hadn't permitted her boots, especially since they had no plans to leave Ranok. She settled with hiking the dress up and strapping the blades to her thigh, which seemed a fair compromise between accessible and appropriate. She pretended not to notice their wide-eyed stares as she did so. Just because they hadn't seen it before didn't mean it was a bad idea. "I will also need something for the outside. Something to wear on the hip, most likely," she muttered to herself. "But there's time to look for that later."

"I'll see what we have, my lady," said one of the newcomers quickly, hurrying out. As she left, the proper one popped back into the room.

Miara raised her eyebrows. Never had she seen such eager servants. Overzealous might be more like it. Miara glanced back at Etral. "What do you think?"

The girl smiled politely. "You're a queen if I ever saw one, my lady. Which I have."

"Wait," said Kalan. She searched in a nearby cabinet, pushing and shoving things like a mother in a market. A moment later, she produced a black cloak with thick black fur trimming its shoulders and on down the edges. "There. That's not a cloak for Queen Elise, but I think it cuts a mighty profile on you. Mighty is what you're going for, I think. Fearsome. But still beautiful, of course. What say you?"

Kalan looked over Miara's form proudly, appraising her like a well-cooked roast chicken, but Miara had to smile. Even with the proper one staring at her as if she were about to break some unspoken rule.

Yes. This was a cloak for ominous glowering. For facing down her former masters as equals. For staring daggers at enemies of the Akarian throne.

That she could do.

And besides, it was damned cold in here.

The thudding of his door woke Thel, morning sunlight slanting sharply into his prison cell. Keys were clanging in the locks, bolts and gears turning, and he struggled to sit up. The rocks dug into his back, and he rubbed the cold, aching skin of his wrists.

Before he was even entirely awake, Alikar swept into the cell, followed by Detrax. Niat trudged in after them, wearing no manacles.

"You're helping them now?" he grunted.

She gaze shifted, but only slightly, not rising above his knees. Her eyes were bleak as they drifted back down toward the floor. Her shoulders lifted in the weakest possible shrug. In spite of it all, he felt a little guilty for goading her. She might have been through the same hell as him or worse.

He ran a hand over his face, trying to shove off the grogginess of sleep. He was aching in half his joints, and the wound in his leg itched, likely infected, but none of that was as bad as the pounding in his head. His stomach let out a loud gurgle. That explained the headache, at least partly.

But... Niat was here. Could this be his chance? He glanced down at the manacles. If only he had some way to get them off. He'd need to convince them to take them off. Or could he crack the stone where the metal attached to the wall and simply drag the manacles with him? Last night's plans hadn't included Niat showing up in his cell.

Alikar stood in the center of the room, just before him, hands clasped behind his back, wearing his typical ostentatious cloak even here. Detrax hung back.

The Gilaren lord glared long and hard at Thel. Silence settled around them for a long moment before he spoke. "Detrax tells me he's gotten what he needed from you. So that leaves you with two options."

Thel didn't like the sound of that or Alikar's brisk tone. He took half his mind and started working into the cracks behind him, where his chains met the wall.

Alikar began pacing back and forth in front of him. "One option is that you agree to help us. Once we return to Kavanar, you can be branded like the rest, if you don't earn our trust."

So they did know he was a mage. The first piece of the wall was almost shattered. He shifted to the other side.

"You will help us with our takeover of Akaria," Alikar continued. "And if you do so faithfully, without betrayal, I may choose to award you a minor lordship when everything is said and done."

"How magnanimous of you." Thel glared at him. As if he had ever cared for such a thing. He just wanted to be left alone in his library, by the gods.

"That is our offer. However, you must make a significant difference to our campaign."

"Or our personal wealth," Detrax growled behind him, making Alikar jump slightly.

"What's the other option?"

"Your death. In a manner of Detrax's choosing." Alikar held out a hand in the creature mage's direction, as if a servant offering him that option. "Oh, and I may let the mage have a few rounds with the priestess before you're done. And you will watch, in case that sways your opinion." Alikar's eyes sparkled.

Thel scowled. Fool was so sure his victory was near. The second stone joint was not *quite* cracked, but close. Thel started on the outer wall. He needed to buy more time. "You really know how to offer a man a difficult decision," he said as slowly as he could.

Alikar narrowed his eyes. "Your sarcasm will get you nowhere with me."

"Really? Detrax seems to like it."

And indeed, Alikar glanced over his shoulder to jump a little at Detrax's feral grin. Then the lord shook his head and opened his mouth.

"Leave her out of this," Thel said, cutting Alikar off. Just a little more time.

"We're not bargaining. Cooperate, or you'll both suffer."

Thel caught Detrax's eye now. "This is between you and me. Leave her out of this."

Detrax shrugged. "Cooperate, and she won't have to be involved."

Thel's eyes caught on Niat. Through all this, she ignored them, bleak eyes trained on the rugged floor. Thel turned his scowl on Alikar. "You're even more vile than I could have imagined. Isn't she supposed to be your wife? And you'd use her like—"

"Oh, he has no plans to marry her," Detrax said, grinning darkly. "As if the lady of Gilaren would put up with that."

"What? I never said that," Alikar said indignantly.

Detrax grinned. "'Course, don't want to be near Lord Sven when he finds out he's been swindled."

"Lies," spat Alikar. "Not surprising from a mage."

Thel laughed outright. "It's really best not to lie to people who can read your mind, you know."

The four-armed mage guffawed and slapped his leg,

even as the color drained from Alikar's face. Had he not realized such a thing was possible? Still, a chill ran through Thel as his mind raced to adjust his plans. He had another obstacle—Detrax. Whatever he had done to thrust Thel into darkness, he could do again. And quickly. Thel couldn't very well escape, and with Niat, if his mind was locked in a prison of eternal, shapeless night. Detrax would have to be dealt with. Somehow.

He glanced at Detrax nervously, realizing the mage could be reading his thoughts even now. But no. His grinning gaze was locked on Alikar, who'd stiffened noticeably. They were probably sharing some kind of silent exchange.

Thel focused quickly on the wall while they were distracted, thrusting the crack deeper, almost to its breaking point.

Alikar spun back to face Thel. "Enough. None of this matters. Your choice?"

He rose slowly to his feet. "It's not really much of a choice, is it?"

"Ah, good." Alikar smiled tentatively, looking relieved, and took a step forward. "I'm glad you're going to be practical about this."

Thel shrugged. "I'll be glad not to die. Nor should the priestess be harmed." However, the shrug was just the slight twitch that the wall needed. Tiny cracking sounds emanated from the end of the heavy chain. Damn, not yet—

The hunk of rock that he'd been severing from the wall broke free and fell to the ground with a heavy thud.

"What the—" Alikar started.

Thel seized the rocks of the outer wall and ripped them

apart, hurtling them inward and around. He had one chance at this. He aimed the wave of stone and mortar directly at Detrax.

The beast mage let out a shout, his hands rising to defend himself even as he vanished under the rubble Thel hurled in his direction. He had been planning to use those to help them get down, but Detrax needed to be out cold. That didn't leave him with many options.

A cry from Niat sent a jolt through him. He searched for her among the dust. She was stumbling back from the moving rock in shock, Alikar right with her. Good, he hadn't hit her unintentionally.

The distraction caused a handful of stones to fall out of Thel's control, crash to the ground, and roll forward. The stones collided with the cell door's bars, embedding them right into the far wall. They weren't leaving the cell that way now, for better or worse. Niat had to jump a foot to the side just for it to miss her boots. Generous of them to replace her sandals. That'd be handy in the snow.

Thel let go of the stones in the corner where he'd last seen Detrax. Underneath them, the stones heaved slightly. Was that just his imagination or could Detrax actually be conscious under there, trying to get out?

He had thrust the pile of stones as hard as he could in the mage's direction, and now he picked up the loose outer ones and crashed them against the mountain of rock one more time, right where it had moved.

He waited. He watched for the rocks to lurch, twitch, anything. Was that a grunt or something outside? Was that blood on the floor, or had that dark puddle been there all along? Another heartbeat. Another.

Nothing happened.

What was he waiting for, a hand-painted sign from the gods? He ripped the other anchor out of the wall, then twisted his hands around the chains, gripping them. Hey, if he couldn't lose them, he'd make a weapon out of them. He'd just have to hope they weren't too heavy. Pure strength had never been his strong suit.

Thel lifted his burdens and barely took two steps toward the gash before Alikar started forward. Thel didn't hesitate. He reared his arm back and then swung the head-sized chunk of rock at Alikar's knees. His head would have been better, but Thel didn't think he was lifting these much higher, he wasn't the type for that—

Hey, Alikar's balls weren't very high either, and Thel wouldn't shed one tear if he managed to hit them. The young lord danced back, losing his grip on his sword. It clattered to the ground. Thel stepped toward him, rearing back for another swing, and Alikar staggered back farther, his eyes locked in horror on his lost sword.

Thel stepped forward, pinning the blade to the ground. He stared down at the hilt. He could end it all here. Alikar was guilty of treason, kidnapping, threatening to murder Thel himself, and much worse. He could gut Alikar with this sword; he could pummel the man to death with the stone.

A ragged breath to his left drew his attention. Niat had sunk into a ball against the cell door, shaking. Thel glanced back at Alikar, then at her.

The hell with this.

He grabbed Niat's arm and hauled her to her feet, dragging her after him to the precipice. Yes, as he'd calculated—three stories down. They weren't getting down without help.

Thel tore the next piece of the wall apart and away from the building. He carefully brought it down in front of them—a platform. Oh, of *course*. He might not be able to heft both of the boulders still tethered to his arms with his muscles, but with his magic he certainly could. How could he be so dense. They rose up in the air like birds following them, chained to his wrists and hovering near his shoulders.

Alikar staggered to his feet. The platform faltered, bobbing slightly, but didn't disintegrate.

"What are you doing?" Niat said, her voice fragile and thin as a fine dish reaching its breaking point.

"I'm getting us out of here."

And then he jumped, pulling her with him.

Niat shrieked as they sang through the air, and he hoped the small boulders didn't hit her. But he wasn't leaving her with Alikar or Detrax, even if her fear of his magic made her think he was just as bad as them. He knew he wasn't.

He and Niat might starve to death. But they'd be free, and no harm would come to her from him.

The mage was dragging her off the platform of rock now, his grip like iron on her forearm. Niat could barely see, the world swam so much. She crushed a slight swell of hope in her heart that this might be a true escape. Didn't she know better by now than to hope? Even if they succeeded, the mage couldn't truly be what he seemed. Oh, he seemed kind, but she couldn't let herself believe it. She'd escape this place, maybe, but it'd only be to some new, fresh hell.

Maybe Detrax's soldiers would shoot them, and she could just die, and this could all be over.

But of course, that didn't happen. She didn't follow just *what* happened exactly. He dragged her down into a stairwell, burst through a door, and they were running past bunks, the rooms dark around them.

"Where are you going?" she demanded.

"Away from here!" was all he responded.

"How do you know where to go?"

"I can feel the earth leading out of here—got to keep away from the arrows!" he shouted.

"The earth?"

"We're underground, did you miss that?"

"So you don't know where you're going?" she snapped.

"I kind of do. But hey, neither do you!"

She shut her mouth; he had a point at that. Her dizziness was clearing, and something caught in her peripheral vision. She turned. "What the hell is *that*?"

"A piece of the wall."

"Why is it floating by my head?"

"So I don't have to carry it! You chose an odd time to ask a lot of questions. And there are two, so watch out."

He still had an iron grip on her forearm, and it was starting to ache, but she didn't try to wring herself free. The dizziness could come back at any time.

Did he actually think this would work and not just get them both killed? Optimistic fool.

And yet, she let him drag her on, ducking through yet another basement barracks, around some crates, and up another stairwell. They resurfaced just before the main gate.

Soldiers readied bows and crossbows at the gate. He faltered for a second, skidding to a stop before looking back over his shoulder.

She glanced back now too. Alikar was not far off, in pursuit. She was mildly surprised he cared to run and not just send others to do his dirty work, but there *had* been other pursuers they'd lost. Maybe he was just the best at tracking them. Or the luckiest.

She reached for the pouch at her belt, some of the few belongings they'd returned to her.

But before she could find the tin in her pouch, she discovered the real reason why Thel had spun to look behind them. The rocks that had once made up their platform soared over their heads and crashed into the gate, their momentum rolling them farther so that each took down more than just one man. Niat gasped and covered her mouth without thinking. Then she snatched it away, concealing the emotion behind her usual mask.

With just three or four boulders, the mage had cleared the gate. All of those who'd been preparing to kill them were dead.

He dragged her forward again, and she ran now with him as fast as her feet could move her. If he'd killed those people to get them free, she'd not worsen their deaths by spiting him, or making them meaningless. That was *not* hope kindling in her chest. She did not hope.

Hope was a fatal flaw. Hope would get her killed. Hope would get dashed when seemingly kind and valiant men proved their true mettle. It was inevitable.

"Miara, this is Priestess Gerana, High Priestess of Nefrana, Elii Temple. Priestess, this is my betrothed, Arms Master Miara Floren."

Miara bowed her head and slightly at the waist too. How deeply was appropriate was entirely unclear at this point. Those were a lot of fancy titles Aven was dishing out. Her blood pounded in her ears. Elise would probably tell her to act like the queen, even without the informal title, but the last thing she needed was to give a priestess of Nefrana one more reason to not support them.

"A blessing to meet you, Arms Master. And betrothed? Congratulations." The woman's voice held a tint of disapproval, but her eyes darted to the emerald and then up to Miara's face.

"Yes," Aven countered. "We haven't had time with the king's sickness and a few other issues—and the war on top of that—to celebrate the matter formally. But in due time, we will. We all thought it best the *arrangement* be formalized, however, with the rest of the chaos." Ah, it was only the lack of due ceremony she objected to, not the betrothal itself, Miara hoped.

We all thought? she whispered into his head, laughing silently. *Did you actually consult anybody?*

The corner of his mouth twitched up in a very slight smile. *I decided you agreed with the proposition when you were kissing me earlier.*

A fair assumption.

"And how is His Highness Samul?" the priestess said smoothly.

Aven looked to Miara. She swallowed her nerves. "No better, I'm afraid. We are searching for medicines, but it is a long process, requiring time we may not have."

The priestess frowned, eying Aven sideways. "You are charged with his care? I hate to point it out, but it would seem to your benefit if he did not improve."

Miara gritted her teeth. "Ranok's healer is charged with his care. I am simply assisting him and Queen Elise."

"Miara has spent most of her life as a healer," Aven cut in. "And she also rescued my father from a Kavanarian ambush only two days ago, for which he granted her her title. Her loyalty to the Lanuken family runs deep and has been proven time and again."

Miara's shoulders relaxed slightly. When had she started clenching them? Aven's words were spoken with conviction, though, and by no means stretched the truth. She *was* an accomplished healer… even if it was mostly of horses.

"I am glad to hear it," said the priestess, but Miara was hardly sure of the truth of that. "I don't mean to monopolize you, sire. I see others waiting to greet you. But I do have more questions. Given your confidence in the arms master's loyalty, perhaps she could accompany me for a walk around the grounds? It's growing icy in here. Some walking would do our blood good, don't you think?" She smiled at Miara, a vague expression that brought little warmth to her face.

Aven looked to her for approval, eyebrow raised.

Is this a trap? she spoke into his mind again.

Perhaps a social one, but she'll have words for you one way or another, now or in the future. Your preference when to spring it.

Miara smiled as warmly as she could muster at the woman. "Agreed, it would. If you don't mind my brief absence, my lord?" Miara said, with a slight emphasis on 'brief.'

Aven nodded. "I'm sure others will want to meet you, but a few minutes couldn't hurt."

The priestess headed for the hall, and Miara fell in step beside her.

"You know, many of us thought that young man might never marry," Gerana said, a touch sentimental.

Miara groped for a response. "I have heard he had many suitors," she replied woodenly.

"I can't imagine what you must have done to capture his interest."

Miara almost laughed. *Capture* was exactly right. But it hardly seemed prudent to point *that* out just now. She only smiled to herself.

"What were you seeking when the two of you became acquainted? How do a healer and a prince cross paths? Was he grievously injured and we didn't hear of it?"

Miara took a deep breath. No avoiding this conversation, was there? She should have rehearsed something. "I spent much of my life as a healer, but I am not only that."

"And what else have you been?" Gerana's voice was patient, as if to say, she could play games like this all day and all night too, if Miara insisted.

"A slave," Miara said coldly.

Gerana stopped short. "Pardon?"

Miara folded her arms across her chest, frowning back at her. "How do you feel about mages, my dear High Priestess of Nefrana?"

The woman tensed, but said nothing.

"And how about the Devoted? Are you fond of *them*?"

Gerana frowned. "Hardly. Their faith is admirable—"

"Is it?" Miara's voice was sharp as the Great Stone itself.

"—but the goddess would never justify murder."

"And what about slavery? Would she justify that?"

Gerana blinked, her lips parted but no words coming out. Finally she managed, "You are… a mage, I hear?"

"As is our king," said Miara flatly. "I'm certain you've heard by now."

The priestess swallowed and glanced around. Calculating her response? It had better be a good one. "I'd never heard of the Devoted practicing slavery," Gerana said softly, "but how could anyone do anything but condemn it? Especially in Nefrana's name."

Miara eased slightly. The words sounded as sincere. Gerana could be a good actress, and what else could she say, with a mage suddenly king? But the words rang true.

Miara turned and restarted their walk, preferring to train her eyes on the marble instead of the priestess's face. The priestess followed her lead, and they strolled out of the main court hall and onto the raised walkway that overlooked the barracks and its yard.

"I had the misfortune to be born in Kavanar," Miara said. "When I was five years old, my mother gave me up to the Devoted upon discovering I was a mage. I was enslaved with magic, branded with fire, bound with a spell I couldn't resist, even in my mind. I was forced to work as a healer. As I grew older, I began receiving other, more dangerous assignments." She paused, waiting to see if Gerana was keeping up.

"I am sorry to hear you suffered at your mother's hands."

Miara frowned, caught off guard at the sudden lump in her throat. Were these sincere condolences or simply a way to tear open the first wound she could find, to throw Miara off-balance? She glared down at her feet and said nothing.

"Tell me, are all mages enslaved in Kavanar?"

Miara nodded, surprised but relieved at the factual question. "And any they can kidnap from neighboring lands too, via the efforts of the Devoted."

The priestess covered her mouth with a concerned hand, and for the first time Miara realized Gerana was deeply disturbed, her brow furrowed and eyes crinkled almost as if in pain. A far cry from Alikar's reaction, at the very least.

After a longer moment of silence had passed, Miara continued. "And that is how our paths crossed. My assignments started off trivial, spying on the Kavanarian king for the Masters, but eventually I was tasked with kidnapping a very prominent foreign mage. You might know him."

Gerana caught her breath. "That… is a far cry from marrying him. Or courting him."

"I did not intend to court him. I hoped he'd defeat me. I had no reason to hate him, and indeed every reason quite the opposite."

"Apparently. How? How did you escape your task?"

"Long story, but suffice to say, I failed." That was not *precisely* true, but it might be the more diplomatic and easier-to-accept story. "Aven freed me in the process, and I have been fighting at our king's side ever since."

She paused, but Gerana said nothing as they walked, sun streaming in and bathing them in warmth for a moment.

"I will continue to fight for him, as long as I am able," Miara continued, softer now. "I owe him everything."

"Well, that explains it." Gerana was nodding now,

although still frowning.

"Explains what?"

"How you attracted him."

"You say that like I had some scheme to gain the throne, and nothing could be farther from the truth," Miara said harshly.

Gerana smiled at her now. "I know. And it puts my mind at ease. Forgive the phrasing, force of habit." She waved her hand as if shooing away a leaf on the wind. "But you must tell me more—these slaves. Something must be done."

Miara's eyes widened. "These *mage* slaves?"

"Yes."

"Surely as a priestess of Nefrana you might have some... *opinions* about the use of magic. You've quite deftly avoided outlining them so far. I can't say I blame you as you stare down a king and future queen clearly on one side of the debate, but..."

"But what?"

"But I would rather know your true opinion and respect it than deal in lies."

Gerana's jaw clenched. "The church's opinion on... mages... is evolving," she said haltingly.

"You can do better than that."

Gerana raised an eyebrow. "You're even more straightforward than he is."

Miara smiled mischievously. "Straightforward, frank, blunt, lacking in subtlety... I think I will choose to take that as a compliment."

"My personal opinion is not terribly relevant," Gerana said. "The official stance of our church is weighed by six separate temples, each with varying exposure to mages and the Devoted. Here in Panar, I have the benefit of seeing many different types of people. Some of the more remote temples may not even hear of this war until it is nearly over. Our Panaran temple also has the greatest, oldest library of any of the city's temples, even those temples to Anara and Mastikos."

"What does that have to do with anything?"

"We have records that date back before the Dark Days. Personal accounts. Journals. Illustrations. The accounts of the Dark Days themselves vary wildly, but if you go back far enough, there are accounts of mages of great faith and service. I have read some of them myself."

Miara frowned. "Mages who abstained from using their magic, you mean?"

"No," Gerana said quickly. "They specifically recount using it in the goddess's name. Alongside something they called the holy connection."

Now Miara did not know what to say. If only Sefim were here. "I've never heard of that before in my life."

Gerana waved it off. "My point is, the church's stance has been evolving for decades, centuries even, and it continues to evolve. My personal opinion is I do not know what to believe. I don't presume to know Nefrana's will *ever*, except when she speaks through my conscience, through guilt, through kindness and charity. I do know that the future queen who stands in front of me has already bestowed remarkable acts of kindness on the Akarian people. And I also know my conscience clearly says enslaving anyone is wrong, and it is our duty to help them."

Miara stopped abruptly and smiled at Gerana, who looked startled. "You are a refreshing change of pace, you know that? When you take the straightforward route."

Gerana smiled back tentatively. "Thank you. I think?"

Miara nodded and began walking again, this time back toward the court hall. It was high time she returned to Aven's side. "We are working hard already to free slaves. Progress has been slow to nonexistent. Our techniques are limited, but it's better than the nothing we had this time last year." Miara shrugged. "I do not know how this war will go, but I hope it brings an end to it all."

Nodding sternly, Gerana stared down at the marble. "I don't suppose there is much my temple can do to help."

"You can follow our orders and send any willing mages to me. You can support our king and his war. And me."

"There was no question of that."

That had certainly not been clear from her first words, but Miara didn't doubt it now. Why the word games, though? Maybe someday—decades from now—Miara would understand how these people worked. But for now, her first altercation seemed to have gone rather well. Had it been too easy? Miara had employed about as much subtlety as a battering ram. If she caught people off guard with blunt frankness, perhaps that was a courtly game in and of itself. In fact, now that she thought about it, Aven and his parents had used it quite often, even on her. Verbal ambushes. Maybe Miara wasn't as out of her element as she'd thought.

"I will keep your interest in helping in mind and advise the king to do the same," Miara promised. "Anything you can do to ease the stigma against mages would be a boon. I have heard rumors your Third Temple is more friendly with the Devoted than you seem to be."

The priestess paled. "You can't be serious."

"It may be only rumors. But it would certainly earn my gratitude if such collusion were stamped out."

"I will speak with Ediama and do what must be done."

Miara smiled as sweetly as she could. "Thank you for suggesting this walk, Priestess Gerana. It has been very thought provoking. And pleasant. And good for the blood." While awkwardly stitched together, Miara thought that wasn't a terrible attempt at courtly etiquette.

Gerana smiled and bowed, more deeply than before. "My sentiments as well, Arms Master. I will not keep you from your betrothed's side any longer. Good day to you."

"And to you as well."

As Gerana led Miara away, Aven had to wonder if this was some kind of concerted effort by the holy women of Nefrana because, of course, Priestess Ediama stepped up next. He'd sent a stern warning to the Third Temple, also known as the Matron's Tears, reminding them that working with the Devoted to kidnap or kill people was completely unacceptable, not to mention against the law. It would not be tolerated.

He didn't know if they'd take heed. They might not understand the force of his conviction until the unit he'd left in charge of the matter had to arrest someone.

If any of this ruffled Ediama—or had even reached her ears—she showed no sign. She smiled and curtsied gracefully, radiating warmth, but also power. Young to be high priestess, she had always been a dark beauty, her olive skin and long, curling, black hair striking against the white robes of Nefrana. Somehow she had managed to finagle an audience with Aven every time he'd visited Ranok. All four of them. Not an easy thing to do.

"Priestess Ediama," he said, giving the slightest bow and head nod in return. "How have you fared?"

"Your Highness," she said a little too grandly. Her wide smile never slipped. "Congratulations on your ascent to the kingship."

He blinked, then nodded again. "Thank you. How fares the Third Temple?"

"As Nefrana wills us," she said dreamily.

His expression had hardened each time she'd spoken, and he glared now. "Does Nefrana will you into the arms of the Devoted?"

She tilted her head, feigning confusion while her smile remained firmly affixed. "Is this about that nasty rumor? Must we talk about such nonsense on such a momentous occasion?"

"Rumor or no, I'm happy to remind you of Akarian law."

"Of *course*, Your Highness."

Don't roll your eyes, don't roll your eyes. "I'm also happy to enforce it," he said, the edge in his voice so hard he could've sliced with it. She had by no means denied anything.

"Of course, Your Highness."

Just how nonsensical of a statement could he utter and still get her to respond the same patronizing way? He was tempted to try it, but it likely wasn't the best way to assert his authority as a new king. When he was gray in the beard, he could try stunts like that. If he lived that long. Still, he couldn't crush the desire to punch through that smiling façade to the truth of her. He sighed. Maybe he *did* prefer Estun to this courtly sort of life, dark cavern or no.

"Did you know I recently had a run-in with the Devoted myself?" he said slowly, hoping to catch her off guard.

And indeed, her smile faltered. "N-no, Your Highness. I have heard no such news."

"Of course. You are one of the select few I'm sharing it with." He smiled even as he wanted to roll his eyes at himself now. That technique might turn his stomach, but it worked. "I had the misfortune of tangling with them in the Gilaren forest, not long ago."

"Oh my," she breathed. If her mix of concerned and impressed was an act, it was quite a good one. She flopped one hand over her heart. "Was anyone injured?"

"They were. All of them." He eyed her hard, and she simply returned his stare, unsure how to respond. "So you see, this Devoted thing is personal. Listen. I know you may have mixed opinions on mages. Even within the temples of Nefrana, I know there are differences in thought on what the goddess approves and does not approve. But I'm a mage, and this is war. Dozens if not hundreds of mages are headed to our doorstep."

Her eyes widened, but she remained frozen.

He lowered his voice. "You don't have to agree with me. But if you want to survive this war with Kavanar, you better make sure *no one* in your temple is persecuting mages. Or working with the Devoted in any way. If I find out they are, I will hold *you* personally responsible. Understand?"

"Of course. Your Highness."

He would have laughed at the same words again, but her tone had sobered and was now more frightened than smooth and buttery. Something about the words "if you want to survive" tended to get people's attention. "If you hear of any mages, I want them sent to Ranok, to the future queen, as the proclamation said."

Ediama glanced around, the sweet-fake smile tentatively returning. "Is she in attendance, sire? I had hoped I would meet her here."

"If you don't like mages, you won't like her any more than me."

The priestess grinned broadly, almost patronizing. "Your Highness, I never said—"

He had no interest being lied to. He cut her off. "Ah,

there she is," he said, gesturing to the back of the hall. "She's just returned from taking a stroll with Priestess Gerana."

For some reason, her brow crinkled at the sight. Didn't like a priestess so familiar with a mage? Some kind of competition for favor or dominance?

"Ah, yes, I see them," she said sweetly. "Sire, you have many others waiting to attend you. Before I take my leave, I did have two requests for you. Well, questions really. Your Highness."

"Yes?"

"King Samul had been planning to support a winter feast in two month's time for the orphans at the Matron's Tears. And for the widows of Panar. Can I still count on your support?"

"Of course." Assuming the city still stood and the war hadn't utterly ruined the kingdom financially by then. He hoped he could assume those things, but he decided not to mention them. This time. He'd scared her enough. "And the other request?"

"One of my priestesses was at a royal function and has not returned. Do you happen to know the whereabouts of Priestess Niat? I've seen soldiers searching the city, but they'll never tell us anything about what they're searching for or if they found it."

He frowned. Could he trust her with news of Thel's kidnapping? Was there any reason to keep such a thing a secret? The guards kept confidence as a manner of protocol, but the woman did deserve to know where her priestess was. And she was probably with Thel, although he certainly didn't know for sure.

"She is a seer, sire, of great power. Her talents are just beginning to develop. I'm concerned for her health outside of the temple. And she could be of great use to you in the war I'm sure in predicting future movements of your enemies." The last bit sounded tacked on, as if she was scraping for a reason to motivate him to bother looking for Niat. Well, perhaps that was fair. He hadn't been concerned about her until now, only his brother.

"A seer? What has she predicted?"

"Only small things so far. She is just beginning, as I've said, and it's been a rocky start for her. I've heard…" She shook her head.

"What? What have you heard?"

Ediama looked down at his feet, no longer smiling. She let out the words grudgingly, although nothing seemed to drain the dreamy, almost sickly sweet quality of her voice. "I've heard she predicted seeing a city fall. Walls and roofs in flames. I didn't want to believe it. I've also heard rumors her father made a deal to marry her off and move her to Gilaren in spite of her vows to our temple."

"Gilaren?" said Aven slowly.

"Yes, the rumors said— Perhaps they involved some sort of deal with Lord Alikar."

"Lord Alikar is already married."

"I know, sire. As you can see I have multiple reasons for being concerned, or I wouldn't have bothered you. I'm sure your time is more valuable than this, but—"

"She may be with my brother Thel, who has been

kidnapped by Lord Alikar. Alikar has also been charged with treason, you might be interested to know."

She caught her breath. "Treason, sire?"

"He tried to bribe two other Assembly members with Kavanarian gold."

"Oh, no. And you think Niat might be with them?"

"She was near them during the attack on the tower, after the function she attended. Her body wasn't found among the rubble, and neither was Thel's. I know Thel is with the Kavanarians, but we weren't looking for signs of her specifically."

"Surely you will send men to—"

"We have," he said slowly, his voice darkening. "The unit we sent was wiped out. We are currently devising another strategy." That sounded better than saying they had no idea what the hell they were going to do.

She stared, mouth open now. "Wiped out...? How? By whom?"

"By twenty Kavanarian mages, who burned our brave men and women alive."

She went nearly as pale as her robes.

"So you'll see why I am deadly serious about my first topic, Priestess. No Devoted. No persecution of mages. It is truly a matter of life and death that we find more to join our ranks."

"I understand, sire," she said very softly now.

"I will let you know if we learn anything of Niat. But I wouldn't count on it. This war is bigger than one seer, or even one prince. Even if he is my brother. We've turned our efforts to the broader war for now. And you will let me know if you discover any mages. Deal?"

"Of course, Your Highness." Her eyes were staring blankly off in thought as she floated away, and the next fine soul stepped up.

Thel dashed into the woods, the wound in his leg aching. The *thunk* of arrows told him a tree to his right had taken the hits meant for them. Their feet crunched loudly in the packed, cold snow. Niat seemed to have gotten her legs under her and was moving faster now, and he was dragging her less, and he was almost tempted to let her go and trust her to run with him. But not yet. She hadn't tried to wrench herself away either, so he took that as a good sign.

He darted toward the densest patch of trees he could find, zigzagging, pulling her along. Another good reason not to let go—she wouldn't know any tricks to help evading arrows, and they could get separated if she tried. If they could just get a little farther into the—

Something hit his right knee, then swung around and hit his left, suddenly yanking them together.

He went down, letting go of her immediately and cursing as he went. Frantically he went for his knees—a simple leather bola had hit him and was tangled there, incapacitating him all too efficiently.

"Go, Niat," he shouted. "Keep going."

She took a few steps further into the trees, but she didn't run. She was stopping. What was she looking *at*?

Only at the last second did he hear footsteps and look up to see Alikar before the young lord fell on him. He reached for the rocks on the chain ends, but too late. Alikar's fist slammed into Thel's face, sending him seeing stars. He lost his grip on the stone—and his magic entirely.

By instinct more than thought, Thel lunged for Alikar's throat, his cloak to choke him with, anything, but Alikar caught the arm and twisted, pulling, flipping Thel onto his stomach and wrenching the arm up behind Thel's back.

He caught hold of one of the chain stones and flung it at Alikar, but the lord ducked as he brought a vicious elbow down between Thel's shoulder blades, splintering his concentration. Pain stopped all rational thought. Alikar's weight sank into him, pinning him down.

Thel tried to heave him off and grabbed for the stone again—or for the earth below him—or anything, but Alikar seemed to have him figured out. A fist dug deep into Thel's kidney, then another collided with his face, stealing away every chance at a thought. Alikar caught his other wrist; the chains attached to the shackles made that all too easy. He held Thel's wrists fast, shoving them viciously into the small of his back.

"You poor thing," Alikar said slowly. "Almost kidnapped by a mage."

"Better than kidnapped by you!" Thel shouted, getting snow in his mouth and viciously spitting it out.

Alikar ignored him. "I'm sure he just dragged you

along. You didn't actually *want* to leave us. Did you."

"Of course not," said Niat's voice smoothly. He heard the sound of a small tin opening, then closing slowly. "But I was afraid he'd crush me. Like he did Detrax." Her voice was different, slow, almost languid. He'd never heard it like that, and a pang went through him, of irritation, of anger, of what?

"*Crush* you!" Thel shouted again, more than a little indignant and not caring any more at this point. "How could you—"

"Shut up, mage, you're not a part of this conversation," growled Alikar, jerking his arms higher. His shoulders split with pain. Thel bit off his scream, but just barely.

"Is Detrax going to be all right?" she said softly. As if she cared. Why was she pretending to care?

"Not likely. Now show me your loyalty. Take that weapon and tie this murderer's hands."

"Even with the shackles?"

"Clearly they were not enough."

Without objection, Niat moved to his legs, untangled the stupid, stupid weapon, and proceeded to bind his hands behind him. He glared at the snow, even if she couldn't see him. "That's what I get for bringing you with me. See if I try to save *you* next time."

Niat said nothing. Alikar laughed darkly and rose off him. Then he was hauling him up to sitting against a tree trunk. He pointed a finger in Thel's face. "You, like your brother, are more trouble than you appear."

"What's that supposed to mean? You don't like that

your little halfwit brain can't figure out why we keep beating you?"

"Who's beating whom now?" said Alikar calmly, propping his hands on his hips. "All that, and I brought you down with a strip of leather. Pathetic."

Thel glowered at him. "At least I still have my honor. At least I'm no *traitor*. At least I can sleep soundly at night knowing I never sold out my country to a corrupt, greedy pack of wolves for an extra chest of silver."

"It was far more than one chest of silver. But that's not the point. The point is, you mages will never rule Akaria. I'd rather have Kavanar as my masters than freaks of nature who must be cleansed. You'll see. History will remember me as keeping *Akaria's* honor. As saving our land from corruption."

"History will look back on you with nothing but disgust," Thel spat.

"When I am king of Akaria, you will eat your words. *If* I let you live to see the day."

"Is that what you think you're getting out of all this? Please. Kavanar wants Akaria for itself. Why would they keep *you*?"

"Because I can make the lords listen to me."

"Like you did with Asten and Toyl?"

Alikar cuffed him across the face.

When the stars cleared, Thel met Alikar's gaze head-on. "And Beneral? You really convinced—"

The young lord raised his hand again, and Thel flinched this time—a tough guy, he was not—but Niat eased closer suddenly.

Alikar stopped, drawn by her presence. She floated up to him, a delicate, glowing ghost of white against the snow, the dark pines. Her lips seemed impossibly red and full and luscious, like ripe cherries from the height of summertime that had somehow been tossed amid the snow. Reaching Alikar, she slowly placed her hand on his chest, and then ran it lower, drifting down his abdomen. Along the belt that held his dagger.

Before her hand could near the blade, Alikar lowered his hand and placed it over hers, stopping it.

"You've already captured him, my lord. Waste no more of your energy on this pathetic prince," she said, voice smooth and honeyed.

Alikar frowned, as if unsure what to make of her words or her hands.

"Detrax has not left us alone for even a minute." She lowered her eyes.

A chill shot through Thel's veins, but he couldn't tear his eyes away from the way Alikar's gaze sharpened on her, the slow way she looked up at him through her eyelashes.

"True," Alikar said, his voice rough. "But Detrax is not here, is he."

"No, he is not." She smiled slightly. "And he's not likely to be anytime soon."

Thel squirmed, both inside and out. Seizing Niat with his other arm, Alikar spun her away as though she was no more substantial than a feather, utterly forgetting Thel.

Gods, let him have interpreted that exchange wrong.

Let him have seen something that wasn't really there. Let him—

The sound of a soft gasp from Niat to his left made him lose a bit of hope. He tried to resist but eventually glanced over. Alikar had drawn Niat under the cove created by the branches of a large pine and sunk to a seat with his back to the trunk. He was pulling the priestess down over him.

"Aren't you *already* married?" Thel snapped.

"Shut up, mage." Alikar sounded highly pleased with himself. Thel gritted his teeth.

"Some holy man you are," Thel grumbled. And he tried to look every which way but there, as the sounds reaching his ears told him he had not imagined anything.

She was *kissing* that traitor with those impossible cherry lips.

The cold forest air was mockingly fresh and smelled of pine boughs and churned-up soil and wide-open wilderness. He had never been terribly enthusiastic about hunts with Dom, but this is what they smelled like. He should have taken them a little less for granted. He heaved a sigh. What else can you do when you're captured and tied up *again*? How many weeks was he going to spend this way? Certainly he'd count it in weeks. They'd either kill him or he'd get away before it got to a year. Wouldn't it? He gritted his teeth and squirmed again, grumbling to himself.

"Must we have an audience?" murmured Niat, as if put out by his sighing and grumbling.

"Fine, fine." Alikar lurched to his feet, withdrew some misshapen cloth lump from his satchel, and pulled it over Thel's head.

Thel rolled his eyes to himself. Well, this was *just* excellent. Now instead of pine boughs and snow, he got to smell Alikar's sweat. A magnificent turn of events.

Alikar plopped back down with a thud, and the mouth noises resumed, and Thel restrained a need to roll his eyes again. It was benefiting no one at this point, not even him. He should be figuring a way out of this. He wriggled a bit, but try as he might, the knots Niat had tied remained snug against his wrists.

He gave up for now and relaxed against the tree trunk. Nothing met his ears but the sound of water flowing somewhere, dripping, wind whispering in the swaying trees, and an occasional bird that was long overdue to fly to Farsa or somewhere warmer.

Nothing. Hmm. Weren't the sounds of infidelity and betrayal supposed to get louder, not quieter? He wasn't very experienced in love, but he knew *that* much.

The silence stretched on, and Thel sighed. Maybe they'd left him here. That's what he got for trying to do something noble—or at least decent. A slow, bitter cold to seep into his bones until he froze to death. Alone.

7 TRANSLATIONS

Niat crouched quietly in front of the mage prince and studied him, now that she had a moment to herself. He'd faired moderately well in their captivity, with one wound partially healed Detrax-style in his thigh and another near his shoulder, but overall he could be much worse for the wear than he was. He didn't look nearly as dirty as she was. The lump in his throat bobbed as he swallowed, and she had to admit it was oddly interesting.

He was a strange combination of masculine grace and lanky awkwardness. If she let herself be honest for a moment, it was a little endearing. For a mage. She'd spent so much of her life only around women, aside from her father, and Peluna had kept her at a protective distance from men as often as possible, either isolating her completely or playing a barrier in their presence. Guards and soldiers had more bulky frames than this mage. She hadn't known many like him. Maybe none.

He was an intelligent fellow, too, with more words than he knew what to do with.

She took one more precious moment to drink him in, to study him and what made him tick, corruption and all. Of course, that corruption had just bought her some measure of temporary freedom. Having all the cards in her control was quite the luxury. It likely wouldn't last long.

Why had he chosen to take her with him?

Failing to think of any answer to that, she moved on to what to do next. What options did she have? They were all bad. Go back to the fortress, or follow this mage wherever he had intended to go. If he even had a plan. She certainly didn't.

She glanced at Alikar's body in the snow, then back at the fortress. Detrax would not recover from Thel's deluge of rock, but someone else might send pursuers soon. And those men would find what she'd done. They would catch her and the mage one way or another. They were simply at too much of a disadvantage and too unprepared out here in the snow.

If defeat was assured, what did it matter what she did? She should simply go back. She was already shivering, in spite of taking Alikar's cloak. Temple gowns weren't intended for the wilderness, and bare flesh was not at all the ideal fashion for snowy expeditions.

They'd likely die out here.

Then again, if one of Alikar's or Detrax's minions catching her—and probably killing her—was inevitable, what *did* it matter what she did? She sat, basking in this brief moment of power, of freedom.

For this heartbeat, all the choices were hers.

Wasn't that what Sister Ireie was always muttering at her? "The goddess judges your choices, girl, and don't you forget it." Niat had often just shaken her head, truly not understanding. When you've seen the future, and seen your visions come to pass, it was not so simple. What difference did choice make then? What difference did it make to the goddess if, in some way, her choice was already made? Though one question haunted Niat. Was it possible for the visions *not* to come to pass? Sister Ireie could not answer that question. No one could, save another seer, and there weren't any. If others had known the answer, none of them had written it down.

On the other hand, she didn't *always* know what would come to pass. She'd seen this young man in her future, but what did that tell her? That death wasn't tomorrow, perhaps, but not much else. He could be in her future if they were recaptured or if they somehow escaped. The latter seemed beyond impossible, but…

She still had to choose.

She knelt beside him and untied his wrists.

He jumped at her touch. She must have approached more quietly than she'd thought. As soon as one hand was free, he whipped the cloth off his head and stared at her, wild-eyed.

He had nice eyes. Pale blue like the sky above the ocean before a storm. Nice for a corrupt abomination that would horrify the gods, of course. But her mind's objection felt rote, hollow. Those nice eyes flicked their gaze to Alikar and widened.

He opened his mouth to say something, but shouts rose up from near the fortress. They both squinted into the distance.

"They're coming after us," he growled and climbed to his feet. "Let's get out of here."

"Wait." She dashed to Alikar, pulled his satchel out from under him, pushing him off it with her foot. She swung it over her shoulder as she raced after the mage. To her surprise, he'd listened to her hasty command and stood tensely until she reached him.

"This way," he said softly, turning toward the sound of water. She followed. Weaving in and out of pines, they reached a narrow stream and jumped across it. "Ideally we'd wade up it," he said as they kept jogging, "but we don't have the boots for that. We'll freeze."

"We'll likely freeze anyway," she muttered.

"Have I ever told you what a ray of sunshine you are?"

She shot a glare at him, but to her surprise, he was smiling. "Is that any way to treat someone who just untied you? I could have left you in the snow, you know."

He eyed her. And to her surprise, he did not point out that she wouldn't have had the opportunity if he hadn't freed himself and dragged her with him in the first place. "Is he dead?" he said instead.

"Yes." If Alikar weren't dead already, he would be any moment now. She pressed her lips together, refusing to meet his gaze. Finally, she set her jaw and glanced at him. He was staring hard at her, but she couldn't read the expression. "What? Don't judge me. He was going to kill us. Well, you. I may as well be dead already. Priestess or no, I know I shouldn't know how to kill people, and I shouldn't do it even if I do know how. But the world should be a lot of ways, and it isn't."

"Keep your voice down," he whispered.

She rolled her eyes and jogged forward more quickly.

"I wasn't thinking any of that," he said between breaths, so soft she barely heard him.

"Well. What were you thinking?" Perhaps he had some other clever angle to judge her by.

"I was thinking I'm glad he got what he deserved, even if I couldn't give it to him." He watched the ground at his feet carefully now, checking where he was going. "I'm glad he can't betray anyone else."

Oh. Not judging, then. Approving? They walked along in silence, boots crunching in the snow and the whistling wind carrying distant shouts. She quickened her pace again. The trees grew thicker, and the shouts quieter as they made their way deeper into the forest. She wrapped the cloak around her tighter. The press of more and more evergreens was reassuring in that it hid them better from those who might pursue them, but the air also grew colder, wetter. More dangerous.

"I don't hear any more shouting, do you?"

She shook her head, slowing to a walk and turning to look back for a moment. "I'm sure they're still coming. But I don't see anything."

"Maybe they went a different direction. Or they found Alikar and had to deal with him."

They both said nothing for another while, walking more slowly now. She strained her ears, but he was right. She couldn't hear them. The forest was simply a few foolish birds and the wind. So quiet, in fact, it made her nervous.

"You were injured," she blurted. "Detrax leaves a mean mark."

His gaze snapped back to her. "You know about that personally?" His voice held a dangerous edge, one she hadn't heard before.

"Injuries don't encourage visions. But I am not unfamiliar with them."

"When? While we were in their dungeon?"

"Just one. I don't think he could help himself. But he seemed to believe me more about my vision than about the bluebell." She hesitated. "There was another time, when he worked for my father. That's when my governess gave me the Devoted stone. To help me spot people like him."

"Oh."

Silence settled around them again, restless and tense. "For what it's worth, I'm glad he got what he deserved too. Even if I couldn't give it to him."

He pressed his lips together in something that wasn't quite a smile—it probably wasn't appropriate to smile when receiving thanks for murder—but he did seem gratified.

"I'm glad to see some measure of justice before we die out here."

"We are *not* going to die out here," he said firmly.

"Oh, I don't see how you can be so sure of that. What, are you getting visions now?"

"No. But we haven't seen Anonil yet. And I think it still stands, based on what I heard. Didn't you say you saw it fall? You'll apparently live at least that long."

She didn't point out that it was entirely possible for her to see things that could happen after her death. In this case, he was right. He was in the vision. Talking to her. The two of them *must* make it that far at least. "True," she conceded. "But nothing says they don't catch us again."

"Guess we'll find out. Does it get annoying, not knowing?"

"What?"

"Well, I'd think I'd want to know everything. If some part of the future can be known, why not all of it? Can't you just look through the rest of your life? I would want to. I always prefer to know as much as possible."

She shook her head. "I don't want to know any of it. I've had enough sickness for one lifetime. I'd love to go a day eating and keeping it all down. Or choose food not based on what it might taste like coming back up." She shivered.

He crinkled his nose at her, and she dropped her gaze to the forest floor.

"What? You asked," she muttered.

"No, no. I just… It's a shame you have to bear that burden."

They walked for a moment in silence. She listened for the sounds of pursuers but didn't hear anything. Odd, receiving sympathy from a mage. "Well, you have your own burden. So I suppose you understand."

"Hmm?" He was eying the terrain around them, searching. "Magic?"

He shrugged. "Oh, it's no burden. I only found out about it a week or two ago. Lost track at this point. But it's a fairly recent development."

"Ah. So if you'd known about it your whole life, you'd have busted out of there earlier? No pleasant cutting?"

He snorted. "I was waiting for you."

"What?"

"I was waiting till I knew where you were. So we could get out together."

Fool. They could have killed him. Her heart pounded a little faster. "Why?"

"Well, it hardly seemed decent to just leave you there. Especially with those blue vials in play." He shuddered.

She frowned down at the ground, unsure what to make of this knowledge. He'd waited for her. He'd made sure she got free too. Very, very foolish of him. He might have lost his chance to escape, she might have been shipped away from the fortress never to be seen again, and likely they'd just be recaptured anyway. It did make her feel a little better about dispatching Alikar with a poisoned kiss, though. Now she and this mage were quite even.

How strange that he'd tried to help her. Wanted to. Looked out for her. As a matter of course, not out of any particular interest, or at least so he claimed. And he'd done it all after she'd treated him with fear and wariness. A sudden, unexpected wave of guilt hit her; he'd been so kind, and she'd been nothing but cold, judgmental, maybe even cruel. Once, she had thought Peluna had been similarly caring and generous, but now that withdrawal had kicked in, it seemed doubtful. Just another agenda, another plan in which Niat had been but a tool.

Her mouth felt dry at the thought of those blue vials, and she rummaged in Alikar's satchel for a bottle or skin. Nothing. Of course. Horrible man. Her shivering was continuous now.

Thel was still inspecting the forest around them, scanning for something.

"What are you looking for?" she asked.

"We need some way to get out of this snow. We're leaving a perfect path for them to follow, even if they're terrible at tracking. We may be faster than them. But I'd prefer to throw them off our path."

She nodded. That was good thinking. A cliffside loomed ahead, and trees all around them, but none thick enough to have blocked much snow.

He stopped short and rubbed his chin, his blond stubble giving him a more rugged look than the day they'd met. His eyes were on the cliffside. "Are you... afraid of small spaces?"

Her eyes widened as she followed his gaze. The earth itself began to move.

Miara awoke the next morning with the same splitting headache as the day before, and now she knew for sure that something was wrong. Her dreams had again been fitful and confining, as though she'd been trapped in them. She ached down to her bones, and the dizziness that hit her when she sat up was as bad as when she'd woken up in one of Regin's tents after healing Galen. Except she hadn't been doing anything nearly that intense.

This time, she managed not to groan—aloud, anyway— and surveyed her surroundings. Could it be something in the room? The too-fine bed? The perfume or incense? The air was heavily scented with flowers, vibrant with roses and orange-blossom oil. But she wouldn't have suspected any of it would give her such a headache.

She slipped silently out of bed. She could hear her attendants in the next room, but she wasn't ready for any of that foolishness yet. She crept toward a soft robe lying across an armchair near the fire. Perhaps a few minutes curled up away from that monster of a bed and the pain would go away.

As she pulled the robe on, however, she stilled at the sound of a man's voice. A man other than Aven likely shouldn't be in the queen's rooms, socializing with attendants while she slept, servant on business or not. She listened harder.

"The knight's rumors were right," said a quiet voice. Miara would have recognized the stiff, proper tone anywhere—Opia. "To think, of all the women, he's chosen a mage. And a commoner. To be *queen* of Akaria. Sleeping in my lady's chambers even now. I had to see it with my own eyes to believe it."

"A true travesty," said a man's voice in a patronizing tone.

Miara silently stepped toward the door. If there was any part of palace life she was made for, eavesdropping was it. Lucky her.

Her attendant huffed. "And now with the king ill, that fool boy has free rein, so there's no one to stop him. We certainly can't appeal to *him* as to the inappropriateness of this choice." The outrage in the woman's voice would have colored Miara's cheeks red if she weren't already red with anger. Who by the gods was Opia to judge?

"So I have your support then?"

Opia sighed. Dishes clinked delicately against each other, then a wooden tray. Footsteps moved softly closer. "Fine, I'll…"

They were approaching the door. Miara backed away, sweeping as silently as a mouse across the floor as she dove back into bed, squeezing her eyes shut and pulling the covers up over her head. The dive didn't do much for the pounding in her head or the dizziness. She felt like the bed was spinning while someone was pounding a hammer on the back of her skull.

Barely a moment later, the door opened, and one pair of footsteps shuffled in.

Miara gritted her teeth, thankful to hide under the white fluff of the bed. What had she just overheard? Certainly the woman had never acted like she approved of Miara, but that had sounded like they were conspiring to do something much worse. But what?

Miara strained her ears, listening. Opia sat the tray

down next to the bed, just the kind she carried the tea on, and Miara braced herself to be woken up.

But there was nothing for a long moment, only silence. A spoon tinkled in the teacup, someone stirring. Then she marched back toward the main doors, opening them, and other footsteps joined the ruckus as she began her chirping. "Up, up! Time to wake and go about the business of ruling a kingdom!"

The sickly sweet cheerfulness of her voice suddenly sounded more sarcastic than prim. Miara opened her eyes immediately but pretended to slowly rise, stretching and yawning widely. The tea sat on the table just in front of her, and she seized the cup and took a sip, glad for something to hide behind. She wasn't sure she could keep the anger from her voice at the moment.

After three large gulps, the pain in her head suddenly lessened.

She stared down at the tea. She'd connected the headaches to her work around the city, but they'd also started when she'd moved to these rooms.

And taken on these new attendants.

She scowled at the back of Opia's head without thinking, and so she had to quickly hide her expression when the woman spun around, ready to pontificate.

Opia faltered; apparently Miara hadn't hidden her glare *quite* fast enough. "The, uh, the king would like to see you in the library at your earliest convenience, my lady."

Miara leapt to her feet, her stomach twisting. The library could only mean one thing.

Tharomar must be done with the star map.

Miara grabbed a dress almost without looking just as Etral was arriving with two bowls of dumplings. Miara couldn't help but eye them with both suspicion and longing. Etral caught the wariness in her look, though, and the girl's eyes widened. Miara forced a smile. Neither Etral nor Kalan seemed like the type to be in on whatever Opia was doing. And they didn't seem to show Opia any particular loyalty either.

"Mushroom dumplings and blueberry dumplings, my lady," she said, voice wavering.

"Thank you, Etral," Miara said, thrusting her arbitrarily chosen dress at the girl.

A shame. Mushroom sounded delicious right about now, and of course she couldn't eat any of that. She needed to get out of the room, talk to Aven.

While she numbly went through the steps to ready herself for the day, most of her mind was carefully scanning her body, looking for whatever had been in the tea. While she couldn't heal any effects a poison or drug might have, she could certainly identify them. And there *was* something odd, something dull about the way her brain lurched and her blood pumped, like she was drunk on too much ale.

The voices had mentioned a knight. She clenched her jaw but tried not to let her tension show. If they were trying to kill her, there wasn't anywhere near enough in her system—yet—to do that. Unless they were counting on the dumplings, which would be a good bet considering the number she'd inhaled the day before. But they might be simply trying to knock her unconscious, which she might be closer to. Either way, something needed to be done. The question was what?

She was relieved to discover the dress she'd blindly grabbed was serviceable—simple and gray, its belt studded with sapphires. After a victorious fight for a simple bun and actually warm shoes, she turned to Etral. "I know the king would like to see me as soon as possible in the library, but would you please tell him I'd like him to come here to escort me? I wish to have a few words with him first."

"Of course, my lady," Etral said, curtsying as she set off for the library.

Miara slid into the nearest soft chair. The headache had totally faded now, and if it weren't for her magic's sense of the drug lingering in her system, she'd have thought things were very normal. She glanced at the table. A rooks and pawns game sat abandoned halfway through, its pieces in grim contrast, some made of bone, others of walnut. It was an ancient game of strategy. Idly, she reset the board to the beginning of play and then stared off at the flowers, the fire, waiting, before an idea occurred to her.

Aven finally appeared in the wide entry bathed in blue and green light. He tilted his head and frowned.

"Come sit with me for a moment," she said, giving him a calm smile.

"They're waiting for us," he said slowly, but he seemed to suspect something because he started forward.

This morning, one of my attendants drugged my tea, she said to him silently.

To his credit, he didn't falter, his eyes only widening slightly. "But perhaps we have time for a quick game. You first?" He slid into the chair opposite her, one eyebrow raised. *What? Which one? Are you all right?*

I'm mostly recovered. I'll be fine. I think they were working up to a larger dose. She yawned and made a simple, predictable move on the board. *It was that one—Opia.* She flicked her eyes in the woman's direction.

He eyed the board, moved his piece in response, then glanced around the room casually. *The one hovering closest?*

Yes. Coincidence? I think not. Speaking silently still, she detailed her mysterious headaches and the conversation she'd overheard that morning.

I'm calling the captain of the guard; we're putting a stop to this now.

No—wait. How will we flush out whoever the man was? Or what if someone in the kitchens was helping her? Besides, I noticed this drug. I'll notice if they do it again.

They could try something else and take you freshly by surprise.

Not if we act like nothing's changed, like they're getting away with it. This way, I can just not drink the tea.

Or eat or drink anything, really, if Opia goes near it. Which is everything. How long can you keep that up? And won't they notice?

She sighed. *Maybe. But I'd still feel better if we could track down the Opia's partner first. Give it a day. We can watch her and wait until they meet again.*

And if they don't? I don't want to put you in unnecessary danger. We'll find another way to flush him out, or maybe seeing his partner imprisoned will scare him away.

It's just one day, and we might find out—

No, Miara. She felt a flash of emotion swirl through him, hot and frantic—a mixture of regret, worry, rage, fear. She raised her eyebrows at the strength of his reaction and faltered before she set down the next game piece in a new location. *Sorry. It's just... I tried "wait and see" with Alikar. With Evana. And look how that turned out. No more waiting.* He absently set down another piece, watching her all the while.

I can understand that, but... She frowned, then glanced down at his latest move and stopped short.

"You... won," she said. Oddly, her shoulders drooped, actually defeated.

"Miara, I— Wait, what?"

"Look at the pieces. See? You won."

He scowled down at them too, then looked up. *This isn't about winning or losing. I just want you to be safe.*

I know.

You could use your magic, couldn't you? Maybe if she thinks of her coconspirator, we can find out that way. Or Perik seems trustworthy. Maybe he can poke around.

She sighed. *All right. You win. On both counts. But rifling through her thoughts when they're so often ill of me sounds painful. Maybe one of the others can?*

Of course. They both rose, and he stepped closer, putting a gentle hand on her shoulder and frowning in concern.

His thoughts were still close, and she could feel him searching for some way to console her, to ease her worry.

It's all right, she said silently, smiling. *You don't need to find the words. I understand.*

He squeezed her shoulder one time, and then managed, "I'm sure you'll win next time," for appearance's sake. And then they headed out, arm in arm. She let her thoughts linger, intertwined with his, hoping it'd make her feel better. Just outside her door, he stopped.

The four guards that were regularly posted there straightened ever so slightly as Aven turned toward them. "The arms master's tea was drugged this morning. Take her attendants and anyone else inside the suite to the dungeon for questioning."

"Yes, sire," said the nearest one. They turned as a unit and stormed in.

Miara's eyes widened as she hurried to follow Aven. He'd already turned to head down toward the library. *All of them?*

If Siliana or my mother is going to dip into their thoughts, might as well talk to them all. Better safe than sorry.

She knew he was right but couldn't keep herself from frowning. Etral was just a girl.

They'll be all right.

Their route took them past Samul's rooms, and Aven ducked inside to quietly explain the situation to Siliana. Miara took the moment to stop at Samul's side. It was hard to see him hurting and not feel she should do *something*. Anything. She laid a hand on his forehead and once again hoped the wounds would respond. Again, nothing happened.

Gradually she had the sense that someone was eying her. She looked around. A man with a hefty tome in his hands stood across from her. Watching her.

She stared him down.

He stared right back. A dozen heartbeats passed, and finally he glanced down at his book.

"Ready," Aven called just as Elise was returning and Siliana was heading out of the room. Miara cast one more long look at the man before following Aven out toward the library.

Who was that man?

That? Nyor, the healer.

He was staring at me.

Odd. Although you are *very lovely today, he doesn't seem like the type to gawk.*

Men don't gawk at me.

I do.

Just you. She found herself smiling as they reached the library, but her stomach sank as she remembered their purpose.

The star map.

A guard opened the door for the two of them. Wunik, Jaena, and Tharomar were crowded around a high library table. Otherwise, the cavernous room was empty, and it echoed as the door shut loudly behind her.

Wunik and Ro were muttering quietly to each other across the table from them, and Jaena eased slightly closer to Tharomar to make room for them around the table. Jaena smiled warmly at her, her dark eyes sliding over the dress. *I know, it's ridiculous, isn't it?* Miara said silently to Jaena alone. *I could feed a family for a year with this absurd finery.*

Jaena only grinned wider. *You look lovely. I wouldn't mind a dress or two like that someday. Oh, I know it's an adjustment, but is it such a terrible hardship? A worthy price to pay to get help freeing our people, is it not?*

If Jaena hadn't been smiling so warmly, Miara would have blushed. Instead, she spoke up, not eager to dwell on *that* particular topic. "So, is this all of us? Sorry to keep everyone waiting."

"It's no problem," said Tharomar, smiling.

Wunik was quickly scribbling some very twisted marks onto a nearby sheet of vellum. "It was a wonderful chance to interrogate him on Serabain, so it's quite all right with me."

"Shall I get started?" Tharomar's eyes flicked to Aven, who nodded. "Well, it's all done. I've made a complete copy here in modern Serabain, which is still a fairly esoteric language, but at least it's only one language and doesn't require any starlight to be read. However, you may prefer it were harder to decode when I tell you more about it."

Miara swallowed and shifted closer to Aven. She didn't like the sound of that.

Ro took the sheet of vellum in front of him. It was a bit longer than Miara's forearm, and he rotated it to face Aven, Jaena, and Miara. Wunik had apparently already gotten his fill; his eyes were dark and his brow creased heavily, which didn't ease the sinking feeling in her stomach in the slightest.

"I can confirm a lot of what you've guessed. The map is a combination astronomical map, calendar, and instructional tool. The stars mapped here are no different than any other map we'd keep these days, but it's the labels that are different. They have some modern names, and some seem to be older. Either that or they're another language entirely, one I can't translate, but I believe they're older names. Beside each name are listed what I can only guess are types of energies. Some aren't even all that surprising." He pointed at a large star drawn in green ink on his version. "The Muses as a whole are labeled 'ARTISTRY.' But some of them have seemingly unrelated labels. Anefin here, the prosperity star, is labeled with the word for 'REVELATION' or 'INSIGHT.' "

"I translated that as 'intellect.' Interesting," muttered Wunik, scribbling more notes.

"Maybe it's talking about insights that lead to prosperity?" said Jaena.

Tharomar shrugged. "Only way to find out is to test it, I suppose."

"About that," said Aven. "You said it's also an instructional tool. Could you find any other information on how to actually use these?"

He nodded. "Some, but it's slight. Included with some of them are some glyphs from a small set of pictograms used even before Serabain. Here with Casel we have a salve bowl in someone's palm, the ancient sign of—"

"Healing?" Aven guessed.

"Exactly," Tharomar said, continuing on briskly. "Anefin's, for better or worse, is a lightning bolt, which I believe is literal. Erepha shows the symbol of wind, and it's labeled 'CALM.'"

"What are these?" Aven pointed at a line that shot across the map in a lighter gray. Miara hadn't noticed it right away. "These aren't on the original."

"Actually, they are. But they only appear after over an hour under the stars, and even then, they're very faint. They appear to connect the stars in pairs, and that's, well, that's…" Tharomar pressed his lips together, considering what to say next. Up until that point the knowledge had come burbling out of him, as if he'd thought little of it except his excitement to share.

But Miara remembered the bit of the map Wunik *had* been able to translate. One word: SLAVERY.

Aven held his breath, waiting to hear this last piece. So much of this Aven had put together on his own, but some he hadn't been sure about.

Tharomar continued more slowly now, like he was sharing bad news. Aven doubted anything Tharomar found in this map could be worse than the news he'd been receiving over the last week. "These lines, they seem to indicate pairs of related energies. And while I've been pointing out some of the more positive labels, they aren't all so cheery. For example, Erepha here is linked to Sagus." He ran his finger along the thin, faint line from the blue star to a red one. "Sagus carries another wind symbol and is labeled something like 'ANGER.' But that's not a prefect translation. It's not just simple anger, it's a word they used sometimes for animals, sometimes for people, like wild or rabid, implying a loss of control."

"And Casel?" Aven said, urging him on.

Tharomar met his eyes for a long, appraising look. Aven waited, staring him down. Did the smith wonder what Aven planned to use this knowledge for? Truth be told, he didn't *have* a plan. More a gut instinct. All the more reason he needed to know every weapon they had inside and out.

When Tharomar spoke again, he kept his voice quiet and lower than ever. "It's connected to Masari. And its label reads 'SLAVERY.' "

"Slavery?" Jaena exclaimed, only remembering to keep her voice down near the end of the word. She clapped her fingers over her mouth. "What the—"

"I think this was the magic they used to create the brand, back in the Dark Days," Aven said.

"And why do we want to know about it?" Jaena shot back, alarmed.

"We need to understand it if we want to undo it," he replied just as quickly.

Jaena stopped, glaring back at the map and then at Aven. In fact, she and Miara were both leveling him the same wary, alarmed expression. When Aven looked back to Tharomar, he tried to ignore the fact that Wunik was eying him too.

"And the symbol?" Aven asked. He might have tried a few before he figured out the star was Masari, but he could have figured it out. The method to use the star's energy… that was what he knew the least about. What he'd had to guess at and reason through for Casel had eluded them for this. Although he hadn't exactly been running around experimenting to find out what might be right.

Tharomar's jaw tensed for a moment as his eyes flicked to Jaena and back to Aven. Then, after another long stare, his voice so quiet Aven almost couldn't hear him he said, "It's the symbol for fire."

Aven almost rolled his eyes. "Of *course* it is. Of course. By the gods, I should have guessed that."

"Why?" Miara asked.

"Because of the brand. That's how it works, through fire. And the energy of it." He shuddered, the feeling of the fiery maggots creeping back in until he shoved the image away.

"Through burns, in particular," Jaena pointed out.

"And you can heal the burn with Casel," Miara said quietly.

Tharomar nodded. "Yes. There are two other pairs. Courage and fear here." He pointed with each forefinger at two stars, again drawn in blue and red. "And over here, joy and something like… despair. Sadness, but much more severe than that. It says literally, 'MIND DARKNESS.' "

Now that Tharomar had explained the other

pictographs, Aven could read them all. Joy and despair both carried with them the symbol of the wind, and courage and fear were marked with a water drop. Fire, lightning, wind—aside from Casel itself, they all seemed like typical air spells, boosted by heavenly energy. The water drop likely meant rain then.

"Can you make a fully translated copy?" Aven asked.

"Should I?" Tharomar replied. "I have no idea how easy it is to learn to use these spells, but right now some fairly esoteric knowledge is still a safeguard. I wasn't sure if I should even make this one, but I needed something to be able to explain it all to you. It occurred to me to burn it after we've looked at it."

"That doesn't sound bad to me," Miara chimed in.

"But what if we need it and Tharomar's order calls him back to Kavanar? Or sends him on some other mission?" Wunik asked.

Jaena shifted uncomfortably beside Miara, her jaw tightening. Aven pretended he didn't notice. He wouldn't be too excited for that to happen if he were in her shoes, either.

"I suppose we can learn and memorize it among us," Aven said, trying to move away from the uncomfortable topic. "The fewer who know, the better. But we do need to learn it first."

Miara narrowed her eyes. "Why? Why do any of us need to know?"

"Pushing magic away and ignoring its power is what put us all in this situation," Aven said. "I'll be damned if we don't learn from those mistakes."

"But this is different, Aven. This magic is dangerous."

"Extremely," Wunik agreed, nodding.

"The temptation alone is worth avoiding, as Wunik's said before," added Miara.

Aven frowned. There was no way he was letting them destroy the only record they had of this magic without someone learning it first. "What if something happens and we need to use it?"

"Like *what*?" Miara's eyes were wide with, what was that, horror? "When will we need to enslave anyone? Or put someone in 'mind darkness'?"

He just stared at her for a moment, his eyebrows raised, surprised at the edge to her voice. The whole argument over what to do about Opia had surprised him, and the edge hadn't worn quite off him either.

"She's right, Aven," Wunik said. "I can't imagine what scenario you'd be in that such spells would be necessary."

"There are other spells on here—courage and fear don't sound useful to anyone?" He glanced around, but all their gazes were guarded. "If we'd shied away from this map in the beginning, neither of you would be free and Tharomar would still be back in Kavanar."

Jaena hung her head, and Tharomar glanced at her, his lips pressed in a thin line. Miara's jaw was clenched and she wasn't meeting his eyes.

He decided to try another tack. "Maybe we need to know how to understand this magic to destroy the brand, to unmake it."

Jaena frowned. "We *have* had no luck with conventional

means of destroying it."

"What?" Miara said.

"You've been trying to destroy it?" Aven said.

Jaena grimaced. "Uh, sorry. I didn't mention that?"

"No, that's great," Aven said quickly. "That's wonderful. Good work. I'm glad you weren't waiting around for a hand-delivered invitation to do so."

"Well, don't be so cheerful just yet," Tharomar said. "It completely resisted melting at temperatures way above normal."

Jaena nodded. "We even dipped it in acid."

"And?" said Miara.

"And nothing. The acid might as well have been water, all the damage it did."

"Still," said Wunik, "this map is just as dangerous as the brand is, if not more so. The right person could use it to enslave people without the brand."

"We cannot let that happen," said Miara, her voice hard. "We need to destroy it."

"Masari isn't the only star on here," Aven said quickly.

"Okay, let's make another map without Casel and Masari then." She met his eyes, jaw clenched.

"But we need to understand it *all,* not just bits and pieces. We have to know how it could be used against us and how to protect ourselves when necessary," Aven replied.

Miara frowned at him, her eyes searching his face. Why? What was she looking for? "You want to be able to use it, don't you?" Her voice was dark with accusation.

Aven glowered back. "Understanding it and using it

aren't the same thing."

"You don't *just* want to understand it."

"I don't know what we'll need, but I'm not turning away any potential weapons when the situation is this dire," Aven insisted.

"To enslave someone is fundamentally against the Way, a serious debt against the Balance," said Tharomar. "As are likely many if not all of these spells."

"No one's talking about enslaving anyone," Aven snapped. "Besides, nearly *every* action we take with magic upsets some part of the Balance."

"The same could be argued of all actions, not just magical ones," Wunik added.

"Sometimes we incur debts, sometimes we repay them," said Aven. "If we limit ourselves based on unbalancing the world, we wouldn't do any magic at all."

"Well, yes." Tharomar smiled darkly. "I believe there are a few who *do* think that's what you should be doing."

Aven just scowled at that, leaning forward onto the table, and Tharomar's smile faded.

Wunik cleared his throat. "Yourself included, our dear smith?"

Tharomar glanced at Wunik, surprise across his features. "Oh, me? No. Ask me a fortnight ago, I would have said yes. Now... it's different."

"Why the change?" Aven asked, not hiding the irritation in his voice as well as he'd have liked.

"On the way here, we were able to avoid a lot of killing with magic. I can't say that I think slaughtering people is a more ethical alternative to using magic to scare the piss out of them and get them out of your way."

"There are no evil weapons. They're all tools. The evil lies in those who wield them, in their intentions and motives." Aven scowled down at Masari. Some deep part of him was screaming that an answer lay here, the answer he desperately needed, buried deep in that dark, maggoty star's energy. What answer, and to what question? And was that the voice of truth or temptation?

Miara's voice cut through the thoughts. "I don't know, Aven. That might be true, but *this* seems like a fairly evil weapon to me."

"I must concur," Wunik agreed.

"I understand your reservations, I really do. But I can't ignore this." Aven spread his hands helplessly. "I need to know the depths of this magic and its capabilities. We cannot allow Daes to know them better than we do."

"He doesn't." Miara's mouth was set in a grim, determined line.

"You don't know that," Aven said gently. "If he knew about this, would he have let ordinary mages know about it?"

"No," she admitted.

"We must understand what damage can be done if we're going to be able to resist it. We're already at enough of a disadvantage in numbers. If we have more powerful magic than they do, we have to at least consider using it. Not Masari, but the others. I'm not suggesting we enslave anyone."

"That's not my concern. I— This magic should be burned." Miara shook her head, her voice hard.

"I don't think you will use them; I just don't want you to be accused of it," Wunik grumbled.

"Destroying this map does not remove the knowledge from our world. If we could somehow be sure no other maps existed, perhaps then it would be worth it. But as it is, for all we know, Daes has dozens of copies of this exact information. He claimed he was making a new brand. We don't know what he knows. Destroying it would only blind us to his capabilities."

Jaena sighed. "He's right."

Miara's jaw was clenched. She said nothing. Aven's stomach twisted into a vicious knot.

"I suggest we study this map, memorize it," Tharomar said, "and then I can destroy this new copy. Most wouldn't be able to read even this. But without it, the old safeguards are very strong."

Wunik nodded. "Most won't know even modern Serabain."

"We didn't have to look that hard to find someone who did, though," Miara said quietly. She was right, he knew. They'd stumbled across Tharomar, but in the middle of Panar? There were certainly others who knew Serabain, just few others they could trust. Even now, Aven hoped that trust was not misplaced.

"We got lucky," Wunik assured her. "But do you agree destroying the new map in a week or so will be enough?"

Miara pursed her lips. Aven held his breath a long moment, then finally released it when she nodded slightly.

He nodded to Tharomar. "Don't let the translation live for more than a week." He hoped pronouncing death over the new copy would ease Miara's tension some, but she didn't meet his eyes.

"I will guard the translation until we're ready to destroy it," said Tharomar, "just as I've been guarding the original."

"And if your order calls you back before then?" asked Wunik.

Tharomar frowned at him, as if he wondered why Wunik was bringing this up. "That won't matter either way," said Tharomar. Jaena stiffened again.

"The map can't leave Akaria," Aven pointed out, in case that wasn't obvious.

"No, I meant—" Tharomar hesitated for a moment, glancing at each of them. "I know, sire. The map won't be leaving Akaria, I assure you."

"It's settled then." Aven nodded. "Let's get to work."

Jaena was glad to return to their rooms after the meeting. Tharomar had curled the star maps into scroll tubes he held under his arm, and now he placed them carefully on the desk, along with a stack of ten other books. She was shocked he could carry it all and also set them down gracefully, but he'd insisted he hadn't needed help. Apparently he'd been right.

She sank to a seat on the bed, watching him as he examined the books, turning them over, looking at their spines. He didn't look much like a blacksmith at the moment, in a dark tunic and trousers only a palace like Ranok could loan to someone. The stubble on his jaw was teetering on the edge of a full-blown beard, as he'd been concentrating on little other than finishing that translation. She'd dreaded the moment, thinking that must be what he was waiting for before... before what exactly, she wasn't sure. Before he finally told her about the message from the temple, at the very least. But he didn't look like a man gearing up for a difficult conversation. He was frowning at the book he'd opened, but if anything, she'd have said he radiated happiness. Contentment. He was absorbed in the book enough to not notice her staring at him. Completely relaxed and at ease.

Not like her. Her guts were coiled up like a snake that'd swallowed a handful of butterflies. She had been so determined to let him broach the subject of the temple's message when he was good and ready to. She also wasn't particularly keen on revealing she'd read it without asking his permission.

But now Wunik had asked him about it. Directly. Twice.

And each time, he'd acted like he hadn't even received any message at all. Like a message calling him back to Kavanar was a near impossibility. Why would he lie, to Wunik of all people? The translation was finished. Ro was free now to do as the womenfolk bid him to, as much as Jaena hated it.

He must be planning to wait a week, until the new copy of the map was destroyed. And perhaps he didn't want her to worry about it or dread him leaving, or he simply didn't plan to tell her at all. And as much as that thought hurt like a knife in her chest, she could see that. He was quite possibly the most self-sacrificing man she'd ever known; she could see him trying to save her the hurt until the very last moment it was necessary.

That might be noble, but it'd also be foolish, because there was no way in all the seven hells she was letting him go *anywhere* near those lying temple women without her.

She rose to her feet, squared her shoulders, and took a deep breath. Ready or not, it was time they talked about that fool message and what they were going to do about it. Together.

"Ro, I—" she started, but she faltered when his warm brown eyes darted up to meet hers. There was not a speck of a secret plan to abandon her in them.

"What is it?" He smiled and set down the book.

She straightened further. She'd try to say her words with courage, with strength, to not hint at the terror shivering somewhere within her. "Ro, I want to go with you."

"What?" He cocked his head to the side. "Go where?" He glanced at the window. "You're not staying here? I was thinking of a nap after all that work last night."

How could he claim to be so utterly confused? The pretense felt like a betrayal, and one that didn't make any sense. She gritted her teeth and tried again. "When you go back to your temple. I want to go with you."

His mouth fell open, and his eyebrows rose, leaving him looking faintly stunned. "I'm not going back, Jaena."

"But when you do," she insisted, frowning. Why was he pretending? They hadn't always been truthful with each other, but to lie at a moment like this… It hurt more than she wanted to admit.

Ro was shaking his head. "I told you, they won't—"

"I read the letter," she said coldly.

"You did?" He raised his eyebrows further, then tilted his head, as if examining her anew.

"I read it the day it arrived. And I'm telling you, I'm going with you. You're not vanishing on me, Tharomar. Why else haven't you mentioned it? Because it's for my own good? I am the only one who can judge that."

"Jae, really, that's not necessary—"

"Yes, it is." How could she explain the depth of her feeling? Didn't he already know? He was all she had in the world, the only one she loved who remained for certain. If she wailed that losing him might break her irrevocably, would that only serve to drive him away? She'd look desperate. Pathetic, even. No. "I want to fight by your side."

"Oh, Jaena." He strode over to her, his hands circling sweetly around her hips and pulling her against him. She rested her head against his chest, clinging to the warm rise and fall of his breath beneath her. There was that earthy smell that never seemed far away. Other women would likely not find it so divine. They belonged together, and not just for this short while. For… much, much longer. Perhaps he disagreed. He must miss home, the village, the women who'd raised him. A wave of sinking dread washed over her, leaving her sure that this fight was already lost. She'd drawn her arms around him, but she squeezed tighter now, pressing her hands into the small of his back, the firm reality that reminded her he was not gone yet.

"That is sweet of you to say," he murmured, his breath hot against her skin as he pressed a kiss to her forehead. The kind of kiss you gave to a little girl before you told her she couldn't have what she wanted.

The hell with that. She drew back from him abruptly and stabbed a finger at his chest. "I *am* going with you, Ro. I won't be denied. You don't think I can help?"

"Of course you can. Would we have gotten this far without working together?"

"Then why can't I go?"

He let out a laugh that mystified her. "I never said you couldn't."

"Oh." She frowned, replaying the conversation in her mind. Hadn't he said… "Then why is it not necessary?"

He strode back over to the desk, opened its drawer, and took out another rolled-up sheet, this one on cheaper parchment that had no seal affixed just yet. Stepping back in front of her, he held out the scroll, his expression almost sheepish.

"I'm not going anywhere." His eyes bored into hers, his furrowed brow intense.

She unrolled it and ran her eyes over it rapidly. "*I regret to inform you… my lord's duties keep me in urgent service.… I am not sure when I can return, if ever.… I accept the consequences and will consider myself severed from the order if you require it…* " She looked up in surprise.

"Did you really think I would simply walk away from this?" he said, his eyes locking with hers.

"This? Akaria? The war?"

"Us, Jaena. You." Gently, he ran a finger along her jawline, tilting her chin up toward him. His lips brushed hers with a surprising tenderness that left her still and dazed, hoping only for more. "You're as fierce as a mountain cat," he said gently, "and it's much appreciated, but unnecessary."

"How can you not go back?" she said cautiously.

He winced. "Well, I never considered myself an oathbreaker, but here we are."

She reeled back. "You're no oathbreaker! What are you talking about?"

"I am," he said calmly.

"How can this be breaking your oath? We need you here now more than ever. What about your duty to King Aven?" What about his duty to *her*? Wasn't she part of their Order's plan? Wasn't it... more than that? She wanted him to have a permanent duty to her, the kind of oath acknowledged before all gods and men. The abrupt realization stunned her.

"I have a duty to the temple too."

"What did you swear, to protect your temple or to protect mages?"

"I swore to fight to end the Devoted blight and protect mages from them."

"And where do you think you can do that more effectively? Here, with the Akarian army behind you, or at a temple in *Evrical* with a bunch of priestesses who can't even be trusted to tell you the truth?" She let out a huff and folded her arms across her chest.

He raised his eyebrows. Perhaps that had come out more harshly than she'd intended.

"If you want to stop them, we need this brand destroyed," she insisted.

"Technically, the brand doesn't belong to the Devoted."

"I don't see how that matters."

"You're right, it doesn't matter. Because I don't care. The Devoted headquarters is in Takar. The temple would be fully within their rights to say, the day has come, we're marching to Takar and wiping the place out. And you know what? I wouldn't go. Because this is bigger than them. I can see that now."

She frowned at him. "Why should you have to choose? If the brand is destroyed and Kavanar defeated, we can make Akaria a place where the Devoted are unwelcome. Outlawed, even. Think of it, a whole swath of the center of the continent. How will that affect what the Devoted can do? Their power? Which will have more impact, this war or that one small temple? *And* if this war is won, the temple can resist the Devoted openly, instead of hiding behind secrets—and lies. Can you even swear an oath to someone who hasn't told you the truth?"

"Yes, you can. I can't believe we're fighting about *this* of all things." He threw up his hands, obviously suppressing a laugh.

"I think oaths to liars should be annulled." She was

really just making this up as she went along, but that sounded good. Even if he was right, she resented the fact his honor could be besmirched by fools—or worse.

"We don't know that for sure. They conveniently left that out of their reply. But I still knew what I was promising, so it's still my oath."

"Oh, they knew." She clenched her jaw, unconvinced. "But it doesn't matter. You can do the most good here."

He pulled her closer, prying her folded arms apart and wrapping them around him. "You're right, of course. But I *want* to stay here with you, brand or no brand, Devoted or no Devoted. Because it has nothing to do with any of that. It has to do with you. And *that* most certainly is against my oath." She simply stared. Could the truth really be so simple? It was not that he'd intended to leave her without a word, but that he'd never intended to leave at all. She found herself hanging on each precious word, even if it pained her that those same hurt him a little too. "I saw that letter, and I gave no thoughts to duty or how best to defeat the Devoted. I didn't care what my duty was. I didn't care what the temple needed. I just knew I wasn't leaving."

"Oath-breaking is about deeds, not motivations. So you have a personal interest. So what? You can still support your cause best here."

"If I had thought of all that myself, I'd be more encouraged. And Akaria doesn't need me. My translation is done."

She straightened to look him in the eye. "We have barely a handful of mages, Ro! Don't you see how dire this is?"

"I don't know any spells. What good will I do?"

"I can teach you. If you want," she said, suddenly tentative. "Or if not, I can use your energy. Even if you know nothing, you still make me twice as strong. Maybe more than that."

How true in spirit, as well as magic.

"Oh, Jae. You don't need to fight for me so hard. I've spent the last week making peace with it."

"And I've spent the last week worrying you were leaving me and plotting how to follow you."

He looked shocked for a moment, but recovered quickly. He squeezed her closer. "I'm sorry I didn't tell you. I didn't think it mattered, since I wasn't going to act on it."

"Well, I'm sorry I read it. I realized afterward I should have asked. It's just there's not much privacy in Mage Hall, and—"

"No, I don't mind. I don't mind at all. And I'm sorry you worried. I had no *idea* you were worrying. I guess I can see it, now that you mention it." There he went, laughing again. "I can't believe you thought I would leave without saying anything."

"You're very self-sacrificing. I thought that you wouldn't want to put me in harm's way, but that you might go even if you wanted to stay."

"Apparently not as self-sacrificing as you thought." He winced again, chagrined.

She pulled him into an embrace this time, and he buried his face in her neck and braids again. She ran her hand over his hair and down his back, calming him. She could feel him aching, though, in spite of all she'd said.

"Listen, Ro," she whispered into his hair. "I don't know much about this whole faith thing. I haven't had a good run with it, between me and the gods. But I take it that what the temple says matters a lot less to you than what the goddess says. So what does your goddess say to you?"

He looked up at her, his eyes a mixture of wonder and sadness and hope. "That I would be spitting on all her gifts to walk away from you."

She laid her hand on his cheek, savoring the roughness of his stubble on her palm. "As would I. That's why wherever you go, I'm going with you."

He snorted softly now, a crooked smile lighting his face.

"Listen to your goddess, will you?"

"All right," he said softly, and as if following orders, he kissed her hard. She barely smothered a laugh.

"I don't care what some lying temple women say," she said when he released her from that kiss. "I don't think we belong apart."

"Yes," he replied. "Especially not for at least the next three hours before lunch." He jutted a chin at the bed and raised an eyebrow.

A giddy laugh escaped her, and she finally started to let herself feel relieved.

"Come here and let me see how selfless I can manage to be."

"Sire!" Lord Dyon's voice echoed up the hallway. Aven turned and waited, and Miara stopped by his side. Their guards halted like pillars of a temple around them. Waves of cold unease rolled off Miara, setting him on edge.

Dyon jogged to catch up, his footfalls echoing mightily. "Good morning, Aven, Miara," he said, breathless for a moment. A few lieutenants, including Jenec, lingered further up the hall, waiting for Dyon to return rather than joining them.

Aven nodded crisply once, impatient for the message.

"Good morning, Lord Dyon," she said politely. Did she look paler than usual?

"Sire, the southern stronghold. Derk just checked again at my request, and we discovered a single soldier collapsed before the door to the keep. The door stood wide open, and the keep looked dark inside. No other movement. I believe whatever's happened there has gotten worse."

Hell. He'd been hoping for some positive news for once. Of course not. "What do you recommend, Lord Dyon?"

"I think it's time we paid them a visit, sire. If Lord Beneral and politics are satisfied."

Aven inhaled slowly, bracing himself. With the map only just translated, that didn't leave much time to learn it. But he relished the idea of being out on the road with Miara again instead of in the palace. Ranok felt more like a trap than a stronghold with every passing day. Even if it might snow out there on the road.

"We've delayed long enough," Aven admitted. "I've got a regiment waiting for our instructions, and the royal guard. I'd prefer to get to the front line soon."

"As would I," agreed Dyon. "I'd also prefer to know if we can count on any troops from the southern regiment at all. If we can't, why haven't the Kavanarians attacked it already? It's been days, but their troops have hardly moved from the brief initial surge. It makes no sense."

"They must be waiting for something," Miara said darkly.

"But what?" said Aven. "Could it have anything to do with Thel? Information they hoped to gain?" Maybe they were waiting for everyone to die of whatever disease they'd infected the soldiers with. He shuddered at the thought.

"Could be waiting for supplies or reinforcements from the interior," offered Dyon.

"It doesn't matter. Dom and the others from Estun are set to arrive tomorrow. Send orders to the regiment they should be prepared to leave after that, as late as midday if we must."

Dyon nodded crisply and headed back toward his lieutenants. Aven and Miara watched him go.

"I still don't think you should ride into that hold until we know what happened there," Miara said. For some reason, the note of concern in her voice reassured him.

He reached out and took both her hands in his. "I promise I won't step foot inside until they've figured out what's wrong. Maybe Wunik's wrong. We could both go. Wouldn't you like to be out on the road again?"

She smiled, then nodded. "I would. Sooner rather than later. But…" She hesitated, then continued silently. *But we told new mages to come here and find me specifically. And who will gather them up and organize them?*

Can we get Jaena to do it?

She's focused on the brand. And she's not even an official resident of Akaria, let alone a representative of the crown.

I should grant her that—remind me. Wunik?

They'd reached Aven's rooms by now, and he headed for the couch that had been too much his refuge as of late. He wasn't entirely surprised when Miara didn't follow him and stopped by the fire instead, staring into the flames. He shooed away all the servants but Perik, who seemed to be better at staying nearby without making a fuss about it.

As much as I hate to think it, Aven, she said silently after a long pause, *I believe I should stay here. Someone needs to help Elise, get the mages together. And by then Dom and Devol will be here, right? We know we can trust them.*

He groaned inwardly. *I knew it was too good to be true that we could get out of here together and back on the road. Okay, fine. You must be careful, though. Siliana can tell you what she found out from your attendants. With Devol here, it would help me worry less about staving off any further nefarious attempts on your life.*

If you're worried about nefarious things, you should destroy that damn map.

He gritted his teeth. The mental connection between them couldn't hide the anger behind her words now.

"Are you sure you're all right?" he said slowly, aloud now and hoping that would diffuse some of the tension.

"Honestly?"

"Of course." When had he ever wanted anything but?

"No, I'm not all right. I don't believe you," she said, almost sounding hurt. The mental connection between them dimmed, her pulling away from him slightly.

At first, he simply stared in shock, but he recovered quickly. Staring blankly never helped much. "Why? About which part?"

"How can you plan on using this magic?" she demanded. "I see your mind working. You're thinking about it. And you're not against using it. Put those together and what do you get?"

"Of course I'm against using it. Do you think I'd have started any of this if I didn't find slavery deplorable? But the map is a weapon like any other, no more evil than a sword."

She rounded on him now, and her eyes were fiery when she met his. "If you use those spells, Aven, we will see our own Dark Days. I don't want the stories our children tell about you to be about—"

She stopped short, and he sat back in surprise. They'd never talked about children before, although given who he was, he'd hoped she understood it was somewhat a given. This was far from the ideal time to bring it up for either of them. She turned away and stared down at the embers, her brow furrowed.

He took a deep breath, stood up, and strode over to

her, determined to reassure her. Her back was to him now, the curve of her neck naked and exposed below her bun. He hadn't seen it like that in days, and for some reason, it felt suddenly like a very precious sight, something that he hadn't realized could slip through his fingers when he wasn't looking. He rested one hand on her shoulder, finding it warm and strong, and she didn't flinch at his touch. He ran a finger down the side of her neck tenderly, trying to find the right words. "Miara, that won't happen. I promise you. We won't have our own Dark Days. If mages get to be free, we'll have… something different. Something new, something good and bad at the same time. But I won't bring what happened back then. We don't even really know very well what happened. I just want to be prepared." He rested his other hand on her other shoulder now, gently squeezing, trying to work out the tension like she had for him a few days ago.

"You know I would never tell you magic is evil." Her warm fingers slipped over his, and her eyes peered up at him over her shoulder, searching his face. Their deep brown was liquid and beautiful, but plaintive too. Still worried. "I'm the one who showed you how beautiful it could be in the first place, wasn't I?"

He nodded.

"Then, please. Please. Listen to me. *This* magic is evil."

"I know. I believe you. I've got no plans to use it, but we *must* be able to defend ourselves."

"Aven," she said gently, "you can't believe that it's evil, have no intention to use it, and also use it to defend us.

One of those can't be true."

He winced. "I truly don't want to use it, but we can't rule out the possibility that it might become necessary. If they use star magic, we need to be able to use its opposite, to undo its damage. It's not evil to re-balance the world."

"Who are we to know if that's what we're doing?"

His jaw tightened. "In this case, Miara, I'm very certain."

"All right, I know, maybe with enslavement. But with the other spells, that's not so certain. Please, *please*, burn the map, Aven. Burn it. Let this knowledge die." She turned slowly, forcing him to abandon her shoulders, but at least she was facing him now.

"I can't. I told you, I can't," he said gently. "Burning it won't take the knowledge from the world, only from us. If Zaera recorded the star magic once, then she could have written down other things. Or written it down again. What are the chances she only wrote it one time?"

"Aven…"

"To defend ourselves, especially when we're outnumbered, we must understand our enemy. Better than he understands himself." A classic tenet, one that he held up in his defense more than he was sure he truly applied it.

She gave him a long, hard look. He raised a hand to her cheek, and she leaned into it for a moment, closing her eyes. But then she pulled away, stepped back, taking his tenuous grip on reassurance with him. His gut wrenched, and ice shot through his veins.

She was challenging him just as she should. And she thought she wouldn't make a good queen? She was already the partner he needed. That didn't make disagreement any more comfortable, though. Even on the road, they hadn't disagreed much.

"Miara—" he started.

She held up a flat palm. "I... I just need some time to think about this."

"Let's—" He reached out toward her again.

"Some time *alone*. All right?" She waited for his slight nod, and then she turned and left the suite as he stared after her, the slight fear that had been pulling at the corners of his mind starting to unravel into panic.

He took a deep breath and viciously tamped the emotions down. He didn't have time for them. And technically, there was nothing to panic over. Just a simple disagreement.

Didn't everyone disagree sometimes?

Try as he might, the thought didn't make him feel any better.

8   Making Plans

Straining his ears as hard as he could for the sounds of pursuit, Thel finished the small burrow into the mountainside and ushered Niat inside. The sweet smell of freshly disturbed earth wrapped around him as he sank to a seat beside her and began closing them in.

Try as he might, he could no longer hear anything of the fortress behind them. Branches knocking in the wind and the creaks of tree trunks swaying, but nothing else. No shouts or footsteps. It was almost eerie.

He and Niat hadn't gone *that* far. Had their pursuers found Alikar—or Detrax, for that matter—and concerns over their health or lack thereof had taken precedence? Or perhaps there was simply no one telling them what to do.

The hollow he'd created was barely big enough for both of them to sit in, but it was dry. And warm, thank the gods, although he wasn't sure entirely why. Maybe it was just enough shared body heat; maybe some part of his magic was insisting on heating the earth around them. Whatever it was, it was a welcome change.

He closed their hollow all the way except for a small opening at the top for air. By the gods, let no one notice. They still had to breathe.

To his surprise now, Niat didn't complain. Or even comment. She just stared wide-eyed and quiet at the earth closing around them.

Between the warmth and the silence, Thel finally relaxed. He leaned his head against the dirt behind him and breathed deeply of the wet earth. He shut his eyes and just listened. Now his and Niat's breathing were the loudest sounds, the quiet forest beyond murmuring in the background. The magic he'd worked was much more elaborate than usual; he just needed a moment to recuperate.

He must have nodded off, for he jolted awake at the sound of voices outside. Soldiers, and they were close. Footsteps crunched in the snow. He sucked in a breath and shifted, rubbing his eyes.

Niat, too, jumped, and her head snapped up from where it had fallen against his shoulder. When had *that* happened? She must have fallen asleep too.

Their bodies touched from shoulder to hip, and he pretended not to notice. It was cold, that was all.

He focused on the sounds outside. Men calling commands, following their tracks in the snow. Dogs too, sniffing, huffing, barking.

Footsteps, all the way up to the edge of the mountain.

He held his breath. Niat was doing the same.

The small opening above let in sunlight at only a slight angle—they couldn't have been asleep for more than an hour or two. It hadn't taken long for these men to catch up.

"What do you make of this?" said one voice outside.

"Of what?" returned another.

"The trail ends here. Just slams into the side of the mountain."

"That's impossible."

"I know, but look."

"Don't be stupid, you must be reading it wrong."

"Two pairs of boot prints are not hard to distinguish from animals, Leul."

The argument continued a while longer, but to no avail. The footprints were a mystery they couldn't solve. Eventually the voices moved off, retracing their steps and certain they must have made a mistake. He breathed a deep sigh of relief.

"You all right?" he whispered.

Nodding, she dropped her head back onto his shoulder. He kept his ears sharp, but all he noticed now was the sound of Niat's breaths slowing as she dozed off again.

Thel blinked in the relative darkness of their hiding spot, rubbing his face with his free hand so as not to disturb her head on his shoulder. He didn't like to admit it, but he liked the feeling of her against him, the light pressure of her head on his shoulder. In spite of all they'd been through, her scent was sage and ocean. Her eyes had flashed like lightning as he'd dragged her through the barracks tunnels. He liked it when she was angry, because then there was fire in her eyes, and passion, and purpose. Not the bleak, hopeless despair that consumed her otherwise, the look that made him feel like she was drowning and he needed to save her but couldn't quite reach her hand. Even now, he could imagine putting an arm around her shoulders and pulling her closer. Just to keep warm. Nothing more. Nothing amorous. He just had a moderate, reasonable amount of sympathy. Any reasonable person would feel the same way.

She was a traitor; he obviously couldn't feel anything more than that for her. Although it did seem her father had put her in a terrible, inescapable position. And she was absolutely sure he was evil. There was really no excuse for that, as he'd been nothing but kind. If his actions hadn't proven his worth to her, nothing would.

But she sighed in her sleep, very softly, and he had to admit any ill will he'd felt toward her was gone. Strange. What actions of hers had caused this? Was it her words? Her proximity to him in this tiny, warm cave and the feeling of her body against his, only insufficient fabric between them? He doubted it was just her presence; it was perfectly possible to feel attracted to someone and still hate them.

He took another deep breath, tasting the warm, humid, earthy air around him. He'd watch the sun. Another hour, maybe two, and they'd get out of this hole and do their best to get the hell away from here.

A young man slunk to a stop in the doorway of Marielle's outer parlor, and Daes beckoned him inside. He eyed the boy like prey. He would do. Daes had brought only a few mage slaves with him to Evrical, and this one was not of the rebellious type, although he was a creature mage like the escaped one. He also wasn't particularly keen to please, which helped. Daes could never stand to be around the obsequious ones for long. Let Seulka keep them. This one was more… apathetic.

"I have questions," Daes said coldly as he glanced over his shoulder. Marielle should be arriving soon, but something had occurred to him.

"Yes, my lord," the young man replied.

"There was an attack on Trenedum Palace at one point. Did you hear of it?"

"I was there with you, my lord," he said.

"Those who attacked," he carefully never mentioned they were mages to his slaves, "they arrived at Trenedum in the middle of the night but were in a city two day's ride away the next. How is that possible? Could they have done something to their horses?"

"I can't say I know anything that could make a horse make a two-day journey in half a day," the mage said. "Nothing that would be comfortable to ride on, sir."

"Then how?"

"Perhaps transformation. With creature magic, my

lord. Change each of the people into a harmless, small animal and carry them."

"Carry them how?"

"The mage could transform into something large and winged. A bird can travel much faster than a horse. Could make a two-day trip in a few hours."

"Is that so?" Daes raised his eyebrows. "What kind of small animals?"

The man shrugged. "Rats. Snakes. Spiders."

Daes winced at the thought of becoming any of those. "And you could do this?"

The young man nodded, looking tired. "Of course, my lord. Any creature mage could."

"Hmm. We'd still have our things to move, coming behind us," Daes said, thinking aloud. "Can you change the trunks into animals too?"

"Afraid not, my lord. Another creature mage *might* be able to carry them and fly, but… they also might not."

Daes nodded and rubbed his hands together, glancing back over his shoulder for Marielle again. What was keeping that woman? He was ready to be on the road.

He turned and appraised the young man again. Daes didn't have the mage-knots with him; they were still at Mage Hall in the Tall Master's hands. And that was probably the safest place for them. As a result, he couldn't compel the man to listen to him quite as strongly, but the fellow did seem to be of a docile sort. An average command should be enough.

"Let's see what we can do, shall we?" Daes grinned,

almost annoying himself at his own cheerfulness. But he was ready to be out of this den of snakes and on the field with swords and men.

Even if that meant being transformed into a rat. There was a first time for everything.

Kae trudged along a quietly burbling stream, the furs and cloaks he'd managed to gather—or surreptitiously "borrow"—swinging around him. Flecks of water or snow flew off from time to time, hitting a nearby log or boulder. He was getting warm enough; he'd probably stop soon. Gods, when would he reach Anonil? Or at least Akaria? He had little idea where he was relative to the border, except that he knew he had continuously gone east and successfully avoided the roads. He used farsight from time to time, but even that glorious magic couldn't tell him quite where the border was without a map.

He was used to living off the land, but he was ready for a break. A city. An inn. Maybe all his days in Mage Hall had made him soft. How long had it been, ten years or eleven now? How could he have lost count? But he supposed it didn't matter. He'd never had any hope of going back before, and even now he held it weakly. It would be nice to see his father again, but he'd have to get the old buzzard to somehow come to Akaria—if Kae could even get word to him. If he was even still alive, Kae thought with more sadness.

Royals had always taken a cut of the harvest on the farm. That had always left them on the edge of starvation before the winter was half over, which had given Kae plenty of experience trapping animals and finding the nooks and crannies of what the forest could provide to eat. Late fall was easy compared to early spring, when deer and other animals had already picked everything over. He wasn't against bark stew to survive, but he wasn't going to go seeking it out if there were other options.

He marched along. He'd have to reach Akaria soon, even if he didn't hit the city at first. Four days of hiking and he should be close. One disadvantage of avoiding the roads was that roads led you straight to cities. Farsight had told him the general direction of Anonil and how to avoid as much civilization as possible, but mostly he preferred to conserve his energy and follow the sun.

With the book he carried, and all its dark secrets, he'd rather die of eating the wrong insect out in the wilderness than risk getting caught.

Speaking of civilization and avoiding people, two voices caught his ears up ahead. He hunkered down behind a tree and listened.

"We're going to die out here." A female voice.

"No, we're not." A man, his voice tired.

Peering around the tree trunk to get a glimpse at them, Kae had to say he agreed with the woman. The two travelers were hardly dressed for the winter weather. Cloaks were the only wise thing they had, and only one small satchel between them. No packs, no warm clothes. They looked better dressed for a court function than hiking in the woods, although they were very dirty.

The man sat down in a clearing near the base of a large, wide pine. A few minutes passed in silence, until the snow around him began to turn gray. It was melting.

Mages! By the gods, a stroke of luck. Finally. The man was warming the earth to keep them from freezing. That sure sounded good right about now.

"Ho, there!" Kae called out, still in his hiding place.

The man opened his eyes, suddenly tensing. "Who's there?" He glanced around. "Who are you?"

"Might you know a mutual friend?" Kae called back. "One Miara Floren?" If they didn't know her, he was heading the other direction fast.

The man's eyes lit with recognition. The woman showed none. "I know her," he said cautiously. "She's marrying my brother."

Kae's eyebrows rose at that. "And you're mages, too?"

"I am," said the man. He heard no response from the woman.

"Escaped, slave, or freemages?" Not that Kae could necessarily trust their answer. It was possible that mage slaves might have orders to lie in order to capture runaways like him. Or could newly freemages be out looking for stray escapees like him?

The man was rising and striding toward Kae's voice. Time was running out for Kae to decide if he trusted them.

"I'm a freemage," the man said, "as all mages in Akaria are."

Kae caught his breath. "Are we in Akaria then? You're an Akarian?"

"Yes." The footsteps in the snow crunched closer. "We're close to the border. Kavanar has invaded these lands, but it won't be long before we drive them back out."

Kae decided to chance it and stepped out, raising his hand in greeting. "Kae Teneen," he said. "I was freed by a friend of Miara's. I have been trying to make my way to Anonil on her orders."

"Ah, that friend would be my brother, I think. I'm Prince Thel Lanuken of Akaria." The young man kept his voice oddly low, as if he didn't want the woman to hear.

Kae managed a hasty bow. He wasn't too familiar with royal protocol but that seemed appropriate. "An honor," he said. "Forgive me, but I was a farmer before they dragged me off. I don't know all the ins and outs of polite manners."

"That's all right," Thel said swiftly. "We're not big on that sort of thing anyway. At least, I'm not."

The woman was eying Kae warily now. She'd entered the circle Thel had started to heat but kept to the very edge of it. "Earth mage?" said Kae, nodding at the circle. "Let's get back over there. That sure looks better right about now."

The prince snorted and headed back, Kae following behind him. The heat immediately bathed him as he stepped into the melting snow, and he grinned, taking a deep breath of the now-moist air rising from the earth. "Ah, you earth mages can't do much, but what you can do! Heaven, on a day like today."

Thel raised an eyebrow, sitting back on the earth again, probably to continue his work. "Can't do much?"

Kae cocked his head to the side. The fact that earth mages were the most relatively useless of the bunch had been ground into the mage slaves in their training at Mage Hall. Didn't all mages share the same impression?

"I'm still learning. Just found out I had the… gift a week ago. Or was it… Well, no matter. I'm still learning. But the only earth mage I know is a woman I'd not trifle with." Thel gave him a friendly smile, leaning back so his hands were embracing the dirt behind him. His fingers were wheedling under the pine needles, trying to get better contact. The prince either was learning fast or had good instincts; that was not a skill taught to young earth mages.

"Wait," Kae said slowly. "What was her name?"

"Jaena… something. Damn, I can't believe I forgot her last name. It's been—"

"You know Jaena too!" Kae couldn't help but grin. "She's all right? Made it to Akaria?"

"Sure did. She's in Panar with Miara, my brother, and the others."

"Menaha?" Kae asked quickly.

Thel frowned, and Kae's heart immediately sank.

"Sefim? No?"

The young prince shook his head.

"Well, at least Jaena is free. Praise Nefrana." He muttered a quiet prayer to himself as he glanced at the forest around them. The woman eyed him even harder at that, but he ignored her. Yes, the clearing seemed big enough by his estimation. "Now, you needn't do all the work. Perhaps a fire is in order?" The thought made Kae feel downright cheerful.

"We were being pursued. I don't think we should draw attention where we are."

"With the smoke?"

Thel nodded.

Kae waved him off. "I can handle the smoke." He began whisking up branches with the wind and rolling them toward the center clearing.

The woman jumped back as a log rolled past her feet. She muttered her own prayer, of protection. What was this? How did some mage hater end up running around with a sapling earth mage?

Kae approached her, pausing his work on the fire, and gave her his best courtly bow, feeling only slightly guilty that it was half mocking. "Kae Teneen, fine lady," he said, "Former mage slave, former farmer, right now absolutely nothing. Except free." He straightened and smiled brightly at her. Her eyes were a nice blue, for all her wary-eyed staring.

She said nothing for a long moment.

Thel sighed. "This is—"

She hastily waved to silence him. "Niat. Just call me Niat."

"Just Niat? Is that what you are now?" Thel frowned at that.

She said nothing, only glared at him.

"A pleasure to meet you, Niat." Kae caught up her hand and kissed it in what he guessed was more of a mockery of fine court manners than anything else. Anything to break the tension between those two. And with that he turned away to sweep up his twigs and build them a fine fire.

Miara trudged down to the stables. Siliana should be looking for her with an update on Opia and the others, but at that moment, the last thing she wanted to think about was the loyalty of her attendants, whether well-meaning or homicidal. The pounding in her head had started to return, but now she was determined to weather it. Scanning her system told her the effects of it had mostly faded, however; the substance must simply be more drug than poison and have extremely addictive qualities. How considerate of Opia. She sighed.

She was used to her life not mattering to the Masters or risking it doing something nefarious. But someone trying to hurt her for being herself? For simply being alive, and in love, and trying to do the right thing? That was new, and surprisingly frustrating. She could only hope that Kalan and Etral had had no part in it.

She stalked down to the stables, using all her skill to get there without being heard or seen. She slipped into Ata's stall and whiled away an hour, brushing her soft, chestnut hair, muttering sweet nothings, and resting her forehead against Ata's quiet, reassuring warmth. Ata didn't have to argue over complex human things, like whether evil things done in the service of good motives were still good. Horses didn't have argue those points with those they loved dearly.

Miara tensed at the sound of footsteps. The stable boy rounded the corner and gaped at her, fumbling and dropping his bale of hay.

"Did you want to go for a ride, my lady?" muttered the boy, clearly uncertain as to any other reason why she'd be in the stables. She supposed it was an unusual place for one to find peace of mind, but it wasn't unusual for her.

Ata huffed and stomped a foot at the words in slight excitement, though, and Miara pursed her lips.

"Yes," she told him, stepping back.

"I'll prepare your horse, my lady." And he tossed the hay out of the way and hurried to get the saddle.

She looked down at her dress in dismay—she hadn't considered that part of the picture. But perhaps it was best she gave it a shot, dress and all, to see how truly bad it could be.

Truth be told, it wasn't quite as terrible as she hoped, and though having bare thighs pressed against the saddle was a little uncomfortable, the stable boy knew more than she did about accommodating her skirt, which he deftly, if nervously, spread out gracefully around Ata's flanks and rump in a way that looked a bit like a covered wagon but also very elegant. She wasn't going to be galloping or jumping any logs, but it would do.

The brisk air and city sights were a welcome distraction.

The stable hand must have alerted someone of what she was doing, because the same four guards that had accompanied her last time appeared out of nowhere to ride in their four-pillar formation. This meant she drew more stares, and suddenly she realized this was a very public appearance and she hadn't given one whit of thought about what she was doing, how she looked, why she was here. She resolved not to care.

He's worried about protecting all this, she told herself. About keeping these people safe, about freeing the mages still enslaved. About fighting off Daes. They were both trying to do the right thing. Weren't they?

The regular clop of Ata's hooves lulled her, and even the people peeking out or standing in their doorways to watch her go by faded into the background, regular little moles popping their heads aboveground, then ducking back inside. Scri soared overhead in hypnotic, lazy circles.

If she was honest with herself, what was she really so angry about? The thought of Aven wielding the same power as Daes? Daes had held so much power over her for so long. Aven held much more power, although she wasn't sure how well he knew that. And he'd granted her just as much power in return. But she couldn't shake the terror, the worry that welled up in her knowing that he could wield the same sort of spell that her former tyrants had. That he would even consider it… An image of Aven holding a hot brand, one lip curled like the Tall Master sometimes did, flashed before her. She thrust it away viciously. Aven was one of the good ones. He fought to

help the oppressed, those like her. Aven and Daes were
worlds apart.

Weren't they? Or was one just lucky to be born with
power, the other grasping for it?

She shook her head. Nothing could excuse the actions
of the Masters or any of the Kavanarians who'd enslaved
mages. Nothing. They had no right. And Aven was terrifying her by even looking at the same star those fools
had used to commit their sins, however indirectly. She
didn't want that stain on his soul, on his legacy, and she
didn't want it to backfire and blow up in his face.

He was right, though, she wasn't being entirely fair. If
he had followed her logic before he'd met her and burned
the map because of the risk it contained, Miara would
still be a slave. And likely Aven would be too. And that
was not a better world for anyone. He'd certainly made
the right choice back then, so why was she so concerned
he wouldn't make the right choice now? Why did the
map bother her so?

She passed a box of roses that had lost their bloom
and started to fade. She reached out and embraced the
plant, and its buds burst into life again, white pools of
beauty in the sun.

When had her roses stopped being bloodred? She
frowned, and then rode on.

All of the star spells were strange to her. Courage and
fear, joy and despair. Revelation. Freedom. They didn't
interact with nature, but with people's minds. Oh, she
supposed minds were parts of nature, but it still felt

wrong. Like cheating. Like messing with something they shouldn't. Yes, that was what bothered her about them. It was one thing to beg a rose to bloom, to ask a falcon to watch your back and reward him for his help.

It was another thing to control people's minds. She never forced tomcats or spiders or robins to do her bidding, and she always rewarded them. People—and tomcats—had the right to think for themselves.

And if there was anyone to whom it would be a dangerous temptation to control minds, it was a king.

She bit her lip. Would he be tempted to calm crowds who were angry about something righteous? Inspire courage in soldiers who didn't want to die—and turn them into wild beasts who sought death freely?

The overwhelming sense of wrongness that filled her was almost nauseating. She took a deep breath, then another, forcing herself to breathe through her nose. Perhaps he might be tempted, but she knew him. Those were not things he wanted to do. Or would even need to do. And she could sway him. If she pointed out the wrongness, how great a debt to the Balance it was, he would listen. Wouldn't he?

Her head was pounding harder now, and the slanting sun was starting to hurt her eyes, but her heart had lightened. Some quiet moments, a noble horse, and brisk winter air really could work wonders. That said, it was full-on winter now, and she hadn't even brought a cloak. She'd been too lost in thought to realize how cold she was, but now she turned back slowly, admiring more of the lovely streets of Panar as she went, the now-lush window boxes she surreptitiously refreshed with a flower or two as she passed.

She remembered sitting by the fire with Samul, everything he'd said about fearing versus knowing. *Fearing* that Aven could be like Daes was extremely different than *knowing*. Aven was nothing like Daes, and deep down, she knew that. It was only fear, torturing her. Very powerful fear she was having difficulty talking herself out of, but simple fear nonetheless. Still, the fear nagged. What if this magic could change him? Make him *become* like the Dark Master—no, Daes.

A man stepping toward them out into the street ripped her out of her thoughts, and the guards tensed, hands gripping their hilts. The man had a respectable-looking burgundy tunic and leather vest but a broad-brimmed hat with a huge feather gave it all a whimsical air. Around his belt hung many pouches and flasks. A merchant?

"Are you the one the announcements speak of, my lady?" he said. His voice was bold and loud, and it seemed to echo as the street around them went quiet.

"Who asks?" she returned guardedly, biting off the urge to add an honorific.

The man swept off his hat and bowed elegantly. "Sestin of Sestin's Drams. I'm an herbalist and healer of sorts." He swept an open hand toward the nearby garden in front of a tall building painted white. The nearby herb garden she'd spelled a few days ago had been carefully cut and harvested. "Are you the one who did this, my fine woman? Arms Master Floren, I presume?"

She narrowed her eyes slightly at that, but nodded. "I am."

"Allow me to thank you for your gifts, Arms Master. They've added three times the yearly inventory to my shop," he said, sounding pleased.

"You're welcome," she said plainly, unable to muster much of a regal air after the exhaustions of the day. Nodding was as close to regal as anyone was getting. She raised the reins to be on her way.

"If I may hold you one more moment, my lady," he said, hesitating.

She lowered her reins, looking back at him but saying nothing.

"Is it true you're looking for mages?"

She didn't miss the slight lift of his chin, the way he flung the words out into the street with a certain boldness that belied the danger in uttering them.

"Why, yes," she said quickly. "Yes, we are. The king is in dire need of more mages." There, that sounded quite like something a royal would say. She raised any eyebrow. "A healer, you said you were?"

He grinned at her. "Oh, I only ask out of curiosity, my lady." His expression clearly said otherwise.

"Well, if you know of any, I can be reached at Ranok." She picked up the reins and started to move away and then added, "Or you can also ask for Jaena Eliar, my... my lieutenant." There. That sounded very official, and after realizing earlier they hadn't even offered residence to Jaena, she resolved to make both official just as soon as she got back.

"Thank you, my lady," said Sestin with another dashing bow. "If I know of anyone, I'll be sure to send them to you. And thank you again for the late harvest."

She gave him another nod that felt quite regal this time. *Come, girl,* she urged Ata. *Let's go back and get you another apple, shall we?*

Thel tore his gaze away from Niat and Kae, down toward where the snow was melting into the dirt to make mud at his feet. He pretended to be studying the earth for something specific—it was his domain, after all—but he was really just staring. His thoughts were blank, but also in a frenzy over nothing in particular.

He sighed. This new mage had friendliness in spades, and Niat was, well—not naturally friendly, if he wanted to be charitable. That hadn't stopped Kae from kissing her hand in a flamboyant courtly display. And that had left Thel frozen, acid pumping through his veins, glaring at the dirt, even as Kae had tromped away through the brush looking for sustenance.

Why? What did he care if Kae kissed her fingers and Niat's cheeks flushed crimson? He didn't, he couldn't. Impossible. Maybe he was just feeling out-of-his-mind exhausted from all the spells and activity over the last week.

Niat came and sat down beside him, and he resisted looking at her. He wanted to ask if there was a reason she hadn't announced she was a priestess, but Kae was not far off, and the forest was dreadfully quiet, as winter often was. It'd have to wait. Some days being a creature mage seemed like it would be terribly convenient.

But Kae was putting on a pretty good display in favor of air mages. Wind swept in all around them, carrying things for him, and he piled them up with lighthearted amusement and set them aflame. He was smiling most of the time, grinning at the warmth of the earth and fire combined. Thel must have been steeped in Niat's wry and pessimistic presence too long, for Kae seemed nearly delirious with happiness.

The two of them just stared at the cheerful air mage like he was some kind of freak.

Kae did not care in the slightest. He clapped his hands together, rubbing them up and down. "All right, then! My instructions were to head to Anonil—"

"We've heard it will be besieged and fall soon," said Thel. "Kavanar's army approaches. If you get there and it's fallen, you should head on to Panar. The White City."

"I thought perhaps we should head there together?" Kae frowned slightly.

"We could. I was planning to make straight for Panar, but…"

"If we don't want to be captured again, maybe we should skip Anonil," said Niat as calmly as he'd ever heard her. Thel pursed his lips. Maybe *he* should have tried courtly displays to mollify her.

"Hmm, but that's where my instructions from Miara

said to go." Kae scratched his scruffy beard.

"I don't know. I'm not sure where Miara is, honestly," said Thel. "But my brother and everyone else has moved to Panar. I think they were going to stay there." Actually, now that he thought about it, he didn't know that for sure. What if they had moved to Anonil? Or Dramsren? Or somewhere else?

"Well, let's see." Casually, Kae made a circle with his fingers and spread it out. As if he were ripping a hole in space, a window of light opened in his lap. Farsight. Niat gaped in wonder and got on her knees, creeping closer. Thel had to forcibly keep himself from glaring at the two of them. Air magic was showy, all right, but which magic had freed her from a dungeon, a near-death rubble experience, certain imprisonment, and indefinite servitude? His earth magic that "couldn't do much."

So what if he couldn't make a window in the sky?

Suddenly he realized the window was pointing at Anonil.

"Looks like it's right at the bottom of this range, here," said Kae. "Which way is Panar?"

"South. That way?" Thel pointed over the window's light.

"Well, then, Anonil is on the *way* to Panar. So we can do both."

Thel rocked back. The fortress at Anonil sat east of the city. That meant... he must have gone north instead of south quite a ways when they'd first run. The important thing had been getting away, and they had done that, so he didn't really mind, and running the wrong way might have even helped them not be found... But he resolved to check the sun more proactively next time. "All right then, Anonil it is. Then Panar, if we don't find anyone."

"So you say Jaena is in Panar too?"

Thel nodded. "You should be able to find her there. Or my brother Aven. How do you know Jaena?"

"We were training partners in Mage Hall. Young warrior mages are paired with older ones to get started."

"You don't seem any older than she is."

"I'm not, but they enslaved her later. Most of us are found as kids and brought in, all alone or in families." Thel glanced at Niat as Kae spoke, wondering if those words affected her at all. She was staring into the fire, her expression unreadable. "She and her sister were brought in late. She's only known she is a mage for about five years. I've been studying for twenty."

"Wait, sister? She didn't bring a sister. Or mention one."

For the first time, Kae's face darkened. "She's dead. Killed herself, some say, although that's supposed to be against the binding of the brand. It's not supposed to be possible. But we all thought for sure she had found a way."

"That's terrible. Why?"

"We don't know. Never will. Maybe she just hated being a slave. Maybe whatever the Dark Master made her do, she couldn't live with it."

Thel glanced at Niat again, more pointedly. She was staring at the snow just outside their ring of warmth. Perhaps lost in thought. Perhaps not listening. "Sorry to hear all that," Thel muttered, feeling like he should have said something and missed his cue.

"Sorry to tell you it," said Kae, smiling slightly again. "Now, here's something you might prefer to hear. About those manacles…"

Thel glanced down at them. "What about them?"

"Where does iron come from, you think?" Kae smiled more broadly.

"Mines," said Thel slowly. Then it hit him. "By the gods, you're joking."

Kae shook his head. "Not joking." He made a gesture like he held both sides of one manacle and cracked it in two.

Niat was frowning and looking back and forth between them.

Grumbling to himself, Thel grabbed the book from his jerkin and started viciously flipping through the pages. There, in the very last chapter—how to manipulate metal. What kind of fool didn't put a basic summary of what earth mages could control at the beginning of the book? By all the gods' dreams. If he ever made it back to Estun, he'd have to write his own damn book.

Kae cleared his throat. "Now, if you don't mind, I'm going to hunt for a bit of food around here. Hungry?"

Thel nodded vigorously, still paging through the book. "Our escape wasn't exactly something we could plan."

"All right then, let's see what I can rustle up. I can't promise it'll taste good, but it will keep you alive. For one more day, at least." He wandered off into the woods, whistling. The fire continued to burn, the smoke from it pouring out to one side instead of up and then dissipating over the wide forest floor.

Niat came and sat next to him again. He didn't look at her, just stared into the fire. All the discussion of Mage Hall had reminded him of the danger in hatred like hers, a danger that was very, very real.

She cleared her throat and straightened.

Automatically, he straightened as well and then grudgingly met her gaze. She was holding out her hand.

"I don't think we've been properly introduced," she said. Her cheeks were flushed again, ridiculous, round, rosy spots on cheeks like the palest birchwood. "Niat. Just Niat."

He snorted but then took her hand and shook it. "Prince Thel Lanuken of Akaria, at your service, my lady."

Her cheeks colored even more darkly, when he'd thought that impossible. "You needn't be at my service."

"That's just the standard greeting." They were still shaking hands, not having unclasped them.

"Oh, so you're at *everyone's* service, then?"

"Pretty much, yes. It's not insincere."

"Oh." She raised her eyebrows. "Well, uh, nice to meet you, Thel."

He caught his breath and then smiled to hide it. "Nice to meet you too." He wasn't sure if that was her starting over again, or just her response to realizing she had no idea what his name was but Kae did. Either way, it was good.

Later, Jaena rested her head on Ro's shoulder and

sighed. They lay side by side, falling in and out of sleep. The sun had shifted to the opposite side of the room, slanting in the sharp angles of winter's early sunset. How long had she slept?

She stared up at the stone above them and took a deep breath of the cold castle air. Out in the streets, the sounds of the market had died down, but the voices of passersby in the streets occasionally sprinkled the room with delighted laughter or indignant calls.

Shutting her eyes, she was about to doze off again when Ro whispered, "You awake?"

She blinked up at him and rubbed one eye. "Sort of."

"I've been thinking… You know, we could probably find a smithy here I could work in. With time, and with the war's end—if it ends—we could buy a house, even. Get my own smithy someday. Or a little shop front for you. Would you consider such a thing? I must say I prefer this White City to the red streets of Evrical."

Was he… saying what she thought he was saying? And did she dare to go with him on this dream and risk seeing it crumble before her? The war was far from won. The White City could utterly fall between now and then, and who knew if they'd even survive. But how often would she have a chance to taste such a dream? "A house with a garden perhaps?" she ventured.

"Certainly, if they have them here."

"I saw more than a few on my ride with Miara. I could finally sell some of your creations."

He laughed. "I'll be waiting on the interest from

those, by the way."

"Selfish bastard." She grinned and kissed him in reply. "There, that should do it."

"Ah, no, not quite enough. I need another."

When they drifted apart again, they lay in silence for a while.

"Have you ever thought about children for that garden?" he said softly.

She blinked. "I suppose if we were truly affluent, we could hire some neighborhood urchins to tend it," she said, smiling. Of course, that was not what he meant.

"Ah, I see," he said, a note of sadness to his voice.

He thought he had her answer. In truth, she hadn't thought about it. She hadn't allowed herself to. When she'd only desired freedom, and that freedom had been impossible, such concerns had seemed very distant. Mages in Mage Hall so rarely had children. It wasn't even until the last few days that she'd employed the use of the seeds that temporarily delayed such an eventuality.

"I'd hoped to avoid marriage, when I was young. My father would have married off my sister for some allegiance or connection, but we were comfortable enough that I might have been able to avoid it and start a shop. A husband would have kept me from that in our circles in Hepan."

"*Finally* I'm getting some details about Hepan out of you," he murmured, his breath tickling her neck, her ear. She giggled, and they settled into silence for a moment. "*I* would never keep you from that, you know."

Her heart pounded in her chest. Of course, she did know that. But she hadn't dared to assume anything permanent might come of this. And yet he had already made some rather permanent decisions on her behalf, nearly from the beginning.

"Have *you* longed for children for that garden?" He was older than her by a few years. Perhaps that brought such things to the fore of the mind.

"Yes," he said simply. Well, at least he was honest. Her heart pounded harder. "But you know, some long for them, yet no children come. Some don't want them and get too many. It's best to not set one's heart too firmly about it when so much of it lies in Nefrana's hands."

And my hands, she thought. She could hardly believe her ears, especially with the pounding of her heart. Did he... Could he really... She bit her lip.

He had been clear, she had no reason for doubt. Suddenly it did not feel so forward to be a little more frank.

"I wasn't saying no, I was just buying time to think."

"Oh?"

"I truly never thought about children. It was always very far away. Not so much now." She blushed at such a ridiculous statement when they lay so close together, as close as two people could possibly be. "I can't promise anything, but it's certainly not off the table. If this war ever ends..."

He kissed her, harder than she remembered him ever kissing her, and she knew already what her answer would be. Oh, she wouldn't tell him just yet. It was far too soon for that, and what if she had regrets in the morning light? But a desire kindled in her to grant him such a joy. After several long, deep minutes of being lost in each other, he fell back against the bed at her side, breathing deeply.

"I know there's a war raging and all, but... I'm sure we could find a priestess, for... you know," she said softly. She thought her heart would pound into her throat. Gods. What if she had this all wrong? What if she had misinterpreted what he'd said—

"Really? You would— I mean, do you think we could? Are you... sure?"

She snorted at his near babbling and drew him closer, back into her arms. "I hated the thought of you leaving."

"As did I."

"Is this too soon?"

He shrugged. "Do you have doubts in your heart?" He ran a finger over her collarbone, down toward her heart, and she shivered with the joy of it.

"No. My only doubt was whether you would let me come with you. Who's going to watch out for me while I'm working spells? And I need to be there to watch your back for deceitful priestesses and an extra-sneaky Devoted or two. I want to be with you all of your days, Tharomar, the good ones and the terrible ones to come."

"Then it doesn't seem too soon to me. Hell, I've already abandoned my whole life twice at this point." He grinned. "Don't see how I'd need to think much harder about swearing my love to you before the goddess. She already knows."

She winced. It was hard to think of Nefrana blessing any union of hers, or *anything* of hers, let alone the union of two mages. Yet, it mattered more to him than it did to her. He tensed, then cursed the Devoted under his breath and bent down to kiss her chest, her shoulder. Thank the gods he understood her reaction. He always seemed to understand her better than she could ever have hoped, better than she understood him.

"There's a temple just down the street," she said instead. "We could go tomorrow."

He pressed his lips against hers again. "Or right now."

She giggled. "Let me make a few preparations first. Nefrana and I have some… making up to do. I should at least wear something nice."

He snorted, then sobered. "You'd marry an urchin like me? You're sure?"

"And you'd marry a mage? A penniless slave?"

"You are far from that."

"So are you. But yes, I'd happily marry you. You may be a street rat, but you're my street rat. And you can read me ancient poetry, too. That's a rare combination, you know."

"I don't deserve a diplomat's daughter."

"Shh," she hushed. "Let's hope some day you can meet my father, and he can tell you that himself. But, personally, I think you do."

"Good thing you're the one that matters."

9 FAREWELL

Aven was waiting on horseback at the west gate when the group from Estun arrived. The cheery morning sun left him scowling at the horizon. The land flattened here near the coast, and so the woman sent to watch for the procession had sent word far in advance of their arrival, as soon as the train of horses and carriage had come into view. He'd ridden out with Dyon and a complement of guards to greet them.

Miara had been in the bath, unfortunately. It didn't matter, he told himself. He'd been sure to verify that claim by calling through the door as to her safety. He'd posted double the usual guards in and around her rooms since the tea situation. Everyone coming from Estun would be here to stay for the time being, so her presence was hardly necessary.

But her absence still made him nervous, rational or not.

Her attendant Opia had had a suspicious powder in

one pocket. The healer Nyor was working on identifying it. Unfortunately, the man who'd spoken to Opia had worn a black hood, probably a Devoted himself. Maybe a squire, since he had referred to a knight, or perhaps just someone trying to hide his identity. The other two attendants had known nothing about the plot, leaving Siliana a little chagrinned and bitter at Aven for making her enter their memories and scare them so.

He trusted her and was glad to know at least those two were innocent. It had powerful implications for the future, if he let himself think about it. But he didn't. He was still thinking about Opia. It had all been wrapped up a little too neatly.

The sight of his youngest brother's surly face and the heft of Devol's clap on his shoulder did wonders to improve his mood, especially when followed with a round of hearty embraces and thuds on the back. Renala and Teron stepped out of the carriage, talking quietly together. But Aven's heart really jumped when Fayton stepped out behind them.

"By Nefrana. How's it feel to see sunlight, my friend?" Aven said as he strode up.

Fayton just wrinkled his nose in amusement and shook his head.

"Miara's sure going to be glad to see you." He clapped a hand over his steward's shoulder.

"Is that so, my lord? I wouldn't have guessed." Fayton raised his eyebrows.

"Nothing like a new steward to make you appreciate

the old one. Telidar is great, of course, but," he glanced at the guards nearby, hoping they wouldn't repeat any of this, "she'll be glad to have you." He gave Fayton a wink, hoping the man knew he meant that Aven was glad to have him back too.

"Any news on Thel? Is he all right?" said Dom, blowing his breath into his hands to warm them as he approached. Their mother had been keeping him informed with regular reports by bird.

Aven winced and hung his head. "We don't know. No news. We sent a company after him, and he was alive then, but… Well, let's discuss it inside. Ranok is much warmer than the middle of the street."

The procession made its way back to Ranok, but Aven's newfound good cheer sank like a stone in the ocean when he saw Wunik and Jenec standing at the gatehouse, waiting for them.

He didn't even have to ask; he just met Wunik's gaze.

"Anonil," said Wunik, faltering. For once, he sounded shaky and older than his usual spry, witty self.

Aven swallowed and frowned down, knowing what was coming. He was surprised it'd taken this long. It'd bought them precious time to prepare, but not enough.

"What is it?" Dom asked from beside him.

"It's fallen, my lords," said Jenec, his voice barely audible over the wind.

Aven inhaled sharply, his grip strangling the reins. He didn't want to fight this war, he didn't want to leave Miara, he didn't want to slog through the cold and snow to a stronghold that might be rife with plague or a trap waiting to be sprung. Why did Kavanar have to long for power, abuse mages, enslave innocents?

He gritted his teeth. It didn't matter. They'd done it, and he was going to stop them. Because it was the right thing to do. Because it was all he could do. Because really, he had no other choice.

"We're headed to the front," he said coldly, glancing back at Dyon. "Send the word. By midday, we take to the road."

The next morning brought clouds peppered across the cool, blue sky. The forest was quiet as a tomb, if tombs had wind, except for the crunching of their boots in snow or snapping twigs from time to time. Thel was just starting to get unnerved by it when Kae started to hum.

The walking kept them warm, though, and Thel asked Kae questions from time to time, trying to work out some of the kinks in his knowledge. His wrists were still a little raw from the manacles, but at least he'd been able to leave them behind at their campsite. He had formed an outcropping out of the mud and rock for them, and with Kae's fire and foraging skills, Thel had been more comfortable than he'd been… possibly since he'd been yanked out of Panar. Niat seemed the same, although she stayed unusually quiet. He had a feeling she was probably trying to figure out when either he or Kae was going to stab her in the back—figuratively, if not literally.

Of course, they hadn't. They'd set off early for Anonil, and it was slowly dawning on him that he hadn't asked her many details about her vision and that she might be dreading seeing it come to life. He, too, had a knot of dread twisting his stomach as they got closer to the city. Possibly because the blue sky had grown grayish and smoky, and thick columns rose in the distance.

As it turned out, Anonil wasn't terribly far. Half a day's walk, and they were nearly there. They skirted around the mountain and followed a path that led higher up into the mountains toward some cliffs where they could hopefully get a good look at the city without getting too close.

When Thel reached the crest of the first cliff, he caught his breath. Niat had trailed along behind him, and she mustn't have realized he'd frozen in his tracks because she ran straight into his back.

"Thel, what the—" Still grabbing onto his arm for balance, she leaned around him. And saw it for herself.

Anonil lay before them, at least what they could see of it. What was left. Some of the town curved farther around the mountainside, but most remained in view.

And most of it was smoking, thick pillars of black coughing up into the air. It hadn't looked anything like this when they'd checked with farsight only the day before.

Soldiers swarmed the parts of the city that were not blacked out with smoke. Gods… Those were not Akarian soldiers. Thel elbowed Kae. "Can you look closer?"

Kae hiked a bit back from the edge and turned his

back to the city to keep the bright light out of view. Bringing up a view portal between two splayed hands, Kae frowned down into the window of light. Thel leaned over it. Sure enough, pennants and flags waved bloodred in the midday sun.

"Anonil—" he started. His voice faltered, so he waited a moment, as he had no desire to reveal how much this shook him. "It's fallen to Kavanar."

"I don't understand why there's so much smoke," said Niat from behind them. He glanced up; she still stared out over the cliff, reminding him for the moment of nothing but a lost little girl. Her hands plucked uneasily at her cloak, the hood pushed back, and her gaze darted around, as if struggling to take it all in. "Oh, by Nefrana, this is it—this is what goes wrong."

"What do you mean?" he said, stepping toward her.

"I— They... Never mind."

"Tell me, what is it? Do you know something about what part Alikar played in this? Or Sven or Detrax or anyone from Kavanar?"

She hung her head, shaking it back and forth unceasingly as she looked at the ground.

Thel scowled and walked the rest of the way over, then leaned closer so he was practically in her face. "They do not care about you, Niat. Why are you protecting them? Why?"

She looked up and narrowed her eyes at him. "No one cares about me. People don't care about other people. That's just the way things are."

Kae dropped the window and rejoined them closer to the cliff's edge. "Aw, now, that's not true."

She folded her arms, probably as much out of frustration as out of the chilling effect of the mountain wind. "Yes, it is. Besides, I'm not protecting them, I'm *scared* of them."

Thel blinked, his gaze on her sharpening. "What?"

"I fear what they will do to me more than what you will."

Well, that wasn't entirely unreasonable. Completely logical, in fact, as he'd never harm her intentionally. How heartbreakingly sad, though, that she had such a dark view of people. "You know, some people actually want to do the right thing *because* it's the right thing."

She shook her head. She glanced out at the Kavanarian troops, again her gaze darting. Searching.

"I can protect you from them," he said.

Her expression turned pained, her lips pressing together. "I know you mean well, Thel, and it's very kind, but—"

"But I'm cursed and corrupted, I know, I know," he muttered.

"—but I don't see how you can possibly protect me. No one can. I've been a failure at protecting myself, even."

"You're here now, aren't you?"

She paused, looking down, then out over the Kavanarian troops again.

"You protected yourself this much. Why do you keep looking like that? What are you looking for?"

"Thinking I should turn myself in."

"What!"

Kae raised his eyebrows. "I've known some like her. They don't long for freedom, after so long in a cage."

She glowered at him. "I'm just being practical. They'll find me eventually. It's inevitable. If I show up willingly, the punishment will be less."

Thel's hand was tightening into a fist, but he tried to hide it in his cloak's folds. "But you'll still get punished, damn it. Don't go back, and you won't be." Stay with me instead, he thought. He blinked at the ferocity of the emotion welling up in him, a deep desire to *make* her stay, to not allow her to leave.

"It's unavoidable." She was shaking her head again, the bleakness snuffing out the fire in her eyes.

He reeled back, and she seemed sincerely surprised. "There are six territories in Akaria. The men you fear have dominion over only two, and one of them has already ceded his land to Kavanar. Before you *killed him* yourself."

Kae's eyebrows flew up even higher now, and Niat's eyes widened. She stared for a moment, then looked away, back at the city one more time. Kae turned and stalked away, as if finally deciding to leave this between the two of them. Thel waited, but she didn't say anything. Just searched the horizon.

That's it, he thought. Whatever was supposedly wrong, she'll never tell me. He turned to walk away in Kae's direction. She was just going to head on back, walk down the trail, and fling herself into the nearest Kavanarian soldier's arms. Throwing away all he'd done to get her free, of a chance at a future of her own making, of a chance of a future with—

"They were not supposed to fight back," she said softly.

He stopped, turned. "Just… let the forces take the city? Akarians sitting by, letting soldiers from Kavanar take their city?"

She nodded, still looking perplexed. "I heard Alikar say he ordered them not to fight."

He laughed darkly. "Well, you can see how well that turned out." He started walking away again.

"Why are you laughing?"

"No soldier I know would follow such an order. It's preposterous. An affront. An insult. Your tormentors may have made some fancy deals and arrangements with each other, but they don't know how to lead men."

"And you do?"

He snorted. "I don't need to, my brother does."

"And yet Anonil has still fallen."

He scowled at her. "If you met him, you wouldn't say that. But thanks for pointing that out, traitor."

"I am *not* a traitor." Fire woke in her eyes.

"Then don't throw the fall of a city and the deaths of hundreds, if not thousands, of good people in my face," he shouted back at her.

"That's not what I was doing. Name one traitorous thing I've ever done," she demanded.

"You voted against my brother."

"I read a piece of paper stating my *father's* opinion," she shouted, and for a moment, he just marveled at the fire and hoped it'd never fade, even if it was aimed at him. "An opinion that was his right as an Assembly Member. Was it not?"

He gritted his teeth. Grudgingly, he had to admit she had a point. "It was. And it still is. Fine. You're not *exactly* a traitor." He forced himself to take a deep breath. "But you have to admit your father clearly is. You can't blame me for assuming things. Especially when you want to run back to them!" He gestured sloppily at the city.

She folded her arms, looking exasperated. "Is that it? Spawned to traitors, betrothed to traitors—what can you expect?"

"I can expect you to make your own choices. To do the right thing, to protect people that need protecting, to treat people with respect. And to not give up before the fighting's done. But most of all, to choose your own path. That's how the goddess will judge you."

Her face went completely white.

He dropped to sit in the dirt, and she spun away from him. Her boots thudded away in the softening soil Thel had created as he'd heated the earth to warm them. Then the sound of the boots stopped. He listened intently for a moment, then another, but he heard nothing. Fine. Let her go back to them, he didn't care. The tightness in his shoulders and the way he glowered out at the city told him he was not exactly being truthful with himself about the matter.

He studied the field, carefully looking for some way he could help. Maybe not turn the tide, but at least be a thorn they wouldn't know they were dealing with.

Kae called from behind him to the left. "I'm going to check the next cliff to see what's visible from there and if there's anything I can do. Maybe put out some fires."

Thel nodded, working his fingers into the dirt. Actually, it was kind of mud. Wet. He shouldn't have liked it. But the feel of cold mud against his palms, his fingers was always more relaxing than not. Even if it got on everything afterward. It always came off. As his mother had frequently found out when he was a child. Mountain fortresses were mostly stone and well civilized, but there was still dirt to be found by clever young boys to play in. His aptitude for finding it more than his brothers made a little more sense now.

Soft, feminine steps came up behind him. He glanced over his shoulder to see her about to reach out and tap his. She pulled her hand away.

They stared at each other for one heartbeat, another. The fire was still in her eyes, the bleakness gone. Well, good. Maybe if he was honest with her, but also respected her right to leave, it'd keep her from doing so. He wasn't quite sure what kind of twisted logic that was, but his gut told him it just might work.

"You can give up," he said, "but I'll be damned if I do. I'm an Akarian. We don't give up. Go on, go down to them if you want. I'll think you're wrong, I'll regret you went, but I won't stop you."

He turned away, turned back to the city. There. A trebuchet on slightly uneven earth. He shifted the ground under one large wooden foot, raising it up just like he'd pull a boulder from the ground. It wobbled off-balance and toppled, the long arm breaking. He smiled wolfishly. Oh, this should be fun.

He jumped at a motion beside him. He'd been so focused on the spell, he hadn't heard her moving closer. She eased to the ground beside him, kneeling in a drier patch over some clumps of grass and clasping her hands in her lap.

"What are you doing?" he said softly.

Her eyes locked with his. A low flame smoldered in them now, and it sent a shiver through him, like he was watching someone that had been pulled violently out to sea get the barest grip on the shore's edge. "What does it look like I'm doing?"

"Kneeling down in the mud."

"You're an earth mage, aren't you? Can't you do something about that?"

"Maybe. I'm not a very good one." He stared a moment longer.

"I'm praying for the city. Obviously. That's what priestesses do."

He snorted. "Obviously."

Aven had received a handful of objections and warnings from Tharomar for stealing off with the translated map so soon, but ultimately the smith had relented and handed over the thick sheet. It was strange to see the map whole, and without its typical shimmering, but it *was* eminently more useful in this form.

Back in his rooms, he studied by the window's light. It had seemed like he'd known it well enough, but dozens of new details crowded the page, and he wasn't sure which mattered. There would be no time to learn it all before he left. He sighed. He'd have to study it on the road.

As he folded the map, the door opened behind him, and somehow against all sense, he knew it was her.

He looked up. Her eyes had halted on the paper in his hand. Then her gaze met his. Her eyes swirled with an intense mix of emotions he couldn't quite understand. Sadness, fear, anger. Was there a hint of betrayal?

"Is that what I think it is?" she said softly.

"Yes." He held it frozen, his fingers gripping it gingerly by the corner, and he didn't put it in his jerkin yet as he'd been intending to.

Who would have guessed that the thing that had once united them would come between them?

"You're not going to destroy it, are you. Ever." More of an accusation than a question.

"I don't know," he said, simple and honest. If this was going to come between them, he didn't need to add lies to it too. "There hasn't been time to memorize it."

She stood frozen as she had since she'd walked in the door. His heart was racing, and a cold sweat broke out on his forehead. Her hair was down again today and inter-mixed with a dozen tiny braids and silver beads, and her dress was silver, pale like a priestess's robe. He wondered if he'd ever see her in a tunic and trousers again. How funny that he should miss that, and so quickly, but it was almost as if the Miara he knew was shifting, twisting before his eyes, and he was waiting to see just who would emerge, and if he would actually know her.

They hadn't known each other even two months. They might as well be strangers. How had he ever been so sure that she was the perfect one for him? Was it all just stubborn delusion?

That didn't ring like truth, though. The thought was frigid with fear. What even was "perfect" anyway? And of all the people he'd known all his life, how many of them had risked their lives for him when they didn't have to? How many would have sought to do the right thing when the world had weighted everything to make them do the wrong one? He might not have known her forever, but he knew the important things.

And that moral compass of hers was pleading with him right now to listen.

Abruptly she rushed close, grabbing his arm like she thought he might fade away. Her sudden warmth, the scent of her drifting toward him—they were all subtle reassurances. When he rode out, when would he feel her this close again?

And if he didn't return?

"Listen to me, Aven," she said. "Some of those spells may seem innocuous, but they are dangerous. You have to believe me."

He ran the backs of his fingers down her cheek, along her jaw, trying to memorize the feel of her. "I do believe you. But where would we be without them?"

She looked down for a moment, then back up quickly. "You're thinking this map has done nothing but good for us. Why assume it can't do more?"

He pressed his lips together. "Yes. Where would we be without it? And I'm also thinking I don't want the last words we ever say to each other to have been said in anger."

She squeezed his arm harder. "Don't talk like that."

"You've heard Anonil has fallen, haven't you? I could see it on your face when you walked in. Now that the others are here, and with that… It's time, Miara. Kavanar's knocked at the door."

"They've been knocking for a while now."

"Yes. And it's time that I answered."

Her grip tightened further. It was almost starting to hurt. "You better come back to me, Aven Lanuken. I didn't rescue you from Daes just so you could throw yourself at him again."

"He'll be the one who needs rescue from me. And I fully intend to return, don't worry. But that's why I'm taking every weapon I can."

His eyes locked with hers as he lifted the map pointedly. Then, after a dozen heartbeats of silence, he tucked the map into his jerkin as slowly as he could manage, inviting her to stop him.

She didn't.

She tore her eyes away, looked down at her shoes,

then the fire. "I hate to fight over this," she said softly, shaking her head.

"You're just trying to help me do the right thing. That's a good thing." He mustered a weak smile.

Her expression turned earnest, and she grabbed his other arm too. "Aven, I thought about it for a long time. With the stars, yes, you've done some good, and I personally have benefited greatly. But people deserve to think for themselves. Everything that map does is the opposite. Anger, calm, slavery, freedom, even insight—it's all mind control. That's exactly what the Dark Days started over."

"You're right. But the map also liberates them from that control. Undoes itself. If people try to abuse these spells, someone needs to be able to stop them. And if I need to use these spells to defend this city—and you—I will."

"You don't just mean the freeing spells. You mean all of them. You mean the ones that enslave, that control people's minds. You want to use them."

"No, I don't *want* to. But I will, if I have to."

"They're evil."

"Evil or not, they're all I've got to work with. Do you think if Daes captures this city—if he captures you—it will feel any better just because we have the moral high ground? 'I might be dead or a slave, but at least I can say I never used any evil spells'?"

She gasped. "Aven! Don't talk like that. Don't *say* that." She was frowning hard, searching his face.

"This is war. There are no second chances, and we're vastly outnumbered."

"If you're using evil methods to win, you might as well sacrifice your soul on Daes's altar."

"We don't *know* they're evil."

"It's mind control! I don't know if I can marry someone who would enslave someone—or who would even *consider* using magic to control minds."

He reeled back. "Miara, the situation is nearly hopeless. We're losing a hundred men to a handful, without the enemy taking any losses. At this rate, we're *doomed* unless we come up with something more. I wouldn't remotely consider it if it weren't so dire, but we have to survive. We can't let them win."

"Promise me you'll leave the slave star alone. Promise me you won't use it." Her fiery eyes bored into him, and the implication terrified him.

He opened his mouth, but no words would escape.

A knock sounded at the door. He glowered at it. Talk about terrible timing. Couldn't they just sort this out for five minutes without interruption? His eyes flicked back to hers.

"Someone needs you, Aven. You have a journey to prepare for and a war to fight. I should go." She took a step away.

"Miara—wait! We can figure this out."

Another knock sounded, and he heard Perik moving from the far office toward the door to answer it.

Impulsively, he crossed the distance between them, took her face in her hands, and kissed her. Let Perik see, or whoever was knocking, he didn't care. If he never got a chance to marry her, he was going to have this one last kiss at least. To his relief, her mouth was firm against his, and he savored her one last time. Her fingers dug into him like talons, reassuring him that she wanted to hold onto him as badly as he wanted to hold onto her. He wanted the moment to last forever so they didn't have to face any of the vileness that awaited them.

She broke away too soon and looked up at him, breathless and eyes wide. Aven had the sense that Perik was hovering near the door, trying to decide if he should answer or not. The knock sounded a third time.

"I'm going to go. But please, Aven, think about what I said. Don't use that magic. People deserve to think for themselves."

"They also deserve to be free. Like you are."

She pressed her lips together as she frowned, clearly upset, but she nodded ever so slightly as she turned to go. Then she slipped out through the door Perik had opened, steward Telidar arriving behind her.

Telidar started peppering him and then Perik with questions, but Aven ignored her, standing numb. He clung to that nod, the look in her eyes. He couldn't quite read it. Why couldn't they have more time? Why couldn't she simply agree with him? Of course, he didn't want that. He'd never wanted that.

The steward's questions finally broke through to his mind, and he answered absently as dread coiled in his gut, deeper and darker than any he'd ever known.

Jaena stared up at the temple steps, a cold wind whipping her cloak's hood against her cheek. What was she doing, coming here? What was she thinking? They'd send her out with curses—if they didn't have Devoted hanging around, waiting to do far worse. She'd defend herself if need be, but she hoped it wouldn't come to that.

Staff in hand, one she'd borrowed from the stables in a moment of fear, she climbed one step, then another. The white marble was rounded down in the middle from years of footsteps. She was not the first to have trodden here, or even the thousandth. How many had worshipped at the temple before her? How many had climbed these steps? She was a grain of sand on the beach, and the solemn stone held no warmth or invitation. Cold and unfeeling as the snow waiting in the clouds above, readying to fall. A pillar on the high crest arching above her had fallen, and the damaged stone itself seemed to frown down at her.

A woman had started down the temple steps but stopped upon seeing her. Her pale, gauzy robe and golden cloak suggested a priestess. The woman paused and waited as Jaena ascended the steps faster now. She had no desire to be seen hesitating or doubting or staring bleakly at the steps.

"Nefrana's blessings, my child. Can I help you?" the woman asked, voice all politeness. Wrinkles around the corners of her eyes gave Jaena the impression of one who had smiled much for many years, and in spite of her desire to dislike the woman, she had to admit the priestess had a kind face.

"I'm a mage," Jaena said. Best be blunt about these things and get it over with. "Do you welcome mages in your temple?"

The woman paled at first, and then straightened a little, as if recovering from a slight. "Nefrana welcomes all in Elii Temple, although we ask that you not use magic within her walls. Why do you ask?"

"I've some questions. But first, I need to pray."

That wasn't entirely true. But she couldn't—wouldn't—explain herself. Not yet, probably not to anyone.

The holy woman held out an arm, ushering Jaena inside through broad wooden doors. Marble columns soared up four, five stories into the air, round slabs of elegant stone neatly stacked one atop another, topped with high, delicate arches. By the gods, were all the great temples in all the great cities like this? Or was this special to the White City? She'd traveled far with her parents, but they'd rarely visited inside temples themselves. And how had anyone built such a place without the help of mages? Could they even?

"Magnificent, is it not?" said her companion mildly.

Jaena nodded. She shivered, then tried to hide it lest the woman think her shivering with awe. No, definitely not, it was just that it was as cold in here as it was out in the street. Only the biting wind was staved off; heating such a large cavern of stone must be next to impossible.

Although, Jaena could have warmed them with her magic. But she would respect the woman's request. For now.

"There are shrines around the outer walls, whichever may suit you. Most priests and priestesses are out in the gardens working, if you have questions."

"In the gardens so late in the year?"

"Rituals cleansing the land after the harvest take time."

"Ah," said Jaena, as if she knew. She did not. Time held captive in Kavanar had not increased her knowledge of those who worshipped Nefrana, and even Ro had said little, shying away from the delicate subject. Her parents had always been busier with politics than religion, and that seemed a common enough attitude in Hepan. Here in Akaria, of course, Anara was easily the most popular deity. What did her temple look like?

She thanked the woman, who headed out of the temple and down the steps again, and then Jaena skirted around the outside, eying the shrines with trepidation.

In truth, she had not come here to pray. She'd been forced to pray enough in Mage Hall for a lifetime. If the day ever came that she needed to pray, it would likely be a long, long time in the future. Maybe never.

Although, Tharomar's prayers seemed... nice. Pleasant. Cleansing, even. Sitting by his side for a solemn ritual wouldn't be so bad.

But no, she had not come here to pray.

She had come to see if she could stand it. If she'd feel like a slave—or like she *should* be one. She would not have them treated like outcasts, and she wouldn't lie about her magic and pretend. Not in front of the gods. If they had to go to the temple of Anara or Mastikos, so be it. But Nefrana was deep in Tharomar's heart, central to his much-beleaguered oath and his embattled sense of honor.

She had to see if she could stand half an hour in this temple. Long enough to be married in Nefrana's golden light.

She hadn't counted on being alone.

Statues of Nefrana circled the outer walls of the temple, each from a different material. The first was carved from white stone, the next from dark stained walnut. One small statue appeared to be blown glass shot through with white, gold, and blue. A few farther ones were crafted in sandy, golden shades. Actual gold inlay shone from a black marble figure.

Jaena walked slowly toward them, her footfalls and the dull thud of her staff rudely loud in the silent, empty hall.

Candles burned before some statues. Many gazed down upon bundles of wheat shorn from the fields. A few altars even held loaves of bread. A standard offering, or the result of creative petitioners? Jaena had no idea.

Walking along, she kept an eye out for anyone. Could the emptiness be a trick? Could the priestess be sending word to set someone upon her, recapture her even now? Surely, with a mage as king, things would start to change, but they wouldn't change overnight. And she held no illusions. She was in the lion's den.

She stopped in front of one of the farthest statues. Wood, she discovered. The figure of the goddess was crafted carefully and meticulously from cream-colored wood, knots and twists and all. This one was not so perfect as the others, not without flaws. Like Jaena herself. It showed the injuries of growth, of years, of the twists and changes of life.

Candles sat on this altar, but they remained unlit. On a whim, she moved her staff to her other hand and took a stick from the altar beside it. She lit the slender stick and carried its light over, lighting not one but all of the candles. This was a beautiful statue, and it deserved equal offerings, even if no one other than her could see it.

Shaking out the flame and returning the wick to the altar, she stepped back.

Why had she really come?

A wave of emotions rose, startling her, the biggest of them all: Why?

Why had she ever been torn from her parents? Why had she been gifted this magic in the first place? Why had she lost Dekana? Why must any of it have happened?

Indeed, what cruel god would let such things happen to innocents?

And yet, she had somehow survived, somehow made it through, somehow escaped. And somehow she'd found this man who loved her enough to walk away from his smithy, his temple, the only life he'd ever known, away even from his oaths and his own sense of honor. And she'd never once asked him to give up any of it. He'd done it all freely, as if for himself.

"What have I done to deserve all this?" she whispered. She wasn't sure which events she meant anymore, the good or the bad. Maybe all of them in concert.

Why did the world give her such gifts after such pain? Was it Nefrana's will? Anara's? The Balance at work?

Dekana would never get such happiness. Where was the Balance in that? And what of her parents? How would they feel when they learned Jaena was alive and safe and free—and Dekana was not? They'd resent her. They'd think she should have tried harder to save her sister. They wouldn't understand what it had been like for her to be a slave, to watch her pillar of strength slowly crack and crumble into broken, bitter nothingness.

How could they understand? She couldn't expect them to. How could anyone? Free or no, the torture of the memories, of the loss, would never end.

And indeed—how could Jaena be happy when Dekana was dead? How dare she ever be happy at all? She deserved none of this.

Why?

She stared into the statue's feminine gaze, not sure what she expected to happen. The world did not make sense, that shouldn't surprise her. It wasn't as if Nefrana or any of them had a single master plan. As if they pulled strings like puppeteers.

And if there was a Balance—where was it? Nothing could justify her sister's death. *Nothing.* How could there be any sort of cosmic equilibrium in the face of tragedy? Of horror?

No, it was all nonsense, designed to manipulate people.

She stepped forward and cupped the candles, ready

to blow them out.

Before she could, a door opened, the frigid wind whipping at the fragile flames. Seeing them fighting for their tiny lives as she'd been about to snuff them out made her hesitate.

She lowered her arm.

What if Dekana had never died?

She shook her head at such a foolish question and turned to leave. She still needed to inquire about marriage, but she'd come back. Just now… she was not in a celebratory mood. They'd think she didn't want to marry him, with the despair that saturated her.

But what if Dekana had never died?

I would have never taken the brand, she thought. Certainly I would have tried to escape, but…

She stopped short. Would she have tried? Escape had been impossible. Dekana's death had been shortly before Miara had left on her mission into Akaria, hadn't it? Jaena hadn't known about it at the time; she'd been too busy mourning and then plotting her revenge.

She took a deep breath, letting her thoughts venture into territory she usually feared to tread.

If Dekana hadn't died, Miara might never have come to Akaria. Dekana would have had the mission to capture Aven. Perhaps she would have failed. Or succeeded. Either way, would her sister have charmed Aven into falling in love with her? Both seemed sensitive souls, but Jaena could not see it. Truthfully, she could not see her sister succeeding at such a trying, brutal mission. Nothing against Miara, but she was not quite so sensitive, and she had determination to match every drop of sadness, it seemed.

What were the chances that if Dekana had undertaken that quest, that she'd have inspired Aven to free her? And if she had failed, then none of them would be free. Aven wouldn't be king. The war wouldn't have started.

Jaena would never have met Tharomar.

She turned on her heel and narrowed her eyes at the statue of wood. She'd never have traded her sister for this happiness. It wasn't fair. But then again, it hadn't been her choice. Dekana had had to do what she'd had to do, much as Jaena might wish she could have stopped it.

The statue's eyes seemed to gaze down at the candles sadly but kindly, as if fixated on her offering. As if acknowledging the tragic and the painful, but also the beautiful that made it all somewhat tolerable in the end.

She shook her head, clenched her jaw, and strode out.

Back in her rooms, Miara lay on a couch by the fire. A gloom had settled over her, a fog of weariness and worry that she didn't have the energy to fight. The words she and Aven had traded kept replaying in her mind, and she kept piecing through them, trying to find some error, some means of reconciliation. In spite of her harsh words, she really didn't want him leaving Panar on a note like this. She needed something to say to him when they said goodbye that would make it all better. But no healing words would come.

Kalan bustled about around her, thankfully returned with Siliana's assurance that the woman had known nothing of the plot. Closets opened and shut, and cloth rustled. Etral had gone home a bit early after the dungeon business, but she, too, had been cleared by the creature mage to return to work. That didn't surprise Miara, and truth be told, it was the best possible outcome because finding new attendants wouldn't have been much of a better bet.

Well, unless they ransacked new individual's minds for signs of betrayal too. Which maybe they *should* be doing, as unpleasant as that sounded. Maybe even everyone in Ranok should be subject to such a check… But she didn't see that winning them any loyalty among nonmages with tactics like that.

"My lady, the healer Nyor sends word that he knows what the substance was that Opia was putting in your tea. He'd like to discuss it with you when you're available. Also Master of Arms Devol hopes to stop by later, and Prince Dom has invited you to dinner after the troops ride out this afternoon."

She sighed, her heart panging just to think of it. "Thank you, Kalan."

"Shall I fetch you some… not tea," said Kalan, smiling shakily. "Perhaps some wine?"

"Certainly, if you bring the corked bottle yourself."

Kalan smiled, nodded, and turned to go, but then

she hesitated in the doorway.

"What is it?"

Kalan eyed her for a moment, then shut the door and scurried close. "You know, it's probably nothing, my lady, but with everything going on... I must say I don't like the healer. I have a bad feeling about him. Take us with you when you go. Or a guard. Or both."

Miara frowned. "The queen had nothing good to say about him either. I mean, Queen Elise. What is it about him?"

"I can't put my finger on it. It's nothing specific he's done. It's just... the look in his eyes. It's like he's more butcher than healer."

"Well, I haven't met him, but I'll be sure not to go alone. I'll wait till after King Aven leaves and take you and a full complement."

Kalan squeezed Miara's arm. "Good. Now let me go see about that wine. You might want it ready at hand, what with your man headed off to war and all."

Miara smiled, her cheeks flushing. "That's very thoughtful of you."

"Well, you've been thoughtful of us. Some would've shut all three of us in the dungeon and thrown away the key." She made for the door, then turned back again. "I'm sorry about what Opia did, my lady. If I had known— I mean, I didn't, but if I'd even suspected—"

Miara held up a hand. "It's all right. She didn't get very far."

Kalan nodded and shut the door behind her.

Miara leaned back on the lounge and took a deep breath of the opulent palace air. While it was so luxurious it almost made her blush even smelling it, she had to admit it did smell exquisite. The smokiness of the fire mixed with the sweet tang of the roses. She filled her lungs again and again, exalting in a moment of pure solitude. The fog of uneasiness had lifted slightly, but now it settled down again around her. She searched again for words.

When she'd sated her need to take in the exotic scent, she glanced around the rooms. The quiet was deep around her, almost oppressive. She shut her eyes and let herself start to hum as she spun her spell into the pots of soil. She hadn't had much time for them just yet. The room had already been breathtakingly beautiful and laden with flowers. But, hell, she'd add a few more of her own making.

She hummed as she worked. The tune was old, one her father had sung to Luha to comfort her when she'd first arrived in Mage Hall, a melody of elaborate beauty but more than one sad turn. Why it comforted, Miara wasn't sure. Perhaps it was because the tune was so powerfully enchanting that one forgot about real sadness and just remembered the song's sadness instead.

The mountains shed the brightest tears
So shed no tears, my love, for me.
I shall love you a thousand years
Whether tempest tossed or thrown by sea.

Torn from your arms that I loved so well

What fate will hold I do not know.
Upon our loss, my love, don't dwell
As to the mountains I go.

She didn't know when she'd switched from humming to singing softly to herself, but when she heard the click of the door, she cut off abruptly. Kalan was sweet, but Miara wasn't so comfortable with her yet that her announced arrival didn't make her blush. She sat up quickly and turned. "Kalan, thank—"

She stopped short. It was not Kalan.

It was the healer, and he was alone. She stood, backing toward the table where her daggers sat behind her. "Announce yourself," she said slowly. "My guards are in error for not doing so." She might be new to this nobility thing, but she knew something was off.

"Oh, I told them not to bother," he said, smiling warmly. That voice… could that have been the voice Opia was talking with? She had met this man so briefly, the day he'd stared at her long and hard, so his voice would be familiar, but her gut told her he'd been at Opia's side that day. Siliana had only seen a man in a hood, and Opia hadn't known who he was or Siliana would have known too.

"It's not appropriate that we be alone," she said, taking a page from Aven's book.

"Oh, but I am Healer Nyor, my lady," he said, smooth and warm. He bowed low with an elaborate sweep of his arm. "Healers at times must visit the ill outside of such rules of propriety. Just as I am visiting you. I'm concerned the substance I've identified for you may have had some long-lasting effects. I've also heard you're an accomplished healer yourself."

"Horses," Miara blurted, as she gripped one dagger hilt behind her and slid it out, holding the hilt with the blade pressed flat against the small of her back. All the while, she tried to look as though her hands were clasped casually and demurely behind her. His eyes flicked to the movement of her elbows. He wasn't fooled.

"Pardon me, my queen?" He strode toward her.

"Oh, I'm no queen. Not yet anyway." If he resented her holding the throne, perhaps she could calm him by pretending she didn't want it. She shifted sideways, circling the room and putting herself closer to the door, and him out of the path between her and her exit.

"And yet, you stay in the queen's rooms," he said, spreading his hands. He stopped for a moment, then took a few more steps toward her.

"I'm just a horse healer. Horses—that's what I meant. I heal horses." She danced to the side again, but this time he came back in her direction, as if he *would* try to block her from the door if she made for it. He didn't ask what was wrong or what she was up to—a bad sign.

She shouldn't be here alone with him.

"Guards," she called. "I'm concerned you may have offended our honored healer, and my sensibilities too. Come here at once." My, she was sounding more and more like a noble these days.

But regal or not, no one responded. Nyor just smiled and drew a small pouch from his pocket.

"Now, back to the substance your attendant was putting in your tea," he said mildly, stepping closer again. He was barely more than a horse's length from her now.

"Stay back," Miara said, anger sharp in her voice.

"It was edder's blood," he said casually. He didn't respond to her command but didn't come closer just yet either.

"Blood?" She'd never heard of a creature called an edder.

"It's from a flower," he said, stepping forward again and holding it out as if to smell it. She took a step back in turn.

But not quickly enough. He lunged forward and tossed the contents of the pouch in her face.

She threw up her arms, revealing her dagger, but it was too late. The powder burned her nostrils, her eyes, her mouth, and she coughed violently, her body desperate to reject whatever it was.

She was still coughing when the door opened again. She could hear it, but she could no longer feel her lips. She looked up through watery eyes but couldn't see who was at the door.

"My lady—"

"Kalan, no—" *Run. Get out. Go.* She shoved the final words silently into the poor woman's mind, but there was no helping it. Otherwise they wouldn't have gotten out at all. She wanted to hurl the dagger at the bastard, but she couldn't see straight enough to know if it was Kalan or him she'd be hitting. Or anything at all.

She groped with her magic. Two creatures were still in the room, closer together now.

"No—leave her—" The coughs were too much. She couldn't make the sounds come out.

Leave her alone, damn you! she screamed into his mind. For once, she thrust herself into his thoughts, dredging out every horrible image she could find—a vicious, leaping wolf, a swarm of angry bees, anything. She forced the sensation of her coughs, her burning, her pain into his mind as well. Anything. Kalan had been kind to her. She didn't deserve this. She had to stop him, to cut him off from reaching her.

She was never certain it did any good, however. The whole world seemed to spin, her eyes swimming with water as she nearly coughed up a lung and fell to her side.

As the powder seized her, she tightened her grip on his mind, dragging them both down savagely into the darkness.

IO   BETRAYAL

Aven's eyes searched the group waiting in Ranok's stable, but Miara wasn't there. Two dozen horses were saddled and chuffing now and then, impatient to get on the road, intended as his personal guard. Men and women bundled in gambesons, cloaks, scarves, and more milled about, finishing preparations for the journey ahead. This part was a small force, but they'd join the rest of the regiment just outside the city. The last few supplies of food, water, and armor were being lashed down to the wagons. Dyon was darting about, overseeing it all with Jenec at his side.

Jaena and Tharomar stood leaning together against a far pillar, chatting casually, and Derk leaned on another pillar, just frowning at everything. He looked more angry than anything else, although Aven had no idea why.

Their presence sent a further twist of worry into his gut for no reason he could name. The fact that they'd managed to stop by to see the soldiers off while Miara hadn't, seemed… off. She couldn't really be so angry with him that she'd not say goodbye, could she?

He took a deep breath. He'd rather not fight. But if the choice was between using the map to save her or not using it and losing everything, he knew what he had to do.

His eyes caught on Telidar standing near the mages, Fayton at her side. He strode over to the stewards. The smith and the two mages turned to listen. As if reading the question on his face, Telidar spoke up as he neared. "Are you looking for Arms Master Floren, my lord?" Telidar had always been one for tradition and propriety, but that seemed an oddly unfamiliar way to refer to her, almost disingenuous considering everyone knew she was far more than just a warrior in his service.

"Yes, have you seen her?" he said simply.

"She sent word via her attendant Kalan, sire, who said your mother the queen requested the arms master watch over King Samul while your mother said goodbye to you. See, Queen Elise approaches, sire."

Aven frowned at that, but he supposed it made sense. He and Miara had already had a chance to say their goodbyes in his rooms. Even if they hadn't ended as he'd have preferred. And indeed his mother walked out toward them from the main compound.

As he waited for his mother to reach him, Aven moved to Jaena and Tharomar and Derk. "Check on her for me, will you?" he said quietly. "Something seems off."

Tharomar nodded, his brow creased in a somber line.

"We will," said Jaena, her expression intent also.

"Running off on her already?" said Derk, the anger in his expression lessening for a moment into a more amused version of itself.

Aven could tell he wasn't serious, but Tharomar looked at Derk like he might like to punch the man himself. Aven smiled and shook his head. "What crawled into your ear and died?" Aven said instead. "You're not the one going off to war this time."

"Thank the gods," Derk shot back, but his face grew grim, not his usual wry smile.

"For the record, I'd rather Miara come along." Aven winced at the wistfulness that escaped in his voice.

"Then why isn't she?" Jaena asked.

"Because she wants to find more mages in the city," Aven said. "Needs to, really. We're vastly outnumbered in mages. She could use your help."

"We'll help," said Tharomar, quick as his last nod. His force of will surprised Aven, but perhaps it made sense with Tharomar's order and all. He likely had a duty to help these mages. None of them were really safe yet. That sent another pang of worry into Aven's heart, but his mother finally reached him, cutting off the thought.

Without a word of greeting, she hugged him fiercely for several long breaths. "You better come back to me, Aven," she said finally, her voice shakier than normal, a little crazed. "Promise me."

"Oh, Dom isn't so bad," he said, trying to laugh it off. "He'd make a good king."

"I don't care. Come back and abdicate, if you like. Just

promise me you'll *come back*." She pulled away and made him look in her eyes, hands on his shoulders, like she had when he was much smaller, a boy refusing to listen.

"You know I can't promise that, Mother," he said, his voice dark. He wanted to pat her shoulder in return, but it was awkward with her pinning him from both sides, so he settled for a shrug. "But I'll try. I'll do my best."

Elise nodded, as if her calm was slowly returning. "That's all I can ask, I suppose."

He squeezed her tightly one more time. "When Father wakes up," he whispered, then faltered. He wouldn't say "if." His father would be all right, certainly. He couldn't die. "When father wakes up, tell him I'm sorry we fought. Even if I was right." He smiled at the silliness of the statement, but while he wanted to believe Samul would definitely get better, Aven was not at all sure that he'd live to see any of them again.

He stared wistfully up into Ranok's pillars and windows, wishing he could have seen Miara's face one more time, run a fingertip along the smooth warmth of her cheek, hugged her body close to his for just one more moment so he could memorize that wild-lavender scent.

But his father's health was clearly fragile. He sighed and mounted up.

He was one of the last to do so; the unit was nearly ready. He spotted Siliana approaching Derk, her arms folded awkwardly at her chest, and Derk's gaze hardened as she approached. So that's what the anger was all about?

"I don't like that he's sending you," Derk blurted.

"It's my choice," said Siliana coldly. "He's not sending me anywhere."

Aven frowned, but something told him they were referring to Wunik, not him. He kept his eyes off them now, so as not to let on he was listening.

"You haven't trained for combat."

"Just because I didn't anticipate this doesn't mean I don't want to help."

"Promise me that if fighting breaks out, you'll stay back. Lay low. Don't get hurt." Pain sheared through his voice at the final words.

"I can heal myself just fine."

"Just come back to us, okay?" he said softly.

"Derk, we've been through this."

"It's not about *that*," Derk snapped. Aven struggled not to raise his eyebrows. Had he been in love with her once? Was he still? "I just don't want all the old man's wrath on me." He paused, and when she said nothing, he continued. "I need you, Sil. To deflect punishment. We couldn't stand to lose you."

Wunik was hardly wrathful, but the return of Derk's sarcasm did ease Aven's mind a little. At least until the man's voice broke on the word "need."

To Aven's surprise, Siliana hugged him, a long hug, a hug goodbye maybe between friends or people who had once been something more to each other but weren't any longer. Pulling away, she clapped his shoulder once and headed for her horse.

Derk stared after her, his eyes an intense jumble. Aven

tore his gaze away and looked over the group. Dyon was mounting up behind him. That was it.

As they rode out into Panar's streets, heading for the north gate, the rumbling of voices gathered somewhere reached his ears. Aven frowned.

Sure enough, as they reached the open market surrounding the north gate, the cobblestones were awash with people, from every storefront to the thick walls that ran around the city here.

The lead riders were slowly stomping forward, urging the crowd to the sides and forming a path. Still, there were enough people to squeeze the procession down to a horse's width.

His people. His responsibility. His duty. Easy to forget amid all the chaos. He met their eyes each in turn, greeting gazes with long stares. Some eyes were curious, some concerned. Now he caught voices among them, shouts thrown up as their group passed through the crowd.

"Is it true there's war coming, my lord?"

"Look, son, it's the new king."

"What about the mages?"

"I heard *he's* a damned mage." That was a new one.

"Kill those Kavanarian bastards!"

He sighed, wishing he had more he could tell them, more time to plan it and overall better tidings, but he reined the horse in. He had no clue how all these people had known they'd be leaving through the north gate, although it only added to the nerves twisting his gut. Someone had spread word of what they were doing.

Hopefully it'd been just an average soldier talking to his family and word had spread unusually fast.

"Halt for a moment," Aven called. The train of horses slowed. "I hear the people have questions. I may not have all the answers. But I may have one or two." He paused and waited. The crowd quieted, now all their attention focused on him like a beam of light.

"Kavanar has moved against us in war." His voice rang out, echoing off the buildings and down the streets. "The city of Anonil has fallen. The border forts are in disarray." That was putting it generously. "We are headed there to meet them in battle."

A few cries went up, some of fear, others of encouragement or bloodlust.

"But they bring with them an unprecedented obstacle for our forces. Mages march with Kavanar's soldiers, fighting on their behalf." The murmurs arose again, angrier and more alarmed now. "Those mages don't choose to fight. They are forced against their will, enslaved to the King of Kavanar to do his bidding." That wasn't perfectly accurate either, as he wasn't sure if Daes was exactly king yet, but proclamations were not the time for subtlety or caveats.

Scowls and grumbled outrage swelled around him, tugging at him like a dangerous current.

"I won't lie to you, we are ill-equipped to face them. Our military is strong, but we're not prepared to battle mages. We believe their mages are five hundred strong. We have but a handful." Some in the crowd fell quiet, stillness settling on them like deer sensing arrows trained on their backs. Among others, the grumbles grew to shouts. "I've put out a call, and I'll say it again. Any mages of Panar, Akaria requests you come to her aid. If you have the courage and ability to stand in Panar's defense—and indeed, in defense of Akaria itself—Arms Master Miara Floren will see you are safe, unharmed, and trained to defend our fair city."

He picked up the reins to continue on but at the last minute added one more thing.

"Pray for us. Sing your hymns of war. Burn incense in the street, and call in that favor from your ancestors. Because we will need everything you have. Even that may not be enough. But we will fight. And we will die if need be. Honor those who stand against death, against injustice. Against Kavanar. We ride to war!"

He thrust his fist in the air. Voices rose to shake the buildings, and more fists clenched in answer.

There. Let them know the drama and the fear, let them know what they were all risking even here, safe in the capital. Let them know this wasn't just politics and men playing childish games.

This was real, this was death, and it was coming for them unless someone rode out to stop it.

Jaena watched the procession trudge away. The air around them felt thick enough to cut with a knife, it was so tense. Many of the servants and stewards had returned inside from the cold, but her friends and allies lingered. Derk scowled after them, Elise wrung her hands, and even Tharomar had a dark expression on his face.

"I had better get back," Elise said, sighing as the last horse disappeared from view. "I hate to leave Samul alone with that healer. I wasn't even going to come to say goodbye, but then he left on his own for a short while."

Jaena nodded. "Will it be harder tending Samul without Siliana's help?"

Elise shrugged. "I couldn't relax even when she gave me breaks. I might as well get used to it."

She didn't look used to it. She looked haggard, but Jaena just smiled and waved politely as the queen walked off briskly, back into the building. She gazed off in the direction the troops had gone, the lingering sense of unease only growing. The tension in Ro's form beside her didn't help anything.

"What's wrong?" she said softly to him. He was still staring after where the soldiers had gone, just as she was.

He raised his eyebrows, his features immediately smoothing. "Oh—nothing."

"You really think you can hide from me? Please. I can read your face like a book." She smiled crookedly at him. Actually, she couldn't read his face anywhere near as well as he could read hers, it seemed, but he didn't need to know that.

"I was..." He shook his head. "Let's go check on Miara."

"Sure. You can answer my question on the way."

He smiled back. "You're the only one that gets to

dodge questions?"

"I don't dodge questions, I just sneak up on them. Very slowly. While asking others."

He shook his head again and stepped away from the wall where they'd been leaning. "If you must know, I was thinking that I couldn't do it."

"Do what?"

"Ride away like that," he said, gesturing at the gate. "From the one I love."

"He's just doing his duty," she said over the flush of heat the words brought. She instantly regretted the words as pain shot through Ro's features. "Just like you are," she added hastily. Obviously she thought being here was his duty, or she wouldn't have even *said* that. But they didn't need to rehash that argument again.

He only stared after the empty gate, just as Derk was doing, saying nothing.

"Well, I'm glad you couldn't do it," she said, reaching out and taking his arm. "I have work for us to do. But first, let's pay Miara a visit like our lord asked."

Ro let her lead him out of the stable courtyard and back inside, staring at the floor ahead of them, lost in thought.

"You know, he's had an easier life than you," Jaena said gently. "Wealth, security, power, education. He's been given pretty much everything he could have wanted for his whole life, in exchange for one thing."

"What's that? What one thing?" His eyes bored into her.

"That if the time came, he'd ride out like he just did." She squeezed his hand. "So maybe don't compare yourself too directly to him?"

"My temple gave me a lot."

"Perhaps. But you had less than nothing to start with." She squeezed his hand again, and she felt some of his resistance melting. "And you have more than ever now."

"So does he," he argued weakly. His eyes were open and liquid though, almost with wonder. "How do you know what I'm thinking so well?"

She thought about making a magic-related wisecrack but decided it wasn't the time. "Because I'm just like you."

"Is that so?"

"Oh, I may have been born to different circumstances, but I, too, had less than nothing as a slave. Somehow, we both found our way out. I know I sure as hell don't want to risk going back to that."

A reluctant, crooked smile took over one corner of his mouth. "Well, you may be right. Or you may just have a way with words."

"Whatever makes you feel better." She grinned.

His stomach chose that moment to growl loudly.

"Maybe we should get some dinner first, in the interest of making you feel better?"

He smiled but shook his head. "First things first. I'm not *that* selfish."

She threw up her hands in frustration. "Selfish. That's what he thinks he is. The absurdity!"

His smile turned sheepish, but he didn't take it back. They'd reached the bottom of the stairs to the king's level. "Wait," he said, stopping. "Didn't the steward tell Aven that Miara was with his father?"

Jaena frowned. "Did she? I wasn't listening. Elise said she left Samul alone."

Ro's eyes widened. "Exactly."

They both turned in unison and raced up the stairs. Miara's rooms were off to the right here, just around the corner—

Reaching the top just beside her, Tharomar stopped short, his face suddenly dark.

Only then did Jaena spot them. The two guards she'd last seen stationed outside Miara's rooms were collapsed on the ground. No blood stained the marble, but they certainly weren't guarding what they were supposed to be guarding.

Ro rushed forward, waking her out of her stupor, and she rushed after him. He leapt over one guard and slammed into the door, not bothering with any kind of formality. The door flew open, unlocked. They spilled into the room.

A body lay on the floor, dress gray, hair red. Blood pooled around its head.

Jaena screamed.

A hand clapped over her mouth, and it took her two long, panicked breaths to calm down enough to realize it was Ro's hand, not some unseen assailant's. But that was what he was worried about, wasn't it? What if whoever had killed her was still here?

She glanced up at him, but he wasn't looking at her. He held her tightly against him, eyes darting around the maze of rooms, watching for anyone else.

But Miara *couldn't* be dead. She couldn't be.

It was probably wishful thinking, but Jaena slid her mind out across the marble floor, reaching toward the body, groping for a sign of life, something. Not that she could feel it like a creature mage could, not like it meant anything, but by the gods, let her not be dead.

The image of the statue staring down at the candles flashed through her mind, and an inexplicable wave of emotion hit her—something between anger and betrayal. All lies. Lies to manipulate. There was no good in this world, save perhaps Tharomar, and she was starting to understand. Nothing good lasted. It was only a matter of time before she lost him too.

As she reeled her mind away from the body, her mind and heart aching, hands shaking, she caught the glimmer of something magical. A spell hung over the body, some kind of creature magic.

She tugged at his wrist, and he looked down at her in surprise, as if he'd forgotten he still had his hand clapped over her mouth. "Gods, sorry," he whispered, "I—"

"I think there's a spell on the body."

"Can you tell what it does? Can you tell if there's anyone else here?"

She shook her head. "We need a creature mage—it's creature magic."

"Hold on. Stay right here, don't move." He dashed back out into the hallway, and she heard the rasping sound of steel against steel. He reappeared, a sword in each hand he must have taken from the fallen guards.

He came close again and held out the hilt of the left one. She took it with a mix of surprise and intense gratification, and then he gestured her to follow him. "We'll see if this place is empty. If it is, we'll get Elise. Unless you have any better ideas?"

She shook her head again. Right now she was barely keeping her ideas in order at all.

They'd checked about half the rooms when they heard the door open. "Miara!" called a man's voice, followed by a gasp. Cautiously, Ro eased his way back to the main room.

Over his shoulder Jaena saw a short, bearded man with his own sword drawn, heading toward the rooms on the opposite side. Who could it be? Friend, or foe returning?

All their feet were quiet on the stone floor, but some clothing must have rustled, because the man abruptly rounded on them.

"Who the hell are you two?" the man growled. "And what have you done to her?"

Ro sank deeper into his fighting stance, so Jaena spoke first. "Aven asked us to come check on her. He was worried when she didn't show to say goodbye."

At the mention of Aven's name, the man's face shot through with pain. "Well, he was right to worry, clearly. But how do I know you didn't do this?"

"How do we know *you* didn't?" she said indignantly. "Me!"

Ro snorted. "He did walk in seeming to expect her alive."

Just then, they heard footsteps on the stairs. They all froze.

Derk appeared in the doorway and stopped, his eyes flicking from the three of them to Miara's body. No, no, it couldn't be Miara's body. Couldn't be.

"Shit," was all he said. The color drained from his face.

"Derk," Jaena said quickly. "There's a spell on the body. We need a creature mage."

He slumped against the wall. "What difference does it make? She's *dead*."

"Someone should call Aven back," Ro said quickly.

"Wait, you know these two?" said the bearded man to Derk.

Derk nodded. "Jaena is—was—a friend of Miara's. If she did this, any of us could have."

"I sure as the seven hells didn't. And who's he?" Jaena demanded.

"I'm Master of Arms Devol. Trained Aven since he was a boy."

They all scowled, at each other, at the body, at the floor.

"Should I go get Elise?" Ro asked finally.

Derk nodded weakly, still staring at the blood.

Jaena moved to stand beside him, finally lowering her sword but keeping her hand tight on the grip. "Who could have done this? Wait till we see what the spell is."

Derk only shook his head, ran a hand over his face, and stared. Jaena faced the opposite direction, toward the door. Staring at the body was unnecessary; the sight was already burned into her brain.

The queen came slowly inside and stopped, her face draining too, as if it hadn't already looked exhausted enough. Ro must have told her some of what to expect, as she didn't look surprised. "This is my fault," she whispered.

"My lady," Jaena said quickly—and perhaps a touch impatiently. Sometimes being an earth mage felt impossibly pointless and ineffectual. "There's a spell still hanging on the body. Before you grieve, can you see what it is, please?"

"Oh. Yes." Elise nodded and stepped closer now, coming up alongside Derk and Jaena and closing her eyes. Yes, that might make it easier to concentrate in the face of horror.

Jaena watched Elise, still too disturbed to look at the body, but when Derk's eyebrows rose and his mouth fell open, she finally turned to look.

The gray dress, the red hair, all of it was gone. A *man* lay where the illusion of Miara's form had been. A man Jaena didn't recognize. She let out a breath, feeling relieved. Then she grabbed the queen's arm and tugged, and Elise opened her eyes.

"Nyor," the queen said, clenching her fists.

"Oh, thank the gods," muttered Derk.

Jaena shook her head and rubbed her brow. "It's got to be a sin to feel as relieved as I do right now. Especially over a dead man's body. Who's Nyor?"

"The healer," said Elise. "He'd only just left a few minutes before I came out to see Aven off. This must have happened in the few minutes we were down there."

"Is he dead?" asked Devol, stalking up to the man and peering at him, but looking like he didn't want to touch him.

"Oh, yes," Elise breathed, as if she found that comforting.

"But then where is Miara?" asked Derk.

"She may not be here," said Devol, "but she could still be dead. There's definitely something foul afoot here. Not a mark on his skin, no injuries. The blood's just run out of his nose. And mouth. And his eyes too, by the gods." He backed away warily.

"Both those guards are dead. No blood. No wounds on them either," said Ro, returning from the hall. "What do we do?"

No one said anything for a long minute.

"Search the castle. We need to get people searching. And call them back," said Jaena. "Aven needs to know what happened. He knew something wasn't right—"

Elise held up a hand to stop her. "No. We can't call them back."

"He'll want to know," said Ro, his voice cold. "And Miara's father needs to know too."

"You're right. Aven would want to know. I promise you I'll send word. And I'll tell Pytor myself. First we must start the search, as you've said. Devol, get the captain of the guard. Organize a search as quickly as you can." Devol nodded and headed out of the room at a run. "I trust you've already searched these rooms?" Elise asked, glancing around.

"We hadn't quite finished. But I think anyone that's here has had plenty of chance to clear out now. But hold on a moment." Ro started on the far side they hadn't yet explored.

"I beg your pardon, my lady," Jaena said, struggling

to be cautious and deferential and failing, "but we should contact the king. He may want to change his plans." She put a slight emphasis on the word "king" because it felt close to disobeying his wishes to *not* contact him about this.

"I understand your concern, and you're probably right. But we can handle looking for her. Him being here or there shouldn't change anything."

"But, my lady—" Jaena started.

"A city has fallen," Elise said, her voice loud and stopping Jaena cold. "The fall of Anonil to Kavanar is likely the result of treachery rather than an actual military gain, but it's extremely serious. We knew Lord Alikar's betrayal would have an impact on Gilaren, but soon they'll be ready to move beyond that. Aven has to find a way to stop them, and I'm not entirely sure he can. And he has to do it *before* they reach the capital."

Jaena's eyes widened. "Here?"

"I'm surprised they haven't headed here first." Elise shook her head. "With mages in their ranks... it's a blessing."

Jaena frowned. "How many mages?"

"We don't know. Think of the destruction even a few could create. Aven has to go north. He has to face them out there, in the open land, in the smaller cities at worst. If he can't figure something out, think of what might happen if their mages and their army arrive here. Or in any large city."

Jaena's mind was already working. Even with a handful of mages, the impact could be devastating. She'd had a fairly devastating impact on the palace where she'd rescued Ro. If she'd wanted to bring the building to the ground, she could have done so easily.

Of course, they'd never taught her tricks like that at Mage Hall. Earth mages had the general reputation of being pathetically impractical, good to enrich a field or two, move a boulder a bit, but not much more. Everyone knew air mages were the most powerful, wielding wind and raging storms. And the stars, although few knew about that.

A chill ran down her spine. Maybe all that nonsense was only what they *wanted* mage slaves to believe. Maybe air mages were not really the most powerful. Maybe the Masters simply wanted other mages to believe that was the case. But why? So they wouldn't attempt to push their powers? Jaena certainly hadn't tried to until she'd been free, until she'd needed anything her magic could dish out.

Maybe I could be more powerful than any of them, a quiet voice said. Maybe not... but maybe. Such a possibility had never seemed even on the table, and now some part of her whispered that it might be the truth.

She swallowed and pictured the city as they'd seen it from the tower while the catapults attacked. She'd been so focused on the brand, the star map, whether or not Tharomar was leaving, that the war hadn't seemed real. It hadn't started for her yet. But now... she imagined if *she* were attacking the city, what she'd do.

She'd start by tearing down the walls. It'd take some work, but if there were ten or even five mages to help, the walls could be tumbled into a small rubble-strewn hill in half a day perhaps. Then there were the towers—already proven easily reachable by catapult. They might be too high and far into the city to be within range from outside, but if she got closer, if she made it inside, she could tumble those stones into a nondescript heap, taking out anyone and everyone inside. The same went for the buildings, but she thought they'd topple the towers, clear and visible examples of conquest. The possibilities for what creature or air mages could do if they came close enough were almost too numerous to count, but in her training, she'd seen the air mages favor fire. Waves of it. Pillars. Walls could easily take out large groups of troops. Wasn't that what Derk had encountered?

Gods, why hadn't she warned them more specifically? She'd been so focused on finding a way to destroy the brand—

Ro grabbed her shoulder. "What is it?" When had he come back into the room? She just stared up at him for a moment, unsure of how to articulate all that had just raced through her head.

"She's realizing we're screwed," said Derk quietly.

"No, we're not," Jaena snapped.

"Miara said they have five hundred mages," he shot back. "Even if they bring only fifty of them, are you telling me you think we can fight them off?"

Jaena jutted out her chin and squared her shoulders, refusing to be cowed. Of course, he'd seen a lot of men killed by magic not so long ago, and she hadn't, but she didn't care. "Are you telling me you think we *can't*? Some big-talking mage you are."

"Now, now, is this really the time for fluffing our feathers and—" Elise started, but Ro surprised her by laying a hand on the queen's arm. She quieted and looked at him in surprise.

"You know, you're right, Derk," Jaena continued. "We should just lay down and put a sign out front saying, *Free city, Yours for the taking!* They stole our future queen so we should probably just roll over and ask for our bellies scratched like dogs."

Derk scowled at her, anger simmering under the surface. At just that moment, the captain of the guard arrived, Devol with him, to tell them a search of the entire city had begun. Elise took the man aside, closer to the dead man's body.

Derk headed for the door, and Jaena followed him, Ro hot on her heels. That bastard air mage wasn't getting off the hook that easily.

"I guess I overestimated you," Jaena said coldly to his back. He stopped ahead of her. "We'll just have to—"

"No, you didn't." He turned, his jaw clenched like he knew what she was doing, but it was working anyway.

"You're right, we're outnumbered, but I, for one, am not giving up."

"Your persistence and stubbornness won't be enough to win the day. Not alone, anyway. Wanting to survive doesn't help you survive."

"You're wrong. It does," she snapped. She had wanted to survive more than anything, and it had gotten her through some very dark days, especially after she'd lost

Dekana, so she knew better than anyone. "Wanting to survive more than anyone else will help us figure out how to beat them. In spite of the odds."

"We can't," he said simply. "We just can't. There's too many—"

"We can't beat them spell for spell, but what if we could keep them from casting them in the first place?"

Derk frowned.

"How?" said Ro quickly, focused only on her.

"We don't let them finish a spell to begin with." She rubbed her chin, her mind racing.

"How do we do that?" Ro leaned forward.

Derk's eyes perked up. "You're thinking… disrupt them?"

"We need some degree of concentration to start and hold a spell," said Jaena. "It's not a lot, but some."

"When the troops trying to save Thel attacked," said Derk, "he was able to knock a few of them down, kept them from being effective. I think he might have saved us from an even worse attack. You're saying, we find some way to do that en masse?"

"Knock people down? An entire army?" said Ro, looking skeptical.

"Well, the soldiers themselves could do some knocking," said Jaena. "But there are other ways to disrupt them. If we could keep them from being able to concentrate, we wouldn't have to directly counter their spells. We could scare or throw them off in any number of ways."

"Why are you thinking about this now?" said Derk.

Jaena stared, trying to figure that out herself. "I guess

I figured Miara or Aven were handling the defense of the city. I had—other things to worry about. And maybe they *were* handling it, but—"

Ro made a hushing sound. "Let's not mention certain recent developments out here, shall we?"

She nodded. "Point being, Elise is right, they could head here at any time. We need a plan. And we need to practice."

"I think we should help in the search first," said Ro. "We can start thinking through things later. When certain other things have been found."

"And you think you're the selfish one?" Jaena shook her head, and Derk looked at them, confused. She waved it off. "All right, let's go and see how we can help."

Thel punched up the ground underneath the wooden foot of another trebuchet. It swayed like a tree in the wind for a moment before toppling to the ground. He grinned. That was nearly all of them.

"How many was that?" Niat asked, still sitting and watching quietly beside him.

"About a dozen, I think." Truth be told, he wasn't counting. He was trying to draw out the time between each collapse, hoping they seemed random. But since when did the earth randomly jut up under such a heavy piece of siege artillery? Never, really.

He glanced up at the path in the direction Kae had taken. The air mage hadn't yet returned. Should he be worried?

A voice drifted up the path and made his blood run cold.

"There's some mage up here, I'm telling you."

He leapt to his feet, grabbing Niat's arm. "We better move," he whispered.

"They figured out what you were doing?" She hurried after him in Kae's direction. Kae was an air mage, a warrior mage, much more experienced than Thel. If they had a chance, it was with him. In a handful of paces, they reached the next cliff outcropping, but Kae wasn't there. He must have meant further on. Thel turned back to the trail to head further up.

A rustle in the brush beside him was the only warning he got. A bear roared out of the forest beside him, careening into him and sending him to the ground.

The creature's massive weight pinned him instantly. Behind him, a man stepped from the forest. Sort of.

"What are you?" Niat whispered.

He had the body of a man, a cloak, a dagger in one hand. But above the cloak, large yellow-orange scales covered his skin up to serpentine eyes. His snout was distended like it could contain fangs, tiny holes on each side for a nose.

Creature mage, Thel realized, thinking faster now. Should he call out and warn Kae? Or would that just alert their enemies to the air mage's existence? Right now they might think they'd caught everyone.

"Got 'em!" the snake-man called. He kept the dagger trained carefully on Niat but didn't seize her. The bear gave a pleased, throaty growl, and Thel realized he, too, must be a creature mage. Of course. Of *course*.

Four more mages trotted up, three men and a woman with daggers in hand. "Well, that worked well."

"Pincer move works every time," said one, giggling and making a crab-like gesture. "Flush 'em out with one side and grab 'em with the other."

"You—you're no mage. What are you doing here?" Their leader, in a blue tunic and equally bright blue cape, jabbed his dagger at her.

"I—uh— He kidnapped me," Niat blurted.

Oh, by the gods. Just when he thought she'd made a breakthrough. He didn't even bother rolling his eyes.

"You can come back to safety with us," said Blue. "Come on."

"Wait a minute now," said Snake-Man. "We could take our time. It's nice up here."

"Yeah, and we'll get killed down there," said Pincers. The two other newcomers and the bear remained quiet.

"Our orders—" started the leader.

"—include scouring these hills for more mages other than him," said Snake smoothly. "Isn't our fault if we're so efficient. We better check we didn't miss anyone."

Blue shook his head. "Fine. Tie him up. You two, stay with him. Girl, come with us. Let's go on a nice little stroll, shall we?"

"We haven't got any rope," complained Pincer.

"I have some!" Niat said helpfully, pulling out Alikar's bolo, which had already taken Thel down once. He hadn't realized she'd kept that. How considerate of her. "Here, let me help."

They looped a string over his neck, and a heavy stone fell against his chest. He reached out to sense it and recoiled. Or, maybe, he just couldn't reach out at all. It was like suddenly he couldn't sense the rock anymore.

Pincer was smirking above him. "That'll keep you from causing trouble." Then he dragged Thel to a nearby tree and knocked him onto his side with a shove from his boot as Niat joined them. Giving her a nod, the mage stalked off past the tree. She helped Thel sit up, just as she had before. Then she knelt and tied his hands while Snake watched her carefully. But it was good and tight. No tricks from Niat. Thel shook his head.

"That way down the trail, now." Snake strode toward the tree line, surveying the area around them.

For a moment there was only Bear beside them. His giant body faced the others and blocked Thel and Niat from the rest of the mages' view. Niat, still kneeling beside him, hesitated to get up. He'd been refusing to meet her eyes lest he explode in anger, but he finally looked up now as he felt her gaze on him.

Their eyes locked, one heartbeat, another. And then, to his surprise, she leaned down and kissed him.

Alikar immediately sprang to mind, and he froze. Gods, she meant to not just get away from him but kill him too? What had he done to deserve this? She kissed him harder, though, her lips warm and smooth and soft against his, and he couldn't resist. It was too late now anyway.

If he was going to die by a poisoned kiss, he might as

well make it a good one.

His heart pounding, hoping the mages didn't notice and the bear didn't turn, he poured his heart into that kiss, all the fire he had to give her, in hopes that the bleakness would never return. That even without him, at the last minute, she'd think, I don't deserve these traitors, and she'd take off, find a life of her own. Find freedom. Find happiness.

But it would have been nice if that happiness had been with him. She kissed him back almost as though she wanted the same thing.

It was the best kiss of his life. Even if it *was* going to kill him. Not that there were terribly many to compare. As the bear started to move, she broke away and rose casually. Like nothing had happened. That was smart, so why did it sting?

"What was that, mercy killing?" he said softly, glaring at her.

Her eyes flicked to his, the sadness in them deepening. She pushed her shoulders back and looked down the path.

"Don't go back to the temple," he whispered.

"What?" They'd notice if she dallied much longer, most likely.

"I understand you have to do what you have to do. But promise me you'll find someone who's not going to hurt you, if you can."

She met his gaze evenly, the sadness suddenly gone, her eyes a cool and collected mask. "I already did."

The words came off like snark. Of course. How many

times had she thought she'd found someone who'd keep her safe, and it'd turned out to be untrue? More than he knew about, he was certain. He scowled after her as she tromped away down the path with the mages on patrol.

One smirked at him over her head. As she passed, he put a protective hand on Niat's shoulder, and Thel could've put a canyon in the ground in front of the man out of spite—all right, jealousy if he was being honest—if it weren't for the damn rock slung round his neck.

They turned, the man moving closer as they went around the bend.

"She's promised to someone!" he yelled out of spite. The bear turned and looked at him, impassive, then looked back out over the cliffs, almost peacefully. Alikar was dead, of course, and already married, but they didn't need to know that. He doubted Sven would be happy with Niat in the arms of any mage, noble or slave. Even if that mage was a prince.

He groaned, leaned his head back against the tree, and tried to memorize the taste of her, the feeling, to keep it long into old age.

If, of course, he lived that long.

Niat was breathing fast as a plan formed in her mind. She struggled to focus on the rocks and roots in the path and not trip over them. The handsy mage beside her was proving useful in pushing limbs out of the way and steadying her on the path, and she almost felt a little guilty at the thought of betraying him. But as his hand slid down from her shoulder blades toward the small of her back—and lower—she felt less guilty by the inch.

"Glad to get away from that fellow?" the man said pleasantly.

Good. He hadn't seen the kiss then. That had been needlessly risky. She wanted to rail at herself, but she couldn't bring herself to regret it. There might not be another chance.

She pretended to stumble and grabbed on tighter to him for support, her right hand going naturally around his back too, now, much to his delight, and she slid her hand to his belt. A convenient way to hold on and nothing more, of course. "Oh, yes. I was terrified, I didn't know what he would do," she lied. "I'm never out in the woods without my mum."

"Well, we'll be back to your family safe and sound in no time," he said smoothly, but there was the ring of deceit to his words too. He had no idea who her family was or where they lived, so she highly doubted he could guarantee that.

While some part of her knew that turning herself in was a wise thing to do, there was a much larger part of her that no longer cared. A rebellious part of her that had long lain in deep slumber, crushed somewhere between her father and the drugs and the visions.

But it was a part of her that Thel, with his determined optimism and frightening ability to sling rocks around, had somehow awoken. Maybe it was the corruption spreading to her. Maybe she didn't care. If he was corrupt, then why had Nefrana sent her so damn many visions of him? Why had he practically spouted off Sister Ireie's own words? Choose your own path.

He hadn't even known her two weeks, she'd spent half of it denouncing him, and yet he had done more than anyone in her entire life to try to make her happy. If he was corrupt, the rest of the people in her life were even *more* corrupt, and they didn't have magic as an excuse.

She wasn't going to let these people capture him again or torture him or kill him or claim Nefrana told them that it was all perfectly justified to do.

She stumbled again, for real this time, and as she recovered, the mage caught her outside hand. She used the moment and the almost-embrace to slide her hand along his side—and slip the dagger from his belt sheath.

Treading along more slowly now, as if struggling to be careful, she frowned carefully down at the roots.

She closed her eyes for a moment, letting herself falter, and she cast her mind up desperately. *Nefrana, gods, whoever you are, if you ever loved me, if you ever cared to help me, grant me a vision now. Some vision—any vision— I don't care.* Something that would debilitate her, throw them off guard. And when they thought she was sick and out of it—that was when she would strike.

Brick to the head, as usual. She fought to keep her hand tight around the dagger's hilt, but she felt it slip from her hand with the last fragments of reality. Her body went limp and fell backward as a vision of a whole other world clouded her mind.

A bearded man lay in a bed, a woman in a chair asleep by his side. Her head had drifted to lie by his arm in an uncomfortable-looking position. A man came in and roused her, and whatever they said, it seemed bad news. The woman's face contorted, threatened tears, but she straightened and visibly willed them away. They continued talking, their words impossible for Niat to hear. She stared at the bearded man instead, feeling a strange and unexpected kinship with him. She'd spent a lot of the last few months that way too, laid up, weak, half dead. She hadn't had anyone at her bedside who cared though, save a priestess or two, and they had only been doing their duty. Did anyone even care that she hadn't returned?

Before Niat's own jealous and bitter tears could threaten, the vision shifted. The bearded man was well, partially armored, and on horseback, racing behind a woman dressed in dark leather, wisps of her red hair catching wildly in the wind. As she watched, an arrow slammed into his shoulder, his back. This must have been how he'd gotten injured.

The vision whirled again to an archer. A hard-faced man with a braided, straw-colored beard was also on horseback, but not riding. He was only paused—just for a moment, Niat sensed. He reached back to a second, smaller quiver. A beautiful green leaf pattern was painted on the top and sides, and he drew out an arrow, the tip of which gleamed a brownish-green.

Poison, Niat knew automatically. Not just any poison,

but anfi, easily made from the heart-shaped leaves of the readily available wild anjunin vine. Peluna had taught her well, and she could see the leaves, the shape, the unfortunately simple preparation, the storage requirements, the antidote.

The man drew back the arrow and let it fly. Niat had already seen where it was going to land, and she winced, even though she was entirely unsure of whether this had already happened or would happen or would never happen at all.

And just like that, her vision cleared. Reality slammed back into unpleasant focus. Her head swam, and she stumbled for real now, everything tilting around her. The mages were in front of her, saying something, or maybe shouting, but her ears rang like she was inside a bell, like a thousand birds screeching, and she could hear none of it.

She collapsed back. Someone caught her. As they lowered her to the ground, the pack of the woman beside her swung awkwardly off her shoulder and bumped Niat, and she stared.

A bow was tied to the pack, as well as two quivers, the smallest of which was painted with a green, heart-shaped leaf pattern.

Niat lunged for the pack, just as the woman was rising, and of course, she missed. She feigned weakness, collapsing back onto the rugged trail, shutting her eyes.

It wasn't really all that hard. For a moment, sleep crept closer. It'd be so easy to just fall into the blackness now. She was tired, so tired, they'd done so much, they'd fought so hard, she deserved a rest. She could still save Thel. She just needed a moment.

No.

The ringing faded, and she could hear their voices now. The weakness recessed slightly, but she kept her eyes carefully closed and her body unmoving.

"What the hell was that?" the man who liked to make crab claw gestures was muttering.

"Didn't they say some seer was missing? She fits the bill." The leader again. Of course he knew what was going on.

"We better haul her back," said Handsy. Oh, how considerate of him. Likely just wanted a grope.

"I'm not carrying her," the Crab shot back.

A thud sounded beside her, which Niat hoped was a pack hitting the ground.

"We don't have time for this." It was the woman now, who'd remained quiet for so long. "She's light, look at her. A waif of a thing. Throw her over your shoulder, and be done with it."

"If she's so light, why don't you do it?" said the Crab.

"You just want to stay here." The leader sounded like he might be shaking his head.

"Damn right. Why are you so eager to return to the fighting?" the Crab man grumbled. Another pack dropped, and then a third.

"I'm not, I just— Brand's telling me to return. This isn't quite our orders, I—" The leader let out a soft sound somewhere between a groan and a growl.

"You just have to be creative," Handsy assured him.

"Look, we had orders to scout this part of the woods. We can do that just as much from right here while we wait for her to wake up as we can from stalking around from tree to tree." Crab Man was determined.

No one responded to the man for a moment. Then the woman growled, "I'm going to take a piss." And leaves crunched as she stalked away.

Niat risked opening an eye just a crack. The leader, the Crab, and Handsy were staring each other down, glaring and ignoring Niat.

The pack with its green-leafed quiver lay near her feet.

Not close enough. She could lunge for it, but they'd be on her in a second. She needed some other plan.

She closed her eyes. Was she really going to do this? Three of them versus her, four if the woman rushed back, and she hoped to get her hand on one poison arrow and do them all in? Was she really ready to poison, injure, and kill these mages on Thel's behalf, and her own? Or at least delay them long enough to get away and free Thel and run? That seemed much more likely. And Snake and Bear were still back with Thel.

But what was really the alternative? Go back to being her father's puppet? Her temple's invalid? Waiting around until she was sold off to someone even worse than Alikar, a traitor who had *already* been married? By Nefrana, Thel was right. Maybe getting caught was inevitable, maybe losing was certain, maybe it would just be more painful in the long run.

Maybe she no longer cared.

She groaned loudly.

"Look, she's waking up."

"Oh, thank the gods."

Rubbing her forehead, Niat struggled weakly to sit up. She wished the weak part were more of an act. "What happened?" she muttered.

"Come on, get up. We need to be on the road," the leader snapped.

"Now is that any way to be hospitable?" Handsy said, his smooth exterior returned. He crouched down. "You just got a bit weak for a second there. Take all the time you need."

The leader glared at his back, either because of Handsy's clearly lecherous intentions or because the man just didn't want to go back any sooner than he had to. Likely both.

Handsy smiled warmly at Niat, and she forced a smile in return. "I'm sure I'll be fine in a moment or two," she said as sweetly as she could.

He nodded once. "See—just a moment or two. Let's see if we have anything to bolster your strength." Smiling even more brightly now, he straightened and moved toward his pack. Both he and the leader bent and began shuffling through their packs, presumably looking for food. A regrettable kindness, but his ulterior motives made things slightly easier.

She reached for the quiver. The lid twisted open quietly, just like it had in the dream, and she kept her fingers silent and fast, daring as a mouse. Reaching in carefully, she felt the feathers of the fletching and quickly withdrew one arrow, setting it beside her before drawing another and twisting the lid closed.

Her heart pounded, and her weakened state left her feeling like the organ might actually explode out of her chest. Gripping the arrows like daggers, she took a deep breath. Was she really going to do this?

Yes. Yes, she was.

The arrows weren't hard to hide in the folds of her dress as she stood and stepped closer. Just as Handsy started to turn toward her, she stabbed.

The arrow hit him in the side, and he staggered back in shock, but not before Niat had buried the other arrow in the leader's ribcage. Blood spilled out of the leader's wound and drenched Niat's forearm in warm vermillion. The woman darted from the trees to Niat's right and stopped short with a gasp. The Crab was frozen, crouched by the tree line and clearly uninterested in helping his friends. Handsy just stared at her in shock, his hand slowly wrapping round the arrow shaft as if he were gearing up to draw it out.

Right. Some of them were creature mages. If so, they could just heal the damage she'd done with a little bit of thought. She wasn't going to kill them. In fact, she *couldn't* kill them.

She could only run.

Niat didn't waste a moment. She grabbed the pack with its poison arrows and bow and fled back up the hill as fast as her feet could carry her.

11   SNAKES

Daes shook himself off in the morning sunshine, along with the memory of the transformation his mage slave had just released. That was *not* a pleasant way to travel, really, but it was fast. Beside him, Marielle was straightening her skirts, hastily brushing off invisible imperfections. He was lucky she was a practical woman and would put up with something other than a carriage.

Smoke was heavy in the air, and he smiled. That was the smell of his victory, or at least one step toward it. Anonil burned, and it was because of him.

He strode toward the fortress, Marielle and a slew of other attendants the mage slave had also transformed following him. It was time to get some better news.

A gaping hole in the side of the fortress caught his eye and made him stop. It was only one small area, perhaps the sidewall of one room on the third or fourth stories up, but somehow that wall had collapsed, leaving it open to the elements. Workers appeared to be trying to replace some of the stones, and some boards were going up to repair it.

Strange. Exceedingly strange indeed.

Perhaps even more strange was the crowd of mages and soldiers waiting at the fortress's gate. One had a horrific second pair of eyes on his forehead, reminding Daes of a fly or a spider blinking wildly at him. Another sported short, brown horns, and a third's skin was an unnatural darkish-green that allowed him to practically blend into the stone wall behind him, if the whites of his eyes hadn't tipped Daes off. Actually, there were several others with similarly altered appearances. Daes glanced at Marielle, who was regarding them with big eyes but her chin lowered in determination. Good.

He approached the group. "I am Lord Consort and Master Daes Cavalion, accompanying Queen Marielle of Kavanar." The group made a hasty, low bow. "We're here to see General Vusamon and Lord Alikar."

A bored soldier to the right perked up. "Will you be in need of accommodations?"

"Yes," Daes said quickly, and the man scampered away.

The multi-eyed one bowed again stiffly, and his voice was like rocks tumbling down a mountainside. Daes shoved down the wave of unease he got from trying to look at the man. "Lord, General Vusamon is in Anonil, dealing with the last remnants of resistance. Shall we send for him?"

"No, I can wait. Let him finish the job. So Anonil is

under our control?"

"Fully, my lord."

"Lord Alikar, then."

"I am sorry to say it, my lord, but Lord Alikar is dead." The mage didn't *sound* very sorry to say it. He sounded as though he was glad of it. Not that Daes could really begrudge him that; Alikar had been a simpering fool. But appearances had to be maintained.

"Excuse me?" Daes said slowly, letting venom sink into his voice. "Dead?"

"Yes. We found him dead in the woods. He left in pursuit of the priestess and the prince he'd captured, and—"

"In pursuit? Wait, a priestess and a *prince*?"

"Yes, they escaped, my lord." Now he did sound a little sorry to admit that.

"They *escaped*?" Daes's voice rose, and he clenched his fists at his side, struggling to keep from lashing out. "Escaped? Before you even thought to send word that they'd been captured?"

The mage winced. "My orders were to obey Lord Alikar's demands, my lord. Lord Alikar did not think to do so."

"Or perhaps he did not *want* to do so." Daes would have rushed to the field if he'd known one of the Akarian royals was here. What other prince could it have been? Could it have been the star mage? He'd have ordered whoever it was executed immediately. He'd have— It didn't matter now. "Who gave you those orders?"

"Lady Seulka, my lord."

"Of course." His voice dripped with disdain. That woman would *still* find a way to ruin everything for him, or die trying. Or without even trying; she seemed to get lucky at it. "Do you know which prince it was?"

"Not exactly, my lord. A blond one?" The mage bowed his head slightly, jaw clenching. He didn't like expressing deference, did he? Just like that escaped creature mage of his.

Blond. Not the star mage then, but a brother of his. Small blessings. "Don't tell me—that's his hole in the wall up there? *How?*"

"He was an earth mage, my lord. Untrained entirely, but still. Our leader believed he was too new and could be controlled—"

"Clearly you believed wrongly."

The mage's jaw clenched more tightly. "Not I, my lord."

"Who is your leader then?"

"He too was killed in the escape."

Daes shook his head, reeling at this bit of incompetence. How could you thwart incompetence you never even knew was present? You couldn't. He couldn't control everything. Although that didn't stop him from wanting to.

He sighed. "Tell the generals and mages I want a full report by this evening. Once Anonil is subdued, we have work to do."

"Yes, sir."

"Mage, how did you... come by those eyes of yours?" said Marielle.

The mage smiled and bowed slightly again. "I grew

them myself, Your Majesty."

"Oh," Marielle managed, her poise only slightly thrown off. "They're quite… impressive."

Impressive? How about freakish, bizarre, horrifying—

"What will you have us do next, my lord and lady?" the mage said. He glanced out at the tree line. "Would you have us go after the prince and priestess?"

He waved off the lost prince and the woods. "We have greater work to do. Our forces must rest and secure our hold on Anonil, but it won't be long now before we move on."

"Where are we going?" the mage asked, eyebrow raised.

"Panar," Daes replied.

"The Akarian capital?"

"Yes. We're heading to Panar. And we're going to crush it."

"Get ready to run!"

Thel was glaring at his boots when Niat's voice split the air. He looked up as the bear raised his head. Just down the path, she was there suddenly. Blood covered one hand and arm, and she had drawn back a small bow. She looked like she was struggling with it, but she was aiming at a creature the size of a house.

The arrow did indeed take flight and thudded into the bear, near the neck, to his surprise. Niat's eyes went wide. Perhaps that hadn't been her target, just luck. Gurgling, the bear stumbled away from them, but barely made it five steps before tripping.

Niat was looking in all directions for the snake man, but neither of them knew where he'd gone. She raced toward him, dropping the bow and savagely undoing the bolo with one quick tug. Huh.

She'd clearly been *much* trickier than he'd thought.

He leapt to his feet and raced after her, up the path, way from the others. The bear had fallen on his side and was thrashing, the transformation starting to weaken. "What kind of arrow was that?" shouted Thel.

"Poison," she shot back. "C'mon. We've gotta get as far away as we—"

Just then the body of the snake lashed out from the side of the path. No, not its body—its tail. It wrapped around her middle. She squawked and dropped the bow and pack as she tried to grab onto the nearest tree.

Thel dove for the bow and grabbed an arrow from an oddly embellished quiver. Poison. Right. Then he scrambled into the brush after her. He'd strangle that bastard, he'd—

He stared. In the clearing beyond, the snake's tail held Niat up in the air. The creature mage's body had swelled to almost two feet in diameter, coiled maybe thirty feet long or more. And it was still growing.

"Put her down or I'll shoot!"

"Shoot and I'll drop her," the snake hissed back. "It'll be much harder to get away with a broken leg, don't you think?"

"Just go!" Niat screamed. "Go on without me!"

Oh, please. He circled the snake, whose eyes watched him, easing closer to the tail, pretending to aim at the head. Then, at the last second, he dropped the bow, gripped the arrow, and leapt.

If Thel was anything, it was tall and lanky, and his weight on the tail brought it much further to the ground, if only in surprise. He ran up its side and then dove for Niat as he stabbed the arrow into the tail.

Niat did fall, though Thel shielded her with his body, and they hit the ground hard, his breath flying out of his chest for a moment. But the arrow. The scales were too hard—maybe the mage had enhanced them. The arrow had broken in his hand.

The rock. He grabbed for the damn weight hanging around his neck, and Niat grabbed too. Together, they ripped it off and tossed it toward the snake's head, sending him reeling back and hissing.

Thel didn't waste a moment. He gripped a mindful of dirt and stone from behind them, ripped it up into the air, and slammed it down onto the snake's head.

"Let's go!" Niat shouted. She was grabbing the bow where he'd dropped it.

He grabbed the pack and raced after her. "South, south—toward Panar! Go!"

"Don't need to tell me twice!" She raced in front of him, out into the forest.

Well, by Anara. She'd come back.

It was hard to hear the silence of the forest over the huffing of horses, the muttering and clinking of men, and the groan of the wagons, but Aven kept sensing it. Like a blur at the edges of his vision that he couldn't quite catch sight of. Every time he thought for sure no forest could be that quiet, another clink, cough, or comment would steal away his certainty. The train of soldiers stretched out in front and behind him, curving along the road. They'd left the fields and plains behind last night before making camp, and the trees had only grown thicker with every passing hour.

Forests in winter *were* quieter. Most birds went south all the way to Farsa or even the Southern Kingdoms, some claimed. The stillness was probably nothing out of the ordinary. And the air was finally starting to convey that crisp cleanness of the darkest, coldest season. After wrestling with a few hours of fitful sleep last night, he'd woken up to a thin coat of frost silvering the grass outside his tent. This evening they'd reach the stronghold, and if nothing was truly terribly wrong—unlikely—they'd all be sleeping inside by nightfall. Hopefully *that* would help him sleep better.

But he doubted it. Miara's absence bothered him more with every step of his horse, but he didn't know what he was going to do to remedy it. Short of a note from her saying she was all right, not much was going to make him feel better.

They'd check out the hold, talk to whatever leadership remained, and determine where the force at Anonil was headed, and soon he'd know their next steps. Falling back to Panar had never sounded so appealing, but it'd have to wait. Better to fight the war out here than in the city.

As they rode, the silence nagged at him. He fought off boredom by working over the maps and pebbles once, then again, the back of his mind pondering options. Too many, and none of them greatly defensible against mages. He sought some advantage, some way to turn things to their favor, but so far, he'd come up with nothing.

They crossed a small bridge that seemed familiar, except that the trees were far thicker than he remembered from last time. He glanced back at Siliana, riding a row behind him. Her dark hair was pulled back in a tight bun, and her wine-colored tunic was shrouded in a brown cloak with mottled fur he didn't remember seeing on her before. To tell the truth, it looked like something he'd seen Derk wear.

"Does this bridge look familiar to you?" he called out to her, and anyone listening, really. "Remember it?"

She nodded once, curtly. "I do. But it's different."

He frowned, not particularly wanting to be right about this one. "What's different?"

"The trees. They're thicker."

Dyon was in the row behind her, frowning now at the trees. Aven nodded back and turned, not caring to say more about it. Especially if the forest was quiet for the reason he feared it was.

Animals froze and hid when predators were around. And humans were predators.

"How can the trees be thicker?" a soldier before them muttered.

"Trees take years to grow," muttered another. "Probably a city dweller. Don't know what she's talking about."

Aven focused on the chestnut's blond mane and tried to think. He'd seen problems coming and not done anything about it before. Watch and wait, let the enemy tell him what they were doing, expose their weaknesses and react.

Perhaps that might work sometimes, but his gut said it was time to go on the offensive. Before it was too late to take that chance. He'd taken the first step, marching toward the border with a regiment, ready to fight.

But only two mages. A wave of acid pumped into his veins at the thought that all this might not be as well-thought-out as he'd like to believe. Closing his eyes, he reached up into the sky, cold and clear and blue, and he caught the cold winds, the wet ones, twisting them together, calling the storm.

Dropping back into his body with reckless speed, he turned again and gestured hastily for Siliana to join him. Even as she made her way up past the others, she spoke into his head.

Something's not right. Isn't it?

He nodded. *Are there people out there in the hills? It's too quiet.*

She lowered her head at the horse, perhaps so others

wouldn't notice her eyes going distant. Her gaze snapped up. *I found one—but he found me. They know we're aware of them now. This isn't good—*

How many? he demanded.

At least four, there's six. Ten. More. Her thoughts came in a jumbled rush as she sought to report as quickly as she could. *They're moving. Shit.*

All mages? What kind?

Aven whirled back, the saddle leather creaking, and he caught Dyon's eye. Frowning, he held up two fingers— for two platoons, that was close enough—and pointed into the woods. The men around him didn't need more warning than that. A few reached for shields belted to the horse's sides. Of course, they weren't wearing armor for such a long ride, but weapons were close at hand, and more than a few loosed them a few inches, if not drawing them outright.

Uh. Her eyes darted back and forth frantically. *There are twelve, they're in groups of three—one air, creature, earth each. Triads. I think. What do I—*

Stay close, Aven replied. *And keep your magic for healing, I think, unless you're fighting to save someone's life. I'll see what I can do.*

Dyon had snapped a quiet command with a gruff word and a hand signal to Jenec and another three lieutenants, who followed suit signaling to the men. The two who'd been muttering in front of him glanced warily up at the sky.

That was the one thing they didn't need to worry about. For now, the sky was Aven's. But if there were three air mages out there, that might change rapidly.

He raised his mind up into the sky again, trying to keep his grip on the reins and saddle's pommel tight so his body wasn't tempted to go tilting off.

From the sky, he could almost see them. A snatch of color between the trees. The new growth worked well to hide them, but every once in a while he could catch one moving.

Where would they come out? What would they try? What if they had a peaceful message and didn't mean to attack?

What if they didn't?

He wasn't waiting to react this time. Aiming for where he'd last seen that flash of color beneath the pine boughs, he gripped the saddle tighter, braced himself, and struck.

A crack split the air, sending up shouts all around him

By the gods, they're attacking— Siliana started.

That was me. Keep watching them and tell me if any were hit.

You mean you're going to—again?

He didn't respond, just stirred the storm's anger. Alongside the lightning, the clouds grew heavy with rain, but he tried to hold it off as much as he could. The lightning might help him, but he wasn't sure whether rain would be a blessing or a curse.

Eleven. You hit one. But they're starting something.

A burst tore through the air up ahead, and Aven snapped his eyes open and reeled back in horror.

A pillar of flame had risen up in the middle of the road,

a towering, fiery inferno. And it was moving. Toward *him.*

"Hold!" a lieutenant shouted. Horses around him were starting, stopping, shying back, not particularly keen on that order.

"Where are they *exactly*?" Aven said quickly. "Left or right?"

Siliana pointed to their left and forward, slightly up the hill. "Most of them. I think. They're spreading out."

"That way," Aven shouted, drawing his sword and pointing himself. "Mages in the woods."

"Flush them out!" Dyon called out behind him.

Aven started forward, steering his horse around Siliana.

"Should I follow you?" she said, not sounding the slightest bit calm at the moment. Derk's warning came to mind. She was not trained for this.

"Well, it's not like waiting for a fiery pillar of death is going to accomplish anything," he said. "Come on."

They eased off the road and into a low area between the trees, but like many forests, the brush was thick here and not quick riding. He scowled. These mages had a good position—high ground, cover to hide them, obstacles to keep the Akarians from reaching them, and they were far from any reinforcements or fortifications the Akarians might use.

This was very well planned.

His horse faltered on a bush as he scanned through the trees. No flashes of color caught his eye now.

But how could these Kavanarians have known to be here? Certainly they wouldn't just be stationed out here in the middle of nowhere, waiting, watching— Even as the thought occurred to him, he knew. He'd been betrayed enough times in the last month that he'd have to be dense not to.

They'd known the regiment was coming. Because someone had told them.

The storm thundered and small bits of lightning crackled above him, and Aven realized he hadn't been tending it. One of the enemy's air mages had probably taken control of it. And indeed he couldn't hear the furious burn of the pillar any longer—maybe they'd dropped it when the men had left the road. He *could* wrestle them for the storm like he had in the mountains, but if he didn't know *where* they were, that wouldn't much help him.

His horse paused again, daunted by the thorns looming from the nearest bush. "Get off," he called to Siliana as quietly as he could manage over the shouts of the men and the growling thunder of the growing storm. He dismounted and hastily tied off the reins to a tree branch.

A scream to his far right made his hand slip. He looked but saw nothing in particular. Others had dismounted and were pushing their way forward. Some horses still fought a valiant fight. Another cry and then a groan sent his heart beating faster, and something told him the creature mages were hard at work. What was it—choking vines? Impaling thorns? The possibilities were endless.

Siliana came up close at his elbow. *He's raising the brush,* she said into his mind. *Making it thicker to hide them.*

Take me to them. If he could nail down their location,

the whole regiment could pour in on them. But until he did, they'd keep picking the Akarians off one by one.

I'll do what I can. They don't want me to see them. And they're moving. She pointed. *This way.*

They bent low and crept forward as quietly as possible, Aven parting the bushes, ferns, and waving stalks with his sword and guiding Siliana through. Clearly she knew enough of the forest to be careful not to touch just anything, but tracking wasn't her forte either.

A string of curses broke out, back near the road, but this time it cut off abruptly with a thud that echoed and shook the tree limbs above them.

Earth mage.

What? What did he do?

Crushed someone. His legs are broken.

Shouts and curses broke into outright chaos on both sides and behind him, punctuated by additional slams of stone into the earth. Siliana pointed to the left again, and he had to hack something out of the way before they could slip through.

Almost there.

The thuds were coming rapidly now, and a wrenching sound split the air that was all too familiar—it was the sound he'd heard when the ravine split the road. The one his father had fallen into. Irrationally, he thought of Dyon.

He plunged forward faster now, and he wasn't quite prepared when the next juniper he fought his way around revealed six cloaked figures, huddled down behind a log.

That's them!

On instinct, he lunged forward and slashed at the nearest one, aiming for his gut. He remembered only belatedly that he had hundreds of men with swords and just *him* with magic.

Vines were snaking up around their attackers. On one mage, the vines groped, then fell away harmlessly. Siliana's work? It wasn't healing—but it did seem to be keeping them from rushing at Aven. Good. He hastily forced a ball of flame into life in his palm and lobbed it at the nearest one, then another.

The first turned out to have been a bad choice, as they caught it and shot it right back, just as Derk had done. The second flame hit another mage in an exploding ball of orange licking over their brown cloak. But the first mage had returned Aven's attack so fast that he barely managed to catch the return volley. Luck and a bit of practice had helped him here, nothing more. He sent the rejected ball of energy whirling back at a third mage, hoping for a creature or earth mage. He was preparing for a fourth attack when the earth tilted beneath him. He stumbled and fell to one knee, then his hip and side as the earth lurched again. He barely managed to hold onto his sword, feeling it slide a bit too far out in his fingers.

Wind whistled past him, blowing his cloak down over his eyes, his hair into his face. Because the wind wasn't whistling side to side, as it usually did, but *down.*

A feminine scream stabbed at his ears. Siliana?

He tried to straighten, to go after her and help, but the earth continued to wobble. Pushing his hair and cloak up with one hand, he caught his breath as he saw why the air was blowing past as it did.

The trees, the mages, the forest itself—they were all gone. The first thing his eyes saw were the pine-needle-covered dirt, a rough, rocky edge about two feet before him, and then treetops. The mountains beyond Anonil were almost visible at eye level.

The earth mage. The rocks they'd been heaving into the air and back down. Aven was on *top* of one.

Or perhaps this was his own special fate, as the rock was flying up and showed no sign of slowing. He rolled to one side to slide the sword back into its scabbard. Trying not to lose it up here was probably a futile attempt, but he had to try.

The storm above him had weakened slightly, but he was still approaching the dark clouds at an alarming rate. What would happen if he hit them? Sometimes mists gathered around Estun, but he didn't make a habit of venturing out onto the balcony in them, and thunderstorms didn't reach that high. At home, it had always snowed.

These clouds were charged with lightning. Clouds he'd summoned himself.

The rock tilted again. He hit his stomach, hoping for traction from it as he slid, headed feet-first toward the edge. Clawing at the dirt, he scrambled but caught on nothing. Of course *this* portion of the forest was smooth. Clear. No rocks or handholds. *Nothing*.

The first wisps of foggy mist flew past him. He'd reached the storm, and soon it would swallow him.

The rock tilted and bucked in the opposite direction, sending his feet flying up into the air as he slid face-first toward the opposite side, heading straight toward free fall out into the storm cloud and open air beneath it. The trees were gone now, and around him was only a grayish darkness. He was immediately drenched and cold, like he'd been flung into a river, except it was so soft he felt nothing except the sheer icy temperature of his skin.

But he didn't have long to marvel at the cloud. The rock tilted and bucked back, and then forward again, and he dug into the very last few inches of the rock, but it was no use.

His hands went over and now groped nothingness. As the rock slid out from under his chest, and then his legs, he had one stunned second to marvel at it all. The air, the thing that gave him so much power, that had called to him every day of his life, that had shown him beauty he couldn't have even imagined…

How ironic that it would be the thing to kill him too.

Miara awoke gradually, fogginess clouding her brain so much that she almost wasn't sure she'd actually awoken. The darkness surrounding her was nearly absolute.

Even after she opened her eyes and blinked into the darkness, the cobwebby, lethargic feeling did not go away. No pain throbbed in her mind, like what she'd expect after expending too much magic or imbibing too much wine, but something sharp jutted into her back, her palms, the soles of her bare feet.

Actually, lots of sharp, pointy things jutted into her. And where were her shoes?

She groped around. Everything was hard, triangular, but smooth. She struggled to sit up, which didn't exactly help the discomfort. The jagged points could not be escaped so easily.

She peered at the wall to her right, inches from her face. The slick surface sparkled faintly, a reflection shining from a dim light off to her left, from beyond the hollow where she so painfully sat.

The sparkles, the shapes—they were vaguely familiar. She held up a hand, running it carefully across the strange, unforgiving shapes again.

Crystals. The smooth planes broke along sharp edges, pyramids jabbing brutally into her body. They held a faint purple glow, just like… the Great Stone.

Oh, gods.

She groped up the wall beside her, circling inward, and her stomach dropped as she realized it really *was* all around her. Her immediate area was entirely crystal, even above and below. The entire space was barely two paces across until she reached cold metal poles that rose up into the air. Bars. She could easily reach the jagged ceiling without fully straightening.

She studied the back of her hand as well as she could in the dim light and reached for her magic. Fur. Claws. Talons. Something.

Change somehow, by the gods. Change. *Anything*.

Like heaving a heavy weight, she managed to grow a few hairs that made her hand look more like a man's than a bear's. She relaxed the spell, which seemed to take nearly as much effort, and they fell away. All much harder than it should be.

Suddenly exhausted, she sagged against the side of her prison. At least until the sharp pokes reminded her that standing up would be more comfortable, as long as she had the energy for it.

That obviously couldn't last, though.

She clenched her fist, thinking of that healer. Nyor. When she got out of here, she'd… well, she didn't know what she'd do, but it wouldn't be good. He'd betrayed her and locked her in a magic-suppressing prison, a rock made of the Great Stone or something very much like it.

And she was trapped inside.

The dim light beyond the bars grew brighter, and a doorway was lit with fiery light from a torch or lantern coming up the stairs toward her.

Miara rushed forward, gripping the bars and positioning herself to grab that healer by the neck if she needed to. Anything to get out of this hell.

But it wasn't Nyor who appeared.

It was a woman's form silhouetted in the doorway. The outline of a wide, sweeping skirt was clear, even in the darkness. She approached slowly, more men filing in behind her in dark hoods, carrying lanterns, some lit by flames, others lit by purple stones glowing with an orange, ember-like light.

The woman's face came slowly into view, and Miara's blood ran cold.

The Devoted Knight smiled at her, insincere and predatory. The knight from Mage Hall, the one they'd also encountered in the woods who'd seemed attached to Aven. A woman who'd already tried to burn Miara once.

Miara tightened her grip on the bars.

"We meet again, mage," the knight said. Delight shimmered in her pale-blue eyes, even in the darkness.

"Give me back my shoes," Miara said bluntly.

"You won't be needing them."

If they'd taken her shoes, what else had they taken? Miara reached for her neck, but only bare skin met her fingers. The queen's pendant.

"You won't be needing that either," the knight growled, "as you won't be going back. Be happy I let you keep the dress. My squires were all too enthusiastic to relieve you of it."

"So generous."

"Your tongue, however, you do not have to keep."

Miara opened her mouth, about to point out that she cold just heal any such injury. But she stopped short. Here, in this prison, that was no longer true. "What do you want?" she said instead.

The knight smirked. "Other than to watch you suffer?"

"Why should you want me to suffer?"

The smirk melted into a glare. "Is it true you're betrothed to him?"

Miara blinked. "What?"

Slowly, almost delicately, the knight held a hand up to her throat, and Miara's eyes caught on the glimmer of emerald in the dim light. "I may be a knight," she whispered, "but I am also a noble. Unlike yourself. I'm more fit to wear this than you are."

"You didn't want it," Miara snapped. "You betrayed him to *them*."

"I am a princess, third born, in addition to a holy woman. Princess Evana Paranelin of Isolte. What are you? The offspring of boot scum and floorboard dust, and corrupted by magic to boot. That he would give you this is a *disgrace*. Not that I am surprised, as he's just as corrupted as you are. Fortunately, I am here to remedy the situation."

"You call yourself a holy woman? A noble? Absurd. You people aren't holy. You're—"

"Silence," Evana snapped. "You'd do well to watch your tongue, or I'll give you wounds to remind you just how powerless you are. I've got you trapped, little mage, and the sooner you admit this, the easier it will be."

Miara scowled at her. Easier? Did she think Miara cared about making this *easier*? When had her life ever been easy? One more torture to add to the list was nothing in the scheme of things. She had a lifetime of experience with tolerating misery. Let the fool knight try to break her. She'd not find it so easy or simple as taking Miara's shoes. Or her magic.

"Where is the brand?" demanded Evana.

Miara smirked. She'd known the knight wanted something other than watching Miara squirm. "It's in Mage Hall."

"Liar."

"Excuse me?" Mock innocence soaked Miara's voice.

"You know where it is."

"It's not in Mage Hall? What happened to it?"

Evana narrowed her eyes, her lips pursed. "You know exactly what happened to it, I think."

"I have no idea what you're talking about. It's been lost?"

"You have it, and you'll tell me where they're keeping it."

"No, I definitely don't have it." Miara gestured at the simple dress. "No brands in these pockets. Or any pockets at all, for that matter." Of all the horrid, impractical things to get kidnapped in. She was *never* wearing a dress again.

"Don't waste my time. You *will* tell me where it is before we're through. It wasn't in your rooms."

Ah, so they had been the ones to do the kidnapping then. It hadn't just been Nyor. Or even Opia. This must have been the purpose of drugging her, so she could be swept into this evil den of misery.

Miara shrugged. "I can't tell you what I don't know."

Evana folded her arms across her chest and walked slowly toward the bars. She came so close, Miara could feel her breath, could have reached out, and—

As soon as the thought occurred to her, Miara lunged, fast as a snake reaching for Evana's neck. But the knight seemed to have counted on that, stepping to the side slightly and reaching out herself to catch Miara by the hair. Her other hand swiftly drew a dagger from her belt and slashed, and Miara fell back, smashing into the stabbing rock behind her.

Evana smiled, stepping back with a handful of red hair. Another chill went through Miara, pondering what the knight planned to do with that.

"We shall see about that," said Evana, and she turned and swept from the room.

And then Aven's boot left the rock too, and there was no mistaking it. He was falling. His stomach dropped like a stone as icy acid surged into every limb and vein. He'd risen up above the cloud in the last few seconds, and it roiled beneath him, not far but how far exactly he had no bar to judge by.

All he knew was that he was approaching the grayish, swirling mass faster than he'd ever thought possible.

The cloud enveloped him, and he was drenched again, head to toe. But this time he felt the hair on the back of his neck, his arms, everywhere stand straight up.

Time slowed and then stopped altogether. A face flashed into his mind, both familiar and not, like someone from a dream he couldn't quite remember. An old woman's face, her dark hair crowned with a circlet of diamonds, like stars plucked from the sky to grace her brow.

What are you waiting for? Her voice into his mind was silvery and ethereal, like a dream, like a ghost. Where had he heard it before?

The woman's brow furrowed, scowling at him as her voice grew commanding. *The sky is yours. Control it. Now!*

Then she was gone.

And he was still plummeting. This was some kind of clue—what was it? She had to be right. There must be some way to use his magic to stop this fall. Mustn't there? How?

He tried to reach for the wind, and he gripped it for a second, pushing himself slightly to the left with a weak gust. But the sheer sensation of air screaming past him fed his terror, threw him off, made him lose it within a heartbeat.

No. He had to forget his body, forget his looming death, forget everything.

Up—he'd go up. His mind rose away from his body, reaching back toward the storm. And the wind. He could see his own body fall now, and he bid the air toward it, flowing up like spring water bubbling into a mountain stream. The sudden change sent a lurch of nausea into his body, almost slamming his mind back down into his brain, but he resisted, clinging to the storm. If he was going to survive, he *had* to.

He pushed the wind further up, up, and over, sweeping his corporeal form toward the nearest tall pine, away from the mages who'd certainly hurl him right back into the sky if he landed too close. He was just lucky that they seemed to have forgotten the storm for the moment. There would have been no time to wrestle for its control.

But his stomach dropped further to think of what they could be focused on instead. Siliana? Dyon? Jenec?

Systematically burning alive the entire regiment?

Now that the air burbled underneath him, he could slide back to his body and try to grab on. It was awkward and he was still falling but not so fast now, and though he flailed dramatically, he could almost manage a little control. When he neared the first tree branch strong enough to hold him, he dove for it, lurching forward and bringing the air spout with him.

His first handhold missed, rough bark scraping a gash into his palm, and he thought he might have to fall farther, but his other hand caught, and soon he was standing on one branch, with another above him, clinging to a thick trunk.

It might be best if he just stayed here a while. Yes. He should just stay here. And never come down.

He glanced over his shoulder. The road, the mages, the fighting—he could hear it, but none of it was in sight. So he technically wasn't in the thick of things up here. But he was probably visible from the forest floor. Yes, much as he might like to never move again, and much as he had absolutely no desire to climb down—or fall from—this tree, this was probably not a smart place to hunker down and figure out what had happened.

How many had he taken out? How many were left?

As he eyed the tree for the next best branch to move toward, he tried to remember. His first hit hadn't taken anyone out. After that, perhaps two, then. If they'd been seriously hurt, which they might not have been. So maybe none. And he'd left Siliana with them, pretty much defenseless. Great.

Unfortunately, there was no near branch. Anything would be a bit of a drop or a leap. Now that he had a moment to breathe, the face from the cloud came back to mind.

Queen Tena. His great-grandmother, the one who'd visited him in the dream not so long ago. She must have been an air mage too. Why hadn't it occurred to him before? Maybe even a star mage, with those diamonds on her brow.

Unfortunately, he didn't think star magic was going to help him now. At least not for getting out of this tree. Although the sun was setting fast, and night would be soon on them, and then the stars might have their chance.

Speaking of trying out new things, he could probably try to shimmy down this tree and hope he didn't break a leg in the process, but considering he had no idea where Siliana was and that wasn't looking at all easy, he summoned up the strange burbling spring of air again.

He stared out at it. He knew it was there; he'd created it. He could feel wisps of wind hitting his face. But it still mostly *looked* like empty space. Maybe he *should* try climbing. He crouched down on the branch, getting ready drop down and swing from it. Of course, if he lost his grip, he'd be plummeting yet again toward the ground. And his shoulders were none too excited about the idea.

He couldn't quite bring himself to do it. He'd always preferred the faster, riskier routes in training exercises. Ah, well.

He closed his eyes, groped for the spinning funnel of air, and jumped.

The air caught him awkwardly, like being tumbled about by a dozen gusts of wind all going in the wrong direction, but bit by bit he lessened the gusts, lowering himself down and away from the tree.

He hit an elbow off one branch he flailed just a little too closely to, but in the end he managed to hit the ground with only a modicum of force that was more awkward than painful.

Rolling to his feet, he straightened and scanned the dimming forest around him. The animals were still quiet, but he sensed no one around, no movement, nothing. A hill provided some denser foliage off to his left. If he could, he'd find some shelter there, open a window, and see what he could see.

Jaena slumped against the wall that ran around Ranok. She might as well go back inside. The gate was only a few yards away. But returning would mean admitting defeat. She could pause here, with the shouting and murmuring of the market and the scent of ripe apples, baked goods, and cooking meat around her.

She'd left her braids free yesterday without much thought, and now they were digging into her back and getting who knew what on them. She reached back, swung them over her shoulder, and sighed.

"It's hopeless," she said softly, rubbing her forehead.

"She's tough," Tharomar said, joining her in leaning against the wall, their shoulders touching. His eyes scanned the market around them cautiously, not looking at her. "Just because we can't find her doesn't mean anything."

"And if she's dead?" She was too exhausted to even sound upset. They'd helped search every room of Ranok and even part of the city with some of the guards, and they hadn't slept a moment. They'd searched all evening and through the night, and nothing. She could barely tell if she was feeling fear or anger or sadness at this point. She was certainly tired.

"She's not dead, Jae. Don't think like that," he said.

"We don't know that."

"We don't know either way. But if they wanted to kill her, they could have just left her there on the floor. Why bother transforming someone else to look like her?"

She nodded grudgingly. "True. I'm still worried."

He folded his arms, propped a foot against the wall, and sighed. "I am too."

"Do you think we're in danger?" she said, more softly now. "Do you think they were after just her or… all of us?"

He glanced around the market again. "I haven't decided yet."

Two people leaving the main crowd and heading toward Ranok's gate caught Jaena's eye. They didn't look like the type to have business at Ranok—not that Jaena did, either. She looked *more* the part now that she'd been living in clothes borrowed from Elise's attendants and the steward, but she still felt very out of place.

The man wore a rather ridiculous hat, the large feather bouncing as he walked. One that big was probably from Detrat, Farsa, or even the Southern Kingdoms. A trader? She eyed him with envy. In another life, perhaps. But as he walked, bottles and pouches also clinked at his belt, and many of the bottles sloshed with liquid behind purple, blue, and red glass. A healer of some kind?

The girl wore a dusty, brown, shapeless mass of fabric, and dirt smudged her face. She carried black cloth slung over one arm, a trim of bright blue peeking out from time to time, and a handkerchief in one hand.

While the man looked comfortable, it was the girl who raised her chin and approached the guards, obviously believing herself equal parts brave and suicidal.

"I'm here to see Arms Master Floren," the girl said.

Jaena's stomach sank. Beside her, Ro straightened, stepping away from the wall as he listened.

"On what business?" the guard said, clearly skeptical.

"We're here in response to her request," said the man, his voice stiffly formal and dramatic. But it sounded less natural than put-on, dramatic.

"Her request for what?"

"The proclamation," the girl said. "And she gave me this." She held out the handkerchief.

The guard squinted at it, then looked at his partner. He shrugged, "It's good stock, embroidered within Ranok. She's probably telling the truth."

The girl scowled at him as if this was a huge affront

to her honor and not completely normal skepticism. Of course, Jaena knew the other reason the guards were hesitating. They were wondering if these people could have had something to do with Miara's disappearance. Of course, if these two *did* have something to do with it, this seemed an odd time to approach Ranok and ask to see her.

Ro waved at the two of them, surprising Jaena by his sudden motion. "Hello, there. I believe Arms Master Floren is indisposed this morning."

The guard looked relieved to have someone else break the news to the wild eyes glaring up at him. The girl turned her glare on Ro.

"What do you mean? The order said to come here."

The man cleared his throat. "When I spoke with her outside my shop," he said slowly, focusing on the guards, "she said we could also see her lieutenant, a Jaena Eliar, I believe?"

"Lieutenant?" Jaena blurted, straightening.

Ro elbowed her in the side. The girl looked like she would object, but Ro spoke up first. "Well, you're in luck, because this is Jaena Eliar right here. We'd be happy to speak with you on Miara's behalf." He gave a little bow that seemed entirely unnecessary, but the girl's face shifted from completely closed to simply wary. "If that's all right with you, Tian." He raised an eyebrow at the guards, who gave friendly nods. Just how many of the guards had he befriended?

"Excellent. Thank you so much, gentlemen," the

man in the hat said to the guards, then ushered the girl toward Jaena.

They were mages, weren't they? Or at least the girl was. That was why she was so afraid.

"Actually, would you prefer to speak inside?" Jaena asked.

"Yes," the girl said quickly. The man glanced at her amicably and shrugged.

"Come on, let's go." Jaena motioned for them all to follow her. She wasn't entirely sure inside was any safer for anyone. But it was a start. "You already know my name. And you are?"

"Sestin, of Sestin's Drams," the man proclaimed with another grand tip of his hat. "I make and sell remedies of all sorts."

Did he have a remedy for missing friends? She doubted it. "Remedies? What sorts are all sorts?"

"Oh, poultices and potions. Herbal remedies, mostly." He smiled, and his eyes glittered with mischief. "And some not herbal at all."

"And I'm Wessa," said the girl.

"Wessa?"

"Just Wessa," she said coldly, keeping her head pointed straight, although her eyes darted around, looking for danger. What had her so spooked?

Abruptly Jaena realized she wasn't sure where she was taking them. Since they still didn't know who'd attacked Miara, how could she know where was safe? She gritted her teeth, then led them to a secluded corner of the grounds between the stables and the barracks.

"This is a quiet spot. Not many around. How is this? I'm guessing that's what you wanted?" she said to Wessa.

"Why do you say that?"

"Because you looked scared as a rabbit that wandered into a kitchen."

Ro smothered a laugh, clearing his throat at the end of it. Now *she* should be elbowing him in the kidney. "You're mages, right?"

Wessa eyed him. Sestin said, "Of course," earning him a glare from Wessa. "What? We said as much walking up to the door and asking for the Arms Master."

"I know. But I'm not sure if I trust her, let alone these people. Or *you*." She jabbed a finger at his chest, and he shook his head.

"I'm a creature mage," said Sestin, waving off Wessa's concerns. "Been practicing most of my life, hiding it behind herbals. People are much less inclined to ask questions when you get the job done when no one else could. And when you give them a little bag of lavender and something they've never seen before to justify it." He smiled brightly. "She's one too."

Wessa shot him a glare but didn't deny it. "I met Arms Master Floren briefly at the Sapphire Temple," she said stiffly.

"Met her? The way you described it, you saw her, turned, and ran like... well, like a rabbit." Sestin grinned.

"I was frightened. I thought she might be Devoted."

"She's not," Jaena said quickly.

"None of us are," Ro added.

"I figured. I didn't believe the proclamation, but then three Devoted were ejected from the Third Temple and sent packing back to Takar." She bit her lip.

"So is there some way we can help?" asked Sestin. "Even if the arms master is predisposed this morning?"

Jaena looked to Ro, and he gazed back, his expression the same as hers. Do we tell them? Scare this already-scared one off so soon? She could sense Wessa's tension building even now.

Jaena looked down at the dirt-packed ground, rubbing her forehead, her eyes. Was there something? There must be. But she was so tired, and her brain felt like it was floating away on a cloud.

"How much training do you have?" she finally managed.

"Nothing much formal," Sestin said, "but I've figured out a lot of healing on my own. At least, I think I have."

"Nothing," said Wessa. "But I do have a few other friends who are mages. I might be able to convince them to come too."

"All right then." Jaena sighed, then looked to Ro. "Wunik?"

He nodded. "Can't hurt to learn a few things."

"You could take that advice yourself," she said, smiling for the first time in hours.

He smiled back but dodged answering as he turned and beckoned for them to follow.

I2 CALM

Aven pushed aside the branches of a spruce near the edge of the cliffside and eased in toward the tree's trunk. He sank to a seat on a low branch. The heavy boughs bobbed lazily in the growing darkness, almost welcoming, and they provided thick cover once inside.

Here, the air was fresh and bright with the scent of pine and fallen leaves, still crisp with an edge of snow, probably because of the storm he'd brewed up. He'd fought his way through at least six feet of evergreen brush to get to this spot, with the hope that the intense light of the farsight spell wouldn't be visible to his enemies with all the dense, dark branches and needles in the way. The generous boughs also blocked the wind, which would have been freezing even if he *weren't* soaked.

His gambeson was too thick for wetness to have seeped all the way through, but his trousers, his boots, his neck had all been near dripping when he'd reunited with the ground. That was a big problem. He'd have to start a fire to warm up and dry off if he didn't like the idea of freezing to death out here, but that could tip someone off to where he was. And of course he couldn't start a fire here, inside the tree, so that meant more wind along with less cover.

But first—he needed to see what he was up against. What had happened. Who had survived.

He calmed his nerves and opened up the window of light.

What he could see was bleak. The road they'd been following was littered with the dead—both horses and people. Nothing moved except a few lost horses milling around, awaiting the return of their riders. Riders who most likely were dead and rotting nearby. No one had even tried to bury them. Not that that surprised him given how long it'd take twelve people to bury that many, but… By the gods, so many. Curse those mages for showing no respect, slaves or no. Those men and women shouldn't have died. They'd been good people who'd been trying to do something right.

Or at least do their duty to him. He swallowed the lump in his throat.

It'd happened so fast. How much of the regiment was dead? All of it? Had they bothered to capture *anyone*? He struggled to think if there was some way this disaster could have been averted. What if they'd brought every mage they had with them? But that would have left Panar completely undefended, and what then? They'd have been even in numbers perhaps, but not in training. And they'd still have had the low ground, the exposed position, and the enemy would still have had the element of surprise.

Akarian forces needed mage scouts to go on ahead and spot enemies both magical and mundane. He'd had the thought before, but they didn't have the numbers for it. He made a mental note that Kavanar could be using such scouts, even if Akaria wasn't.

Notably, the wagons were gone. Not broken, not abandoned, but gone. Tracks and hoofprints lined the side of the road, and some bodies had been cleared to make way for the wagons to get through. Others had not been cleared and simply been crushed. He gritted his teeth.

The wagons held food supplies, yes, but also a large amount of armor. Wunik had said Kavanar appeared short on that. Aven certainly hadn't wanted to be the one to supply them with it, by the gods.

The thought that someone had tipped the enemy off returned, persisting in his gut, although he could just as easily imagine this had been an opportunistic attack. They might have seen the regiment leave through farsight. This was one of the main roads north, the one Aven's forces would likely take. The mages could have found a good spot and waited.

But the idea itched at him. Something about it wasn't right. If this had been an opportunistic ambush, would they really think to take the wagons? Perhaps. Or had that somehow been part of the plan?

Aven slowly guided his view of the road north in the

growing darkness. It was black enough he feared he'd miss the wagons, but as it turned out, the darkness helped him find them. The huge blazing fire and the camp circled around it were hard to miss, about a mile or so north of the carnage.

He eased closer to the fire, and he spotted brown cloaks and colored tunics, like those on the mages he'd seen. Four stood by the fire, speaking with… Akarian soldiers.

Aven caught his breath.

As his view swept closer, he stopped and glared. One soldier speaking and standing in front of a group of others was none other than Jenec, Dyon's lieutenant. Who'd been privy to all their plans. Who'd *made* half of them.

Who'd clearly been leery of mages, and Aven hadn't done a single thing about it, hoping to win the lieutenant over eventually.

Another time he'd waited to act. He'd hope to convince the young man in the long run. And *this* was the result. A thousand good soldiers dead. He cursed under his breath, a stream of swearing that went on and on. What could he have done differently? Banned anyone from planning who didn't support mages? Would that even have helped? Any of them could have simply lied. Aven sighed. It was too late to change it all now.

He peered further around the camp. A dozen men—a dozen armed *Akarians*—stood guard around a group of figures seated on the ground, and peering closer, he caught sight of Dyon's scowl. His heart leapt—at least the old curmudgeon was alive. And apparently not in on the betrayal, thank the gods, because he looked more prisoner than bargainer. Another form sat on the ground behind him, and there was a flash of red—Siliana? Although how could a creature mage be bound? Perhaps she was simply waiting to try to escape when there weren't so many guards to sneak past. Even a fly could be swatted, he supposed.

Well, that told him everything he needed to know. He was headed to that damn camp. But first, he'd look at one more thing.

He slid the farseeing window up and higher into the sky now, racing along the road north that they should have been traveling, and then slightly west, until he found the southern stronghold.

His stomach dropped like a slab of ice in his core. What he saw was worse than he'd have ever guessed. The entire hold was on fire, wooden fortifications blazing orange fury into the night. Men and women had spilled from the open keep doors, but none of them were moving. They'd tried to get away, but failed.

Almost without meaning to, he dropped the spell, his hands falling weakly in his lap.

He took a ragged breath. This shouldn't faze him. He'd known the southern hold was likely a lost cause, not something he could count on, that something terrible had happened. He'd been going more out of duty than out of optimism that they'd find any reinforcements.

But with the loss of so many at once tonight—so many dead, and how many others injured or lost or taken prisoner—it was hard not to simply fall back on the pine-needle-strewn ground, stare at the sky, and despair. He'd left Panar with a thousand allies and then some.

And within the span of a few hours, he was now completely alone.

He did have one thing they didn't, though. He staggered out of the spruce and stared up at the sky. The stars.

He had the stars. He just had to figure out how to use them.

What are you waiting for? The words drifted back into his mind. What, indeed.

Eventually, Aven stalked back up the north road until he reached the chaos. Apparently he had ended up south of the devastation, which was lucky, as the enemy camp had set up farther north. Perhaps they meant to meet up with the Anonil forces. With only twelve mages, it shouldn't have mattered, but of course, the chaos around him proved it did.

Time was of the essence, but he did need to warm up at least a little before charging in like a mad bull, or at least not turn to ice before then. So he lit a small fire on the edge of the road. He checked a few bodies for anyone alive and found none. He considered burning the dead, finishing the job they'd started. It would be the best death rites he could manage at the moment, but he quickly realized it would take him hours—and probably more energy than it was wise to spend.

If he was alive after going after Dyon and Siliana—and confronting Jenec—he'd come back here and help them.

He gathered up some of the horses instead and removed

their tack. If he survived, he could take many of the surviving horses back, but if he didn't, at least getting their
bits out of the way would help those horses survive the
winter by themselves. They might wander to a town or
be found by whatever unlucky travelers next happened
upon this mess.

His boots and such were never going to dry before
morning, even with the fire that burned with the zealous
rage that stirred in Aven's own chest. So, he settled for
less frozen and studied the star map. He kept waiting for
some clear advantage to reveal itself, some method that
would guarantee him the win, because he was on the side
of justice, the side of right. And how could the world be
Balanced if the side of justice got massacred by the side
of the road? There *had* to be a way.

Nothing screamed out to him. He settled on Erepha.
Calm. Wind. Perhaps he could somehow force a civil
discussion with her energy. He certainly wasn't jumping
in trying to enslave anyone, nor was he sure how he'd
combine that with "fire" for such a large group. And Casel
wasn't helping in this battle, that was for sure. Perhaps all
these spells could only be cast on one person at a time?
He was about to find out.

He gathered the reins of three horses and led them north.

Niat had followed Thel down from the cliffs, and
they'd skirted their way along the south road. A network

of caves had been tempting them to seek shelter, little alcoves appearing rather frequently. Their darkness would normally have frightened her, but she'd become more acquainted with earthen hollows on this journey than she cared to admit. Now, they looked positively inviting. But distance between them and Anonil sounded appealing to her too, so they'd trudged on.

Eventually, though, they'd tired enough to pick a larger cave and head inside. A complex latticework of interconnected caves stretched out beneath their feet, and they began searching for one that was relatively cut off from the others.

She stopped still. Had she heard something? Thel had frozen too. She listened harder.

Voices echoed in the caverns around them. They were coming from the road that ran alongside the caves, the one they'd just left.

"This way," said Thel, gesturing in the direction of the voices.

"No, c'mon. Let's hide." She pointed in the opposite direction, further inside the caves.

"I want to see who it is. Maybe they have Kae."

She pressed her lips together. "Fine." She didn't want to abandon Kae. But she didn't see what good they'd do him that he couldn't do himself.

Thel did an admirable job of creeping quietly up a sharp ledge and out onto an overhang. She was less quiet but further back, and when she lay down beside him, she could see more mages, including another dressed in a blue tunic and cloak like the leader of the last group.

"Let's take him back! Easiest. Then we can interrogate him."

They were arguing. Over a prisoner. Apparently these people needed better orders as to what to do with prisoners once they found them.

"Let's just kill him and be done with it," said another.

"But they might want to know—" Voices broke out, talking over each other, none of them making any sense or listening.

Thel rose to his knees and took the bow from the pack.

"What are you *doing*?" she hissed even as he pulled an arrow from the quiver.

"Trying to help him, what's it look like?" he whispered as he inched forward, raised the bow, and lined up an arrow.

"Stop it, Thel. They'll notice us."

He dropped the bow slightly, easing the tension in the string, and turned to glare at her over his shoulder. "You would rather cower back here and watch him die, then?"

She glared right back. "Your foolhardy bravery will be the death of you."

"Sounds look a good death. I could do worse."

"We don't know that that's Kae. We can't see anything."

"And we don't know that it's *not* Kae."

"And I don't want to die trying to save some stranger. Please, Thel."

"No. Go hide from danger. I can't take that path."

"Thel—" She wanted to say more, but the words caught in her throat. "Thel, stop—" Still they hovered there on the tip of her tongue. I don't want you to die either. Whoever had raised him had either given him an extra helping of courage or a very strong aversion to injustice. Possibly both. But beautiful as it was, she couldn't thank them now if it got them both caught by these mages.

She reached up and put a hand on his upper arm, the rough linen warm, as though she could feel his heat just below. His gaze caught on her fingers, staring for a moment.

Then he shook her off and gestured with his chin. "Go on. Head back a few outcroppings, and if they come, they'll find me and not you. You can head back to Anonil, and you'll be all right. Take the pack but leave the arrows."

He turned away and focused on his target again. She didn't move.

"Well? Are you going or not?"

She sighed. "No. Go ahead and shoot."

"What?"

"I'm not leaving."

He squinted at her. "Fine. Think of a way to help. Or hide quickly when they come in here. Hold the pack and be ready to run."

He pulled back the bowstring again, much more easily than she had and further too. He let the arrow fly. Something in a tree far on the other side of the men thunked to the ground.

"What was that?" she whispered, as the men's cries of alarm went up.

"Bee hive," he said. "Sorry, bees."

"Someone's coming—just do it!"

"No, by the goddess—"

A gurgling sound made her clutch Thel's arm, and he hung his head. The men surged forward toward where the hive had fallen.

"They killed him *anyway*," he whispered. "Faster because of me. Maybe they would have decided not to if I'd—"

"Stop. Just stop. You tried." She couldn't stand for him to regret doing the right thing when she'd urged him not to. "C'mon. Let's get further inside. This is as good a place to camp as any, right?"

He said nothing, just turned and led the way inside, head hanging.

Aven crouched behind a large thicket on the edge of the mage camp. Muffled voices drifted toward him, the smoke of their fire on the wind. It blew toward him, the wrong direction for the spell he was about to undertake. Fortunately he could take care of that.

The thicket provided some cover, but he still needed to be able to see those in the camp and their reactions—if this worked at all—so it wasn't a complete block. He also needed somewhere with a clear sky above, which limited his options further. He studied the traitors and Kavanarian mages and prisoners for a few more moments and then took a deep breath.

He turned his eyes to the sky. Casel winked at him, and he caught sight of Erepha's sparkle just above the tree line. It was lucky these trees weren't taller, or he might not have been able to see the star.

Miara might hate him for what he was about to do. Might never forgive him. Much as his chest ached at the thought, he swallowed and steeled himself. He was one man against two dozen, maybe more, and he was going to have to use this magic if he was going to win this war. Or even get out of these woods alive.

If he could win this war and she never forgave him, at least she'd be alive. And free.

It was a risk he'd have to take. Gods forgive him. Balance protect him.

He reached out to Erepha. Similar to Casel, a cold, delicate energy wormed into him, twists of white smoke swirling down. He pulled it down, urging it beyond its initial wisps into its true form.

The energy pouring into him expanded, multiplied, like a river overflowing a dam. Except where Casel flowed like a stream of water, Erepha was more like a gale off the ocean. Which figured, he supposed.

He needed to direct this energy somewhere before he drowned in it. No time for analysis now.

He twisted to peer at the camp and pulled the energy along with him, trying to force it into the air around him, into the wind. The wind blew, but the energy in him stayed the same, filling dangerously fast.

He gritted his teeth. Think, Aven, think. Casel had

been marked with a salve, a healing icon. But he hadn't had to literally find a salve and imbue the freeing energy into it. He'd simply reached out with his mind.

Maybe he didn't need to put the energy into the real wind, but to simply move it like he moved the wind.

A breeze blew against his face, back in its natural direction, and he smiled, feeling as if the air itself was agreeing with him. He closed his eyes now, simply willing the energy out and over the encampment, spreading it like that same gentle breeze, a fog drifting in to hopefully calm those before him and give him some way to negotiate, to talk, to rescue Dyon and Siliana.

The frigid, powerful wind blew out of him, leaving him empty. He opened his eyes.

The camp at first was so still he wasn't sure what he was seeing. All of them had utterly frozen, and he blinked and rubbed his eyes.

The first sign of movement beyond the blazing of the central fire was a man who sat on a log near the fire; he tipped over and fell to the ground. Aven stared, unsure what to make of that. A loud snort and then a string of snores rang out.

The man had fallen asleep?

Indeed, another few fell over as the next few heartbeats passed. Cautiously, Aven scooted around the thicket, moving closer to get a better look. The silence of the camp made his twig-cracking footsteps seem even louder. He couldn't avoid one or two in the darkness, no matter how carefully he trod. Still, no one glanced his way.

As he neared the edge of the clearing, they all came into view. Jenec and one of the mage leaders, in a blue tunic and brown cloak, had been talking in front of the one tent that had been erected, and even they stood silent, as if paused in thought but facing each other.

Aven crept closer, and then, at the edge of the clearing, he risked standing up.

No one moved.

He took a step forward, then another. The whole scene was entirely frozen. More like dolls than real people. Except they *were* real people.

He glanced around nervously. He hadn't exactly expected this. What did he do now? The most important thing should be getting Dyon and Siliana and anyone else held prisoner freed. That would give him allies, no matter what these people had planned. They could execute their prisoners at any time, though thankfully they hadn't yet.

At that thought, though, he stopped cold. These people *were* either traitors or outright enemies. Plenty of laws justified the deaths of every one of them, and as their king, he had every right to make that decision.

A knot of dread twisted in his gut. Their own Dark Days indeed. He swallowed, trying to imagine himself slaughtering these people while they sat here like docile lambs.

The sight of the smoking dead strewn across the road came back instead. Good men and women, butchered like cattle going to market. He found Jenec in the crowd and glared. Maybe he could slaughter *one* of them.

These mages, these soldiers, and Jenec would fight

against him and against all of Akaria if he let them live.

He had no choice but to end this, here and now.

Not the mages; they were slaves. It wasn't their choice to fight this battle, just like it hadn't been Miara's. He should be *freeing* them, not enslaving them. The thought was even tempting, but alone he was too at risk of an imbalance and passing out. The spell was too difficult. Erepha's calming had been easier, really.

Panar flashed through his mind, its subjects sitting sullen and comatose in the streets like these people. Ripe for slaughter, abuse. He shook his head. Miara was right. This was a truly horrifying spell. A single air mage could murder dozens, hundreds, maybe even thousands if they so chose.

On the other hand, he was right too. It was a powerful weapon, and he'd have no hope of freeing the prisoners without it.

He shook off his thoughts and strode toward the group of prisoners, eying the people around him warily. Eight traitors guarded perhaps twenty prisoners. So few had survived. And less than a dozen traitors had taken down a thousand men—with the help of mages, at least. He shuddered.

His footsteps sounded loud as felled trees falling, but none of them moved. He found Siliana first. She was bound at the wrists to his surprise, and a rock hung from a thin chain around her neck. But *she* looked up and met his eyes.

"Aven!" she whispered. "What's going on?"

He quickly stepped past one soldier standing guard and untied her wrists. She rubbed them, glaring down at where the rope had been. "I could ask you the same thing. Can't you just shift out of that?"

"This rock," she said, pointing at the stone before she pulled it off over her head. "It suppresses magic, so I couldn't. But what by the gods is going on?" She gestured at the prisoners, all also still and really, really, excessively calm.

"It's a long story," Aven said. "I tried another kind of star magic we found in our research. It seems to have worked... surprisingly well. Here, help me with Dyon."

Together they untied Dyon and pulled him to his feet. At the physical movement, his eyes cleared slightly, but not all the way. He looked around himself in a daze. "Aven? Is that you, my boy?" He reached out as if to tousle Aven's hair, like he had when Aven was little, barely hip-height, but Dyon faltered and ended up resting his hand on Aven's shoulder and squinting hard into his face. Some unseen film clouded his vision.

Siliana let go of his arm to let Dyon stand on his own, but the lord immediately stumbled, almost into the wall of soldiers around them. They both caught him and straightened him, but he was clearly going to need help, at least until the spell wore off.

Great. Aven glanced at the other prisoners. No way they were getting them all out of here if they couldn't walk. "Untie them," he told Siliana. At least it would give them a better chance. "While I figure out what to do next."

Glancing around the frozen encampment, he struggled to think. He could tie them up, but what would he do with them all? Leave them here to starve or freeze? Even if there were more loyalists than just Dyon and Siliana, they would still be vastly outnumbered.

He guided Dyon out of the prisoner area, then stepped away from him. The man stayed put, waiting patiently for direction. Gods. This was a dangerous spell indeed. He guided Dyon the rest of the way to the edge of the clearing, then returned.

Siliana was nearly done untying all of them. He walked up to one of the Kavanarian soldiers and gripped the man's sword hilt. No reaction flickered in his eyes. Slowly, Aven drew the sword free. Aven still had his own sword, but the escapees would need ways to defend themselves. Eventually.

Aven kept glancing around the encampment. The spell should wear off *sometime,* shouldn't it? They couldn't be like this forever... could they? Would he need to apply the opposite star's energy to make them snap out of it?

Maybe. Except the next two times he glanced at Jenec, he could have sworn the man's head had moved. Had swiveled toward Aven.

When they'd fully armed all the prisoners with two swords each and strapped more weapons to Dyon's and Siliana's hips—and a second sword for Aven because why not—he headed to the wagons and hastily dug out some supplies. He set Siliana the task of waking up the remaining prisoners and getting them walking as quickly as she could. The spell had to weaken *sometime*, and they needed to be gone by then.

A plan hadn't entirely formed in his mind—where should they go, with the stronghold in flames?—but if they had food and horses, they'd have time to figure something out.

When Aven stepped away from the wagon, his eyes caught on Jenec. The lieutenant's head had fully turned and was staring at him.

"You," Jenec whispered, the word slurred and seemingly loud in the utter silence. Siliana looked up from where she'd been shaking one prisoner's shoulders and patting his face.

Aven casually slung the sack of supplies over his shoulder and smiled at Jenec. "Didn't think you'd see me again, did you?" He gave Siliana a subtle nod, hoping she took that to mean she needed to keep going. They might have even less time than he'd hoped.

"Curse you." Jenec spat on the ground. "You're going to lead our land to ruin for your own selfish purposes."

"Selfish? Trying to defend us from Kavanar is selfish?" Aven swaggered toward him, taking his time, emphasizing that he wasn't affected by the calming spell.

"Selfish. You're just under the spell of that mage. You're doing whatever she tells you, including putting a mage on the throne."

Aven snorted. "A mage is *already* on the throne, if you hadn't noticed. And magic doesn't work like that." At least her magic didn't. "And this war has nothing to do with her."

The war would have happened with or without Miara. Wouldn't it have?

Just then, Aven caught a hint of movement by Jenec's belt. His hand had found its way to his sword pommel. Aven had been leaving that group for last to disarm because if the mages woke up, it would change the situation dramatically.

Aven stopped about five feet short of the group. Siliana had made her way closer and stood at the tent's far side, eying Jenec warily.

"This war has everything to do with her. I don't think you'd be fighting it if it weren't for her. All those dead are *her* fault and *yours*." Jenec was trembling now. Aven wasn't sure if it was from rage or because he was fighting against the calming spell or something else altogether.

"Her fault?" Aven whispered. "You have some audacity to blame your treachery and betrayal on a woman who's not even here."

"You're the traitor!" Jenec hissed, succeeding in drawing his sword an inch from the scabbard before stopping. "Evil, filthy mage scum—" As if he was heaving a great weight, his neck muscles strained and his face contorted as he forced his arm to move and his blade to slide from the scabbard. He staggered a step toward Aven.

Aven shook his head, not moving. "You sold us out to Kavanar. Death is the *least* you deserve for all the lives you've taken."

He tossed the pack aside, drew his sword, and rested the

blade against his shoulder, staring Jenec down. Waiting.

Jenec started forward, at first halting and uneven, then growing more certain. Aven steadied his breath. The footfalls sped up.

The lieutenant's blade flashed, and Aven caught it, blocking and twisting it aside. Jenec countered with a slash upward, and Aven hopped quickly aside as he easily brought his blade to bear again. He heaved a gust of wind forward at the same time, knocking his opponent back.

Jenec's wide eyes hardened to a scowl. "Fight fair, you bastard."

"Like you fought the thousand who lie dead in the road?" Aven snapped. "Was that fair?"

Growling, Jenec surged forward again, sword raised overhead for a powerful blow. Aven's blade hovered at eye level, and he shifted, expecting a feint, but no. Down the blow came.

Aven caught it near the cross guard and bound the two blades together, the two of them nearly eye to eye. He could feel Jenec's breath—breath stolen from a thousand others who lay rotting on the road.

Lightning flickered up his sword, unbidden, and he twisted, driving down, forcing Jenec's wrist back and the blade toward his feet. The flash of lightning charged down the length of Aven's blade and up Jenec's, and the sword fell from his hands, even as Aven continued the twist and drove the point of his steel into the traitor's gut.

The lieutenant froze. Hands burned black hung limply for a moment before clutching at his stomach. Blood, dark and red, soaked through his gambeson and peeked out along the blade's edge. Aven drew back viciously at an angle. Jenec groaned and collapsed to his knees.

"How could you betray them all?" Aven whispered. "What, was it for coin?"

"I did, and I'd do it again." Jenec spat again, and this time blood splattered the earth. "And no, not coin."

"What then."

"Magic is too powerful to sit on the throne. And too evil. Even now, look at you. You're corrupted by it."

Aven narrowed his eyes. "They were your friends, your colleagues. They *trusted* you. I trusted you, and so did Dyon."

"An unfortunate but necessary price."

"Why? Why is it necessary?" Aven kicked dirt at the man in frustration.

"Because you've corrupted our monarchy. The Kavanarians were willing to help us restore leadership untainted by mages."

"Restore leadership?" Aven laughed incredulously. "You mean, *their* leadership. After you help them wipe out our entire army, who would oppose them? By the gods."

"No!" Jenec said, blinking. His hands clutching his stomach were almost fully red with blood now, but he wasn't pale. He had a lot more bleeding to do before the gods would judge him. "No, they wouldn't—"

"Oh, you fool," Aven whispered. "Of course they would."

Jenec raised his chin. "It doesn't matter. Anything is better than a mage as king."

Aven took a deep breath, knowing what he needed to do, something hardening inside him. "Lieutenant Jenec, you are hereby accused and found guilty of treason against the crown and the murder of hundreds of your fellow soldiers. I sentence you to death."

Aven raised the sword and swept it down, slashing into Jenec's neck just deep enough to draw blood before pulling back. That was a wound that would hasten his meeting with the gods.

Jenec, eyes wide with surprise, fell from his knees to his side, sputtering. Coldly, Aven wiped the blood off the blade on the traitor's trouser leg and watched the life drain from him for one heartbeat, two. Finally, Jenec's eyes stared out into the forest, empty and blank.

Justice. But it wouldn't bring back a single one of the people he'd lost.

He swallowed. One traitor down. Eight more to go. "Siliana."

"Yes, my lord?" To her credit, her voice was solid, and it steadied him. She strode closer but stopped well short of Jenec. "Most of the prisoners are recovered and can follow, when you're ready."

"Good. Take that stone they had on you and put it on their leader. Then bind the mages every way you can think of. Vines, webs, whatever you think will hold them the longest."

"Just the mages, sire?" She hadn't caught on yet.

"Yes, just the mages. They're slaves; they had no other option than to attack us. The others... Well, they made their choice."

He wasn't sure if the sadness in her eyes was more for him or them, and he didn't care.

The discomfort of her stone prison was starting to become unbearable, and it had only been a few hours. Or so it seemed. The room around her prison was still hopelessly dark and perfectly quiet, except for the sound of a fire burning in a hearth somewhere she couldn't see. If it cast much light, it wasn't doing her any good. It seemed to be night, unless she was simply deep underground. The lack of any references to time or geography left her a bit disoriented, and her swimming, pounding head didn't help matters.

Incredibly, she must have found some way to sleep in spite of the torturous stone—or she'd passed out from exhaustion, because she roused to something cold poking her calf.

"Tell me where the brand is." A lantern sat on the floor, sadly well out of reach, and its light was just enough for her to make out the wide skirts and scowling features. Evana. She had an iron hearth poker in her hand and was prodding Miara's leg. Finally awake, she kicked the thing away, only regretting the hurt to the sole of her foot a little.

"I told you. I don't know where it is." At this moment, that was technically true.

"I have something that might change your mind." Evana gestured to the doorway, and the form of a woman appeared out of the darkness. She walked in slowly, dragging her feet, as if she knew something dreadful awaited her here.

She was probably right.

"This is the mage who helped us capture you. After you killed the healer—"

"Killed him?" Miara exclaimed. "I didn't kill him. I don't kill people." Except for Sorin, but that had been part accident, part self-defense.

Evana raised an eyebrow. "Oh, I'm fairly certain you did. Not a wound on him but the blood from his nose. And elsewhere. Crushed his brain like the evil monstrosity you are. There was no one else there when we arrived, so it must have been you."

Miara tightened her hands around the bars at that. "What about Kalan?"

"Who?"

"My attendant."

"*You* had ladies-in-waiting, even?" Evana scoffed. "Those Akarians should be ashamed of themselves."

Well, at least that meant maybe Kalan had gotten away.

"No matter. This mage also helped us transform the healer's body into yours. So likely everyone you love thinks you are dead." Evana smiled.

Miara narrowed her eyes. "You're not going to get away with this," she said softly.

"Watch me." She looked to the mage and pointed at

the floor. "Kneel down." The woman complied, her face darkening further.

"What are you doing?" Miara whispered.

"Tell me where the brand is. Now."

"I told you I don't know."

"Tell me, or I'll kill her." She looked to one of the Devoted who stood guarding the door. He stepped forward, dagger proffered. The mage woman's eyes widened, and she looked up at Miara with pleading green eyes.

Miara stared back, faltering. Could she give up the brand and her friends? Could she watch this woman die for not doing so?

An impossible choice. Jaena and Tharomar, compared to this stranger? How could she choose the life of a slave over giving them the power to enslave hundreds more? All mages everywhere?

No. The brand must be destroyed. Even if it cost this mage her life. And Miara's too.

"Kill me instead," Miara offered quickly. "I can't help you. I don't know where the brand is. You can still use her."

But Evana was smiling. "You reveal yourself, foolish girl. Do you think I haven't been paying attention, watching you weigh her life against the brand's location? You've made your choice but told me what I wanted to know. You know exactly where it is."

"Then you don't need to kill her, if you learned what you want to know," Miara said desperately, hope kindling.

"I'm afraid I do. I want the brand. Unless you'd care to reverse your decision?"

"I can't," Miara whispered, more to the woman than to Miara. That didn't lessen the panic in the woman's eyes.

"So be it."

Miara reeled back, sharp crystal or no. Her whole body ached, her feet screamed with pain, and now her soul and her mind shrieked too, but she couldn't look away as she watched the knight slice the woman's throat.

The blood spurted fast, then slower, draining into a huge, languid puddle on the floor.

"What do we do now?" Siliana said, mounting up one of the horses Aven had led and tied off along the road closest to the camp. "How long do you think *that* will last?"

"The calming spell? I have no idea. Never tried it before. You seemed to get the prisoners out of it quickly enough." Along with twenty or so escapees, they had about half that many horses, which was an immediate problem. They might have to leave some soldiers behind and send help back from the next town they reached. Perhaps Siliana could transform them and carry them somehow, but he wasn't sure the men would be up for any more magic so soon. Or ever. "Dyon, are you feeling all right?"

Dyon cleared his throat as he settled himself in the saddle. "With so many dead? I've been better."

"But after the spell. Are you feeling normal again?"

Dyon nodded. "Mostly. I think what's left is only

shock."

"Well, there's that, but we woke you up. It could last indefinitely, for all I know. If that's the case, fine with me. But the safest course is to assume it won't last much longer." He didn't mention the dead man, but Jenec had fought his way through the spell at the end too, so he assumed that meant it had been weakening. "We should get moving."

Still, he didn't move his horse.

"Which way?" Siliana asked.

"Keep going to the southern regiment?" Dyon asked, turning his horse north. Aven was impressed the man knew which direction was which.

"About that." Aven winced now. How much bad news could this day bring? "I checked it when I was looking for you two. It was… in flames."

Dyon's eyes widened slightly. Too slightly. Yes, shock indeed. "So…"

"It and its regiment are lost."

The tirade of swearing that erupted from Dyon was like nothing Aven had ever heard. He glanced up the road. Anonil had fallen, and the southern stronghold too. There were towns along the road to Anonil, but they were likely beset by Kavanarians too. They could head south, fall back to Panar, maybe even give those bodies the rites they deserved. Or he supposed they could try to head east to Dramsren, although there was no straight road leading that way until closer to Anonil, which could mean they'd run into Kavanarians before then.

And there were so few of them now.

"I'm sorry, my lord, my lady," Dyon said, recovering slightly.

"Nothing to be sorry for," Aven said.

Siliana shrugged. "You said what I was thinking."

At that, Dyon snorted. "All right. She's right. What do we do?"

"We could try to head north and then east into Dramsren, or cut straight east through the forest. But it's a few days' ride. I could probably keep the snow off us if it threatens, actually, but still. No one's expecting us there. Or we could return south."

"With our tail between our legs." Dyon spat in disgust.

"Focus on what comes next. If we head to Dramsren, and their forces head to Panar…"

"Beneral is there, with two regiments. Plus the city guard. Miara, Elise, Jaena, the others. They're not without defense."

Aven nodded. "True. And there are no mages in Dramsren right now. You can see what kind of slaughter it could be."

"But there's still only two of us," Siliana said. "We couldn't do much against twelve."

"And there could be more than twelve that show up there." He sighed. "A lot more." The truth was even being outnumbered two-to-one was a huge disadvantage, and they were looking at much worse odds.

"I know you don't relish returning in defeat," Siliana said, "but after all this, I have to admit I think we should pool our forces. Our magical ones, I mean. All in Panar."

Maybe he should have brought all the mages with them here. Then maybe they'd have had a shot. But that was impossible. The brand had to stay as far from enemy hands as possible, and they couldn't recruit more mages if no one stayed in Panar. But was there even time for that? Things were getting worse very, very quickly.

"How many mages were we facing?" Dyon asked. "It looked like only a handful."

"I counted twelve."

The lord winced. "And you said there are five hundred, Aven?"

"Well, we haven't confirmed that. We haven't seen where they have which ones and how many. We can't tell which are unarmored soldiers and which are mages—and technically the mages could be armored."

"I suppose it's too much to ask that they wear a sign."

Aven snorted. "You could send them a letter perhaps. Also ask them to please leave, while you're at it." He glanced back over his shoulder toward the campsite in the distance. They were a half mile perhaps down the road, not at all close, but it also wasn't wise to linger. "Let's start south."

Dyon swallowed even as he eased his horse into motion. "Then we'll pass... the remains again. There might be more horses for the others."

"Yes." Aven nodded gravely as his horse began its way south. "I had wanted to give the dead some kind of rites—"

"We can't," Dyon said quickly. "The mages we escaped

will know right where to look for us then. They'll check there first."

Aven groaned. "Can nothing go right today?"

As it turned out, they ran into other people before they reached the bodies. As they rode up, they spotted new fires blazing on either side of the road. Aven stopped, dumbfounded. The night was pitch-black, the moon hidden behind clouds, but in the dim firelight, he could see people moving from one fallen soldier to another in the darkness.

"Scavengers?" he whispered, barely containing a swelling edge of rage.

Siliana put a hand over her mouth. But Dyon surged forward, undeterred. Or perhaps indignant.

"Halt. Who goes there?"

"Who wants to know?" called a voice farther back. It sounded strangely familiar and carried a hint of authority. A thin figure straightened and began walking toward them.

"I am Lord Dyon of Liren, in the company of the king. And who are *you*?"

Aven winced, not entirely sure he wanted that to be known. Too late now.

"The king?" someone said, laughing a little.

"What's the king doin' out here with a lord and lady and a bunch of fools on foot in the middle of the night?"

"The king of tricksters, he means, methinks. What does he take us for?"

Dyon cleared his throat and glared haughtily. "I command you, in the name of King Aven Lanuken of Akaria, not to take anything from those bodies."

"He thinks we're common thieves," another voice muttered, amused.

"Barbarians, eh?"

"We didn't leave the road full of the dead," said another.

The thin figure who'd first spoken had almost reached them now, coming into the light of the nearest fire. "King *Aven*, is it?"

"Regin!" Aven dismounted as fast as he could and ran to the wiry old man, throwing his arms around him. "I never thought I'd see you again."

"Certainly not here, I'd wager," said Regin, patting Aven's shoulder and smiling slightly.

Dyon cleared his throat. "You two—know each other?"

Aven nodded. "Our paths crossed ways once, not so long ago."

"He didn't tell me he was a king," Regin said to Dyon.

"You didn't ask." Aven smiled crookedly. "And I was only a prince then."

Regin's expression faded as he looked back out over the carnage. "I… What happened here, Aven?"

"Sire," Dyon corrected.

"Kavanarian mages attacked," Aven said quickly. "It was a disaster. We barely survived."

"How *did* you survive?" Siliana asked. "Last I saw, you were airborne and flying into the clouds on a hunk of earth."

Aven wished he had something remarkable to say, about how he'd mastered the rock or the storm or figured his way out of it. Instead, he shrugged. "I fell. Tried to break my fall with the wind. It worked, mostly."

"You fell—"

"Let's talk about it later," Aven said. "Regin, tell me your people aren't looting these bodies?"

"And who exactly are you people?" Dyon added.

"Just some wanderers," Regin said mildly. "We live a nomadic life, moving town to town, camp to camp. We aren't camped far from here, but we saw something strange was going on and came to check for danger. It seemed to have passed. And *no,* we weren't looting them." He glared at Dyon now, even though Aven had been the one to ask.

Aven glanced over his shoulder, up to the north. "It's not clear if that danger has entirely passed. The mages who did this are still alive, about a mile up that way. They could come back."

"We were hoping to bury them, but there are so many." Regin scowled.

"Regin, if your people would do us the favor of tending to our fallen comrades, we would be very grateful. A funeral pyre would be acceptable if you can't bury them all. Come to Panar after, bring what effects of the dead you can manage, and you will be greatly rewarded." For that, and for explaining the truth about Miara, and for everything else. Without Regin's help, he might have never freed any of them.

Regin nodded sagely. "We don't usually travel so far south, Aven—sire."

"I might suggest you consider it," Aven said, looking

pointedly at the bodies. "War has reached this place, and it'll be moving to Panar soon."

"War?" Regin breathed. "With Kavanar?"

Aven nodded. "Anonil has fallen, betrayed. The south stronghold is in flames. We were headed there when this regiment was ambushed."

Regin scowled. "I can't say I want to be anywhere near where the folks who did *this* are."

"Well, they're just up the road. Panar may be their destination, though. Your choice."

"We'd be happy to tend to them, with or without reward," Regin said, clasping his hands in front of him.

"Thank you," Aven said, genuinely grateful. "We can leave some of these soldiers to help you, if you'd like."

Regin eyed the men. "No, they look like they've seen enough death. We tied some horses off down that way, though."

"Good."

"Aven, should we try to send word back to Panar?" Siliana asked. "I'm sure I can find a bird."

He turned to Regin. "Have any parchment? Yet again, I owe you."

"You assume this nomadic wanderer can write?" Regin said with a twinkle in his eye.

"Yes…"

"Well, you assume right. Hold on."

Aven scribbled a hasty note, and Siliana woke up some poor bird and sent it off. Then Aven gave Regin one last hug goodbye. "We should keep going then, head south, I think."

Regin nodded. "Safe travels, Aven. Sire. Safer than this. Anara watch over you."

"I hope I'll see you there, my friend." He nodded, and they rode off down the road, none too soon. The more time passed, the more certain he became that he agreed with Siliana.

Pooling their forces in Panar was quite possibly their last hope.

I3 DUTY

When they'd reached the inside of the cave, Niat had collapsed. From the running, the arguing, from all the walking that morning—everything—it was too much. She'd gone down and been asleep almost immediately on the rock floor of the steamy cave he'd found with a bright blue pool in the center.

She awoke sometime in the early morning hours, before the sunrise. The warm, humid air around her confused her as to where by Nefrana she'd woken up, until she finally remembered stumbling in here the night before. The beautiful sound of the running water and the way it sapped into the air and dampened her gown all had probably helped to lull her to sleep; the symphony of echoing sound was astonishingly relaxing. She simply sat listening to it for a while. When had she slept so well? She couldn't remember a time she'd slept better, and she was sleeping on solid rock.

But where was Thel? She scanned the darkness—there.

He was sitting up about a dozen feet across the cavern from her. His profile was outlined in moonlight, which trickled through a crack in the cave's ceiling. She could just make out the barest suggestion of his forehead, his nose, his hand cupping his stubbled chin in the silvery light; he looked noble, thoughtful, pensive. Handsome. How had she ever thought any differently?

"Thel?" she whispered. She sat up and stretched, her body aching.

His face turned toward her voice. "I can't believe they killed him because of me. I was trying to help."

"Thel—"

"No need to gloat." He held up a hand. "You were right, clearly. I should have stayed out of it and played the coward."

"Coward?" She was fully awake now. Had she not just saved him from five mages all by herself, including one giant snake? She stabbed a finger at him, not that he could see it. "Hey, I've lived my whole life hiding from danger. Don't judge me for trying to stay alive."

He glared. She could tell, even in the low light. "Can I judge you for weighing your own life versus his and choosing your own?"

"Oh, fine. Judge all you want. I shouldn't have expected you to understand."

"I *do* understand," he said quickly. "I just—"

"No, you don't. You don't know me, Thel."

"I—well, tell me then."

"What?"

"Give me something to think of other than that sound."

Her heart leapt in sympathy for a moment. She'd forgotten it that quickly, slept peacefully afterward. A man's throat was sliced, no big deal, time for bed.

He shook his head. "What danger did you spend your privileged noble's life hiding from?"

Her sympathy evaporated, and she wanted to throw the sand at her feet in his face.

"My father, among other things," she snapped.

His gazed hardened, intensified on her. She suspected the look wasn't meant for her.

"What happened to your mother?"

"She died. When I was born."

"In childbirth?"

"No. They caught her trying to smother me with a pillow. I was off to a nurse after that, then a governess. But my mother threw herself off a tower a week or two later. Or so they all told me. I don't know how much of the story I can trust, but it seems true. I changed her. Made her sick." Shouldn't be a surprise, since she'd spent plenty of her life sick herself.

His head hung lower now. He didn't say anything. There was only the soft burbling of the water in the pool beside them.

"They say she was never like that before," she continued. "My father insisted he didn't blame me, but I know he did. We never spoke."

"So who raised you then?"

She shrugged. "In some ways I raised myself. But I had one governess for quite a while at the end. I was a fairly ill little girl. Peluna was the one who suggested the temple could get me away from my father. She taught me a little, but mostly she taught me what to be afraid of. And she was afraid of everything, saw evil in everyone. Perhaps that's why she pushed me toward the church." Peluna had especially been afraid of men, Niat recalled, thinking of the way the woman's rough knuckles would whiten on the arm of her chair when Lord Sven came near. "Some of her fears were realistic. Some not so much. It was hard to distinguish as a thirteen-year-old."

It still was, truth be told.

"She taught me poisons. To defend myself, she said, as I'd surely need to. And other tricks and tools of a… less than honorable trade she had once been employed in."

His head snapped up. "That sounds… inappropriate for a governess to teach her—"

She snorted. "She wasn't a courtesan. She was an assassin and a poison taster in Takar."

"Ah. Useful skills. I am relieved on your behalf."

"I suppose the other skills would be useful, someday, if taught in a more appropriate setting," she muttered. What the hell was she saying? She cleared her throat, glad he couldn't see her cheeks were flushed hot. She was *supposed* to be telling him off, letting him know why he was an ass for questioning her instinct to preserve her own life. And instead she was flirting? She cut short the slight smile that had crept onto her lips.

"When my blood moon came, it was like some kind of debt had come due. My father persisted in attempting to marry me off to the highest bidder and be rid of me. At least his greed made him hold out a bit for a higher price."

At that, Thel threw up his hands. "As if he's short on money. Not that there's any justification for such behavior." He scooted a few feet closer to her, but still under the moonlight.

"Well, you don't see how much he spends on wine. I think he still missed her, under all that vileness."

"Hmm." Thel didn't sound like he cared much for that excuse.

"This set my father and my governess at odds. Peluna was absolutely positive that a husband would be the death of me, and I don't know, maybe she was right."

"I would think your father has plenty of resources to protect you."

"To do that, he'd have to choose to use them, though. Or care to."

Thel snorted. "I still think she was wrong. Marriage is not death for most people."

"Perhaps. But especially considering what happened to my mother, I'm inclined to agree with her. My luck clearly hasn't been good so far."

"I think you are due a turn of luck in your favor."

There she was smiling again. Damn it. "Do you, now? Let's hope." He almost seemed like he might be smiling over there. He scooted another foot closer again.

"Did your father succeed in his quest to marry you off?"

"No. Peluna and I were able to get the temple to accept me before he found a suitable price. I'm sure he's still looking, though. Well, I suppose he thought he'd found a deal in Alikar. *Lord* Alikar, sorry."

"Don't be. He's probably been stripped of that title."

"You think so?"

"I don't understand why you persist in being so unsure of the monarchy that rules the country you actually live in, but can't you take my word for it? It's my family, by the gods."

"My family has been nothing but a source of terror, betrayal, and insecurity."

He ran a hand over his face, briefly illuminating contours of pain further.

"See, I told you you didn't understand," she said, feeling less triumphant than she'd thought she would.

"Just because it hasn't happened to me—"

"There's more," she said quietly, holding up a hand.

He stopped. "More? Niat, I'm so—" He actually got on his hands and knees now and crawled toward her. Her heart was pounding. Why was it pounding? Why were her eyes glued to every shift of his tall, powerful form in the moonlight?

He stopped just beside her and held out a hand, just barely visible in the dim light. She looked away, hoping that would rebuff him and also hoping that it wouldn't. But she also moved her hand toward his, hesitating.

His hand closed, warm and smooth, over hers. She smiled. Not a soldier's hand, that was for sure, but she imagined it would feel good against—

She focused on the dirt, still looking away. "When I got to the temple, I was finally free of them. But I got sicker. And sicker. I was frequently weak, couldn't eat, feverish, and none of the priestesses could determine what was wrong."

His fingers squeezed hers.

"That was when the visions started."

"Visions? Of what?"

She took a deep breath. *Of you, among other things,* she thought. "War, mostly. Anonil. I told you of those. But there are others. I've seen... many battles. Some of them are ancient, some of them— I don't think they've happened yet. Many deaths."

She turned finally to meet him. His eyes were brighter in the moonlight than she'd have thought, and they locked with hers. They were concerned, the blue pale like precious glass in the darkness.

"The thing is, visions don't start so late. Shouldn't. Seers don't come into their power so long after blood moons. I should have been having visions my whole life."

He frowned. "But you hadn't. Are visions supposed to make you sick?"

She shook her head. "No. But as the priestesses started to acknowledge what I was—am—must be—whatever, I realized there was one explanation that made sense. There was a poison Peluna had taught me about, called pale dove. A pink powder. It's supposed to be fairly tasteless if a little sweet, and it's highly addictive. It makes you mildly weak and feverish, and it suppresses visions of all kinds." She ran the back of her hand over her forehead. She was suddenly sweating even mentioning the stuff.

"Someone was giving it to you? To suppress your visions?"

She nodded. "I can only think that it was Peluna, given all she knew. Now with each vision, I go into withdrawal, craving the drug, and that lasts much longer than the visions. Perhaps I told her of the visions when I was very young, young enough not to remember, and she started it then. I don't know. She could have taken me to the temple then, and if that was always her goal, why didn't she? Why try to smother the visions away? She must have known they would return as soon as she and the drug left me."

"Did you ever ask her?"

"I tried. Weak as I was, I went looking for her. She'd gone missing. Her rented room had been abandoned. No one knew where she'd gone. I fear my father took revenge on her, as in many ways she'd won in the raising of me, getting the priestesses to accept me into the temple and depriving him of his wedding bounty."

"That's terrible."

"Then again, it could have been my father giving me the drug, or ordering her to do so. Maybe that's why she had such handy skills. She could also have simply left. I shouldn't blame him for something that I'm not even sure happened. Also… if she was so concerned for my wellbeing and wanted me in the temple for my own good, she could have easily done so. There was something more to it."

"Like what?"

"Well, she could have told me about the drug. She must have known I'd figure it out once it wore off and the effects of the addiction took hold. I'd been on it for years. Who knew what it might have done to me to take something clearly harmful for nearly my whole life? Fifteen years? Eighteen? Who knows."

"Gods. How old are you, Niat?"

"Twenty."

"That is a long time, indeed."

She studied his face thoughtfully, what she could see of it in the darkness anyway. She could more feel his presence now than see him, as his face was no more than a foot from hers.

Huh. He had listened for a long time, not turning away. He hadn't even mentioned himself, save that bare tangent about Alikar. People were usually more self-centered. And here he was trying to add pieces to the confusing puzzle of betrayal that was her life. Trying to help her put them together.

"How long did it take to get over the addiction?"

"I'm not sure I am over it," she said quietly. "But after a year, the constant fever went away."

"A *year*? No wonder you're so thin."

She blinked, her mouth falling open and searching for a clever retort. But nothing came out. She only had a sinking feeling, a sudden dizziness with all her discussion of those difficult days. She didn't care what he thought of her; what did she care if he found her plain? What had they called her, a board? A rail? She didn't care about any of that. Still, a surprising swell of disappointment hit her. She'd thought—he'd kissed her back, when she'd stolen that foolish moment beside the bear. No, no, what did she care? She didn't want him. Or need him. Or...

She glanced back at his blue eyes, then back to the sandy distance she'd been staring into. Now, that wasn't true at all, was it.

Was it. Don't delude yourself, like Peluna or your father did.

Best to move on with the conversation. Pretend it didn't hurt. He hadn't meant it in a hurtful way. She was thin, and it was because of the drug, both the withdrawal and all the years on it as well. But she couldn't figure out how to go back to talking. Where had they left off? What had she mentioned and what had she forgotten to say?

She glanced back at him and sensed he was frowning. "You're pretty thin yourself," she blurted instead.

He laughed outright. "I know. Too much time with my nose in books, not enough time with arms heaving stones, I guess."

That explained the hands. And the vocabulary. She smiled down at her lap. "Or not enough time lifting forks in kitchens."

"That seems to go for both of us."

"Hey, I had a drug making me throw up half of everything I ate for years and years. What excuse do you have?" She grinned playfully, but his face fell at that. She supposed that was probably what he *should* do. Wouldn't it be unkind of him to laugh at that? But damn her for ruining the moment.

Especially to bring up vomit. Gods. This was becoming a bad habit.

"Sorry," she amended quickly.

"Don't be. I mean, you were right. I didn't understand."

Her eyes widened as she gazed down at her lap, only to notice that his hand had come to rest over hers on her thigh. If this was the victory she'd been shooting for, she didn't feel very victorious. She'd expected more shouting and bitterness and… less hand-holding.

She was staring. Slowly, he started to withdraw his hand. Did he think it unwanted?

She recaptured it with her other hand instead and brought his hand back into both of hers. It all seemed insanely forward, but what did she have to lose? And the darkness seemed to cloak her, hide her blushing cheeks, her tentative eyes.

He didn't object. In fact, he shifted closer again. The cold of a slight wind whispered around them, moaning as it hit the tiny crevices and holes in the caverns.

"I'm sorry I judged you," he said softly.

"No, no, don't be," she muttered. "I'm just being stubborn."

"How so?"

"I just… I've never known anyone who would put others ahead of themselves so readily, so frequently, with no ulterior motive."

"Yes, you've made that abundantly clear. It's amazing

you survived your childhood at all."

"At first, I didn't trust it. But I've come to see that, no, you actually aren't looking to gain anything. You're actually looking for the right thing to do."

"Well, I do it to save my self-respect. So I can look myself in the eye, so to speak."

"It's just—when you act like that, it makes me defensive."

"Defensive?"

"Yes. It makes me want to…" Stop you so you don't get yourself killed. Be like you. Sacrifice like you—and for you. Be a better person, so that you… So that he would what? None of the words would come out, and her thoughts froze. "It makes me want to tell you to stop being so damn virtuous," she blurted. "You're supposed to be evil, mage."

He chuckled. "That's not what you were going to say first, was it?"

She turned to face his crooked smile. "No, it wasn't." Just because she couldn't get the truth to come out didn't mean she wanted to lie. "You *are* supposed to be evil, though."

"Do you still really think that?"

She shook her head. "No. I think your goodness is going to get you killed."

"Good. Between your father and your governess, I would have a lot to do to prove the true corruption of my soul. They've got a real head start on me. And I haven't got any drugs or the ability to hire governesses or arrange marriages, so I believe I'm at a distinct disadvantage."

She realized abruptly she was staring into his eyes, his

face so close she could feel his breath. She was just staring, saying nothing. She should respond. Something. Anything.

"Yes," was all she managed.

"Sorry. I shouldn't joke about such things."

"No, it's fine. That wasn't it. Don't worry about it."

"What was this 'it,' then?"

"Nothing."

He smiled crookedly again, but he seemed willing to let it drop. "Thank you for staying with me back there."

She shook her head again. "It was nothing."

"You were right to be wary. I was too harsh."

"No, no. It might have worked if they weren't such bloodthirsty bastards. That wasn't your fault." She poked him in the shoulder to drive the point home.

"Or they might have caught us and killed us too."

She lowered her gaze, but a bit of courage had taken root, a bit of honesty for just a moment. "No, I was glad to stay. You were right. I wish I were the kind of person who tried to choose his life over mine. I'm not that person yet, but... you make me want to be."

He frowned, as if surprised by her words. Had she truly been so opaque? She looked up at him through her eyelashes. His eyes were searching her face intently. She darted her gaze back down. It was too much. She couldn't take the earnestness of his expression even in the darkness, those pale eyebrows, those soft blues. She tore herself away, turning so only her hair faced him, though she did not release his hand in hers.

Deep breath. Maybe another. Maybe that would help

her calm down.

"Niat?" he said softly. A thrill ran through her at the sound of her name on his tongue. A finger from his other hand touched the back of hers, tracing slowly up her arm.

"Yes?" she said, without turning back. The soft touch passed her elbow, sending shivers cascading through her, sliding up to her shoulder, along her collarbone, up her neck.

"Can I kiss you again?" he whispered. "In less of a rush this time?"

She whipped around to face him. He had been thinking the same sorts of things she had been? He wanted to— He didn't think her selfish and boring and too thin and plain? She could only stare in shock for a moment, then another.

"A kiss without poison would be preferred, but I might settle for either at this point," he said, his voice rough. At this point? By Nefrana. He was much closer now, his forehead nearly touching hers. The fingertip against her neck turned into a warm hand that curved around and cradled her, his fingers brushing into her hair.

"I'm all out," she said softly, a little too stunned to make sense.

"Of kisses or poison?"

"Poison."

"Oh, how convenient for me."

She laughed softly. He slid even closer to her, and his chest brushed her shoulder. His fingers were strong, entwined in her own, and she could feel herself gripping back fiercely. Still, he waited. What was the question again, exactly? Oh, yes.

"You want to kiss me, after I berated you for trying to save a man's life?"

"Yes," he said simply. "You also, wisely, tried to convince me not to risk my life unnecessarily for someone we couldn't even be sure was an ally."

We. The word seemed significant—why? "I *was* concerned about you," she blurted. "It wasn't just about me. I'm not a totally selfish person. That's why I got angry that you wouldn't listen. And I couldn't explain all that, and—"

"So you... wouldn't be against a kiss then?" he said, laughing lightly.

"Um, no. I mean—"

Even as she spoke, he leaned forward, and she shut her eyes and shut off her words and leaned in herself. The soft, warm pressure of lips met hers. The hand curled around her neck tightened, an exquisite pressure, sending a shiver through her. The sweet protectiveness of the gesture was thrilling, and she opened her mouth, kissing him harder. His tongue met hers, slowly in a caress at first, then more eagerly, and she responded in kind. Warmth flooded her. By the gods. By Nefrana.

At that thought, something in her recoiled and drew back in fear. What was she thinking? Could this be some sort of mage trick? How could she— But he was—

Oh, shut up. Have you learned nothing? Thel was the first person she'd ever met that seemed worth any trust, and... he seemed worth quite a lot. What did it mean that he was a mage? Did it mean anything at all? It seemed at best an arbitrary label, meaningless. At worst, it was yet another way people had manipulated her for too long, without her realizing it.

What if she had never realized it?

His hand leaving hers cut her thoughts short. His fingers brushed over her hair gently, running down her neck, tickling the skin of her shoulder, of her arm. His other hand drifted down now and curled around the small of her back, encircling her.

A flash of a vision stole her attention for a moment, causing her to gasp for breath, her eyes jumping open. But this time before her there wasn't a cave, but instead a snow-covered mountain peak. Thel was in much the same position—did he look a little different? A little older? A pale-gray stone bridge stretched out behind her, and before them a gray fortress nestled into the mountainside. Snowflakes fell, dancing around them, and—

Back in the cave, staring into concerned eyes.

"What just happened?" he breathed.

"A vision," she muttered, feeling her cheeks flush. She couldn't even kiss someone without proving she was a freak. He'd push her away, if not now, eventually.

"What did you see?" He ran a gentle hand over her cheek.

She hesitated. She wasn't sure what she'd seen. Did she really want to tell him?

"Was it more battle?"

She shook her head. "I saw you," she whispered, forcing the words out. "And me. And a lot of snow. A mountainside, with a gray sort of fortress in the background,

I think? Heavy wood doors to the gatehouse."

"Estun, maybe?" he muttered. "Was there a bear on the doors?"

She pictured it carefully. "Yes."

"That's... where I grew up."

She raised her eyebrows. "Really?"

He nodded.

She gazed at him, trying to comprehend. He seemed unsurprised by this casual prediction of hers. Of the idea of visions. And in particular visions of the two of them together, in the future. Well, perhaps she hadn't mentioned that the activity seemed to have been the same...

"Will you come to Estun with me then?" he said, his voice surprisingly eager. "There's a lot—well, I think you'd like it there."

She smiled. "Well, apparently I have already answered yes, but yes, I would love to see a fortress these fools couldn't get at me in. And I'd also love to not be hunted by men in the woods or my family's minions, that would be very nice."

He gazed at her, his eyes warm. "You will like it, I promise. Also, I'm fairly sure those men are quite far away and not going to bother us tonight. Maybe tomorrow, but not tonight. For tonight, we have this cave all to ourselves."

Her eyebrows rose, and the warm, humid air pressed in around her more heavily now, her body coming alive to its sensations. He leaned closer again, and she threw herself into his kiss. His hand slid between her arm and her body, running along her hip, up to her waist, pulling her suddenly closer, and she caught her breath.

"Perhaps there are some… useful skills we could learn while we wait," she said against his lips. He nestled his head against her neck now, brushing his lips against her hair, her skin, her earlobe.

"You know how to excite a man, all this talk of learning," he whispered into her ear, tickling. Shivers shot through her. "I find you a very challenging subject to study, but a rewarding one."

She smothered a giggle. "That's not what you said when we first met. Or two days ago."

"We live, we learn." He kissed her hard again.

Perhaps her luck had taken a positive turn after all these years. Perhaps not, as she was falling for a mage, one that would certainly complicate her past if not her future. But such considerations seemed petty, bureaucratic, in light of the fire flowing through her veins. How could any of that matter, in the face of a man such as this, his profile in the moonlight forever burned into her memory, a man who made her feel brave? And alive.

"Yes," she said into the darkness. "Indeed we do."

Aven stared into the flames. They'd made a late camp—such as it was, without bedrolls or tents—for the night near the same spot down the road where the regiment had camped, although now of course they didn't need nearly as much space. He'd eased a snowstorm away from them and farther west before it fell, which was a boon. But not much of one.

Dyon and Siliana had fallen asleep quickly, in spite of it all. Fighting and riding and stress would do that to you, leave you sore and tired and a heap of bones that could even sleep on your arm and a pile of pine needles. The small remaining force also didn't gripe about their lack of—well, everything. Everyone was just happy to be alive.

More than a few clapped his shoulder or gave him quiet nods of thanks, and he knew he'd won loyalty for life from this few. He'd never have chosen to pay the cost of all the others, but he was glad to have saved them. Not even half an hour after they'd made camp, nearly everyone was asleep. A few stared quietly at the stars. Like he did.

Aven didn't find sleep so easily. In a few minutes, he'd lie down and try sleeping again. They weren't going to make an early start; they were all too exhausted. But the last thing he needed was falling off his horse because he hadn't had enough sleep.

This was a situation he'd been in more than a few times as of late, camping with not enough equipment in a lonely wood. Except those other times hadn't been lonely. There was one person whose presence was glaringly absent.

He sat cross-legged at the campfire and closed his eyes, calling back to mind the day she'd returned with his father. The way he'd fallen asleep at her side rather than leave her. He could feel her hands digging into his shoulders even now, calming him, running through his hair, easing his tension, the heat of this fire just like that one.

She might turn away from him when he explained what had happened, the calming spell and all. He might be able to persuade her how important the star magic was and fix things. Either way, he would find out what fate held in store for him soon. Tomorrow. It wasn't that long.

He took the map out of his jerkin and unfolded it, eying the keen and beautiful letters that Tharomar had penned. A gorgeous piece of writing and art in and of itself, now that he could see its entirety, without need of the stars.

He knew much of it now. He knew all the key stars and their associated spells and the pairings. If he shut his eyes, he could still see the map floating in his head. And perhaps if there was something he'd missed, maybe he didn't really need to know it.

He hadn't been able to promise her that he wouldn't use the magic. He most certainly *was* going to, if it kept them all alive and free men. But there was one promise he could keep.

Carefully, he refolded the map, eying it one final moment. And then, almost casually, he tossed the sheet gently among the flames, watching as its swirl of smoke twisted up and into the sky and vanished among the stars.

The sun had barely risen when knocking on the door got Tharomar out of bed. He wasn't sleeping, as usual, just staring at Jaena while she slept. He answered quickly, glad they'd successfully fended off Telidar's attempts at getting them a servant. Uneasiness nagged at his mind about the steward but was forgotten when the door revealed Prince Dom's worry-creased brow.

"We got a message, by bird," he said, his voice rough. "From Aven." The youngest Akarian prince had a full beard, broad, stocky shoulders like the king, and dark eyes that smoldered with worry.

"Did your mother send word to him about… ?" Ro trailed off. He wasn't sure if they were telling anyone outside of the guards what exactly had happened yet. He glanced at Alec nearby, who gave him a slight nod. The captain had assigned a rotation of guards to their rooms; Ro knew nearly all of their names by now. Only one on duty at a time, not too conspicuous, but it did relieve Tharomar slightly to know he wasn't the only one who suspected every one of them was in danger. Even if he wasn't admitting it to anyone just yet. No reason to cause panic.

"No, she didn't send any word," the prince said. "And she may not, because he's headed back here."

"Headed *back*?" said Jaena from the bed, alarmed.

Dom glanced behind Ro but had the foresight not to come in. Tharomar's body physically blocking the doorway might have helped. "Yes. Aven's news is grim. The entire regiment was destroyed, or nearly so. Aven was able to rescue Dyon and Siliana and a handful of others. So they're on their way back."

Ro swore under his breath. Jaena was scrambling out of bed.

"Did you hear from Beneral?" Ro asked.

"He agreed to our meeting. He should be here in an hour or so. We can talk then. Here's the staff Jaena asked for."

Ro nodded, taking the plain wood pole a little taller than him. "See you then." Dom turned away, and Ro shut the door behind him. He leaned the staff carefully by the door.

"The entire regiment," Jaena whispered.

"Would that be difficult? What does that tell us?"

"It doesn't tell us anything that I'm sure of." She rubbed her forehead. How many times had she done that in the last day or two?

"We better get ready. Get something to eat."

She nodded.

Jaena shifted her weight from foot to foot, clutching the smooth, reddish wood of her new staff. Holding a staff felt good. Official. Like she was actually somebody's lieutenant and qualified to tell everybody what to do. She wasn't, not exactly, except through the hearsay of some random Akarian mages in Panar's streets. Close enough. She was going to tell them all what to do anyway.

Because nobody else was. And it needed to be done.

Telidar announced Lord Beneral, Assemblyman of

Panar, and in he swept. He wisely came alone; he must have sensed mages were up to magical business. He wore his typical white robes in honor of his city and carried his own ebony staff, and he was one of the few men she'd met with skin darker than hers.

His eyes smoldered like angry coals as his gaze slid across the group, taking them in. Beside Dom and Elise, Jaena stood at the head of the long, silver-inlaid table in the meeting room and secondary library. Ro leaned against the table just around its corner at her side, and Derk was beyond him, glaring down at the maps Jaena'd brought and spread across the table. One was of Panar and its surroundings, and the other, eastern Akaria. Wunik stood beyond him, talking quietly to Devol of all people, who'd somehow managed to weasel his way into this meeting even though he wasn't a mage. The other side held Miara's sister and father, Luha and Pytor, and a Takaran named Teron who'd arrived with them all from Estun, along with his father Jerrin. The new mages Wessa and Sestin had been talking brightly and laughing at the far end of the table, although they quieted as Beneral entered.

The lord of the White City clenched his jaw as his gaze returned to the table's head. To her. Probably processing that this was a meeting of mages. He didn't want to be here, did he?

"Thank you for coming," said Dom. "We have some… unfortunate news to share." Checking the doors were firmly shut behind Beneral, Dom took a deep breath before he continued. "Miara is missing."

The lord's eyebrows shot up, some of his anger fading. *That* he hadn't been expecting. "What happened?" he said, voice rough.

"We don't know," said Elise.

"We suspect she's been kidnapped." Dom folded his arms across his chest.

"Maybe worse," Jaena grumbled.

"Are other mages at risk?" Beneral asked.

"We don't know," said Dom simply. "But I thought you should know. We already mounted a search with Ranok's guard. It's turned up nothing." He paused, swallowed. "But that wasn't the only reason for this meeting."

"What is it then?" said Beneral.

Dom looked to Jaena. She sucked in a breath. Here goes. "I believe we need to organize a defense of this city, urgently, both magical and traditional."

"You believe… ?" asked Beneral, sounding skeptical. "I assure you our traditional forces are already well organized, although were an attack imminent we might—"

"I promise you, it is imminent. I asked Wunik to check the other cities last evening, and again this morning."

"I had been checking regularly," Wunik added, "but with Miara's disappearance, I…"

"It's fine, Wunik. We all understand." Beneral's voice was much more understanding for *Wunik*.

Jaena cleared her throat. "It appears that three Kavanarian regiments have started down the road toward Panar. Our best estimate is around three to four thousand men and two hundred mages."

A long silence stretched on as everyone fell still.

"Well, it's not five hundred mages," Derk mumbled. "That's something, I guess."

"It still leaves us outnumbered twenty to one." Elise's eyes were large and round. "Or even worse than that, perhaps."

"I've played worse odds," Devol said, patting her on the arm.

"I'll order the army to begin preparations," Beneral said quickly. "Is there anything else you need from me?"

The quiet in the room suddenly became brittle, ready to crack at the slightest touch. Derk coughed, and Jaena shifted her weight again.

"I think you know what we need," murmured Elise. Beneral frowned.

"Your *help*." Jaena pursed her lips at him, words heavy with meaning. "We need all the help we can get."

His dark-brown eyes locked with hers for a long moment before he sighed slowly through his nose. "Fine. You shall have it. Just tell me where and when. And what. But I need to see to the city first. It must always be my first priority."

"You'll defend it best by offering your aid alongside ours," Jaena offered, but he didn't look convinced.

Elise was nodding. "Our subjects must be warned."

"Is there any possibility they could be heading to Dramsren instead?" Beneral asked. "Or somewhere else? I don't want to create fear unnecessarily."

"We can't know for sure," said Wunik. "But the best

road for Dramsren was one they've already passed. They will pass another two less direct routes. I can report to you each time they do."

"Yes, please, Elder. I'll figure out something in the meantime. Now if you'll excuse me, I'll go get started. Let me know of your plans and how I fit into them, and I'll do as you ask."

"Thank you, Ven," said Elise softly.

He bowed low to her. "It's all right, Elise. I may be stubborn, but I want to live too." Then he turned and strode out.

Jaena took advantage of the moment of silence. "Wunik, have you seen anything else we should know about?"

"As Aven reported," Wunik chimed in, "we confirmed the southern stronghold is gone. Only ruins and embers remain."

Elise rubbed her face. "So many lost…"

They couldn't think about that now. Time enough for it later, if they survived. "All right, if Beneral's too busy for the rest of this, that's fine, but I wanted to meet with you all today because I have plans. Plans for how to maybe even defeat them, or at least save some of the people of Panar, if not ourselves."

"Don't sound so confident, General," Derk said, folding his arms with a smirk.

She rolled her eyes. "At twenty-to-one odds, I think acting confident might actually make you feel *less* sure of me."

"A good observation, that," said Devol, chuckling. Next to him, the young bronze-skinned Takaran snorted, and his father, standing at his shoulder, smiled.

"Now, my plan is this. We can't win fighting them spell for spell. We can't win catching their spells either; they'll be too many, and we might miss. We need to keep them from even casting. Stop them. Distract them. Annoy them. Whatever we can manage. And I think there are ways we can achieve that with spells that are cheap in energy cost. Meaning we can do them again and again and again. We've got lots of options. In fact, I made a list."

Glancing to her side, she caught Ro smiling crookedly as she unfolded her sheet. Derk and Wunik were sharing a look, eyebrows raised. Elise was still rubbing her face.

"How many creature mages do we have?"

"Me, my mother, and we'll have Siliana when she gets back," said Dom.

"And Luha and I," said Pytor, Miara's father.

"Us too," said Wessa, raising her hand halfway in the air. "I don't know how much we can do, but…"

"You certainly may be able to help," chimed in Wunik. "Or you can always support with energy. We'll see how far we get between now and then."

"I'm hoping to get some friends to show up too, but I can't guarantee anything," she said quietly.

Jaena nodded. "Good. We won't count on them till they're here casting spells, but that's great that you're trying. All right—seven creature mages. That's excellent. Now, we need some to focus on healing. If not of the soldiers themselves, then of lieutenants, commanders, and us mages. Anyone at a critical location in the battle."

"Siliana and the queen would be best," said Pytor.

"I'm a gardener, not a healer."

"Perfect—then you use vines. Brambles. Flowers to make them sneeze. Anything botanical you can think of to reach out to mages a mile across the battlefield and distract them from casting their spell." Jaena scribbled their names down, with "healing" and "gardening" next to them.

"Got it." Pytor nodded.

"I'm great with pranks," Luha chimed in.

"Why does that not surprise me?" Derk muttered.

"That leaves me," said Dom, "but I've got very little training. Wunik's showed me a thing or two, but…"

Jaena frowned. "Hmm, I want someone on insects. Wunik, do you think you could teach that to any of the new mages?"

"Insects?" Dom said, looking dumbfounded.

"Bees, mosquitos, beetles, flies—they're all hard to catch, hard to stop, and horribly annoying and distracting, don't you think?"

"I guess?"

"If there's a swarm of them? Coming at your face? I thought charming some into helping us could be a good strategy."

"I can try to learn." Dom looked to Wunik hopefully, who gave him a slight, optimistic nod.

"We'll work on it with all of them," Wunik said.

"All right." Jaena nodded. "If not, you can pull energy for the healers."

"I suppose that's what I'm going to do too?" Tharomar asked.

"Moving on to earth, then. No," said Jaena. "You're going to be heating things up."

"Excuse me?" coughed Derk.

"Metal things, Derk. Like armor and swords. As a smith, maybe he's thought about doing that once or twice before in his life?"

Derk snickered. Ro was eying her with a mixture of surprise and amusement, and perhaps incredulity that she was assuming he'd go along with actually using magic. She wasn't truly assuming that. She half expected him to say no. But she hoped this meeting would illustrate that they were counting on him. Sitting out of the fight at this point could get them all killed. And he'd already been doing magic at the smithy anyway, dozens or probably hundreds of times without knowing, so what was the difference? She just needed him to make it explicit.

"What good will heating things up do?" asked Ro. "If you're not in a smithy, I mean."

Jaena blinked. "Well, you can't kill anybody with a sword if you can't hold it. Or wear armor if it's scalding you."

Teron's face lit up. "Oh, I like that. That sounds fun. Can I do that, too?"

"Sure. Unless you want to be on boulder-throwing and sinkhole-creating duty with me." She was actually leaning more toward earth-quaking and monster-building, but really, whatever he could do to shake things up would be better than nothing.

"Tempting. Do I have to pick now? Which is easier to learn?"

"Heating metal is easy as hell," she said, smiling. "But moving the earth itself usually comes pretty naturally too."

"Oh, great, you assign me the easy spell," grumbled Ro.

Jaena smiled, deciding to feel heartened at his seeming acquiescence. "Well, it better be easy if you need to do it three or four thousand times. Or two thousand if Teron joins in."

"A fair point."

"All right, is that all the earth mages?" No one said anything, which she took for a yes. "So that leaves air: Derk, Wunik, Beneral. And Aven when he returns. Did I miss anyone? Four. Could be better, but let's hope it's enough. I was the least sure of what you should do. Everything seems so... expensive and lethal."

Derk smirked at that. "Yes. But storms take up the same space. If their mages are trying to use storms on the city, we'll have to fight for them. Only so many will fit."

"We could try to squabble for them," Wunik said, "simply to slow them down. Go through the air picking fights but jumping to the next one without finishing them. That should come naturally to you." Derk narrowed his eyes, still smiling. "What can I say? You're an inspiration to me. And then that should throw them off their actual goals, if temporarily, while they prepare to fight. A fight that won't actually be coming, 'cause we'll be moving on to alarm the next one."

"In their training, I saw the warrior mages favor fire quite often," Jaena added, tentatively now.

Derk's face darkened. "Walls of it, that's what I saw. Built as a group. Not your typical projectile. Completely unavoidable at close range. Could easily… take down a regiment."

The group fell silent for a moment, as if they were all wondering if that was exactly what had happened.

"Is there any way we could mess with that?" Jaena asked quietly.

"We could fight over it the same way," Wunik shrugged. "Pick holes in it."

"Or you could light their shoes on fire," said Luha, smiling. Everyone turned to look at her, eyebrows raised. "What? It's a classic. Prank, that is."

Jaena nodded. "Yes, that's it. That's exactly what I'm talking about. Derk, you can alternate between that and picking fights."

"Shoe fires. Right. Children's pranks will save the day." Sarcastic as always, but he looked heartened.

Jaena scribbled down more notes. "Would lighting their pants on fire amuse you more?"

His eyes sharpened, smile widening. "Why, yes. Yes, it would."

"Then, by all means."

"I have a few ideas up my sleeve," said Wunik, smiling. "My students tell me I'm a nuisance, anyway. There's a lot of sand and dirt on that plain that can be blown into eyes. The simple spells can often be quiet disruptive. And fog can be a serious distraction too, especially for creature or earth mages who will need to find an air mage to clear it. I can manage to make an annoyance of myself."

"Can Beneral? What job should we give him to do?"

"Maybe he should be held in reserve," offered Ro. "To defend the city if we fail, with whatever means he can. He's trained, isn't he?"

"Yes, he's very well trained," said Wunik. "He studied with Elder Staven. In secret, but for several years."

"Speaking of elders," Devol asked. "Wasn't there another elder that was supposed to join us here? Or was it Estun?"

Elise swallowed. "Dead."

"We found him along the side of the road on our way here," Dom said. "He was nearly to Estun. Mage slaves or Devoted must have gotten him."

Devol swore and shook his head, looking down.

"Nevertheless," Wunik said, his tone clearly trying to buoy the mood, "Beneral and I are well trained and can easily be rocks in people's shoes while keeping an eye on defenses."

Jaena finished scribbling the last name down and looked over her list. "Defenses…" she grumbled. "Ro and Teron, one of us may need to be able to shore up the walls as well. If *I* were them, the first thing I'd do would be to attack these walls. I hope Beneral knows that."

"Write down your thoughts and send them over," Wunik offered. "It can't hurt, and you won't have to wrangle him into your presence. He'll read it. Warn him the soldiers could be dying if they're up on the ramparts at the wrong time."

"Is there ever a right time? But, yes, I'll do that. The city guard off the walls would be best, I think. We can make use of the towers here, here, and here, starting with that one."

"This is a good plan, Jaena," said Derk. "And not just 'cause I like the idea of pissing all these bastards off."

Devol propped his hands on his hips. "Sounds like you'll make their lives a living hell. Which they deserve, for attacking the White City."

"I hope it doesn't come to that, but if it does, we'll be as prepared as we can be," said Jaena.

Derk nodded. "I don't know if it'll help us win, but it will sure as hell slow them down."

Her eyes lit up. "Slow them down? Yes, we *will* be slowing them down. But maybe we could do more..." She scratched her chin, thinking. "Yes, yes. That's brilliant."

"What is?" Derk mumbled.

"Let's set some traps for them along the way too. Put some obstacles on the roads they travel." She pointed at the map. "Make them lose momentum. Destroy the bridges, if we have to."

"Sink the swampy parts even further. Make the forest grow over the road," Pytor offered. "Or tangle it with thorns. I can help with that."

"Wunik, can you bring up farsight of the road after this? We have some chaos to cause."

"Yes, of course." Wunik was nodding, his eyes looking a touch excited now.

"Anything else? We should go get to work." Jaena picked up her notes, ready to leave.

"Uh, Jaena?" Luha said softly. "I was wondering about

that... thing you brought back? Any luck getting rid of it?"

Jaena frowned. She wouldn't normally talk about it in front of this many people, but...

"We have not been able to destroy it," she said as softly as she could manage. "We tried heat. We dipped it in acid. Transforming the metal into stone. Nothing works. It's resistant somehow."

A dark hush fell across the room.

Jaena dropped her chin, not wanting to lie but hating to end on a note of defeat. "We're facing the very real possibility that it might not be possible to destroy the brand at all."

Suddenly, with a crack, the doors across the room flew open. The steward—Telidar—and four armed men charged in. But the men didn't wear Akarian colors or any uniform she recognized.

Jaena's heart leapt into her throat. Something wasn't right. Telidar raised her arm, eyes narrowed, and pointed straight at Jaena. "Start with *her*."

Ro didn't give them a chance. He dropped to a crouch, seized the knapsack, and raced away behind her. Ice pumped into Jaena's veins as he gripped the edge of the balcony and vaulted over it, plummeting down.

"Ro!" she cried, feeling like he had ripped her heart from her chest and taken it with him in that sack. "Wait!"

The guards rushed past them all, Telidar on their heels, and jumped over the balcony after him.

14 CLIFFS

Ro held onto the edge of the balcony as long as he could as he went over, seeking to ease the fall. He hit the ground with a poorly executed roll, but it was better than nothing for all the preparation he'd given to this idea.

He leapt to his feet and raced off toward the gate. Hopefully Tian or Pekar were on duty. Someone he knew. A peasant man with a knapsack racing out of Ranok with the steward on his heels probably would look mighty suspicious.

Wind rustled behind him, and something crashed hard into the marble wall behind him. He risked a glance back. One guard was slumped at the bottom of the wall, unconscious. On the balcony above, Derk and Wunik were leaning over the balcony, glaring.

Helping him.

Another gust of wind swept through the air behind him, and he heard bone hit marble with a sickening crack. By now he could see the guards—and neither Tian nor Pekar were there. Of course. Just his luck. Maybe he should try anyway—or just turn around and give himself up or—

He turned and raced toward the king's smithy.

Sprinting inside the door, he glanced over his shoulder. Even though he was sure the air mages had taken out two of them, there were now five men racing after him.

He slammed the door shut and barred it to slow them down. He looked around frantically. The smithy was empty except for one apprentice pumping the bellows at the fire, who looked at him in shock.

"You better get out of here, kid," he grunted. He didn't have time to see if the apprentice heeded his words as he veered further into the smithy.

The hearth wasn't working hot quite yet, but it was getting close. A barrel of tools sat on the far side of the hearth, and he bolted past the anvil and shoved the knapsack down into the barrel, hastily shifting some tools over it. Then he pivoted and glanced around frantically.

In addition to the usual hammers on the table nearby, a sledgehammer leaned against the anvil. He grabbed it and lifted it over his shoulder.

And just in time. The first two soldiers burst through the door and pointed. Ro sank to a hasty crouch. They weren't wearing Akarian colors and weren't any of the guards he knew. Mercenaries? "You don't have to do this," he called out in warning.

It took them a few seconds to spot him, but they lunged blindly in his direction.

It was a slaughter.

He lunged to his feet and brought the hammer down with practiced force. He aimed for the man's shoulder, but the sellsword tripped on a floor bracing, and the sledge hit him in the head with a sickening crunch as the man's eyes went blank and glassy.

Ro didn't have time to draw the hammer back again as the second assailant slashed at him with his drawn sword. Taking a split second to aim—and to dodge the flashing silver blade—Ro brought the hammer's head up and slammed it into the man's chin. His head snapped back with unnatural speed, and Ro knew he didn't need to worry about the second merc any longer. He hadn't fully dodged the blade though, he realized, as hot, wet blood was oozing down the left side of his face.

Three remained, and they surged toward him all as one. He got the sledgehammer back up over his shoulder but not before a sharp icicle of pain stabbed into his left side just below his ribs.

This next blow had to count.

Swinging down and at an angle, he managed to hit two: the one that had stabbed him and another to the right. No time for a full swing, he hastily switched directions, raising the hammer again.

Blood was soaking his tunic and the hip of his trousers. Another sharp pain carved along the skin of his left shoulder even as he ducked, the blade slicing off fabric and skin besides.

At the last minute, instead of raising the hammer fully,

he settled for stopping it at waist height and thrusting it forward, slamming the head of the hammer into the last merc's gut and sending him flying.

He collapsed on the ground at the apprentice's feet, and the boy held out a shaky sword at the man's throat.

"How do you know I'm on your side?" Tharomar croaked as he lurched toward the barrel and grabbed the sack and the cursed brand inside. His vision swam as he collapsed against the side of the barrel, his blood-wet hip against the wood and metal bands.

"You know your way around a smithy," the apprentice said. "And can lift a hammer. That's my side, if you ask me."

Yellow splotches danced before his eyes. Then black ones. "Thanks for your help, but…" He struggled for breath, to make out where the apprentice even was between the splotches. He slid down the barrel to a seat, leaning against it, his strength deserting him. "I think those broken ribs will keep him… Can you… can you get my friends?"

His head fell back against the wood, black splotches covering his vision like bats closing in. He shut his eyes, but they didn't go away. He opened them again, but the room barely came into focus. He couldn't tell if the boy was still there, was talking to him, or if he'd gone for help. He couldn't tell anything.

My life for Nefrana, he thought. And for Jae. In some way, in his heart, they were one and the same, as one had brought him the other.

He shut his eyes, knowing at least he'd done all he

could. He let go and fell into the darkness.

Evana swept into her cold prison chamber, and Miara stifled her shivering. The midday sun was barely enough to warm this place, and nearly every part of her body screeched in agony. No position was relief from the pain.

But she'd show no weakness to this woman.

"I have a very special someone we've recaptured you might like to meet." Evana stopped against the wall and folded her arms over her chest. From the doorway that seemed to be the only entry into the room, a man's form appeared.

She gasped. "Aven!"

"Miara." His voice… it *sounded* like him. But no, no, it couldn't be. How could he have been captured? Then again how had she been captured? She reached out for his mind automatically, but of course nothing happened. Like trying to move her arm, but the arm wasn't there. *Damn* it. Damn Evana. "I thought you were dead," he said. "I came looking, hoping you weren't—"

"Why?" she whispered. "The war—"

"Doesn't matter. I needed to know you were safe. I guess now I do."

"I am far from safe. Are you all right?" Miara winced. What kind of inane question was that?

"Not exactly. They got through my defenses."

Miara's stomach dropped to her feet. No. It couldn't be. "The brand?"

Evana folded her arms. "I told you we made another. Go on. You can have a few words."

Aven strode cautiously up to the cage, his eyes warily trained on Evana. Like he feared some correction from her. Stopping just in front of the bars, he turned toward Miara.

"Did you tell them anything?" he whispered.

"About the brand? No. Did you?"

"No, of course not. But... I'm not sure how much longer I can hold out," he whispered. "I already lost it once."

Miara frowned harder now. What were they doing to him? She couldn't imagine much—or really anything— that Aven wouldn't strive to endure to keep information from them. She inspected him quickly but didn't see any wounds; what could they possibly be doing that he thought he was soon to break? She reached out and put her hand over his shackled one. "Hold on," she said softly. "I know you can do it. It can't be much longer, right? I'm sure help is coming." She paused, smiling nervously, because she was *very* far from sure of that right now. "I... well..." She glanced at Evana awkwardly.

He squeezed her hand, leaning forward. "What is it?"

"I'm sorry we fought. That I didn't get to say goodbye. They'd grabbed me. I just want you to know... I love you, Aven," she whispered. She squeezed his hand harder.

He stared back, blinking, almost as if he didn't understand. As if he didn't *want* to hear those words from her just now. Her heart froze in her chest. "You too," he muttered.

Evana approached and grabbed the chain.

"You had your chance." She smiled wickedly, pulling Aven away and out of sight. "He's mine now. And when I'm done with him, maybe you'll reconsider my request. Or this can continue for as long as I desire."

Miara scowled after them at the empty air, then shifted again in her pained spot. What could continue? What was she going to do? What horrors would Miara now have to listen to?

Whatever she had expected, it was not what transpired next. The sounds that filled her ears made her blood run colder than she'd thought possible, icy with bitter shock. First there were commands, then gasps, then grunts. Her body shook, and she slammed her fists against the bars, her forearms, everything, blind and futile in her rage.

Those were sounds only the throes of passion could evoke.

Miara gripped the bars of her cage, determined to bend them apart by sheer force of will. No, no, no, after all they'd waited for, after all that they'd struggled to overcome. This couldn't be happening. Where was the Balance? What did the Way matter if this was the reward? What kind of world left her in this hellish, brittle prison while the man she loved lost everything he honored to a knight who despised him? No, it just couldn't be.

Was this what was breaking him? It certainly felt in danger of breaking her.

Weakening, Miara collapsed against the bars, stifling a sob. She would not let Evana see her suffer. She would not let any of them know of the ache exploding in her chest, or how it threatened to shatter her soul. She crushed her hands over her ears and screamed at her brain to think. She had to find a way out of here. Now.

She just had to.

Jaena had never run so fast in her life, certainly not down stairs or with a staff in her hand.

Gods, she should have never mentioned the brand. She knew better. She knew better. And now Ro was determined to pay the price.

She pounded out into the courtyard, looking both ways. A shout came from the right, and she sprinted toward it, just as a young man came blinking out of the smithy. His leather apron told her he belonged in there in some capacity.

"Are you his—" the young smith started, faltering. "I think he needs a healer. Fast."

"Tall man, white streak in his hair?" she shouted.

"Yes. Hurry, I—"

Jaena whirled, turning back without waiting for another word. She discovered that Devol of all people had raced behind her, and seeing her turn didn't slow him down. He headed on toward the smithy.

Many of the others were crowded at the bottom of the stairs, although Derk was running in the opposite direction. He hadn't heard the shout.

"Derk! The smithy!" Even as she shouted in his direction, her eyes searched the crowd for Elise. Finally—there she was, at the back, two actual royal guards in midnight blue flanking her. Jaena dove into the crowd, her friends scattering. "Elise! We need a healer—hurry, please. The smithy. I'll lead the way."

Where was Telidar? Was it true? Was she a traitor?

Thankfully, Elise didn't hesitate. She ran alongside Jaena just as fast, in spite of her pallor, her cheeks far more sunken now than when Jaena had first met her. She wasn't sure the queen was eating, but she'd need to after this.

Jaena was first to the smithy only by a hair. She flung open the door and raced toward the young smith, who was crouched by a barrel. He backed away just enough to allow Jaena to see he'd gotten a filthy rag and pressed it to a wound in Ro's side. The rag was already soaked through, wet and shining with blood.

Jaena stopped short, frozen. Fortunately Elise made it past her, pushing her out of the way, stepping over bodies, and crouching on Ro's other side.

His eyes were closed, his head fallen back against the barrel he'd sunken down against. He wasn't moving. She couldn't even tell if he was breathing.

"He's lost a *lot* of blood," Elise was muttering, mostly to herself. "I—gods, I don't know—"

"What do you *mean* you don't know?" Jaena's voice sounded hysterical, nothing like her own.

"You're helping me with this." Elise's voice was hard, all business, which helped.

She nodded numbly and felt the energy start to drain from her almost immediately.

"They got lucky, hit a main artery." Elise was shaking her head, ripping fabric apart and handing it to the young man to add to the wound. She adjusted his hand, then turned and looked Jaena in the eye for a moment. "I'll do my best."

It was what she *didn't* say that sent Jaena staggering back against the far wall of the smithy. Fortunately she couldn't think on that, because Elise turned and went to work, and the energy drained out faster now.

Jaena reached out savagely and ripped power from the earth beneath her feet, the tools, the walls, everything, funneling it up and holding it on a platter for Elise to take. Anything, anything, she'd shatter this entire smithy, sacrifice every stone of Ranok if it was enough power to save him.

Because what Elise hadn't said with her words, but had said with her eyes, was that he might already be dead.

The energy flew out of her, and she tore more from the world around her, bending it to her will, begging for its aid. A pair of tongs to her left shattered into dust, followed by an anvil on the right, and she refocused her efforts on the abundance of the earth itself.

Not a sound came from Ro. There was no scream, no nothing.

Healing was incredibly painful. If you were alive.

She fell to her knees, and a prayer welled forth, shocking even her. Gods, please, gods, not him, why, gods, he doesn't deserve this, damn you, damn you why must you take everything from me—everything that I've ever held dear—he adored you and you abandon him—how dare you how dare you—

Her eyes squeezed shut, her body starting to ache from

the power flowing from the rock and into Jaena and then into Elise. And then, even though her eyes were shut, she thought she could see it again.

The statue with the kind, sad eyes.

Oh, don't you give me that. She wanted to scream, to rail, to tear it all down—what was the point of any of it, if it all ended in suffering, what was the—

The statue was gone. She could hear herself sobbing, as if from a distance, feel the hard dirt-packed floor of the smithy pressed against her side, but also as if it were someone else. Had she collapsed? Should she open her eyes? She could hear nothing but sobbing.

The massive drain of energy had stopped.

Ro.

Her heart ached, like it had broken in two. Or maybe a thousand. Heart dust. Nothing was left of her. Let Kavanar come, she'd be lying here.

She should have gotten him to that temple right away. She should have gotten over it and married the man. She should have told him she'd have been happy to fill a garden with tall, black-haired children that looked just like him but with skin the color of the forest.

Why? Why must everything she ever loved be destroyed?

Then again, would she have had it another way? She sucked in a ragged breath. Nothing could have ever justified losing her sister, being ripped from her parents, but... what if she *had* snuck away from Ro's home in the night and tried to make it on her own? Before she'd known of his mission, before she'd trusted him, before she'd admitted to herself she'd fallen in love with him? Then he'd still be alive. And she wouldn't be sobbing.

No, she thought. She'd take twice the pain to have known him. Three times. Although, perhaps that was still coming. She couldn't imagine having walked away and never known everything that had grown between them.

She sat up and opened her eyes, solidly back in her body now. Her chest still heaved like she was sobbing, but almost no sound was coming out. The apprentice was looking from Ro to Elise and back frantically. Elise's eyes were closed.

Gods, she'd passed out.

Jaena scrambled on all fours over a body, not caring what she crushed with hand or knee, and knelt beside Elise, shaking her shoulders gently.

"Elise!" she said desperately. "My lady. My lady! Are you all right?" She was shouting now.

Elise's eyes fluttered open, and she looked around, disoriented for a moment. Another great bout of energy left Jaena, and a chill kindled in her core. She reached out desperately again, down deeper to the warm center of the world. If Elise needed power, Jaena had it.

A soft exhale caught Jaena's ears. The young smith? She leaned over Elise, looking at Ro, holding her ear up near his mouth and nose.

A slow, weak breath caressed her skin. Never had a sensation been more welcome, more holy, more beautiful.

"How is he?" said Elise, her voice breaking.

"Alive," Jaena replied, embarrassed at the incredulity in

her voice. But hadn't even Elise doubted she could do it?

"For now," Elise said gently. "The wound is healed. But he lost a lot of blood. I need to get inside—rest, eat—and so does he."

"What..." said the young smith softly. "What just happened, Your Highness?"

She looked at the teen as if seeing him for the first time, then smiled gracefully, all benevolence and kindness. How she could muster that expression at a moment like this, Jaena had no idea. Probably a lifetime of practice. "I saved his life, son. With magic."

"Is he... did I help the right person?" the young smith managed, glancing at the bodies.

"Yes, son. Yes, you did. This man has helped Akaria greatly, and hopefully thanks to your help, he'll live to do it again. Now, we're very tired from healing him. Can you go get our friends who are waiting on the nearest steps to Ranok?"

The teen nodded, stood, and wiped the blood off his hands on another rag that only seemed to replace the red with black. Eh, probably suited him better anyway.

As he left, Devol suddenly appeared in the doorway. "Your Highness," he said, with a stark air of formality.

"Yes, Dev?" she asked.

"I... I regret to say your steward appears to have been part of the treachery. Or more accurately, your steward may have been murdered and replaced. I watched her change into another person entirely. A man, in fact."

"Did you catch her?"

"Killed her. Him. I couldn't risk him escaping."

"We could have used the information."

"I'm sorry, my lady. There may be some in her belongings."

"Yes. Have the captain of the guard search Telidar's things. Or should we be looking for Telidar? You with him, please. Take charge of this one." Dev nodded and bowed, taking off at a jog. Elise glanced at Jaena. "Who *can* you trust, anymore?"

Jaena couldn't respond to that and only glanced back at Ro breathing shallowly against the barrel. The knapsack was in his hand. She took it from his fingers tenderly and slung it over her back. No need for the loyal guards to wonder what it was and if it belonged in the smithy or on him. Or why so many men had chased someone carrying this bag.

Guards funneled in, followed by Derk and Wunik, and they lifted Ro not as carefully as Jaena might have liked, but they carried him outside.

In spite of the sun nearing its zenith overhead, she followed numbly, like the moon trailing its way across the sky, unable to alter its path, locked in its endless pursuit of the horizon until it finally fell to its goal and achieved oblivion.

"Have you reconsidered telling me what I want to know?"

Miara looked up weakly. That's right. I'm exhausted. I'm crushed. Come a little closer and gloat. Come see the broken shell you've left behind. Make the same mistake twice, you fool. Miara wouldn't miss this time.

Evana did take a step closer. Then another. "Tell me where the brand is."

"I don't know," Miara muttered, barely forming the words.

"I don't believe you."

"I don't care what you believe," Miara bit off.

"Fine. We'll continue where we left off yesterday. Send for my slave," she said to someone at the door. Moments later, a shirtless and shackled Aven walked past. He caught her eye briefly, and his gaze flicked to his shoulder. The brand's wound looked almost entirely healed. Strange. But he was still following her orders. She tore her gaze away; she couldn't look too hard, not knowing what was to come.

She covered her face with her hands to hide her grimace. She tried again to shift to a less painful position, but there wasn't one. She hadn't slept soundly in so, so long. Was this plan even a good idea? Was she even rational at this point? She'd hoped Evana would ask again, threaten, even gloat a little. Give her the chance she was looking for. But no. Evana was moving away, following him.

Miara had to delay, draw her in. She owed Aven that much.

"What kind of holy woman rapes a man?" Miara whispered at her back.

Evana stopped still, clearly hearing the words in spite of the whisper. Then she whirled to face Miara, jaw jutted out, nostrils flaring, eyes flinty with barely repressed anger. "What did you say?"

"You? A holy knight?" Miara said, louder now. "You're no better than a tavern drunk."

Evana took a measured step closer. "You're *no one* to judge who is holy and who is not."

Miara gritted her teeth, lurching awkwardly and painfully to her feet. "What, you can't attract someone without having to enslave them first?" She leveled her most withering look at Evana and dared her to come closer.

"How dare you—" Evana rushed forward.

"You can claim noble birth, but how do you spend your time? Like the most low-brow thug."

Evana stopped short, eyes widening with cold, fierce rage. Miara's heart surged, hope blossoming. It was working.

"Is that why you couldn't earn a kingdom of your own?" Miara inched up against the bars, raising her chin in challenge.

Evana's hands clenched into fists at her sides. She stepped closer again. She was barely more than an arm's length away now. Almost enough. "You have no idea what you're talking about. You're a *peasant*. A slave."

"Everyone can see right through your façade. Pretend all you like to be regal. You're not fooling anyone."

Evana hardly moved, but the muscles in the knight's neck twitched in barely restrained fury.

"Nobility isn't just about money," Miara whispered. "To be truly noble is to be on the side of what is good. What is right. And you couldn't be further from it."

"Shut up!" Evana's voice was rough, brutal in its anger. "What do you know about what is right?" Evana stepped forward one more time. Just a little closer…

"More than you." Miara dropped her chin and narrowed her eyes, glaring through the bars.

Evana seemed to understand she should resist, laugh it off, walk away, not step forward. But Miara's words had struck the right weak point, and the knight was frozen, caught between moving forward and back again. Agonizingly slowly, the knight stepped forward again, arms tensed like she had half a mind to attack.

Miara had a whole mind to do it, though. She thrust her arms through the bars and seized her, catching Evana just barely—by the thin silver chain of the queen's necklace. While Evana was still surprised, Miara groped for something—anything—with her other hand to give her some advantage. She caught the top edge of Evana's bodice, the rigid construction and lacing serving as an excellent handhold.

She drew back viciously with all the force she could muster, slamming Evana's face into the iron bars just inches from Miara's. The knight cried out, trying to stumble back, but Miara held her, close as a lover. If lovers had bars between them.

"You will pay for this, mage," Evana growled, hot breath hitting Miara's skin. Blue eyes burned as she clawed at the hand clutching her bodice, at Miara's arms, but Miara held fast.

"Not as dearly as you will," Miara said. She tugged at the necklace, then flipped her hand, creating a twist in the chain closing around Evana's throat. The chain cut into Evana's skin, and the knight grabbed for her neck, but the twisted chain wasn't having the strangling effect Miara'd hoped. She didn't have the strength after all this imprisonment, nor the time for it. Dropping the chain, she thrust her fist forward, slamming Evana in the throat. Coughs and choking sounds sputtered out of the knight.

Now that was more like it.

Evana's nails dug even harder into her forearm, but Miara ignored the pain. What was one more pain at this point? She groped down Evana's form, searching for the key. Just one... more... moment. She dodged as the knight reached through the bars herself, nails slashing at Miara's face. She leaned her head back as far as possible, ducking while still groping for the key.

Not finding it, Miara thrust Evana away from her a foot, then drew her back again, slamming her against the bars a second time. Evana staggered, gripping the iron. Her nails found Miara's wrist and dug deep.

Miara's grip faltered, loosening and losing an inch before grabbing on again.

Groping desperately, Miara's fingers brushed a leather pouch along Evana's belt. She might not get another chance. Her hands feeling more like tangled thread than useful tools, she awkwardly fought the stupid clasp and ripped open the pouch, delving frantically inside.

Cool metal hit her knuckle. There—there!

Just as Miara twisted her hand around, struggling to reach the key, Evana recovered and swept an arm down viciously. Something struck Miara's searching hand. Her forearm slammed into the heavy iron bar, and she cried out. Then, the knight lunged for Miara's neck through the bars.

Miara didn't have much more time. She had to do this now if this was going to work. In a last-ditch effort, Miara dropped down, squatting while still holding onto Evana's dress as best she could. She spotted the pouch dead ahead of her, and she dove at it, again groping for the key. The pouch ripped half open.

Her fingers closed around metal.

Miara jumped to her feet as she shoved Evana away with all the power that arm had left. Shaking now, she searched frantically for the lock and jammed the key inside.

It turned. And clicked.

Miara forced the door open with a shoulder, staggering out.

Evana's icy eyes locked with hers, widening briefly. Then they narrowed slowly as she shouted, "Archers!"

Glancing at the door, Miara dashed blindly in the opposite direction. Eyes searching the room, she discovered little. Nothing but the bed and a low balcony lay out of sight.

She faltered, tripping over her own feet. The man still slept in the bed, the chains on his wrists familiar. But it was not Aven. Not any longer.

A trick. By the gods. It had all been a trick. *That* was why he hadn't understood what she'd tried to say to him. That bitch—all a cruel deception. A devious, perfect trick.

A shrill cry from Scri brought her attention back to the balcony. He'd settled there on the ledge and beckoned her. She sprinted toward him.

His alarmed dive was all the warning she had. An arrow sailed by and out into the empty air. She whirled, the fabric of her dress swishing around her. A dozen archers had assembled at the doorway to the suite, Evana beside them, a jewel-encrusted bow in hand.

Miara dashed back toward the balcony edge. How far would the drop be? Would she be far enough from the stone to use her magic at all? Did she have any energy, or would she need to steal some?

Reaching the ledge, she glanced down and reeled back before she could stop herself. The drop was hundreds of feet. Hundreds. Pine forests stretched out to a lake in the distance. Where the hell *were* they?

She reached for her magic. It was there—but weak. Much too weak. She needed more energy to do anything, and yet she could still feel the oppression of the stone, like the sun's glare in her eyes, pulling her down and away.

Evana laughed bitterly, striding toward Miara while keeping her bow drawn. "You know, I had envisioned a different end for you. Something a little more painful for our dear prince to suffer through."

"King," Miara said, calmly as she could. She reached out for their energy to steal. Evana was close to the stone now—maybe if she tried the farthest archers, she could work around the stone. Out of the corner of her eye, she watched as Scri alighted on a side window and hopped forward toward the table beside the bed.

Evana smiled. "Not going to be king for long. It's about

time some blood is spilled. I must balance the corruption you two have brought to this world."

"This is not the Way," Miara whispered. "How can you justify this?" To the side, Scri leapt into the air, wings flapping. Energy was funneling into Miara now, a slow, syrupy drip rather than the usual torrent, but it was something. She tugged harder, and one of the archers further back collapsed. The mage, even asleep, was a greater danger; she sapped his energy next, as low as she dared. Still not enough. The transformation into Aven had drained him.

"Nefrana commands it. Who am I to question the gods?" Evana narrowed her eyes and continued forward in earnest.

With blazing speed, the falcon shot between Miara and the knight. Metal glinted and slid past her feet. Miara dove, groping for it. The dive somewhat saved her, as the next volley of arrows peppered the path behind her. Agony flared from one that caught her in the calf.

The dagger Scri had tried to toss her slid off the end of the balcony and into the sky.

Miara cursed, turning back to face Evana even as she pulled harder on the archer's magic. She didn't look straight at them, but out of the corner of her eye, she spotted two more go down. Scri dove after the falling weapon.

"You don't know the gods' will," Miara whispered.

"Yes, I do."

The cold certainty in her voice almost made Miara believe her. Almost.

"No one can."

"I do." Evana's eyes narrowed viciously down the length of her arrow, and her voice rose, dripping with cold, bitter hate. "You are a mockery to their honor. You are an aberration in their glorious plan, and I am so, *so* honored to kill you in Nefrana's name. Your evil comes to an end." She drew her bowstring taut.

Miara tucked her feet under her and rolled to a crouch, coiled and ready to make one last dodge. She'd almost enough energy to feel normal now, but the final archers closest to the stone were proving more difficult. The new energy had slowed to a trickle, and she still did not have quite enough to be sure she could fall from such a great height and survive. If she could dodge this blow, get herself just a little longer, or drain Evana even… She tightened every muscle down to her core, ready to spring, and she narrowed her eyes at Evana.

"I'd rather be born evil than become it," Miara whispered.

Wings flapped behind her suddenly, and she instinctively ducked. Evana, too, was thrown off, glancing up, her aim rising ever so slightly.

The dagger fell and landed a handspan before Miara's feet. She lunged for it and caught the dagger's blade as it sliced into her left palm. She frantically groped for it with her right hand, seizing the hilt point down over the pommel. Then she winced, bracing herself—it'd taken too long, there was no time left to dodge the arrow.

Except it never did come. The vibration of the bowstring still rang in Miara's ears, then the shrill avian cry.

Mental pain slammed into her, unbidden and unintended to be shared. *No,* she thought, not Scri—he doesn't deserve this. He was only trying to help.

Her friend crashed to the ground beside her, Evana's arrow piercing his wing near the shoulder. He wouldn't fly again like that.

Miara staggered to her feet and charged toward Evana. The knight hadn't yet drawn another arrow and moved to block Miara with her bow. Seizing the delicate wood with her bloodied palm, Miara twisted and yanked, hoping to catch Evana off guard. Indeed, her blue eyes widened in surprise as the top of the bow swept away but it didn't leave her grip. Miara didn't hesitate, plunging the dagger into the gap between her chest and her arm, aiming inward for her heart. If the knight even had one.

Evana screamed. No, more a growl of rage. The bow clattered to the floor. Even then, she lunged for Miara. The dagger was still tight in Miara's grip, and she drove it further into the woman's chest.

Warm blood flowed from the wound. Miara scampered back, squeezing the last energy she could from the archers. A quick glance showed only two Devoted remaining, and those were checking on their fellows, highly alarmed. She wrenched the blade free and shoved Evana back, leaving her staggering, gasping for breath.

Evana collapsed back on the ground near the stone. That was no small wound Miara'd inflicted. She hadn't wasted her chance. There'd be no recovering from it, not without magic.

Evana clearly didn't want that. And the stone would have prevented Miara from helping anyway.

She scooped Scri's body into her arms, a faint flicker of life still beating slowly through him. She'd failed to free that raven so long ago in Mage Hall; she wouldn't fail this time. She would save him. She had to. She lunged toward the balcony edge.

Damn it all, the queen's pendant.

Hastily, she dashed back to Evana's side. The icy eyes were empty now, coldly staring into nothingness, the pool of blood growing. She gripped the emerald pendant and yanked with all the force her unbloodied arm could muster.

The chain finally snapped.

She sprinted toward the balcony, Scri under one arm, the queen's pendant clutched in the other. She leapt atop the low railing and gasped, the treetops looming tiny below her. There was no time, no time to hesitate or fear.

She jumped up and dove outward, plummeting from the cliff into the open sky.

15   RETURNS

To his surprise, Tharomar opened his eyes to a familiar stone ceiling and late-morning sun streaming through the windows. Jaena's scent surrounded him, and he breathed it in, heady, heady stuff, and he could smell baked breads and spices too, calling to mind cinnamon, apple, clove, honey. A familiar, shockingly soft bed cradled him, warm under the lush blankets of Ranok. A fire crackled. Birds sang. The wind whistled somewhere in the higher arches.

Everything was perfect. Beautiful. The best way he could have ever imagined to wake up, save for a home of his own someday. That would be better. With Jaena by his side. But this, this was suspiciously perfect.

Jaena's face leaned over him, and without saying a word or acknowledging he was awake, she kissed him softly, just for a heartbeat or two. Then she smiled. The brightest smile, brighter than the sun.

"Am I dead?" he said softly.

She snorted. "Does this look like Nefrana's golden fields to you?"

"Yes." He was still staring at her, taking in every curve of her face, the way the sun played across her beautiful skin, her twinkling eyes.

"Well, if so, Nefrana's fields must have stolen the chef from Ranok along with you, my holy knight, my sweet love, because this heaven comes with tea and dumplings and Corovan cheese. Would you like some? Can you sit up?"

He tried. He managed. He took the cup of tea.

"You lost a lot of blood," she said softly. "You almost scared me down to the seventh hell all by yourself."

He simply gazed at her. She'd worried? Thought he was dead? What had happened? But he couldn't bring himself to speak, to ruin the heaven he'd found himself in.

"Here." She maneuvered a small tray over the bed and set it in his lap. "Eat up. Elise tells me you'll need to after the blood you lost."

He nodded. He ate.

There were fluffy apple dumplings, and he demolished two quickly, discovering that he was suddenly ravenous. But there were also beef and pork and cherry, and fairly soon he'd emptied the tray.

She was smiling, her eyebrows raised, evidently delighted at the effort he'd put forth. "You didn't hold back, did you?"

He shook his head.

She took the tray away and then eased to a seat on

the bed, sliding her arms around him. She rested her head against his chest, her braids pressing into him, a wonderfully ever-present reminder that she was real, and she was there. Feelings and thoughts welled up in him, longing to be expressed, but he couldn't form the words. Couldn't say anything, lest it shatter this moment he'd never thought he'd have.

Unfortunately, a knock on the door handled that for him.

"Sorry to bother you, my lady, but there's a fellow here asking for you at the front gate who's quite persistent. I thought it might be one of those recruits and told him to come back this afternoon, but he said it can't wait. Said his name was Tay or Kay or something."

"Kae!" Jaena exclaimed. "I do know him. I never expected to see him here. Yes, please send him up."

"Someone you know?" Ro said as she sank back down beside him.

"An old friend from Mage Hall, freed by Aven before they cracked down too tightly. I don't know how he got out, though."

Ro frowned. "What kind of friend?"

She tilted her head, confused. "What kinds of friends are there?"

"I'm your friend." Or he had been, once upon a time.

She snorted, shaking her head. "You are much more than a friend. Don't be silly."

Still, she didn't complain when he managed to snag her and draw her into *his* arms this time. They sat quietly in the warm sunlight until the knock sounded again.

"Kae!" she said as she opened the door. He couldn't see their visitor until she was throwing her arms around a young, blond man who was covered in the most insanely bizarre collection of cloaks, furs, and rags he'd ever seen. Aside from his fresh, almost innocent-looking face and golden hair, the rest of him looked like he could have been a monster from the woods in a child's nightmare.

"Jaena! I'm so glad to see you," he said, in a lilting northern farm accent, with sincere warmth in his voice. It didn't help Ro like him more.

"You made it!" Jaena exclaimed, laughing. "You got free! How did you know to head here?"

"I ran into someone lucky."

"Who?"

"An Akarian prince."

"An Akarian *prince*! Prince Thel?"

"Yes, actually." Kae frowned. "How did you know?"

"He was captured by Lord Alikar. So he's escaped? Was he okay? Why isn't he with you?"

"We were separated at Anonil, unfortunately. Some mages came after me, and I had to make a run for it without warning them. Hopefully they will be right behind me."

"How did you come all this way?"

"I walked," said Kae, shrugging.

Feeling forgotten, Ro cleared his throat. "You walked all that way?"

"I walked to Anonil. I managed to get a ride on a

wagon going south the last few days."

"That's still quite a walk," said Jaena.

"I grew up far from other people. Used to it, I suppose."

"I'm so relieved you're here." Jaena ushered him into the room and finally shut the door.

"Thanks. Frankly, so am I." He started shedding some of his many bizarre layers by the fire. Ro wanted to tell him not to, that this was *his* heaven. That he wasn't invited. "But boy, I've got something to show you," Kae was saying.

"What?" Jaena approached and was helping him with a cloak caught on a button of something else entirely.

"Is there somewhere more private we could talk?" He glanced at Ro pointedly.

Ro narrowed his eyes. Kae regarded him evenly and, to his credit, didn't flinch.

"Oh, anything you can say in front of me, you can say in front of him. This is Tharomar Revendel. We're…" She faltered, as if unsure how to define them. His heart lurched. Or was it that she wasn't sure she wanted this man to know?

"We're going to be married," she said abruptly, snapping him out of his wallowing. She met his gaze, smiling almost shyly.

"We are?" he said. "I mean, we are."

"Later today, in fact," she said, to Kae. Ro's eyebrows crept even higher. "If he's up for it…" She was staring at him now, an unexpected vulnerability in her eyes.

"What's a little blood loss?" he said. "It can't keep me

away from you."

"Clearly," she said, laughing.

"Well, congratulations, then! But blood loss?" said Kae. "Something happened?"

"We had some… violent adventures yesterday. Nothing a creature mage couldn't fix." The way she said it, though, the way her voice shook a little over the words, he knew it had hardly been that casual. But this was enough of an intrusion. Kae didn't need every damn detail.

Kae had shed the last of his many layers and looked much more the farm boy underneath it all in a simple, rough, brown tunic and trousers. He bent down amid all the things he'd shed and drew out a book. The leather cover looked like it had been black to start with, but now it was burned, rough, and warped. Old and beaten.

"That binding is old," Ro mused. And maybe he was hoping to point out his usefulness a little more. "Old as Zaera, at least."

Kae raised an eyebrow. "Funny you should mention that, 'cause I'd guess she or a friend of hers wrote this book. Here, take a look." He handed the book to Jaena, who brought it to Ro's side and opened it. The pages crinkled and complained, warped from water damage. The burned edges left soot on her fingers as she turned the pages.

"What *happened* to this thing?" said Ro.

He hadn't really expected an answer, but suddenly Kae looked sheepish. "Well, I was set by the Dark Master to find a way to make a supposed second brand, see? But

I was already free then. So I hurried to find something faster than my fellows, and I was determined to destroy it. But then after I'd lobbed it into the fire, it occurred to me, maybe Jaena took the brand, maybe that's why we were all locked down, maybe that's why they had me really looking for this. Not to make a second one but to make a replacement. And then I thought—maybe Jaena needs this to unmake the thing, too. So did you? Do you?" He smiled hopefully.

Jaena blinked. "I did. I did steal it." Her eyes flicked to the knapsack, on the other side of the bed beyond Ro. "You figured out all that from throwing it in the fire?"

"Well, yeah, guess fire made me think faster than usual, but then I had to put out the fool thing, so there you have it. It was in rather good condition before I did all that."

Jaena shook her head and grinned down at the book. "This is incredible, Kae. I can't believe it." She met Ro's eyes. "Maybe we can finally find a way to destroy it, after you almost gave your life protecting the thing."

He tilted his head and gave her a serious look. "I wasn't protecting it. I was protecting you."

"Quite selflessly, I might add," said Jaena, narrowing her eyes at him.

He opened his mouth to disagree, but for once, finally, he knew she was right. About the oath, about selfishness, about everything. In the split of the moment, when no thought could intrude, he'd happily risked his life for her. And he'd do it again.

Niat had thought the first half of the night had been the best sleep she could remember having, but the second half of the night put it to shame.

She woke again to even stranger sensations than she had the first time. Not only was she breathing the warm, humid air swirling around her, but her head was resting on something soft and warm. And it wasn't a pillow.

Opening her eyes, the night came rushing back. Her back was warm where he was cradled behind her, and his breath came in soft puffs against her neck. One arm draped over her waist, and the other lay just under her ear.

She stayed stock-still for a while, listening to water and breath and the wind blowing through the tiny crevice in the cave above them that now let in some sunlight. The whole moment felt nigh on impossible, it was so peaceful.

She didn't want to move. Or leave. Ever. Maybe they could just stay here and live in this damp cave. It was warm enough. She didn't know what they'd do for food, but surely there must be a way.

Reality tugged at her, though, her mind reminding her that he was a prince and highly unlikely to want to live in a cave with a mad seer. She'd also clearly seen visions of the two of them together somewhere other than this cave—his home, he'd said—so she already knew they couldn't stay. That made it all the more disappointing.

He would have things he wanted to do when he awoke.

For her, staying in this cave might be the safest she'd ever been, but he'd want to get back on the road. Get back to Panar, probably. She sighed deeply.

His arm tightened slightly around her for a moment, then relaxed again.

When they got back on the road—the events of the day before hit her. The man he'd tried to defend. The one those thugs had killed. When they headed out to the road, they'd see whether it had been Kae or someone else who'd lost their life.

Unless…

Slowly but surely, she eased herself away from him. He must have been sleeping deeply for it to work, but she managed it. He stirred and tucked the arm that had been wrapped around her up in front of him, but ultimately he settled back to sleep.

She picked her way out of the caverns. They'd ventured far from the cave network's entrance, his magic telling him this strange cave and its hot water spring lay deep inside. She hoped she could find her way back without disturbing him. Ideally, she'd make her way out here, see who had lost their life, and… well, she wasn't sure what she was going to do. Maybe try to drag them out of the way so he didn't have to see, or cover them somehow.

Or at least she could warn him personally if it *was* Kae.

Thankfully, it wasn't. She hadn't seen the man before in her life. She stood for a long while, staring at the body, trying to figure out how she could move it or give it some sort of final rites.

A throat cleared behind her. She jumped, catching her breath and whirling.

Thel stood leaning sleepily against the entrance's side. She smiled, but he was rubbing the sleep out of his eyes. Finally he blinked warily at her. "Everything all right?" he said softly.

Her body was blocking his view of the dead man, she realized. She froze. "Yes, I... I just thought I'd come out and see if I could honor the dead somehow. So you wouldn't have to see him when you woke up."

His eyebrows rose, and he appeared to have been stunned silent.

"It wasn't Kae," she said, probably too cheerfully.

He said nothing for another long few breaths.

"Are *you* all right?"

"I thought you'd finally gone." His voice barely carried over the wind.

Shaking her head, she strode back to him, stopping just short. It felt strange to have been so close so few moments ago, but now she didn't know what to do. How to act. How to cross this kind of distance. Tentatively, she reached forward and laid a hand on his forearm.

"No, I'd stay here forever if I could," she said. "But I imagine you want to get back to Panar." She tugged on his arm, trying to pull him closer.

Smiling now, he gathered her into his arms. "We could stay a *little* while longer. For one thing, there's a hot spring in there, and neither of us has bathed in days."

"Weeks, maybe," she agreed, laughing.

"Oh, I don't smell that bad."

"I meant—"

"I'm joking. Come. I can bury this man, and we can go back inside. Want to say a prayer?"

"All right." She dug through her memory for some invocation, and it was no effort at all for once to reach up and offer up her thanks, her wishes that this man find peace and order in the Balance and in Nefrana's golden fields.

And just like that, it was done. They headed back inside to their warm sanctuary, their damp clothes almost frozen by the chill winter wind. They could spend a few more hours, maybe another day. Panar and the rest of the world would come calling, but not just yet. Not today.

The window of shining light glimmered in a circle before Jaena, showing the road to Anonil and north. No matter how many times she saw this air magic, she never got used to its beauty. Or its power. Kae was asleep, and Ro was busy studying Kae's book—and clearly feeling better, even if he was still in bed—so Jaena had headed to see Wunik. She still wanted to throw obstacles in front of the Kavanarians, but between everything with Ro and the brand, there hadn't been time. She would only get so many chances the farther the enemy marched south.

Wunik slowed the window's speed. Spelling the earth was harder than normal, *much* harder at this distance, but she was glad she could do anything at all.

The earth of the road cracked, split, and this time shifted up, rising like a cliff. The precipice was three-men high, the other side breaking into a rocky tumble.

She sighed. "The mages are just going to put the road back together when they arrive."

Wunik gave her a tight, but encouraging smile. Pytor surprised her by speaking up. "Ah, but think of how they'll feel with each obstacle they encounter. This will be the most trying, awful road for anyone to ever trod on. I hope it demoralizes the hell out of them."

Jaena couldn't help but smile at that.

"And even if it doesn't, we tried. Maybe it will slow them down."

As they'd spoken, a thick bramble of thorny vines had grown around the base of the small cliff, and a few pines spiked up into the sky for good measure.

"It does make me feel a little better," said Jaena, sighing.

Pytor's face darkened. "I'd feel better if I knew where Miara was."

Wunik patted him on the shoulder. "We're looking. We're going to find her."

"I hope you're right." Pytor sighed.

"For Miara, then. Let's keep at it keep at it, and give them a fraction of the pain they've given her."

Jaena nodded, determined now. "Canyon this time."

"Nicely hidden by some leaves. And with brambles at the bottom." Pytor frowned, concentrating.

Wunik cleared his throat. "Let's not let them forget *this* road for a long, long time."

The wind rushing past her, Miara fought back panic and reached for her magic, desperate, her thirst for it frenzied beyond just the terror of the fall.

Yes. Finally. The energy she'd stolen rushed through her, racing like a wild stampede through her veins, and she tucked in her knees. There was only one way out of this fall—to fly out of it.

Or die.

She managed to keep her clothes and the pendant within the change but lost her grip on Scri in the final moments. The hundreds of feet *might* work in her favor now while she struggled to right herself and take her eagle form. She surged up with one wingbeat. Then another. And then she was soaring through the air, still a dizzying lurch but not an outright plummet to her death any longer.

Scri, though, continued down without her.

She dove, chasing after him with furious beats of her heavy wings. He wasn't far, but she'd gone forward, out of line with him, and she needed to swing around her talons to grab him. She got close to his level, twisted, trying to reach him—and missed.

No. *No.* She would not let him die for trying to help her.

She dove again, flapping again and then spinning, reaching with one desperate talon.

Feathers brushed her skin. Her claws found purchase, wrapping around him. She headed quickly toward the earth, the obscurity of the treetops. Those archers could still shoot her, and an arrow whistled by to prove it. She pumped energy into Scri as she struggled to control her flight, dodging the first limbs she passed.

One wingbeat, then another, then she finally slowed enough to alight on the earth. Setting Scri gingerly aside, she wasted no time abandoning her eagle form, shutting out her discomfort as the shape unraveled. She focused only on Scri.

The slow pump of his blood sped up slightly. The first vein closed, then the second, and then the skin. She eyed his chest weakly, sprawled on the ground beside him, waiting for a breath.

There. His chest rose and then fell, and she heaved a sigh of relief.

Of all that might yet still go wrong, neither she nor Scri had died this day. As if to threaten her relief, the whistle and *thunk* of an arrow sounded not far off in the trees. Well, at least they hadn't died *yet*.

She staggered to her feet, but her limbs shook weakly. Magic or no, she hadn't eaten much in days, and the intensity of leaping from a cliff and fighting to survive hadn't done much to calm her nerves.

She glanced down. The dress, now much bloodstained and crumpled, was still fairly intact but wouldn't provide much warmth. The emerald was still clutched in her hand. Moving quickly, she tried to clasp the necklace behind her only to see she'd broken part of it ripping it from Evana's neck. Fiddling, she found a way to clasp it on a lower link in the delicate chain. Good. She didn't want to loose the thing again, and carrying it would very much get in the way.

Scooping up Scri under one arm, she crept forward slowly, hugging the trees. Soft *thwunks* told her the archers were still hoping to luck into a blow, but she'd give them no such satisfaction.

She lost track of time, moving quietly through the shadows of the trees as the sun sank lower toward a horizon that seemed strangely flat and far away. She hadn't seen land so flat since they'd left Kavanar. Where was she? Where had Evana taken her? Was she still even in Akaria?

Her limbs grew weaker, her blood rushing in her ears, as she struggled forward. She reached a road and followed it south as best she could. At least that ought to take her toward the sea, and she could follow the sea to Panar. If only she could be sure whether it lay east or west...

She hadn't made it far enough to decide before she drifted and fell, a rock digging into her knee. She groaned and crawled away from it, not sure she had the strength to stand. At the base of a tree trunk, she collapsed, every part of her feeling both too heavy to move and too insubstantial to try. She closed her eyes. Just a brief moment of rest, and she could continue on to wherever this road led.

Before the span of one breath, she fell deeply asleep.

Darkness had almost fallen on Panar as they trudged the last few miles to the city. Its white towers still soared into the sky, banners crisp and whipping in the wind, and Aven could just smell the salt of the sea and the smoke of the city over the sharp winter wind.

Siliana sent off another sweet, generous bird with a message and a fruit, and soon they were approaching the north gate. The same gate he'd left with a thousand men.

And he returned with twenty of them. His chest felt heavy and simultaneously hollowed out, like someone had taken his heart and replaced it with a lead weight. They were mothers and fathers, daughters and sons, husbands, wives, lovers—all not returning to someone, tonight or ever again.

His mother caught his eye, waiting at the gate as they finished the tired last hundred yards. She, Dom, and Beneral, it looked like. Miara was not among them, and the ache in his gut returned.

It redoubled when he was close enough to see their eyes. Suddenly it seemed less paranoid.

Reaching them, he didn't dismount, just stopped.

His mother opened her mouth but didn't say anything for a long moment, just looked at him, the sadness growing.

"Where is she?" he said softly.

Dom looked down at the horse's hooves, clenching his fists at his side. Elise closed her mouth, then opened it again, but still nothing.

"What happened," he demanded. He felt stiff, frozen, like he couldn't have gotten off his horse if he'd tried. His fingers tightened around the leather of the reins in his hands, and he was glad they couldn't tell.

Dom glared at Elise for a long moment, then met Aven's eyes with a smoldering, angry glare. "She's missing. We don't know exactly what happened. Someone tried to fake her death."

"And you didn't tell me?"

"I didn't let them," his mother said softly.

"Why?" He barely kept the anger from his voice.

"I wanted to look for her first," she replied. "I thought maybe we'd find her, and then you wouldn't have to worry."

"What do you mean fake her death?" Maybe this wasn't the time to ask for details. Maybe he couldn't handle it, on top of everything else.

"Someone killed the healer Nyor and transformed his body to look like her. But we haven't been able to…"

Dom kept talking, but Aven wasn't hearing him anymore. He stared off over their heads into the city, forcing himself to take deep breaths, but his heart was racing.

She's disappeared before, he told himself. The last time it was because she knew best. And there was a body that time too. Surely nothing horrible's happened. Miara's tough. She can defend herself, she can survive anything, she can—

But of course, no one could survive everything. Why had he left her here? He had been a fool, and now Miara was paying the price.

Just like his soldiers had paid the price—the ultimate one. He should have known this would happen, should have done better, should have done something differently.

He wasn't sure when the horse started walking, and

if it started on its own or if his boots had subconsciously flinched and urged it forward, but at some point the creature wandered forth. Dom was still trying to talk to him, his mother adding things in Dom's wake, but nothing got through the thick fog that seemed to have settled over Aven's thoughts.

He just rode toward Ranok, less riding than letting the horse carry him home, not responding. Eventually they gave up and followed him. Still the mental fog didn't lift, words rolled over him, in one ear and out the other and he merely drifted through the motions of getting off his horse, getting inside, getting out of his filthy clothes.

The star magic. Was this the price he paid to the Balance for using it? Had he truly had no choice, no other way? No, it couldn't be; he'd been saving his soldiers, saving Dyon and Siliana. He couldn't have just left them there.

At the door to his rooms, he shut the door behind him, cutting them off. He didn't answer whatever Perik asked him.

Hot water waited for him, and for the first time he wondered if he deserved it. Why not Dom? Why not a thousand others? Why should Aven be a king and not a slave?

Maybe someone else could have kept everyone alive. Maybe someone else wouldn't have utterly failed nearly everyone they'd ever loved. Maybe someone else could have not been a mage in the first place, not started any of this trouble, not even been tipped off to the tragedy occurring a nation away. Maybe someone else could have blissfully ignored it all.

He splashed the water on his face, ignoring the voice. For better or worse, it came down to him. He was the king, he'd been singled out, and he had to make his choices and play his hand.

Truth be told, he didn't know that she was dead. She could be alive. When she had disappeared from Estun, it had worked out all right. But then she had been planning to make the journey. It'd made sense that she'd disappeared. This? This didn't make sense. He should wait to grieve—and panic and despair—until he knew the truth, but that was more easily said than done.

The logical part of his mind knew to be patient. To wait and see. The rest of him was in control, however, and it dragged him half awake into his bed, where he collapsed weakly. But again he couldn't sleep. Couldn't calm down. He stared at the ceiling, unblinking and unfeeling and at the same time raw.

He remembered that last kiss, the way her fingers had dug into his arms like talons, the way it'd ended too quickly just as he was trying to memorize her taste in case he never returned.

It hadn't occurred to him that he could return and still lose her.

16 PROMISES

Miara awoke and clutched at her neck. The emerald was gone. So was… well, everything else. Rough burlap scratched across her skin, and straw crunched underneath her. A far cry from Ranok or Estun, that was for sure.

She raised her head and scanned the room quickly. Her things were nowhere in sight. The ragged bed was broad enough for at least two, if not more, and nothing else filled the dim room. The only light came in under a dark door, dim, like firelight from a hearth.

A foggy memory of the home she and her parents had shared before the betrayal, before the Devoted, before Mage Hall, reared up and tightened her throat. She shoved it away and clutched the rough burlap as she sat up. The room was as empty and as poor as a room could be.

She swung her legs to the floor and winced when her ankle slammed into a stool, pain shooting through it. She reached down to rub the pain away, nudging the stool aside. It scraped loudly across the floor, and she winced again.

And to think, she prided herself on her stealth.

Footsteps sounded outside the door, and Miara caught her breath, clutching the blanket harder and tensing for whoever might open that door. A lock clicked open, pouring ice into her veins. She anchored her feet against the floor, ready for a fight with whomever would steal the queen's pendant and lock her in this dark room.

She needed to get back to Aven, and if Evana hadn't stopped her, this certainly wasn't going to either. Whatever it was.

Warm firelight poured in and revealed the silhouette of what looked to be a pale-haired woman—and a veritable herd of children clutching her skirts. Behind her, two older girls peered curiously over their mother's shoulder near a far wall. A boy of maybe fifteen eyed her more warily, face stony and eyes narrowed.

"You're awake, my lady?" said the woman, in a voice sweet and lilting.

Miara blinked. Well, this was not exactly what she'd expected. "Where are my things?"

"Just out here. My girls and I washed them for you. Dress is almost dry. The emerald is lying on the table where we've all been admiring it. I hope you'll pardon us the violation, but the rain had gotten them muddy as a pig in his sty."

"Why did you lock the door?" she said, a note of

warning in her voice. A lock hung from the latch on the outside—it wasn't even built into the knob. In fact, the door had no knob, or even a handle.

The woman glanced over her shoulder, revealing for a moment rosy cheeks and full features, a blond braid swinging over her shoulder. "I beg your pardon again, my lady, but our constable, if he found you…" she trailed off.

"What about him?"

A long, tense silence settled around them.

"We don't know what he'd do," said the boy by the fire.

"Aye, that's a fair description of it. Thought it best in case he came nosing around, but he hasn't. Can we get you some food, my lady? Meager as it is, I figure you must have been quite ill to collapse like that. Are you feeling well?"

"Quite better now," Miara said. In truth, magic and sleep had worked wonders. Her stomach growled as if to willfully spite her. "But, uh, I am a little hungry." She hated to even admit it, what with the number of them and the look of the house. They couldn't have much to spare.

The mother looked back, and one of the girls scurried out of view. "All right, you've got your chance to gawk, my sweet ones. Go play and leave the fine lady alone."

"I'm no fine lady," Miara said reflexively, and then winced. That was really no longer true, but she didn't want them to think of her as above them. She'd spent her life in just this sort of situation. Even if Mage Hall had had food and shelter to go around, it had still starved and tortured the soul.

"I beg your pardon again, but I've never met someone who wore silk dresses in the rain or emeralds around her throat who wasn't a fine lady."

"Thank you for bringing me back here," Miara said softly, remembering herself. "I, uh, I have come into those things only recently. I suppose you are right. But there's no need for such deference. I'm not so different from you."

The woman stepped aside, the light from the fire revealing sharp, dark eyes and a stained, amber apron over a dress brown as soil. One of the girls came through and brought a hunk of bread and stew Miara quickly discovered was more water than anything else.

"Check her dress, sweet," the woman said to one of her horde, turning her eyes back to Miara. "I'm sure you'd like to be back in your own things. I am Vayna." She bowed now, the children studying her. "And you might be…"

"You can call me Miara," she said.

"Only that, my lady?"

Miara hesitated, unsure exactly what answer she preferred to give anymore. Vayna wanted to know not her name, but her station. She was unpracticed at her new truth, but even Vayna knew she was no average woman. She weighed whether there was a risk in the truth, but there were too many unknowns to be sure. They'd brought her back here and hadn't killed or hurt her, so she'd just have to hope they were worthy of her trust.

"Miara Floren, arms master of the realm and… betrothed to the king."

Vayna's eyebrows flew up as a flurry of murmurs swept

the children. Only the boy didn't react much, narrowing his eyes at her.

"That is, if we are still in Akaria?" said Miara slowly.

"Yes, of course we are."

"Where are we exactly?"

Vayna frowned. "Faeren territory, near the northern border to Shansaren. The deep forests begin not ten miles to the north."

Good thing Miara had decided to go south, then. "And how far from Panar?"

"I couldn't say precisely, my lady. I've never been. I believe four days' ride. Maybe five."

Thankfully still a flight she could make in a few hours. That made sense; the Devoted couldn't have taken her far. Thank the gods she wasn't in Takar. She'd feared perhaps they were near the main Devoted monastery. It must have been some monastery, just not the important one.

"If you're an arms master, why weren't you armed?" said the boy, eying her like a wolf in the forest.

"My weapons were stolen."

"But not your emerald?"

"I grabbed that on the way out." She smiled wolfishly at him and ripped up an unladylike hunk off the bread with her teeth. She was too tired and too starving to be bothered with manners here.

"Is it— You said betrothed to the king?" said Vayna.

"It's the queen's emerald, yes," Miara said matter-of-factly.

Even the boy's eyes widened this time.

"It's dry, Mum," said the girl, approaching.

"I, uh, yes," Vayna muttered, looking flushed. Miara tore off another hunk of bread and chewed it, eying her. "Well, then. That is something. Um, here—you put this on and come out, and we can eat and talk like civilized folk." Vayna smiled, bowing again. She sat the dress beside Miara on the bed and scurried out, pulling the door shut behind her by its top edge.

Setting the bread and bowl on the stool, Miara cast aside the rough blanket and dressed quickly. The dress was indeed in better shape, cleaner and softer, although no washing was going to hide the tattered hems or the extra gash or two she'd picked up.

Murmurs from the children and the sound of a flute drifted in, and Miara paused to listen for any cause for concern. For once, she found none.

Wolfing down the rest of the bread, she picked up the bowl and swung the door open cautiously, but sure enough she bumped it into a small child anyway. A little girl as high as her hip laughed once and skittered away.

"It's here," came Vayna's voice.

Most of the children were gathered around a large table, peering down at the emerald that lay quiet and inconspicuous on the dark wood.

"Thank you," she said softly, quickly drawing it up and reclasping it as best she could around her neck. She took a deep breath, and indeed it did feel better to have her things back. How odd that such fine things were hers, and that they provided any comfort just from their familiarity. "I need to get back to Panar," she said quickly. "If you have things I could borrow, I can pay you now or send payment when I reach the city."

"Do you have news from the city?" Vayna said softly, not reacting to her other words. "We've heard civil war is imminent, the prince deposed, the lords at war with each other."

"Did you now?" Miara couldn't help but smile. "From Lord Sven, no doubt."

Vayna nodded slowly. "Well, from the constable. But he gets all the official word from the city. Is that not true?"

"It's not. The Akarian Assembly voted in favor of Prince Aven's ascension to king. Unfortunately, King Samul has been gravely injured. He's chosen to abdicate, so Prince Aven has been crowned king. I know not what he'll make of Lord Sven, but I can't imagine he'll forget his lack of support."

"The prince is king?" Vayna said slowly. "And pardon me, my lady, but, did you say—"

"She can't be," the boy cut in, glaring at Miara. "Lies. What would a future queen be doing out here in Faeren anyway?"

Miara narrowed her eyes and scowled right back. "I don't need to convince you," she said, surprising herself with the touch of disdain in her voice. She'd been through enough, though, she had no interest in convincing anyone of anything. "I just need boots and a cloak to get back to Panar."

"Just boots and a cloak?" the boy shot back. "For a four-day ride, with no horse? You'll freeze to death, fool woman."

Vayna caught her breath.

Miara scowled harder but ignored the comment. "If you have a dagger, that might come in handy."

"I might. But that won't keep you alive in the snow."

"I'm not worried about snow."

He scoffed. "It'll be here any day now."

"I'm sure I can find some boots," Vayna said, nervous.

"That's all right. I'll be back in Panar in a day." Although, she'd likely need to take breaks to rest and eat between flights, especially with her recent troubles. And night was not far away. Perhaps it'd be more like two days.

"You can't walk to Panar in a day," he snapped.

"You're right, I can't."

He blinked. "Then how—"

"I'm going to fly."

His mouth dropped open, eyes round like an owl's. Miara smiled at him and turned back to Vayna, who mirrored a similar expression. "A cloak, my lady?"

Flustered, Vayna jumped to her feet and started hunting through her things.

Bare minutes later, a threadbare cloak graced Miara's shoulders. The boots were a little big but better than nothing, and she'd be transforming into some other form in a few minutes anyway.

"Uh, my lady, pardon me but..." Vayna started.

Miara raised an eyebrow.

"Your hair... One piece is shorter than the others."

She looked down. Ah, yes. Evana and her dagger. "Ah, I forgot. Thank you. You couldn't... trim it for me, could you?"

"Are you *sure?*"

"It will grow back."

As Vayna buzzed around Miara's head, nervously wielding their one dagger, Miara hoped she hadn't put her trust in the wrong place. But crooked would be better than a chunk missing. She glanced at the boy, who'd returned to glowering suspiciously at her.

"Are you willing to sell your dagger or no? I hear arms masters should be armed."

"How did you get to Faeren?" he said instead.

"I was kidnapped," she said plainly. "I escaped, though. Where is my bird, by the way?"

"Oh, you're the reason that falcon keeps diving at me at the door?"

She sighed and smiled in spite of herself. "Oh, good, I'm glad he's all right. Nearly died in the process."

"All right is a matter of opinion I guess." The boy rubbed his neck absently. "How are you going to fly? Ride the falcon?"

"I'm a mage," she said simply. If they were ever going to make it safe to be a mage, this seemed like a good place to start. "I won't ride the falcon. I'll transform into one. Or maybe an eagle. I prefer their size."

"You're serious," he said incredulously.

"Yes. Now, dagger or no? I need to be on my way."

"Uh, what are you willing to trade for it?"

Miara looked to Vayna. "What do you all live on?"

"We've got a field for turnips and potatoes, but it hasn't been the best since my husband ran off last spring." Ah, that explained the boy's attitude then. He knew someone should be playing the role of protector but wasn't quite sure how to do it himself. "We forage in the forest when we have to. Which we were doing when we found you, if that tells you much. We don't have much saved for the winter."

"It'll be enough," the boy said sharply.

"Not at this rate," she shot back quickly. "We can't be stubborn about this, Serol, or we'll starve to death."

"Where is the field?" Miara said briskly.

Serol jerked a thumb over his shoulder. "Out back. Now, back to this trade of yours. Since you don't seem to *have* anything—"

Miara held up a palm as she groped for the soil of the field, sensing the few struggling turnips remaining in the ground, perhaps missed or perhaps not worth harvesting just yet. "One moment." Yes, she could make this field work. It was overgrown a bit, the soil overworked. Hmm, what did the gardeners at Mage Hall follow potatoes and turnips with? "Can you grow other things?"

"Nothing's worked," Serol said quickly. "We tried radishes and beets, but they're as bad as the turnips."

"Never mind the past. If you could grow whatever you like, what would you choose?"

"Oats will last," Serol replied. "And catch a fair market price. Why, though? Don't see what that has to do with my dagger."

"Beans can be dried and cellared. Peaches would be lovely, but they don't grow well up here," Vayna mused.

Miara nodded crisply. "One moment, then."

Closing her eyes and her fists to concentrate, she called them up, slowly at first—turnips and potatoes, but also beans, oats, carrots. A peach tree just outside the garden. Lavender could be sold, couldn't it? It was all over Estun, and Ranok too, though she'd rarely seen it in Mage Hall. As she pushed the field to ripen, she found an open spot nearby. Lavender burst into life and bloomed fiercely, long stalks waving in a breeze.

She opened her eyes. "Let's go see our payment, shall we? And see if you think it adequate."

She strode outside, Vayna following her now bare-foot. Scri dove angrily at first at Vayna, but then righted himself at the sight of Miara, changing course to land on her shoulder. She winced as he landed; she really needed to get some shoulder padding for him. Good thing she could heal herself.

The dim twilight couldn't obscure the now-crowded field, and Vayna stopped short, hand over her mouth. Serol ran forward, stopped, and ran a hand through his hair in shock. He whirled back on them. "You did this?"

She nodded, her expression neutral. "Tell me truly, can you trade it for what you've given me? If not—"

"Oh, this is much better than that," Serol breathed. "This could feed us for a... a long time."

"But you'll need to replace those things. Can you—"

"Yes, we'll find a way," said Vayna. "Aros, Leso, Peras, go help your brother bring some of that inside. Hurry."

Miara frowned. "Even in the twilight?"

Serol strode over and frowned right back. "A dagger doesn't go too far in defending something this valuable, especially if I don't tell them I have it. I keep it for emergencies."

She winced. "You'll get one right away then?"

"I'll get something better if I can find it."

"Who will this need protecting from?"

"The constable, for starters."

"Tell me about this constable."

Serol shook his head. "You don't want to hear about him, my lady. An awful man that."

Miara stifled a smile, amused that her honorific had appeared now that she'd helped them. But her smile faded quickly. "He'd come after your livelihood? In the name of the king?"

"Taxes," Serol said, practically spitting the word out.

"Hmm. Give me a moment," said Miara. She closed her eyes, reaching out into the forest. Looking for friends. A ground hog, a beaver, a hibernating bear—no, no, no. Then off in the distance, she found them. A wolf pack.

She opened her eyes and looked at the boy. "You do any hunting?"

"I did when we had a bow." He shrugged. "Can't kill much with a dagger."

Scri, she whispered. *Go to town and see if you can steal one of these.* She sent him the picture of a bow. Hopefully he'd pick the constable to steal it from.

Then she reached out to the first wolf that perked up at her mind's brush. *Care to make a deal, young wolf? In exchange for some meat?*

The wolf laughed softly. *I'm not young. But I do like meat.*

There's a field—territory I need protected. This family needs the food in it. If you defend it from anyone other than them for seven days, the family will leave what meat they can out for you this winter. All winter. She pictured rabbits, foxes, deer hanging on their back porch.

What they can? Hmm.

Ah, but aren't you also looking for something different? Some new game for your pack to play? What better to toy with than evil humans? She softened her tone. *Please, Sir Wolf, they deserve the food. The human pups will die without it.*

She could almost hear the wolf sigh. *Tell them I like birds. Big ones. They catch those, don't they?*

I'll tell them. Seven days? And leave these ones alone.

Seven moons and suns. On our way.

She opened her eyes. "Some rather vicious friends are coming to defend the patch. They'll be safe for you—but no one else. That should buy you some time to store things. You've got seven days." She explained the rest of her deal to Vayna and Serol just as Scri returned and dropped a longbow, knocking the boy in the head with it. He swore, but stopped short when he saw what lay at his feet.

"You'll have to hide that," she said. "And make your own arrows. But pay back the wolves for this deed they do for you, please. And I'll do my best to return to you and address this issue of the constable in the future."

He nodded. "May the Balance protect you, my lady. Good luck in Panar."

"You as well." She smiled and turned away, heading for the road as she twisted herself into an eagle and took to the sky. Yes. Good luck. She was going to need it.

Aven awoke, not remembering when he'd fallen asleep. He simply opened his eyes again. He was not in the same position, flat on his back and staring at the ceiling, though. No, he was curled in a ball like he'd be trying to find something and kept missing it, kept curling in on himself in hopes of finally capturing it.

Miara.

The thought was almost too much to bear, and he sucked in a ragged breath. Squeezed his eyes closed again. He couldn't get out of bed. He'd just make another horrible mistake. More people would just get hurt because of him.

Unfortunately, Perik had other plans.

"Sire, the mage Jaena Eliar would like to see you. As soon as possible, she requested. She said it's about something the two of you are mutually concerned with destroying?"

The brand. He'd almost forgotten. Well, he could listen to what Jaena had to say. That didn't require any decisions, most likely. That wasn't something he could screw up.

He dressed, but ignored the food Perik brought him. His stomach felt like the roiling sea, and he didn't need to add throwing up on anyone to his long list of failures.

Jaena, Ro, and a newcomer awaited him in the library, as usual, and he stopped short as Jaena's mouth fell open and Ro's eyes widened.

"Aven—sire—you look…" Jaena started.

"That terrible, huh?" Aven said. His voice was rough as gravel. He swallowed and waved her concern off. "Never mind how I feel. What is it you wanted to share?"

"This is Kae, an old friend of mine from Mage Hall."

Aven mustered a weak smile. "I remember freeing you," he said. Those were simpler days. When it seemed like perhaps he could have solved this whole mess by simply freeing each of them one by one from the inside. He should have known it wouldn't be so simple.

The blond man grinned at him. "And I remember being freed. Probably will never forget that. Mighty grateful, sir."

"Sire," Jaena offered quietly.

Kae nodded quickly. "Sorry. *Sire.*" He had a good-natured smile and a bit of a sheepish, relaxed disposition. On another, brighter day, Aven might have wanted to get to know him better.

He was about ready to bark at them to get to the point when Jaena spoke again. "We've learned that after you freed Kae, he was tasked with searching the library for books to recreate the brand."

"All while he was free," Ro added.

"It was too quick, and I hadn't had a chance to escape," said Kae. "So I had to act the part. Not my greatest strength, but I did well enough. Thought maybe I could beat them to the book, if such a thing existed."

"Did you?" Aven asked.

Kae smiled slowly and picked up a rather shabby leather-bound book. "Actually, I did."

Aven took a step forward, some of the fog clearing in spite of himself. "This describes how to create a new one?"

"And it also describes how to destroy it," said Tharomar, "although not in the common tongue."

"And thank the gods for that," Jaena muttered.

"It's not *that* uncommon," said Kae. "Lots of spells are written in Anovan."

"Well, finding out how to destroy it is great news—" Aven started.

"Sort of," said Tharomar.

Aven raised an eyebrow. "Why sort of?"

"Well, we've reviewed the steps," said Jaena. Her face, her voice—she looked nearly as tired and beaten down as he was. Her tight braids were swooped back into her usual larger braid, but her cheeks looked sunken and tired. "And it's… Well, you need thirteen mages to complete the process."

"Thirteen?" Aven stared up at the ceiling for a moment. Could they never win? Did they even have that many, much less ones they could trust?

"The worse thing is that in the process," Tharomar said, "I believe each mage would have to understand the brand and its star magic inside and out. Enough that they'd likely be able to recreate one."

"What?" Aven snapped. "Thirteen people with this

knowledge, instead of none?"

"I know. Not a good trade, if you ask me. It's like this damn thing doesn't want to die. Even to kill it, we'd increase the likelihood it being reborn. And I've counted; I don't think we have thirteen mages we can be sure wouldn't want to recreate it—if we can ever be sure of that. We also may not want to burden them with this knowledge unnecessarily."

Aven ran a hand over his face. The temporary rush of energy gone, he felt even more exhausted now. "What do we do?"

"I don't think we do anything yet," Jaena said.

"Aside from guarding this book with our lives." Tharomar glared at the thing.

"As we've already been doing," said Kae rather pleasantly. He shrugged.

Aven swore. Unless he wanted nearly every mage in Akaria to know just how to enslave people and create the brand, they were stuck. And even if he trusted every one of them, it would still make all of them a target for Daes and the others to hunt down. Then instead of one inconspicuous bar of metal and a book, they'd have a dozen people moving around, trying to live their lives, forever targets. No. At least for now, hiding it was better. Destroying it might never be an option at all.

Another dead end. Great.

Tharomar clapped a hand on his shoulder. "I'm sorry about Miara, Aven. We went to check right away."

"Not as sorry as I am," he muttered and turned to go.

"I've got six new mages recruited," Jaena said, as if trying to keep him there. "They're training with Wunik now."

"And actually—I should be joining them." Tharomar started toward the door again. "You stay here with her," he said sternly to Kae, who nodded.

"You should be joining them?" Jaena started. "I mean, yes, you should be!"

"I'll see you later," Tharomar said, but his voice was heavy and intense with some other meaning Aven couldn't detect.

"I'm counting on it."

Aven turned. Jaena was smiling brightly after Ro, and in spite of his own stubborn resistance, it eased him a little, somehow. She caught his gaze.

"I have some thoughts, my lord. On how we can defend ourselves when outnumbered. I've organized the mages into teams around them and given them each jobs. I... hope that was all right."

"Some thoughts?" Aven said weakly. "You organized them?"

"Yes. Was that all right?"

"Of course. That's wonderful."

"Can I show you?"

"Wait—that reminds me. I've been meaning to grant you permanent Akarian residence, if you so wish it. I kept forgetting. Tharomar too. Stay as one of our own, if you wish."

Jaena's eyebrows rose. "I... hadn't expected that, my lord."

"Of course, you may want to return to Kavanar or Farsa or—"

"Hepan," she said quickly.

Ah, so he *could* do something wrong even in the most basic, generous act. "Akaria is open to you. You've done us a great service. But you're always welcome as a foreign person too."

Jaena blinked. "No, no, my lord, I'd *love* to stay in Panar. Hopefully things will work out."

And hopefully it would still be standing for her to do so.

"Now, can I show you what I've planned?"

"Yes, yes, of course." Plans were good. He couldn't fail at listening to plans. He stepped back and took Tharomar's seat at the table.

Leaving the cave was harder than Thel would have expected going in. It'd been their first moments of comfort since being swept away from Alikar's carriage, and he was *really* not looking forward to finding another cave or camping under the stars. Especially because as they neared Panar, the hills would smooth into plains, and there'd be no caves unless he created one himself.

But the lure of real safety in the city was strong, and also he wanted to be as far as possible from the Kavanarians as he could get, so they'd set off along the road. Actually, they stayed near the road, but off it when they could, picking through hedges and along deer paths. Thank Dom for teaching him how to follow the things. If there was one way to run into Kavanarians, it'd likely be walking blindly down the road. And thus, except for some bogs or excessively thick brambles, they traveled for a full day in unusually happy and mild spirits. They were lucky to find a large outcropping in the woods to camp under again, and it was a lot warmer combining his magic with her sleeping in his arms.

The peace that had hit them like a storm's deluge surprised him more than anything. Niat still seemed frequently on edge, and he caught moments where he could sense suspicion in her. And fear. He pretended not to notice.

The second day's walk was much the same as the first. The trees were starting to thin, which made Thel nervous with less to hide behind, but it did mean they were getting closer. The forest was a little less quiet today, as the day was a bit warmer than the last few, and he could hear an overwintering bird or two and other creatures scrambling around in the trees. The air was cool and crisp with snow, but the walking kept him warm enough. Not long now and they'd be back with a roof and a fire and actual food and books and—

On the even path, Niat suddenly stumbled, then collapsed forward.

Rushing to her side, he found her eyes closed but moving behind the lids. As she'd fallen, she'd hit her head on a log off the side of the path and scraped her temple badly, blood starting to trickle toward her ear. He scrambled to open the satchel and rifled through it till he found an old scarf of Alikar's. Ripping off a portion, he held it over the wound and propped her up in his arms, hoping the bleeding would stop by the time she woke up.

Must be another vision. Strange timing on this one, though. Would she be sick when she woke? He scanned the forest around them and waited in the quiet, looking for somewhere to shelter. He didn't see much, but they had passed a sturdy pine over the last hill back…

The deep, thrumming sound of a horn cut through the air, and he jumped, looking around. He saw no one nearby, but the sound came in the direction of Panar.

That was no Akarian horn.

He never had asked her if she'd seen any other city burn. She did seem to drag her feet about going to Panar, but he'd thought that was because she didn't want to deal with her father or her temple or any of it. Couldn't blame her for that. But could there have been some reason more? Some reason she wasn't telling him in case it was too traumatic?

The horn sounded again. Was it closer this time?

He struggled to his feet with Niat in his arms. Good thing she was barely a feather, or he wouldn't have made it far, but as it was he made it back to the pine he'd seen, pushed through the spikey branches, and found something of a hollow inside that hid them well from the outside world.

Her grip suddenly tightened on his shoulder. Her eyes were open now, her face pale and brow sweaty as usual.

"Where are we?" she croaked.

"We're inside a tree. Are you all right? You hit your head on a rock when you fell." He held up the bloody rag by way of explanation. In truth, he thought it had already stopped bleeding.

She struggled to straighten up and kneel in the earth beside him, looking ill. "Vision again."

"I gathered." He sat the rag aside and tentatively put his arm around her, rubbing his hand up and down one arm. Happily, she didn't tense this time. "What did you see?"

"Troops," she whispered. "Kavanarian ones." She looked out, her eyes almost as if she could seeing something more than the empty forest around them. "They're not far."

"I heard a horn. That's why I decided to carry you in here. In case they were coming this way."

Her eyes locked with his now. "I think I know how to find them. If you want to try and stop them."

He scowled. "One man against regiments of Kavanarians?"

"Three large units," she said. "I'm not sure how big a regiment is. And yes. You've got that little book, don't you? Look and see what it has to say."

He pulled out the book obediently even as he grumbled, "I don't know what good this'll do, if they can skewer me three thousand times over."

She wrinkled her nose at him, and for a second he thought she was nauseous before it hit him that she was also smiling. "Who's taking the coward's path now, Prince Thel Lanuken of Akaria?"

"Oh, leave it to *you* to bring that up now." He snorted, opening the book and flipping through the pages. This was ridiculous. He could have no hope of—

His eyes caught on a spell he hadn't paid much mind before, one of the last few listed in the final chapter. Perhaps, maybe...

Yes, that just might work.

What do you wear to promise yourself to someone forever? Something special? Something new? Something treasured? The white tunic and leather vest you met him in? Did it even matter?

In the end, her mind had persistently concluded that it did not matter. But some other part of her had been equally uninterested in the same tunic and vest she'd worn so many days before Ranok had started heaping new piles of comfortable clothing on her like she was some kind of minor noble. That other part of her had whispered that a pale-blue gown wasn't so bad, or so outlandish.

It didn't really matter. His hand was warm around hers. *That* was what mattered.

She gazed up at the temple as they started up the stairs. The high pillar was still toppled, still frowning down at her. Perhaps it hadn't been judging her. No one at the temple had. Perhaps the temple was frowning because it was broken, out of the indignity. And how would they fix it? It had to be a major undertaking for a nonmage.

"Wait a moment," she said softly, pulling him to a stop with her on the bottom of the stairs.

She reached up with her mind and eased the piece back, melding the fracture that had let it fall, restoring it to its former glory. As she worked, the same crinkle-eyed, kind-faced mage emerged from the temple and followed their gaze up. Then she met Jaena's eyes, the knowledge in them clear. There was no escaping she'd used magic, perhaps not *in* the temple, but on it.

Well, so be it. She was a mage. She was honoring Nefrana. They could accept her, or they could not, and she and Ro would march on to the next temple.

For now, they marched up the stairs and met the woman at the top.

"Welcome back," she said to Jaena alone, her small smile pleased.

Ro shot her a glance, one eyebrow raised.

"Thanks," said Jaena weakly. "Can we go in?"

"Of course. Everything is quiet today." The priestess gestured inside, then continued her way down the steps.

A man was sweeping the floor near the front of the temple. Golden light spilled through the large leaded windows of white and orange and yellow, making the dust motes he blew up shimmer and glow.

Jaena started back toward him. She passed the wooden statue without looking at it, although it felt like walking past someone staring at her, demanding her attention. He looked up as they reached the archway, but said nothing.

"I'm looking to get married," she said. My, this temple put her in a blunt mood.

The priest tilted his head, glancing at Ro. "We don't

keep husbands in stock here. Candles and meditation beads, maybe." He smiled very slightly.

"I have a husband," she said quickly, gesturing at Ro, and then balked at the sound of those words. The word "husband" as something she might actually *have* felt strange on her lips, awkward—terrifying. "I mean, my intended and I would like to be married in this temple. Right now. If that's a thing you do here."

The priest nodded sagely. "Let me get High Priestess Gerana."

"Wait," she said, holding up a hand. He had turned away but now stopped and looked back. "I'm a mage. We're both mages. Is that going to be a problem?"

"Are you planning on celebrating by controlling anyone's minds?"

Ro snorted. "I should think not."

Jaena frowned at the priest. "We can't do any of that. Nor would we. Of course not."

"Then I think you shall be fine as wine."

To Jaena's surprise, the discussion with the High Priestess was a rather simple one. In Takar, a wedding could be a highly elaborate affair, going on for days, every family invited. In Hepan, it was smaller but still rather an extended affair, sometimes going for more than a week. But of course they didn't *have* a week. And Jaena and Ro had no family, really. His was all gone—or liars—and what was left of hers might be a continent away. Unless they counted their friends.

"Akarians tend to consider marriage a very private

experience," the high priestess explained. "Many worship Anara for marriage and venture into the waters, the ocean or the midcountry lakes, alone under moonlight to be wed. So you see, a simple ceremony is quite what we do here. If that is all right with you."

"Yes, of course," Jaena said.

Ro smiled up at the arches above him in amusement. "In a temple like this, I don't know if we can call it exactly 'simple.' But short and sweet is fine with me."

But in truth, the words were simple, and honest, and that made them all the more sweet.

The priestess put Jaena's hand in Tharomar's and wrapped her hands around them as she spoke about love, about life, about family, about pain, about persistence and devotion. About faith to each other and faith to the gods.

Jaena squeezed his hand, and he squeezed hers back.

And then, just like that, it was done.

"By and in Nefrana's golden light," said the priestess, "I declare you are married. Go and bring prosperity to her fields, and give glory to her name."

At those words, Ro's face broke into a grin. "Oh, we will. Won't we, Jae?"

She smiled back and nodded, but it wasn't until they had turned and were making their way out of the temple when she whispered to him, "She has *no i*dea."

I7 SIEGE

The forest stretched on endlessly for the first leg of Miara's flight, until the trees started to space out a bit, the dark pines thinning to oaks. She flew on into the night's darkness, forest had given way to grassy hills dotted with herds of fluffy sheep wandering over the rolling land in the moonlight. They looked like schools of fish from her height. Scri flew alongside her, occasionally amused or even mildly irked by the breaks she took in human form. But she had a very different definition of acceptable dinners than he did.

Finally, sleep demanded its due. She spent the second half of the cold night curled in a thicket—thankfully in her own body, although she broke down and grew extra fur to keep warm. She took to the air again far after the sunrise, for once allowing herself time to fully rest. She'd need the strength for the rest of the trip.

By the time she took to the sky again, Scri was eager

to sore. Time seemed to slow as the sailed over the grassy hills. As the sun reached its zenith, a small stand of buildings to the north caught her eye. What looked like black sheep and dots crowded at the horizon line.

Too large to be a herd, of sheep or even horses. It had to be men.

Men forming up for battle?

She adjusted her course and soon was gliding over ranks and ranks of Akarian soldiers, some on foot, some on horse. Archers and crossbowmen, swords and pikes. No mages, of course. A few hundred yards back from the line, she found a small tent and perched on it, searching for anyone she recognized. Reaching out to into the distance, she could just barely sense the Kavanarian troops that loomed in the eerie quiet. Some were dousing cooking fires, but most were preparing for battle, forming up in ranks. She searched among them for what she most feared.

Yes, there they were. Mages. Hard to get a count, but perhaps twenty-five. Their energies were predominately wild—mostly creature mages and perhaps one air. Unless there were more somewhere else.

Twenty-five creature mages to one. And what would Daes have them do? She was tempted to simply try asking when a familiar head of blond hair caught her eye, on top of a white warhorse she knew as well.

Miara fluttered down, transforming on the way and hitting the ground with a running step. "Warden Asten!"

She needn't have called out, because Asten saw her immediately, even as the transformation was completing.

She reined her horse to a stop, startling the two riders behind her.

"Arms Master! Well met." Without wasting a moment, Asten was dismounting and heading for her. "What are you doing here? Visiting Dramsren stronghold?"

"Not exactly. Long story. What's going on?"

"One of the Kavanarian units is closing in on us. The battle will soon be joined," said Asten, her eyes flicking to the emerald and widening slightly. "Is Queen Elise unwell?"

Miara shook her head. "She devotes herself to Samul."

A dour man looked down from over Asten's shoulder and sniffed, running an eye over the dirty and now somewhat ragged gray dress that had once been so fine. He likely didn't even recognize that now, did he? "*King* Samul, you mean."

"This is hardly the time." Miara narrowed her eyes at him, then turned back to Asten. "There are—"

But the man started up again first. "Warden, we need to get to the front line. There'll be time for catching up with old friends—or *mages*—later." He said the word with distaste.

Now it was Asten's turn to shoot the man a harsh look. "This may be your regiment, General, but I decide when I get to the line. I am not one for turning aside knowledge of our enemy if it's available."

He clenched his jaw but said nothing.

"I estimate twenty-five creature mages on their side," Miara said quickly, striving to ignore his fluffing and posturing. "At least one air. Could be worse, but not a great combination."

"What do you think they'll do? Any way to inform our tactics?"

Miara shook her head. "The creatures mages can heal troops, so only fatal wounds might get by their efforts— aim for the neck, the armpit. Anything that kills quickly. The smaller the wound, the easier they can undo it."

The general's eyes widened. "Undo it?"

"Yes, I—" She started to say more, but the sound of a horn split the air. From the far side of the field.

"Get her a horse!" Asten barked at a nearby mounted soldier, shouting over the din.

The soldier glanced around and suddenly dismounted. "Here—I'll find another one for me," he shouted, handing her the reins as the horn faded into the pulsing of drums. The man trotted off and back toward the hold behind them even as the general opened his mouth.

"No!" shouted the general. "We need every man we've got. She can fly, as she's clearly demonstrated."

Miara mounted up, frowning but trying to keep her eyes trained ahead. Where were the mages on the field? Could there be more she'd missed? How the hell was she going to go up against twenty-six or so mages? What could she even do to stop them?

No plan was coming to mind.

"Shut up," snapped Asten at the general, her patience gone. "You know they have archers. Flying over the battle would be suicide."

"All battle is suicide. Who the hell is she?" he shouted,

all directed at Asten. The warden only glared, then looked at Miara as if for permission to tell him.

Miara met the general's eyes instead. "I'm Arms Master Floren; you heard the warden."

"If you're what you say, where's your sword? Your shield? *Anything?*"

"*I* am my sword and my shield."

"And she'll been your queen too, someday," Asten added.

The general's mouth fell open. The thunder of the troops moving cut off the fool argument. Asten turned and rode for the front of the troops, the general spurring his mount on and following after.

Miara straightened, keeping her eyes on the empty field that was about to be bathed in blood. She reached out to the horse below her without tearing her gaze away. *Hello there,* she whispered. *I'm Miara. And your name?*

She sensed the horse's surprise first, then his wary interest. *Trenor.*

Well met, Trenor. Are you ready to gallop?

Trenor whinnied and tossed his head enthusiastically.

She shared the idea of protecting a foal, a barn, a stable, the herd. Did horses conceive of bravery? Of protection?

Memories of his training flicked past her, the excitement and speed of battle. Good. He probably knew better than she did what they were getting into. She patted his chestnut coat, not so much darker than Kres's had been, and a pang stabbed at her chest. She ran her fingers through Trenor's mane as she reached out toward the mages again.

If she knew one of them, and if they hadn't been spelled too completely, perhaps they could tell her what they were planning before the brand's compulsion kicked in. The first few were unfamiliar, but then she caught her breath.

Sefim!

The mild worry that had been brewing in his mind bloomed into a joyful warmth. *Miara! What are you doing here? So the Akarians have mages, then? We thought not.*

It's a long story. And no, there's just me, and I wasn't planned. What are you *doing over there?*

They've ordered everyone out. Everyone. Brother Lithan made it extra pleasant by proclaiming that the evil we were forced to commit was barely adequate penance for our deep, deep sin. He mentally shook his head. *I figured there'd be more of a chance to escape out here than on the road, which proved true, but we've been in the middle of nowhere. I've been looking for the right opportunity, but I'm no outdoors-man. Even flying away—where would I fly? No idea where your inn was or if you were still there.*

Well, you've lucked into the right place. If we survive this.

Cheery thought.

Can you tell me anything?

He's ordered us to heal wounds the soldiers receive and to make any sacrifices necessary.

Miara's eyes widened, a chill shooting through her, and she dug her fingers deeper into Trenor's mane. Sacrifices? *Who's he?* Daes? Was he here?

The Tall Master.

Miara gritted her teeth. Almost as bad. Maybe worse,

in his own way. *What sacrifices?*

Starting with the forests. And the enemy.

The Akarians themselves? By the gods.

I know. I've been ordered to do some awful things, but that tops them all. They're hoping it will lead to surrender. Said the only thing that'd give them more bragging rights than defeating the Akarians would be actually forcing them to give up.

And if they don't surrender—they'll kill them all anyway, and half the plants in this territory. So why not?

I'm afraid so.

We have to stop them. How?

Before Brother Sefim could respond, she saw both sides lurch into action—both through his eyes and hers. Akarian riders started the charge, war cries filling the air, and the first line of mounted Kavanarians rode out to meet them.

"Pikes!" the general shouted. The Akarian troops shifted with precision, some forward some back, and pikes lowered toward the oncoming riders. The general and Asten were in a small group with two lieutenants and a handful of wardens, all mounted at the back of the line.

The scent of the air changed, and Miara looked up. Sure enough, the formerly clear sky had begun to thicken, the clouds coalescing out of nothingness and darkening, heavy with the threat of rain.

"Asten! Spread out the command group!" she shouted. "You remember what happened—"

She didn't get to finish. The crash of steel on steel rang

out. The screaming of horses split the air. Miara felt more than saw the first injuries, then deaths, and her instincts begged to heal the wounds. But that was unsustainable. *She* wasn't going to sacrifice whole forests if she could possibly help it. If she wanted to win, she'd need to try something else.

Trenor fidgeted underneath her as Asten rode up alongside. "We'll spread out," she said quickly. "Good reminder. What's your plan?"

Miara could only glance at Asten, keeping her eyes firmly trained on the battle. "Plan?"

"Yes."

"I'm… still working on it."

Asten clapped a gauntleted hand too hard on her shoulder, right over Scri's talon wounds. Miara stifled her wince. "May the Balance protect you."

"And you as well," she replied before the warden rode off further down the line.

Miara's eyes had been searching the opposing line automatically, hunting for inspiration. Now her eyes caught far in the back, a figure tall even on his mount, cloaked in dark cloth. The Tall Master glowered out at the beginnings of the battle. And beside him, another cloaked rider held a staff propped on a mount by his foot.

"Crossbows, now!" the general was shouting. Another line of Kavanarians, footmen this time, had charged forward, and the next line of armored men surged forth screaming as well.

Easing her mind toward the air mage cautiously, the

crackle of lightning and the sharp smell of sulfur accosted her brain, and she reeled her mind back, hoping to go unnoticed.

No luck. Even at the distance she could see the man with the staff—the air mage—turn his head and speak.

The Tall Master and the air mage. If she could stop *them* maybe she could stop the battle. They were only two men, after all.

Thunder crashed above her, shaking the sky.

Shit. If the air mage knew where she was—

Before she could fully finish the thought, Trenor had felt the danger. He broke free into a gallop parallel to the enemy line, diving behind the ranks of the mounted Akarians. It wouldn't hide her entirely. She had to keep moving.

She racked her brain. How? How could she stop them? Gods, to be an air mage, rather than the rabbit the air mage was hunting—

A rabbit! That was it.

She had no idea if it'd be enough, but she pulled Trenor to a stop and gripped the air mage in her mind, pulling life energy out of him and pouring it back in. His cloak collapsed in as his body twisted into that of a small, fluffy, gray rabbit.

The staff tumbled down, and she felt him slide from the saddle as if she were the one falling. She yanked her mind away, not wanting to find out if a fall from that height would kill a rabbit.

She rushed into a gallop again, back the other direction along the line. She had to stay one step ahead, hidden. Trenor reached the end of the line of Akarians and turned back, but no more thunder echoed.

She cautiously slowed and eyed the spot again. The Tall Master was there, alone now. Creature mages crowded around the air mage's horse. The energy that vibrated from the spot felt hot and intense with life.

He'd be back. Maybe she'd drained him and injured him too, but it wasn't enough. She stopped, glancing around, looking for an idea.

What she saw was carnage. The field before her, usually green and pleasantly pastoral, was now a sea of swinging swords and axes, grunts and groans, broken up by shields gleaming red with blood. Hoarse screams and savage battle cries rang out, horses stamped and reared, and the smell, gods, the smell. Blood and worse. She coughed, trying to block it out. Men and women lay crawling, flailing, dying... dead.

She tried to reel her senses back, but their outcry of pain caught her like a wave, minds clinging to what life energy they could, groping for it in the air with all the desperation of death. One light winked out, suddenly falling still. Then another, drained nearly dry before they gave up from the pain and agony of it all.

This was just what Sefim had warned her of. Creature mages killing the injured to heal the living.

How could they do it—how *could* they—

Her eyes flicked to the far line, to the Tall Master, some instinct telling her something was wrong. His arm pointed in her direction as he shouted orders. She looked to the cluster of healers, several of whom were breaking off and transforming.

She'd stopped too long. They were coming for her.

She turned and raced Trenor back behind the Akarian cavalry, but deep down she knew that as the only mage on the entire Akarian side, their magic would always help them find her. Always.

Hiding was buying her nothing.

At the end of the cavalry line, she turned Trenor toward the battle, and together they surged forward. Skirmishes filled the field, and Trenor leapt over one fallen man only to dodge right as another two swordsmen staggered in their direction.

If she could make it to the Tall Master before the creature mages made it to her—

Wind blew furiously, swirling above her, the sky crackling with energy, and she cursed. Spotting the air mage, she seized him again and twisted him anew. A flea this time. Let them find that in the chaos.

Her victory was short-lived. The largest eagle she'd ever seen dove from the sky above, its scream piercing her ears in pain. She ducked close to Trenor, but the transformed mage didn't falter, scratching at her back, trying to claw her off.

It relented, gaining air again, but then she felt something leap and collide with her side, knocking her from the horse—and the sword from her hand.

The heavy, furry thing came down on top of her. She writhed, determined to get away, but a large paw came down on her neck, claws just barely drawn enough for her to feel them.

She froze, the message clear. She could heal a lot of things, but not a neck wound. She blinked up at a large orange and white cat, its head easily the size of a shield.

Miara, it's me. Don't react.

Her eyes widened. The voice was Sefim's.

He's ordered us to bring you back. So he can take you back to the Dark Master. A trophy, I think.

No chance she was letting *that* happen.

What are we going to do? he whispered to her.

I don't know. Get me closer, and I'll try something.

He didn't acknowledge her, but he got up, transforming back into himself. The eagle landed beside them and twisted back into a human woman, except that she kept her talons. Grasping the back of Miara's neck with them none too gently, the mage grabbed Miara's arm and pulled her forward. Sefim grabbed the other and followed along, stoic as always.

Miara had made it well beyond the main line of fighting, although not to the Kavanarian reserves just yet, so they had a fairly uninterrupted march. That is, except for the dozen other creature mages that had been after her circling around her and closing in. Just when she'd gotten used to having guards to protect her, now she had ones who wanted to skin her alive.

They marched her straight up to the Tall Master. Miara noted with a slight bit of satisfaction that the air mage had not returned to his mount. Hopefully he was still a tiny jumping creature somewhere on that horse's hide.

"Well, well," said the Tall Master, smiling darkly. "Thought you could get away, did you?"

She spat at his feet. The former eagle mage tightened the talons behind her neck ever so slightly.

Miara's mind raced. She was free. Sefim was free. Surrounded by enemy creature mages. What spell could she work that there weren't ten more here to undo? Even with Sefim's help, they were outnumbered.

"Where is the brand?" he demanded.

She stared him down, saying nothing. She could lunge for him and try to take him down with her. She couldn't expect to live with so many adversaries, but if one less Master was in the world, perhaps it would be worth her death. But it would have been such a short taste of freedom for one life…

If Aven were here, he'd use the star map. She pursed her lips. Of course, that didn't help her. She wasn't an air mage, and it was day, not night. But he'd had a point, she could see it now. At that moment, she'd have tried anything to stop the Tall Master—even slavery.

"Search her," he ordered. She had no idea what he thought they were looking for, but Sefim obliged, looking excessively thoroughly over her cloak. "And bring me a stone. Tell me where the brand is, and I'll consider protecting you from the Dark Master."

She only narrowed her eyes further.

He stepped closer, looming over her and casting her form in shadow. "You wish to kill me," he said. "I can see it in your eyes. This is why your kind must be enslaved.

Corruption? Deviance? It's all priestly poppycock. It's because you're dangerous. You can't handle freedom."

"Seems to me you can't handle mastery," she whispered.

"Ah, finally she speaks. I thought you might have lost your tongue. Now tell me—the brand." He reached out and seized her neck with one hand, fingers slowly tightening.

Lost your tongue. She caught her breath. That was it. If he couldn't give orders, the mages wouldn't be bound to help him. If she could silence him or kill him quickly enough…

She closed her eyes, feigning pain but truly to concentrate. Reaching down into the earth, she summoned a single vine, coiling it and building up its strength even as his fingers slowly tightened against her skin.

Sucking in a breath, she struck, launching the vine from the ground as fast as she could manage. It caught the Tall Master at the throat, wrapping around insidiously and pulling tight.

She opened her eyes. The vine yanked him down to the ground savagely as his hands left Miara and clawed at his neck. She tore power from Sefim to strengthen the vine as it clenched tighter against the earth. Luckily, the talons at her neck were frozen still, the eagle mage staring in wonder.

But, no—she could feel the Tall Master fading, but it wasn't enough. He might pass out from lack of air, but how long would that take? How much strength from her would it require? No, it was time to end this.

Ripping another vine from the ground, she gripped

his head from another angle and twisted. She winced at the sickening crack as his neck broke.

The eagle mage's grip loosened on her arm. Sefim stared down darkly at the still body. For a long moment, none of them moved, and it seemed the whole world had gone still.

Of all the places Daes had traveled, Akaria hadn't often been his destination. Although he'd ridden through Akaria to reach Takar a few times, he'd gone by ship much more often. None of his trips had taken him through the White City.

Now, though, the road finally opened up from the forest, and he could see the city in the distance, a long and mostly flat plain full of grain fields between him and his prey. The towers rose up boldly before him, spires of white defiant against the sea and dusky horizon beyond. A worthy adversary, for once. But one he would still crush under his heel. The cold, bitter wind whipped around him, as if excited on his behalf, encouraging him. The sun was setting on the Akarian kingdom, and in its place, Daes would build something new. Something great.

Yes. This was his time now.

The Akarian capital's walls were maybe four men high, just as his reports had showed, and the three gates were all where he'd expected them. Good. No failures there. Not yet at least.

"Vusamon!" he called out. The general rode up to his side. "Are you ready for a battle, my old friend?" Daes took a deep breath, almost *tasting* the anticipation in the air.

"As ever, Lord Consort."

"Please. No formalities on the field. I'll be dead before you can tell me what I need to know."

Vusamon snorted, smiling a little. "I am ready. The men are ready. But night will fall within the hour. Shall we camp and wait for the morning? Let them stew in their fear?"

Daes frowned, shifting uneasily. Night was when the stars were out. When the star magic would be at its greatest. When he suspected they'd use it to free more mages. Could they free his whole force in the night, stealing away his advantage and leaving him to pummel the city with only swords, sticks, and rocks? They hadn't even brought artillery, as it would have slowed them down. They *shouldn't* need it. Assuming the slaves remained slaves.

"No," he said quickly. "That's what they're expecting. They'll use it to heat oil, load artillery. To prepare. Let us begin."

"But my lord, the men need rest. Marching all day, and four days straight—"

"They got to rest at every lovely break in the road my mages had to fix. But let them rest here on the road. We'll send the mages first and pummel them at night. Hold our soldiers in reserve. Maybe they'll even think we're camping—until they're dead."

Vusamon grinned. "As you wish, Lord Consort."

"I told you, don't call me that in battle."

"We're not in battle yet, Lord Consort." And then with a broad grin, he angled his horse toward the mage leaders and lieutenants. "But soon."

"You killed him," whispered one of the mages.

The stillness of the area around Miara hung in sharp contrast to the clashes and screams of the battlefield behind them. Every mage stood stone still, the wind blowing the stench of the battlefield past them. Their cloaks flapped against their legs. Thunder broke over their heads from the storm the air mage had stirred—or was still stirring.

"She killed him," another whispered. "What does that mean?"

The question pushed her into action. She ripped her eyes away from the Tall Master and glanced around. "It means you're free. Or you will be. Now heal the Akarians," she ordered. Sefim met her eyes, his expression a mix of darkness, sympathy, and hope. The other mages glanced around nervously at each other.

"Now!" she snapped. "We're putting an end to this madness, *now*."

One turned immediately, then another followed. A third caught her eye.

"Can we bring back Rikor?"

She frowned, not understanding.

The mage pointed at the horse. "Our air mage."

"If he's not going to cause trouble."

"He won't." The mage inched closer to the horse, looking around for her friend. A few moments later, the rescued air mage twisted into a human form once again. He eyed Miara warily, shrinking against the horse.

Are we going to have a problem? she asked silently.

Are you going to kill me? he replied.

No. As long as your mission to kill me has ended.

Indeed, it has.

Clear up the sky then.

Yes, my lady.

Interesting. A Kavanarian wouldn't know the meaning of the emerald. But she *was* handing out orders like she owned the place.

Which, now that she thought about it, she did.

"Are you all right?" Sefim asked.

"Yes," she said briskly. "But we have to end this battle." She spotted the mage-knots on the Tall Master's belt. Bending down, she took the knots and his belt too and wrapped it around her waist. Strictly speaking, she didn't need the knots, because she hoped not to command these mages ever to do anything other than stop fighting. But she certainly couldn't have it falling into anyone else's hands. She tied the leather knot and strode to the air mage's horse, mounting as he backed out of the way. The soldiers still fought, but now some on both sides were healing.

A battle that could go on forever, people only dying when someone got lucky. Was that more horrible or less?

She charged forward through the line, taking no time to introduce herself to her poor mount while men and women were dying. "Stop!" she shouted. "It's over! Stop!"

A few paused, but most opponents took that as an opening, and it left her words having little impact.

"Stop," she barked, shouting now with both mind and voice at once. "I command you to stop!" She stretched out her mind over the battlefield, steeling herself against the pain and horror and suffering emanating up from the ground.

I command you. Stop at once.

She had rarely talked to two minds at once. Screaming out her words to all of them was far from easy, or pleasant, and the staggering drain of energy hit her almost immediately, but she reached for the mages to replenish her. They'd stolen most of that energy anyway.

This war is unjust. Akaria has done nothing. Your leader is dead. Kavanar is defeated. These slaves will be freed. You, soldiers, lay down your arms and surrender.

Around her, slowly, some of them began to comply. Across the field, a flash of blond caught her attention. Warden Asten caught Miara's eye, and they held each other's gaze for a long moment before Asten nodded, her face grave but proud. Miara turned her eyes back to the field of fighters.

I will be your queen. I will not be denied. The mages are mine now and under my protection. They will no longer heal you. Fight till you're dead, kneel and surrender, or turn your tail and run. It does not matter to me.

She raised her voice to a deafening roar. *Drop. Your. Swords. Surrender!*

Around her, wide-eyed soldiers staggered away from their weapons, abandoning them in the morass. One mage stumbled, another slumped against a companion, as she drained energy fast and hard. A handful of soldiers turned and ran, and more than a few cavalry at the edge of the battle headed for the hills. The thuds and clangs of weapons dropping were dull, muted by the squishing mud.

But they were the sweetest sounds she'd ever heard.

What Thel would have given for a creature mage right about then. His plan would be a lot easier if he could just be a small fox. A white one, preferably, to blend in with the snow. Or maybe a snow owl. Or a smaller white bird…

As it was, he was a dark blob of brown cloak that barely blended in with the trees. Low brambles abounded in the forest, and so they stayed hunched over, even crawling, as they inched closer to the Kavanarian troops.

They seemed to have stopped. Were they making camp? The sun was rapidly setting, so he supposed that made sense. They'd wait till morning to attack, hovering menacingly outside of Panar before striking.

He squinted at the troops and flattened himself against the ground, and Niat followed suit beside him. Neither of them were particularly stealthy, but being "scrawny" did have some benefits on occasion.

Time to give his ridiculous plan a shot.

His mind slid out from him, following the dirt, tracing along root and rock and rivulet toward the camp and then down along the road. He followed until he reached the most southern troops, and then he groped upward, reaching for anything that felt made of the earth.

A sword. He found a sword and infused it full of energy. It had to be blazing hot now, but it could also be in a scabbard. And he was going to have to heat way more than one sword before anyone would take much notice.

It was hard, slow, painstaking work, but soon he saw Niat's eyebrows twitch. She smiled and glanced toward him, nodding. She must have heard something he didn't. He didn't see anyone remotely near them, so he let his mind expand back out into the earth and kept going.

The murmurs among the troops picked up, and soon some of them were speaking rapidly. Others were rushing back farther north into the camp.

Buying him some space. Away from Panar. Good.

He met Niat's eyes, giving her a significant look, and she nodded once sharply. He returned the nod and then trained his eyes back on the camp—or more specifically, the land just beyond it.

He inhaled slowly, pulling in energy from the warmth of the earth as he went. Filling himself fuller and fuller, he reached farther down, until the warmth grew hot. Angry. Restless. He could feel its pent-up tension like it was a crick in his shoulder. Liquid pressed hard against solid rock, locked in an endless battle, no relief in sight.

But he could offer relief, couldn't he? Following the convoluted description from the book, he reached down gently and created an opening. Pushing the earth apart just slightly. Then a little further. Then more, each time widening the gap beneath the ground. The liquid rock flowed and surged, following his path.

He could bring it farther. He could set it free.

In one final, wrenching blow, he cleaved the earth, and the hot, molten rock surged up and out, filling the broad canyon he'd torn in the rock and soil. The sides of the canyon surged up, but even still, the hot, liquid rock kept coming.

Screams from the camp told him they'd noticed—and that the bright-yellow rock was flowing over the heightened edges of the canyon.

He wrenched it farther, for good measure. He couldn't see it with his eyes, but if his mind's estimate was accurate—which was a big if—the canyon full of molten earth was at least four horses wide.

Another wave of rock surged over the sides, bigger this time. And there was no sign of it stopping… He glanced around. The encampment was transfixed by his handiwork.

"C'mon," he whispered. "Let's get out of here."

Another wave of hot rock rushed up from closer to the earth's center and poured over the canyon's rim, Yes, that was much too close for his tastes, even at a few dozen yards away.

She grabbed his hand, tugging his mind out of the earth and back into his body, and they ran as fast as their legs could carry them.

Jaena gaped at the mound of black welling out of the forests on the horizon. Like ants, the Kavanarians seemed to writhe and spill over each other. They were a black pool spilling from the forest onto the plain, growing ever larger. Headed toward her.

From the north gate, they watched—she, Ro, Aven, Wunik, and Derk. Peering out, hands raised to block the last remnants of the setting sun, the cold wind whipped plaintively at her cloak. She could hear artillery being cranked back farther down the wall, the shouts of soldiers preparing.

"Don't worry," said Aven, trying to sound reassuring. "They've marched far. They'll camp and wait for morning. Then we can free some of their mages, thin the force a little. Reduce their numbers."

"How many can we really free?" Derk shrugged. "And make sure we aren't out of commission in the morning?"

"We have to try," said Aven.

"I agree. One less slave attacking me is worth it. But I just don't know how far we'll get."

"I know."

"Look," said Wunik, pointing. "Tents. They *are* camping. They'll wait till morning."

Aven nodded and turned away from the sight of the oncoming army. "All right. I think we should get some rest. At least a few hours. When the stars come up tonight, Derk and I can take a shot at freeing the slaves. The rest of you, rest up for the morning. And be ready."

Nodding, Jaena dragged herself away from the pool
of Kavanarian soldiers and mages oozing across the plain
toward them. Her hand still in Ro's, he led her down the
stairs and along the street back to Ranok. "Easy for him
to say," she said to Ro. "Rest? How can we rest?"

"I'm pretty sure I can think of a way to tire you out."
Ro grinned.

"Oh, and is *that* the way to spend our energies, with
an enemy on our doorstep?"

"No better way, I should think." He pulled her closer
and slid his arm around her waist. "Especially if they're
the last energies we ever spend."

"Don't talk like that. It won't be."

They hadn't mentioned their ceremony to anyone
other than Kae. Not with Miara still missing. Oddly
enough, in some ways nothing was different at all, and it
all felt arbitrary. And yet in other ways, there was a subtle
difference. An expansion, a sense that they were on this
adventure together not just for today, or for next week,
but for as long as their hearts were beating.

The streets were empty, save a few folks nervously eying
the troops and then rushing back home. Those in homes in
the outer rings had been ordered to move to more central
buildings and temples, now crammed full of people. An
eerie quiet had settled over the city, tense, waiting.

Afraid.

They were almost back to Ranok when the sound of
stone crumbling, loud and harsh in the distance, reached

her ears. She spun around, eyes searching the end of the long street for the walls, the gate.

But she didn't need to see. She knew.

"Ro!" she whispered. "We were wrong. It's beginning."

He caught his breath as another loud crumbling crashed down. "C'mon," he barked. "To the tower, like we planned."

They sprinted down the rest of the street and up the tower they'd chosen for the mages to meet in. Stair after stair after stair after stair, and finally she was at the top, lungs burning to explode, legs aching, panting like an overheated dog. They were the first to arrive. Shit, should they have shared their realization before taking off up the tower? Were they wrong and all that sprinting had been for nothing?

She stared out at the city and its surrounding lands. There *were* tents. There were also mages approaching. A much smaller cluster was moving out from the group on horseback, headed for the city.

She could see the walls easily from here, too, one of the reasons they'd picked this tower. The north gate, the place where they'd just been, had been smashed into nothing but rubble.

She took a deep breath. Well, she couldn't rebuild a gate accurately, but then, she didn't need to. A pile of rubble was harder to cross than the gate, so let them destroy it. She just hoped no one had been inside. Hastily, she piled the rubble up even higher, making it as steep as she could.

Then underneath the small group of mages and horses,

she gripped the earth and thrust it up into the air, sending bodies and unfortunate horses flying.

"How's *that* for a distraction?"

Ro let out a bitter laugh. "Now let's just hope they don't do the same to us."

"I'm ready," she said, lowering her head. "C'mon, Kavanar. Show me what you're made of."

Aven staggered as the earth shook beneath his feet, acid shooting into his veins. By the gods—the north gate had just crumbled behind him.

He stood staring at it, his pulse racing. There had been three guards in there, three people with families and—could he save them—

No. It was already too late for that. He had to *run.* He dug in his heels and raced back to Ranok. Clearly the Kavanarians *weren't* going to camp. At least not all of them.

Perik met him at the entrance—had the crash been heard even here?—handing him his pack. Aven spouted a list of orders for whom to fetch, what to tell them, where to send them, where to go. Before he charged off, Perik forced a horse's reins into his hands. Although the tower wasn't far, in the end he did appreciate the rest from running, especially when he was climbing as fast as he could up to the top. As he neared, he could hear Jaena's laughter rolling down the stairwell—dark, almost manic.

At the top, nearly every mage they had was waiting

for him. All except Miara, of course. He pushed the bitter pain aside. Dropping the pack near the low lookout wall, he collapsed to his knees and looked out over the city.

"North gate's gone," Tharomar said quickly. "Jaena's rather… gleefully causing havoc. Some mages attacking, but not two hundred. Not yet, anyway."

The normally flat fields outside Ranok were already marred with three strange, dune-like hills and one gash in the earth. In much worse shape was the city wall. Two men thick and five men high, it lay crumpled not just at the north gate but stretching out in both directions. He swore under his breath. Mages to take down defenses in preparation for the soldiers in the morning? Yes, that must be their plan.

Aven peered down, eying the mages. With a small group, freeing a few could make more of a difference. He glanced up at the sky. Darkening, but not yet black, and certainly no stars.

As he looked around for something else to try, he noticed a group of troops scrambling in the distance. He took the spyglass from his belt and looked out. All he could see was a slight hill he hadn't seen before and an eerie glow.

"Siliana, Jaena—any idea what those troops out there are up to? They're swarming away from their campsite, but not in this direction."

The two women were silent for a moment. Jaena slowly raised her eyebrows. "Can I see?" She held out her hand.

He gave her the spyglass and waited impatiently,

tapping his foot and searching the field below for the next best move.

"Well, by the gods." She lowered the glass. "There's some earth mage at work out there, but not any of ours. I can't feel the mage, but I think he opened up a canyon blocking the troops for at least a mile. And it's getting wider. Should I add to it?"

An earth mage—like Thel? He crushed the surge of hope. "Yes, by all means!"

She nodded and handed him back the glass, her eyes glassy and focused off in the distance. Before she could finish, the rock of the tower beneath them shook violently.

Stumbling, Aven swore as his shoulder thudded hard into the wall.

"They've got tons of earth mages," Siliana shouted. "At least ten out of that small group. At least half of the mages I checked. Unusual."

The tower shook again, and Aven grabbed onto the top of the low wall beside him. "Are we going down in this?" he shouted. "Do we need to—"

"They're just shaking the ground, I think—" said Jaena.

"No," Siliana said, cutting her off. "I'm in their heads. I can see what they're trying to do, and that's crumble this on our heads."

"Over my dead body!" Jaena snapped.

"Not literally, please," said Ro.

A loud crack sounded above them.

"That's it! Everybody—go, go, down the stairs," Jaena shouted through gritted teeth. "Get down. I'll hold it for now. Go. Hurry!"

Aven didn't need encouragement. He raced back down the stairs, racking his brain for a better strategy than fleeing down the stairs with his pack. Where next? Where wouldn't they expect? Where would be so obvious they'd never think to attack there?

He glanced up at the sky. Clouds covered half the darkening sky. They'd be out soon, but could he reach them if he couldn't see them? What if he grabbed the wrong one?

Another loud crumbling of stone reached his ears, and he darted farther away from the tower he'd just abandoned, staring back over his shoulder.

The middle of the tower had fully collapsed, but true to Jaena's word, the top of the tower floated in the air, bobbing slightly, but mostly staying up.

Aven just stared. By the gods, that woman could move the earth. Let it be enough.

Slowly the rocky top of the tower drifted down to the ground. First Ro stepped out, then Jaena. Then after she was a few paces away, the tower's top collapsed into a pile of stray, disconnected stones. But it didn't linger for long. The giant, thick bricks were floating up into the air and out toward the field at incredibly fast rates.

Jaena and Ro, he realized. Lobbing building materials at their enemies. Thank the gods for them.

But unfortunately, the mage slaves could lob building materials too. He heard the whistling—and felt the fire with his magic—before he could see the huge rock hurtling toward them. Straight for Jaena and Ro.

As he dashed for a side street, he thrust a massive gust of wind, hoping to knock it aside, but it had no effect. A mage caught it before it could land. Aven did successfully suck the energy from the flames on the rock, but only just barely before it slammed into the spot where the tower had once stood.

He caught his breath. Had it hit them?

Another whistling projectile caught his ears. He reached out for it, to thrust it back, and found the energy of at least five mages pushing the rock forward—and Aven out of the way.

Siliana and Teron were huddled in a shop doorway, glancing around frantically.

"Over here! Come on," Aven called.

As they ran toward him, Derk emerged from the next side street over and jogged toward him too. All three mages stopped when they reached him.

"Where to, my king?" Derk said, his snark just this side of bleak despair.

"This way," said Aven, turning and motioning for them to follow. "We need another tower."

Ro dove out of the way just in time, finding himself sprawled against other warm, bony bodies. He hauled himself to his feet and found he'd crushed Sestin, the healer. Wessa bent down to help him up.

The three of them looked around uncertainly.

"Jaena!" he called. "Jae!" He took a few steps toward the boulder. He didn't think it'd hit her, but he couldn't see her anywhere else.

A whistling sound caught his ears, and someone caught his hand, dragging him back against the side of the building.

"Look." Wessa pointed to a nearby section where a building wall had collapsed. A woman had been crushed, two children trying to frantically uncover her.

Glancing back once more in hopes of finding Jae, he turned and started toward the wall at a jog. "Come on. We have to help them."

The other mages didn't disagree. They followed closely behind him, eyes darting around the torn-up square around them. By Nefrana, just their luck—three mages with barely a week's training combined, and they'd gotten themselves separated.

"We'll help them, then we have to find the others," he grumbled.

"Of course, of course," said Sestin.

Ro heaved the rock off the woman with mostly physical force, aided by a little magic. Or maybe a lot. He wasn't really sure, but the two healers quickly went to work, mending her legs. One of the children clung to his leg silently. The other hung around Wessa's neck, crying, while the mother tried to pat their back.

"It's all right," he said to the quiet child. "Help is here. But when she's better, you all go as far south in the city as you can. All right?"

The wide blue eyes looking up at him nodded, still fearful but determined now.

He wondered if all that was all a lie. He knew full well things did not always end up "all right."

By the time Aven and his small group had located another tower and raced halfway up—as Teron was not going to be pulling any of the tricks Jaena had—night had completely fallen. Aven lit each torch they passed idly, and they gathered around an arrowslit to stare down at the raging, chaotic mage battle below. The stars should be out by now…

He had to try.

He chose a mage near the outside, so tiny from that height he couldn't even tell their gender, just that someone was there. He batted some of the clouds away above him and hoped the mages would be distracted long enough to let him through and find the right star. Yes, he could see it and its neighbors. Reaching up to Casel, he gripped the now-familiar, beautiful white smoke, and twisted it down, calling it out, summoning the icy water deep inside—and funneling it at the mage. As he worked, he sensed the others at work around him, focused intently on the battle below.

Unlike when using farsight, he had difficulty aiming. The mage was small and hard to hit, and at first it seemed he wouldn't be able to make contact long enough to get a spark. Then he thought he'd hit the mage spot-on, but nothing changed. He couldn't even see the mage clearly enough to determine if they were itching their arm. One boon was that Aven didn't feel as drained as usual. He was getting better at throttling it and channeling the energy where it needed to go.

"Siliana—that one on the far right," he said, pointing. "I've freed them, I think. Can you tell them—"

"On it," she said quickly, glaring intently at the tiny mage far below them. "Found her. Telling her—"

The freed mage turned and ran east, toward Takar. She didn't make it far before an arrow sent the mage sprawling. She collapsed on the ground and moved no more.

"Damn it," Aven muttered. "The soldiers are watching them. *Damn* it."

Dark, thick clouds had gathered, and icy rain started to cascade down.

"What do we try now?" asked Teron. "They don't have many swords for me to rob them of. I'm just shaking the ground over here."

"Not too close to us, I hope," Aven said. He sighed, searching his brain for the next move. "Or maybe closer is what we need to get…" He glanced up at Derk, who smiled crookedly.

"We need horses," said Derk, nodding. "Warhorses. I'll get on it." He started for the stairs.

"No, I can find some and call them here," Siliana said in a rush. "If we all go down now to greet them?"

Aven nodded. "Let's go."

Jaena staggered out of the dust, coughing and desperately sucking down air. She collapsed against the nearest wall, sliding to a seat as she struggled to breathe. Of course the dirt cloud had hit her—just her luck.

"Are you all right?" a young voice said.

Bleary and blinking, Jaena struggled to see—there was dust in her eyes too, damn it.

"It's Luha and Pytor," said Miara's father's voice. "We can heal you if—"

"No, I'm all right," she managed, hacking out another cough. "Just a little dust, that's all."

"Mother—this way, *now*," someone shouted. The voice drew closer, and she struggled to see. Prince Dom was dragging his mother around the corner toward them.

"But Aven went that way—"

"And we're unarmed and unarmored and not going with him." Dom stopped, seeing the three of them standing, and approached.

"Has anyone seen Ro?" Jaena asked, her voice finally almost working. They all shook their heads no. "Tharomar!"

The silence of the response was deafening.

"How about we get back to the north gate?" said Jaena. Dom turned an incredulous stare her way. "I mean, what's left of it. We could build up a barricade, and they won't look for us there; they think they've already torn that down. And we would be able to see a little better."

"And also get stuck by swords," Dom replied, clearly dubious.

She pointed up at the sky. "Would you prefer giant boulders? Hiding inside is not going to help in a fight like this. Nothing is going to stop them." She glanced around at all of them. "Now, c'mon."

Jaena took off back the way they'd come, and the others followed. Yes, this was a game of hide and seek, and their enemy had already checked this spot.

Before their small ragged group could reach the gate, two platoons of city guards surged past, heading toward the mass of mages on the field. Gods, she hoped some of the air mages were watching this, understanding. Unless Akarian air mages fought whatever the Kavanarian mage slaves threw at them, these troops would be toasted in no time.

Icy rain finally reached them, and she was soaked through before they reached the remains of the north gate. Well, at least that would help with the walls of fire.

They hunkered behind the largest bits of rubble, and Jaena looked out along the walls, expecting to see a large section of wall torn down. In truth, she couldn't see *any* wall remaining standing. Shattered walls curved away and disappeared out of sight. Houses, too, that had leaned outside against Panar's walls for security, for trade, many of them had been crushed to little more than piles of rubble.

The troops surged past them, and sure enough, a wall

of flame materialized. Jaena focused on the mages, jiggling the ground and finding a breastplate and heating it red-hot. Its owner staggered back, as though to avoid the heat strapped to his chest.

The wall did falter somewhat. A storm cloud coalesced inside the wall of flame, lightning snaking out toward the mages nearby, upsetting the wall or at least the mages' grip on it.

Some troops were caught by the flames, but others surged and sprinted around it.

Jaena did her best to help them as soldiers reached mages. She knocked a mage off-balance behind a soldier who wasn't looking. Then she lobbed a stray boulder to finish the job. Mages finally drew their swords in combat, and she poured energy into the metal. Six swords dropped in a matter of seconds.

In spite of the determined efforts of the healers around her, both forces slowly dwindled. Two platoons hadn't been much to send up against this handful of mages. And then, before the last mage slave had fallen and faded away, another twenty poured forth, like they were nothing. The new mages trudged—clearly already exhausted—on foot toward the battle. She gritted her teeth. They deserved better than this. Better than no choice but to march to their deaths. Or their mass murders.

Still, though, it wasn't even two hours before all the soldiers of the first wave were dead. She didn't catch quite when it happened, but all of a sudden, she looked up and couldn't spot any Akarians. Stands of archers took over behind her now, peppering the battlefield with arrows. Some of them burst into flame as they approached their victims.

Seven hells, the destruction.

The death.

The mage slaves might be exhausted. But maybe they weren't. Maybe they were just getting started.

The buildings outside the wall started to fall now. Systematically, each was torn asunder, wood splintering when rock tore through it, stone sliding and grinding apart—and then flying into the city, impromptu artillery.

Another wave of troops surged past Jaena and her creature mage fellows. Pytor and Luha were hard at work on bees, brambles, and vines, while Elise was healing and Dom guarding their backs. Which, frankly, was nice in this situation. Certainly he was probably donating his mother power too.

But it wasn't really working. It wasn't really enough. Almost pointless, even. In next to no time, the new wave of troops that had been four times the size of the last were melting already.

She winced. These mages would destroy everything in their path. Everything. Every beautiful white tower and sunny, tree-covered garden, all the way to Panar's quiet docks. Step by step, these mages would work their way through the city, until all the buildings were gone.

Where Panar had once stood, only a dusty field, bloodstains, and skeletons would remain. And all of her dreams of making a life here with Ro would be gone too, sand blown into the wind.

"Tharomar!" she yelled. "Ro! Where are you—"

Dom grabbed her arm and shook her. "Keep it down, or they *will* come looking."

"Or drop a boulder on us," Luha mumbled.

Forgetting the battle—no, she wasn't giving up, she just… needed to know what had happened to Ro—she grabbed Pytor's arm. "Help me find Tharomar. *Please.*"

With one quick nod, the creature mage shut his eyes and began searching.

Aven didn't bother to question whether riding out into the fray was a bit suicidal. It was definitely suicidal. But he had no other ideas, and so he fell back on what he knew best.

The kind of war that involved swords and horses.

Derk at his side, Aven raced out toward the mages. A wall of fire appeared, predictably, and Aven started grabbing energy left and right, ripping the wall apart. Derk followed his lead.

The formation fell to pieces, but now he was too full, too hot. He seized hold of the energy, formed it into lightning, and flung it at the Kavanarians closest to him.

Three mages went down, writhing. Aven searched for the command tent and its red flag, but the fog and the smoke obscured nearly everything.

Abruptly, he felt himself falling, almost as if—as if— No, it was really happening. The warhorse Derk had found was shrinking down beneath him.

He landed awkwardly, stumbling onto his side. He glanced up just in time to see a boulder flying toward his head.

He rolled, dodging. A sword left its sheath behind him. He staggered to his feet, whirling as he drew his own sword. Keeping the blade low, he waited. A burly mage with feathered wings on his back stared him down. Damn, a creature mage. He'd have to strike a killing blow.

The mage seemed determined to out-wait him, so Aven lunged forward. His opponent's sword rose, but not fast enough, almost… intentionally slow. His blade sunk into the man's ribs. Aven straightened, yanking the sword away, alarmed.

Just then another one of the mages leapt in front of him, but facing the other slaves. Almost as if she were ready to face them. But that couldn't be, she was a—

"Who are you?" he demanded. "What are you doing?"

"Menaha," the woman growled. "And I'm defending you, obviously."

Menaha. Menaha! "From Mage Hall?"

"Good guess," she said wryly.

"I freed you!"

She whirled to look at him incredulously. "You—it was you?"

He nodded, but lunged around her to block a slave who'd sought the opening. "Time for getting to know each other later!"

Derk joined them, and together the three of them

fought their way through the rest. But even as the last one fell, forty more mages marched forward.

Enough. Time to get back. But first…

The new mages hadn't yet taken control of the skies yet. Aven brushed a hole through the clouds and yanked down every bit of Erepha's energy he could. He blew the spell across the wind, and the forty approaching mages gradually slowed to a stop.

No… only thirty or so did. Some of them, the furthest out, didn't feel it. In fact, they were already shaking awake the others who did. Moments later, the sky split with lightning, vicious attacks beginning to fall.

"Come on. We better get back in." He gestured to Menaha to follow.

"I thought you'd never ask," she said.

They took off at a sprint for the battlement—or what was left of it.

Kae dashed up the steps of the second tower two at a time. At the top, he stopped short, panting.

"Only two?"

Elder Wunik turned and nodded darkly.

"But this was the second meeting point," Kae said weakly.

"No one else has made it here yet," said Beneral. "It's just us air mages now."

"Fortunately," said Wunik, a touch proper, "we can do quite a lot."

Kae strode to the tower window and looked out at the battle. To his surprise, where there had been twenty mages, there seemed more like thirty now. More were falling every minute, but he could also see more mages readying to join the field behind them.

"Lightning," Beneral suggested.

Kae nodded. "Yes, all three of us together. Let's take some part of the storm over them and shock them a little."

"Or a lot," grumbled Beneral.

Wunik led the way, and the three air mages poured their energies into a twitching ball of lightning, swinging it out over where the mage slaves fought. And then, when it was just so—they struck. Kae's fist tightened as the first bolts darted out.

But even after attack after attack left a mage smoking on the ground—more were still coming. They could barely handle these twenty. How were they going to handle nearly the whole two hundred?

"That way—down by the shop with the green sign, see it?" Pytor pointed across the square and down the street. "Right there."

"Got it. Be right back." Jaena darted away.

"Wait a minute—" Dom started. "Maybe we should come with you."

She stopped, already shaking her head.

"If you don't return and the situation is dire," said

Pytor, "we're falling back to Ranok."

She nodded sharply and took off through the fog.

Down the street, and toward the green sign. The street was empty. So was the side street. Where was he? She stepped forward and opened the door of the shop.

The shop… was no longer a shop. The roof had fallen in—or been crushed—leaving only a raw husk. But inside, healer mages and nonmages buzzed around, patients laid out in a semi-orderly fashion.

One thing her eyes didn't see was Ro.

She ducked as another incoming boulder shook the earth, and when she straightened, Ro came around the far corner, stepping gingerly over the rubble and holding a young man in his arms. He was dust-covered, and his face was tight with worry, but there was no blood. Well, only a little blood that didn't seem to be his. No missing limbs.

Thank all the gods and all the ancestors.

She ran to him even as he sat down the man, dodging mages and the injured, and once the man was out of his arms, she threw hers around him.

"I was so worried," she said softly.

"Jae!" He nodded against the side of her head. "We're here now."

"But the battle isn't going well, Ro. This is a losing game. We're only delaying the inevitable."

He shrugged. "We knew the odds were stacked against us from the start."

She pressed her lips together, unwilling to take failure

as an answer. "Come on. We aren't stopping them; at this rate, they'll level the city. We need to find Aven."

There had to be some other path to victory. She just couldn't think of it.

Aven stared out at the battle, panting as he knocked yet another air mage on his ass for trying to toast a soldier. It didn't feel like nearly enough. The darkness fell like a smothering cloak over him, choking hope.

Calling down Sagus, he tried another star spell. Anger, this time. Maybe he could turn them on each other. But no. He winced as the Kavanarian mages only fought harder, sudden ravenous beasts but still single-mindedly focused on Panar. And still only two dozen or so. He couldn't reach them all, and it wasn't helping. If anything, it was hurting. He swept the calming spell across them again, lulling the enraged ones into a temporary sleep. This one didn't last much longer than the first.

He fought off the icy rain, and each time others fought to bring it right back. The earth around Panar was churned and raw; gods only knew what was happening to it back by the camp line. Flames flickered in the darkness before being snuffed out. Lightning struck at the fighting mage slaves, followed sometimes by screams, sometimes by silence.

Screams rang out when mages hit brambles or were assaulted by beetles. The city's catapults loosed stone after stone, most deflected or dodged.

Nothing was working. None of it. Sure it slowed them down, but these mages fought on, losing fewer troops and doing greater damage. It was an equation that was not in Akaria's favor at the moment.

The mages had no choice, really.

They weren't the real enemy. Daes was.

If Aven could cut off this monster's head, the limbs would stop flailing. Or maybe stop collapsing buildings with innocent, unarmed people inside.

Twenty more mages joined the current twenty, then an hour later another twenty, and still the fighting raged on. Somehow distracting them *was* slowing them down. Fog blinded, swords rebelled, vines hindered. But he couldn't free any. He couldn't even *see* Casel now. And eventually he and his friends were going to get tired first, and what then? He needed something better—a plan—but no one had come up with one for actually winning. Only stopping, delaying. And they were doing that.

But this wasn't just ceding the city to an enemy. The entire city was being *destroyed*.

A messenger caught his eye, running fast in royal leathers toward where they were hunkered. "Sire!" the messenger shouted. "Lord Beneral sends word. Ships approach. Armed! From Reilin."

"Reilin—why—" Aven stopped short and swore. Of course. Queen Marielle was from Reilin.

By the gods.

"He's readying the fleet, but if it gets colder, they'll

be trapped in the ice."

"Got it. Go, get out of here." The messenger raced back away from the battlement. He wanted to offer help, maybe some way to melt the ice, but who knew if there'd be a mage available to do it?

Aven caught his breath as a new crushing sound rang out, close by but *behind* him. He turned to see a shop crumble, then the house behind it.

Then another. And *another*.

He offered up a hasty prayer that no one had been inside, but a chill ran down his spine. It wouldn't take terribly long for them to do that to the *entire* city.

He had to do something. *Anything*.

He whirled back, glaring at the Kavanarian mages, the tents across the chasm beyond. Actually, on *this* side of the canyon, one tent sat slightly bigger than the others, and its top was flagged red on top. The head of the monster.

Daes.

He turned his attention to the sky. A backup plan had occurred to him in the dead of the night, and he knew it was time. He was out of other options, besides letting the city be flattened.

Frowning, he pushed the clouds apart and reached up. Not for Casel. Not for Erepha.

No, not this time.

He winced and gritted his teeth as he reached for Masari and pulled down its essence—thick, hot, squirming, rotten. He poured its rage and heat into the dagger in his belt, poured until it would fill no longer. It flowed into the metal, settled there. Kae's book had taught him that much.

Letting go, though, the energy started to race out. He clamped down on the dagger, gradually refilling it back up.

He would have to hold it closed, like a damn bottle with his thumb over the lid. He sighed. Let his opportunity to use it come soon.

He unstrapped the dagger sheath from his belt and wrapped it around his forearm, covering it with his gambeson and the mail that Perik had so valiantly brought. The boy deserved to be more than a servant. Too bad Aven likely wouldn't survive this to raise him up.

Hand and mind clamped over the dagger, he turned back to the field. Devol was hunkered nearby.

"Dev! Devol, I need you to send word. A messenger. Tell them we want to negotiate."

"Negotiate! Aven, you can't. Not with *Kavanar*."

"Look around you, Dev. They're going to destroy the whole city," he shouted. "We have to try."

No one else needed to know. It was too great a risk they'd give the truth away. The dagger felt warm, writhing like a snake inside his sleeve.

Devol's face was dark as he scanned the wreckage. Buildings had collapsed all around them. Rubble was on fire. And that wasn't even on the battlefield yet, where real chaos reigned.

"All right. All right. I'll go. Be careful, son."

Aven nodded, gripped the dagger tighter, and waited.

18   SACRIFICE

Morning light had just cracked the horizon when the Kavanarian group rode out and stopped on the field, signaling they'd accepted his offer to negotiate. Aven sighed, feeling a sense of victory that no other Akarian did. He hid it deep down behind the sigh and got on his horse. The fighting had drifted down to nothing in the wee hours of the night, and Aven had sent his messenger, and here they were.

His finger stayed clamped on the dagger, along with his mind, but he blinked, exhausted. How long would he have to maintain this? He couldn't do it forever.

The Akarian group that rode out was nearly all mages. Devol and Derk rode on either side, Siliana, Jaena, and Ro at the back. All of them armed and armored to the teeth.

Aven stared down Daes the minute he could spot the man. The Kavanarians had their mages too, and a few average soldiers posted around the corners of the group.

But Aven wasn't worried about a violent altercation. Not with what he offered. Daes looked much the same, if better dressed and with a circlet of rubies this time. The queen was there too, to Aven's surprise, placid and statuesque on horseback beside him.

"So, we meet again," said Daes.

"Unfortunately," growled Aven. No reason to feign politeness. Daes wouldn't buy it.

"No courtly formalities?" Daes grinned at the queen. "Not much of a king, is he, Marielle?"

"You're Queen Marielle?" said Aven, faking surprise. "You're not what I expected."

"Why do you say that?" she said in a perfect courtly voice, neither challenging nor sweet, hard to read.

"Well, you're quite lovely, for someone as ruthless and self-serving as Daes."

A corner of her mouth quirked. "Ruthless and self-serving was a welcome change."

"Enough," Daes said, cutting them off.

"Enough courtly niceties for you?" Aven pursed his lips.

"You call that nice?"

"Akarians clearly have a thicker skin."

Daes clenched his jaw for a moment before speaking. "You said you wanted to negotiate a surrender, not trade insults. What do you want?"

"I don't want to see the White City destroyed. Neither should you. And I want us to be left alone, of course. What do *you* want?"

A slow grin spread across Daes's face. "Ah, but what

have I ever wanted? You, of course."

"Well, you can't have him," barked Devol from behind.

"Wait." Aven held up a hand.

Daes's eyes twinkled with amusement. "You know, I didn't believe you when you said you were the only one with the star magic. But now I see it's true, you really haven't told anyone. I want the star magic destroyed, above all things. I want mage slaves never to be freed. Ever. And I want you to become one of them."

"No, Aven, you can't—" Devol started.

Aven held up a hand to silence him again. "If I go with you, you'll leave the city? Leave Akaria? End the war?"

"Well, I can't go quite that easily. I suppose I need the brand too. How else will I make you a slave? I will rip every brick from this city and toss it into the ocean until I find it."

Aven could feel Jaena tense behind him, and what he was about to say was only going to make that worse.

"I'll make you a new one," he said.

Daes stopped short. "What? Liar. You don't know how."

Aven carefully drew out the tattered, leather-bound volume from his cloak, keeping the dagger's energy carefully sealed. "I do know how. Been looking for this?"

Daes hesitated, scowling at him. "If you fail to create it, I'll return. The brand *will* be returned to me, one way or another."

"Yes. It will be," said Aven softly, his voice dark.

"A fair exchange you propose." Daes sounded mildly surprised at that. "But we cannot trust each other. It's doomed."

"Send your troops back first. And your mages. And your queen's fleet of ships. When they're all a day away, I'll go with you."

"Aven, no," Jaena whispered behind him. "Miara wouldn't want this."

That hit him like a stab in the gut, but he showed nothing. "I won't see the city destroyed over me." He turned back to Daes. "The book stays here. When all your armies are back in Kavanar, along with me, they'll send the book by bird, and I'll do what you ask."

Daes had raised his eyebrows. "You… have it all thought out."

Aven nodded.

He could see Daes's wheels turning, but he wouldn't find the catch. There was none. It was a better deal for Daes, who could just wait a week and turn his armies back around to attack Panar without its king. Or its star mage. Aven would never have agreed to it, unless he was truly, truly desperate. Like how he'd feel if he watched his city flattened building by building.

"Fine," said Daes. "My armies will back off. We'd appreciate a clearer road this voyage."

"No promises," Jaena muttered behind him.

"Excellent," said Aven. "I'll have the formal treaties written up and sent to you for signing. And I'll see you here this time tomorrow morning."

Daes nodded, glaring at Aven, searching for the trick. "Indeed."

By the next dawn, Aven was battling exhaustion bordering on delirium. For some portion of the night, he'd fallen asleep for a few hours, Masari's energy dissipating, and he'd had to draw it all down again. The rest was probably worth it, but it racked his nerves. It was too easy to lose the magic, too easy to fumble. And if he did, he'd lose everything.

His mother had obviously not been a fan of his plan. In fact, no one was. Probably because he wasn't telling them the real plan. But even if that plan failed, he still would rather see the fighting stop.

The only positive was that the fighting *had* stopped. Everything had stopped. The creature mages fanned out, attending to the wounded, and earth mages tried to reform the walls as best they could.

The lack of Miara's presence was a constant weight on his shoulders, leaving him a ghost among the living. Without her, there was little for him here. The future he'd wanted was long gone, crushed like the city walls, and if he could go out with a blast and save them all for a little while, it was something.

That mission steadied him as he mounted up and rode out to meet his fate.

"Ready to become a slave, little prince?" Daes called from a distance as they rode up to the meeting point, glee in his voice.

"King," Aven said almost out of reflex, dismounting quickly.

"Neither of those any longer, if you're fulfilling *your* half of this bargain."

Aven stepped forward, headed to Queen Marielle's horse rapidly, and grabbed her hand just as a guard's blade came to rest calmly at his shoulder. It hovered icily by his neck. "I'm pleased to make peace with you, Your Majesty," he said formally, kissing her fingers. She returned the appropriate nod, flushing.

Aven strained his ears, listening, hoping his gamble had paid off. He didn't want to unleash the dagger on Marielle, but he could do it now if he had to, and that would be something. He could ransom her freedom, and perhaps delay the war even longer. But still not forever.

Huffing, Daes dismounted and rounded the horse, snatching Aven's hand away from Marielle's.

Clear of the queen now, a kick came at his side from her guard, and Aven staggered and fell to his knees, being sure to fall forward toward Daes. Daes wisely moved back. Just a little too far. He needed him closer. He couldn't quite get a grip, as Daes had torn his fingers away from Marielle.

"Oh," Daes said, feigning disinterest, but his voice and face were more dark and brutal than ever. "Before we get too far, I have a message for you."

"A message?" said Aven slowly. He inched forward, away from Marielle and toward Daes.

Pulling something from his black gambeson, Daes dropped it on the dusty grass at Aven's knees.

Strands of red hair, tied with simple twine. Not as long as Miara's, shorter. But he knew.

Daes bent down and glared at Aven. "Your knight friend sends her regards."

Aven glared back, eyes suddenly wild and breath heavy. "Where is she, you bastard?" he whispered.

"I actually don't know. The knight won't tell me. I presume she's alive but who knows. The Devoted prefer to kill their prey, you know. If not now, then eventually."

Aven was still shaking with rage when he realized Daes was moving back, his opportunity passing. No…

Daes grinned. "But now there will be nothing you can do about it, really. Let's get on with this. Oh, also, seize them." He pointed at the rest of the Akarians.

The guards rushed forward, and swords slid out of scabbards, ringing in the morning air.

"No! Just me was the deal," Aven shouted. "You can't take them."

"Looks like you're no longer in much position to bargain, Star Mage." Daes stepped closer and moved to push Aven to the ground, glowering again.

Aven ripped the dagger from the arm sheath and lunged.

Daes was enough of a fighter for his instincts to flare. He staggered back, blocking with his arms. But he was expecting a stab. And that was not at all Aven's goal.

Aven's free hand snaked out and caught Daes's, and Aven viciously pressed the blade to his palm. The blade glowed with red, fiery, writhing energy, and it hissed as it met flesh like it was truly on fire. Aven pressed down, determined to pour every ounce of energy he could into Daes.

He held it as Daes screamed.

He held it as the guards rushed him, as chaos broke around him.

He held it as the star magic, the evil star magic, flew out of him and bound Daes to Aven's very soul.

Masari. Slavery.

When he finally let go, Daes fell back, skittering away like a crab. Staring at his palm.

Around them, everyone else was fighting. Except Marielle, who stared, fear in her eyes.

"Order them to stop," Aven said, rising easily, voice hard as steel.

Daes glared incredulously, then cried out as the pain seared his hand anew. The horror in his eyes only grew.

"By the gods…" he whispered. "No, it's not possible, *I'm* the Master, not you—"

"Do it!" Aven ordered. "Now."

"Stop, stop—" Daes shouted. "All of you!" Then he looked shocked at his own words as the men backed away. The tumult quieted, except for the sound of feathery wings landing.

Aven stepped closer to Daes.

"You're supposed to be coming with me," Daes said weakly. "I… I won."

"I'm not going anywhere." Aven shook his head.

"But—but—"

"Get up."

Gritting his teeth and clutching his palm, Daes rose.

"How's it feel," Aven said, "to do things against your will? Things you wouldn't choose? Things you hate?"

"No," Marielle whispered.

But Aven had no sympathy for her or any of them now. "This is over. From now on, you belong to me."

Daes's eyes widened in horror. Then, a heartbeat later, his gaze darted over Aven's shoulder and widened even further.

Aven spun around.

He caught his breath. For a moment, he wondered if the exhaustion or the awful magic was making him hallucinate, but no. It was her.

Miara stood before him—a beautiful, magnificent thing, a gorgeous creature, radiating might. Her hair was chopped short, falling bluntly to her chin, and three pairs of massive wings like an eagle's stretched out from her back, the largest the breadth of a man, all the way down to the smallest near her elbows. Relief cascaded over him. She was alive, truly alive, more alive then ever.

But her eyes were dark.

Gods and ancestors. He swallowed hard. This was the price he'd thought he'd been willing to pay, the risk he'd been willing to take. He'd saved the city.

Had he lost her in the process?

"Miara—" he started, and he took a step forward, but the realization that this moment of victory was truly a defeat had drained him of all strength. He stumbled and collapsed to the earth.

Miara landed and shook out her wings. Growing wings from her own body had the convenient side effect of allowing her to land faster, without transforming, and she dropped to the earth in an immediate run. "Aven!"

He didn't hear her. He was standing by a horse, talking to someone. What was this strange meeting? Why was there no battle, even though huge swaths of Panar were devastated? What was going on?

He finally turned toward her as she stopped, a few feet short of him. His eyes met hers in a bleak look of surprise. "Miara—" He looked relieved to see her, but stunned. Wary, even. He took a step forward.

And collapsed to the ground.

She rushed forward, barely able to hold him up. She poured energy in, stealing recklessly from those around them. "Are you all right?"

"I'm sorry," he whispered. "I had to. I—"

She pressed a finger to his lips to quiet him. But he lurched away from her, collapsing to the ground again, and he let out a groan.

"By the gods, Aven!" She crouched at his side and poured more energy in, but it didn't seem to do any good.

He glanced at a man behind him, and Miara followed his gaze. She gasped and took an involuntary step back.

Daes.

"Get on your horse and send your guards back," Aven

ordered hoarsely.

Daes's face contorted in an expression she knew all too well.

"Don't make me kill you," Aven growled.

Daes gritted his teeth and let out his own low growl. "You vile son of a—"

Aven narrowed his eyes, and Daes gasped, shaking his hand, clearly in pain. "What, you don't find being a slave pleasant? I can do worse than this," said Aven calmly.

Daes gasped for breath, falling forward, and then reared back. "Fine! Fine!" He strode over quickly, got on the horse, and looked at his guards. "Go on. Take Marielle and go. Retreat. Go back to Kavanar."

Miara's mouth fell open as she realized what she was seeing. What Aven had done.

The groans—he must be in extreme pain. She tightened her grip on his shoulder, helping him to his feet. He looked down at her, nodding his gratitude for her help.

A man from the right cleared his throat. "Why should I not just crush this city to the ground anyway?"

Aven turned sharply and glared. "Who are you?"

"General Vusamon, commander of these Kavanarian armies. My lord and lady are clearly under duress; perhaps I should execute their former orders…?" His voice was leading, as if suggesting Aven present another option.

"Without your mages, we can still fight you off," Aven said, an edge of threat to his voice.

"Who will rule Kavanar?" the general asked briskly. "Will you to turn it over to some minor noble you can puppet? Do you mean to take the nation as your own?"

"As a matter of fact, I do," Aven said slowly. "It may take an order from Marielle. Or it may take a longer campaign to force the nobles to accept it. But I won't tolerate the evil that's brewed in Kavanar any longer."

Miara caught her breath.

"Hmm," said Vusamon thoughtfully. "And when this conquest of yours is over—"

"Spoken like a true patriot," Daes snapped.

"—do you plan to extend your typical Akarian practices to the Kavanarian military?"

"Such as?" Aven said, frowning.

"Such as a standing, paid army that's trained and well-supported by the crown?"

Aven raised an eyebrow. "If your soldiers can swallow their rivalry, that's how I'd prefer it."

Vusamon smiled. "Then our goals are in alignment. I offer my regiments to your command, Your Highness."

"You traitor," Daes snapped.

Vusamon looked at him through slitted eyes. "As if you'd do differently in my position. The Kavanarian monarchy is rotten and impotent. You are defeated. Why should I not choose my own master, one that will value my skills and my calling rather than neglect them?"

Daes scowled bitterly, but didn't disagree.

Vusamon glanced back at Aven. "I will return to my camp and await your orders, Your Highness."

Aven leaned hard against her as they watched the general ride away. The guards were gathering around

Marielle, preparing to escort her in the same direction.

"Well, that was unexpected," Miara said.

"You look magnificent," he said quietly. "I thought you were dead. I thought I'd never see you again."

"Well, my dress has seen better days. But I'm no worse for the wear." She smiled, crooked and a little shy.

"No." A powerful word from Marielle cut through their reverie. She'd started to follow the guards, but turned and angled her horse back. "I'm not leaving."

"Marielle, you will do as I say—" Daes snapped.

"No." She glared daggers at him. "I am the reigning monarch here, and I choose my actions, not you. And I'm choosing to go with you."

Daes opened his mouth to argue again.

Aven turned to Devol. "Take them to Ranok. Put them in the dungeons until we can decide what to do with them."

"He will not!" Daes shouted.

"Yes, he will, and so will you," said Aven, voice brutal. Daes stared, then looked down at his palm once again. "You will go wherever Master of Arms Devol tells you to, and you won't put up a fight."

At that, Daes was too stunned to do anything other than be led away, Marielle in tow.

"You did it," Miara whispered. "You really did it."

"C'mon," called Jaena. "Let's go back inside."

Miara helped Aven to his horse, and she flew alongside them back into the battered, beaten shell of the White City.

Inside, he had no time for prisoners. No time for planning. No time for responses. Nothing. There were others who could handle it. He dragged Miara into the nearest room, which happened to be a library, ordered everyone out, and slammed the door, so they could be alone.

He had to know. He had to get what was coming, so he could start dealing with it or die trying.

"Miara, Miara, I'm so sorry, I had no choice, I—" What he'd hoped would be a rational explanation came out a wandering, incoherent mess as he gripped her shoulders and searched for words to forgive the unforgivable.

She covered his apologies with a sudden kiss, brief and firm. And he stopped still for a heartbeat before returning her kiss—ravenously. Something in him cracked and broke, something made of fear and despair, and his heart soared up through its remnants, casting the brittle pieces of horror and anguish aside as it headed toward the sun.

He broke away abruptly. "You're not mad? You don't hate me?"

"No," she said softly. "Well, I'm a little bit scared of you, to be honest. But how could I hate you?"

"I had no other option. I swear to you. They were going to level the city."

"I know. I know. I saw the walls. I saw the Tall Master, too."

"You did? Where?"

"Near Dramsren. I killed him."

"You killed him?"

"Yes. But before that, I finally understood. The map could have stopped him. I'm sorry for judging you so harshly. I've seen a lot of evils in the world, but all-out war was something… different. I underestimated it. The senseless loss, the chaos, the pointlessness of it all…" She trailed off, blinking away tears.

He clung to her, wrapping his arms around her shoulders and pulling her closer. "Don't be sorry. Let's not be, either of us."

She nodded and started to smile, shaking off the sadness a little. "We were both sort of right."

" 'Sort of' right. How's that for justice? For morality?" He smiled down at her bitterly.

She smiled more brightly back. "Maybe 'sort of right' is the best anyone can really do."

He nodded. "And maybe, just maybe, it's over now."

She sighed and clung back to him. "Yes. It's time to rebuild."

19   BEGINNINGS

The clanging of the dungeon doors was all the warning Daes had. He staggered forward, and was not surprised to see the star mage entering, the rebellious creature mage by his side. Daes gritted his teeth.

Marielle stood and came calmly to the front of her cell, separate from and opposite Daes's, to his dismay.

"Queen Marielle," the Akarian started. "I'm of a mind to believe you were an innocent bystander in this, even with a fleet of your ships at my doorstep. I think perhaps I should send you back to your family on said ships, who've claimed this was all a miscommunication and they were just looking for safe harbor. Am I wrong to assume so?"

Daes wanted to lunge through the bars and shove him away from her, but that would only reveal another way to control Daes, if the Akarian hadn't guessed it already.

"Your Highness, if I may..." Marielle clasped her

hands gracefully in front of her and glanced at Daes. As their eyes locked, she hesitated.

Daes gritted his teeth but held her gaze, forcing careful, deep breaths through his flared nostrils. He knew what could come next, and none of it was something he'd ever wanted to see. What would come out of her mouth? What would it be—vying for a place in Akarian court, an offer to be mistress rather than prisoner, lies, groveling on her knees, what? He pressed his eyes shut, not that that did much of anything. He would still hear it all, see it burned in his memory.

He wished he could shut them out completely. The Akarian should have killed him already.

"I know I am in no position to make requests, Your Highness," she said. "I hold no particular claim over Kavanar, so it does not pain me to quit it. If you should order me to return to my father, if you were to be so magnanimous, I would readily obey your wishes, of course. And if you were to ask for my head on a platter, you would have every right."

"I have no desire for that," the Akarian said, surprising Daes a little. In fact, it sent a sliver of fear into Daes's heart, much as he didn't want to admit it. If the Akarian didn't mean to execute Daes and Marielle publicly, then what might he have planned? Torture? Public humiliation? The gods knew there were many things worse than death. He had a feeling he was about to learn some of them firsthand.

"I know it is sometimes customary to have defeated

queens marry those in power to solidify their hold over newly acquired lands," she said, sweet and smooth as ever. Daes's fists tightened around the bars, but he said nothing.

"That is not our custom," said the Akarian coldly. Daes glanced at the creature mage standing beside him. Betrothed, they had said. Indeed. That did ease Daes's mind a bit.

"Well, I am coupled but as of now not married, should you be concerned about the option. However, I would make a different request of you, if I may."

"Request all you like. What is it?" The Akarian's voice was wary.

She curtsied low now, knees almost touching the floor. Here it comes, he thought. What ploy would this be? "I would ask, if it would at all please you, Your Highness, that I stay with my lord in his sentence. Wherever you are taking him, I would like to go."

Daes felt his heart skip a beat. "Marielle—no," he said without thinking. She didn't turn toward him, but her shoulders straightened, pushed back slightly, her chin raised. She was set upon this, he could see. But why? "Think about what you're doing. Don't do this to yourself."

Now she finally glanced at him, but her look told him nothing. She turned back to the Akarian, waiting.

Why would she—oh.

He finally had a definitive answer, didn't he? If she really felt anything for him. If she'd only wanted her husband offed, or if she'd actually wanted *him*. Here was his answer. Was it the one that he wanted?

"I'll think about it," growled the Akarian. "Later."

The two of them walked out, leaving Daes and Marielle alone in this part of the dungeon. The very minute they were gone, he set upon her.

"How can you do this?" he demanded. "You have your whole life ahead of you."

"A life of what? I have spent my whole life alone. I have searched, I have talked, I've rolled between the sheets of both highborn and low. And yet never have I found anyone loyal. No one who treated me as a friend."

He said nothing for a moment, thinking. Highborn and low? He'd have to ask about that—some other time. If such a time ever occurred. Had her days truly been so uniformly lonely?

"Until I met you," she said, "I'd gone from loneliness to horror to torture to apathy, then back around the meadow for another tour of pain."

"But I've *failed*, Marielle. I've failed at that as completely as I possibly could have. You're not safe, and how can you be happy? Why they haven't killed me, I'll never know. I've got half a mind to try to hang myself from these bars."

Even as he said it, though, the burning in his hand told him that doing so was not truly an option. But she didn't need to know that.

"Please don't," she said, the perfectly soft command of a true queen.

"I don't know why you are doing this, Marielle."

"Why? Have you even *tried* to see this from my point

of view? I know you cared much about Kavanar, and this war. I have cared for none of it but you."

He opened his mouth to speak, but faltered.

She shrugged. "If the choice is between safe agony and happy death, I choose death."

He reeled back an inch at the bluntness of her words, at the sincerity creasing her brow, at the entreaty in her frown. "I don't want you to choose death," he said numbly, for once letting his guard fall away. "I have destroyed nearly everything I ever fought so hard to have. I will not destroy you too."

"It is not your choice," she said gently. "And besides, you aren't destroying me. I don't think they are going to kill us."

He scowled bitterly. "They are most likely waiting to publicly execute us in the most horrifying way they can think of. And they need time to think of it."

She shook her head, smiling. "Then we'll die together."

"Yes," he said simply. "Yes, I suppose we will. I hope you don't live to regret this."

"Who doesn't have regrets? But if we live, I do not think you will be one of them."

Niat wasn't sure anything could have been stranger than arriving back in Panar with Thel at her side. They'd left under duress, sneering enemies, and had returned... something much more. People who had spent long nights huddled together for warmth—and for the joy of it—kissing sweetly until sunrise some days it seemed, but never any further. People who had once argued bitterly now discussing all manner of science and history as they walked and rode their way back south.

People who had stalled an army together.

And to think, all along, she had been so afraid to love him. But following her temple, her governess, their teachings—it had all gotten her nothing. Less than nothing, in fact. It had destroyed her faith in other people.

Instead, following her heart had gotten her everything. Was it her heart she'd followed? Some keen sense of intuition? Her mind, even? It had always known better than anyone that Thel had offered the best chance of survival all along. Could it have been something deeper? The voice of the goddess herself? Perhaps there was no difference between that holy voice and the voice of her own heart, speaking one and the same.

Whatever the source of inner wisdom, however long she'd fought it, she was glad she'd succumbed.

The two of them walked through the rock-strewn streets. Whole buildings lay as piles of rubble, and large boulders sat in the streets. People were quietly buzzing around them, beginning the repairs, looking for any dead, but the damage to the city was shocking. Niat had never seen anything like this.

They arrived on foot to the gates of Ranok, and when the first guards spotted Thel, he ran out, shouting, "Fetch the king! Get King Aven! Prince Thel has returned!"

"*King* Aven?" Thel mumbled behind her. "That's new."

Niat was glad that it was actually Queen Elise that appeared first. That whole horrible vote was like something from another lifetime—something she wanted to forget.

Elise flung herself wildly at Thel, a wild storm of laughter and tears and hugs. Niat smiled as she dismounted, although inside there was always that slight ache, that knowledge that something had stolen her mother from her. Not Niat, whatever her father thought, but something. Ah, well… She was glad to see Thel happy.

"I missed you, too, Mother," he said, laughing. "But is there any sign of Father?"

Elise stopped short, frozen. "Oh. I forgot you didn't know. He's… yes, Miara rescued him from the hands of Kavanarian mage slaves. But he hasn't recovered. We can't seem to heal him. I've spent days trying to heal him, this way and that, fighting it. But I think it's a losing battle, Thel."

Thel only stared, as if such a development was impossible, inconceivable.

"Aven has been made king, for this whole time you've been gone," Elise muttered.

"Can we see him?" said Niat, stepping up to Thel now and eying him with concern. She took his arm, as she had a dozen times on their journey back.

Thel nodded numbly. "Yes—yes, can we?"

Elise's eyebrow rose, her eyes flicking to their interlocked arms, but she said nothing of it. "Come. This way."

Thel rushed to Samul's side, but Niat stopped cold in

the doorway, the vision flashing back through her mind. The poisoner, the arrows, the man riding, the woman tending him. Gods... she'd seen all this before.

She knew the antidote to anfi, too. The hard part was determining if it *was* anfi at all, and the vision had handled that.

She seized a nearby servant's arm. "Get me eight selnoetia branches, three apples, a handful of sage, three drams of maple sap, a walnut, and a mortar and pestle. Can you do that?"

"What is it?" said Thel, approaching. "Everything okay?"

"I had a vision of him, Thel. I saw the poison they put on the arrows." She was probably saying that with entirely too much joviality.

Elise darted forward. "What does that mean?"

"I can cure him."

Aven sighed, eying Jaena and Miara talking by the fire. He sat behind his desk in his rooms, waiting for Marielle to be brought in. He'd consented to her request to discuss her plea once again only because he still didn't know what to do with Daes. Killing the man seemed both unjust, as he was now utterly defenseless, and also not nearly enough punishment for someone who had made so many suffer for so long. But if he was going to talk to the Kavanarian queen, he wanted Miara and Jaena present. Those he'd made suffer personally, beyond Aven, would be his advisers.

"Good evening, Your Highness," said Marielle as she arrived, curtsying low.

"What did you want to speak to me about, my lady?" he said, trying not to snap at her. Different nations had different courtly standards, but he had little patience for pomp and spectacle.

Fortunately, Marielle cut to the chase. "I think he's a good man, you know."

He raised his eyebrows. "A good man who's willing to kidnap his enemies from their homes, when they haven't done anything against him? Who's willing to kill anyone who might endanger his power?"

"Are you not doing the same thing?"

"No. We were at peace with Kavanar."

She sighed. "I know, I know."

"What about a man who forces hundreds to work against their will, without pay, for their lifetimes, under threat of torture and worse? All for his own selfish needs?"

"Truth be told, sire, I don't believe they were for his selfish needs. Not in his mind, anyway. But I know it is unconscionable. I have always known, and turned an eye away."

"Why?"

"Because he was kind to me," she said simply.

Aven blinked. He wasn't sure what he had expected, but it hadn't been that. There was a tenderness to her voice, a real concern. He had assumed it had all been a plot for mutually greater power, but... was it? "And what about your former husband? Quite convenient I facilitated him falling out of that window."

"I imagine without your assistance, we'd have had a much harder time. You certainly made things easier for us." She stopped and smiled slightly. "Bet you didn't count on that."

He snorted. "No. I didn't."

She furrowed her brow. "What makes a good man? I have endured many unkindnesses, but none from Daes. My husband was… Let's just say I feel I no guilt for what we did. The world is better off without him."

From his encounters with Demikin, Aven did not find that particularly surprising. But he said nothing.

"Let me ask you, my lord—what do you think Daes's life would have been like if he'd been born in Akaria?"

Aven scowled at her, silent. He wasn't sure that was a question he wanted to answer.

"Daes is quite possibly the first person ever to be kind to me."

Aven leaned back in his chair and propped a boot up beside him, putting his elbow to his knee. "Not without gain for himself."

"You would think that, but I believe he would have preferred not to take the risk. Perhaps I am the fool." She looked thoughtful. "But I think not."

"What do you want, Marielle?"

"I want you not to execute him, of course."

"Can you truly tell me the world will be better with him in it?"

"*My* world will be."

"What about everyone else's?" He glanced at Jaena and Miara by the fire. They were rapt, faces sad.

Marielle sighed. "Perhaps not. But I have had enough life without purpose. Without kindness. Without love, to be frank. I don't care to continue without it."

He said nothing to the threat.

"I came to ask." She paused. Again, he sat in only stony silence. "Or to barter or negotiate, if possible." She stepped forward, closer. "I have little left. Is there something… I could offer you?" She swallowed and raised her chin, threw her shoulders back, whether to draw attention to her fragile, exposed neck or to cling to her pride, he wasn't sure. "In exchange for his life, I would do a great deal, as much as he'd prefer I wouldn't."

He shook his head, just staring, tired, exhausted. But mostly surprised. Surprised that she had actually swayed his opinion with such an argument. Surprised that someone like Daes had attracted anyone who loved him, let alone someone logical and well-spoken. And self-sacrificing.

"Perhaps it is true even the most evil have their reasons to sin," he said softly. "I know I do."

She swallowed. Was she shaking? He frowned. Ah, she thought he meant the price was steeper than it truly was. "Is there something I can offer, sire? Only in exchange for his life."

"Yes, there's something," he said, not disabusing her of her fear just yet. "But what about his freedom?"

"How could you trust such a thing? I don't see how

you could grant any such request."

"That is very wise of you. But you're sure you would join him? In imprisonment? In relative poverty to what you've known?"

"Do you mean to starve us in the dungeon for the rest of our days, sire?"

"I don't know what I plan to do with you yet."

Her face fell further. "So… you do mean to keep me? Us?"

He looked to Miara and Jaena again, standing arm in arm by the fire. Miara gave him a subtle nod, and although Jaena frowned, she gave him a slight nod too.

He must never go free, said Miara silently. *And we must give him something awful to do.*

Aven snorted, trying not to reveal the silent exchange. *I have enough coal mines to keep him busy till the end of his days.*

Are they very dark and dirty? Awful places?

Yes, quite.

Then that sounds excellent.

"Yes. You've convinced me. But in exchange, you'll live in confinement, under guard. And you'll promise me you and your husband— You do intend to marry him, do you not?"

Relief washed over Marielle mixed with shock. "Yes, my lord. That had already been the plan."

"You must promise me you'll find some way to make the world a *better* place, on top of your assigned work." Her eyes widened as he spoke. "For mages," he added harshly.

She stared, unsure now.

"Now go. I'll send you off to work soon, but I will return to check in on your progress."

She turned and was led out by the remaining guards, still looking stunned.

He got up and strode to the fire beside them. "Odd, wasn't it?"

They both nodded.

"Do you think we should have killed him?"

Miara shrugged. "What does the law decree?"

"Wise woman. But for war criminals, death or imprisonment indefinitely are both just punishments."

"He deserves to rot in seven *thousand* hells," said Jaena, glaring at the fire. "But killing him? Then I won't get to see him suffer in any hells at all." She gave them a stern look that faded into a smile. "Just promise me you'll find some way to make him work for his livelihood, Aven. He shouldn't get to lie around plowing her all day. That's no punishment."

Miara burst out laughing. "At the very least, snow shoveling in the streets right away, eh?"

"I know, manure shoveling in the spring," said Jaena, still smiling.

"I'm thinking the family coal mines," Aven said, shrugging. "Or all of the above. But trust me, the frustration and humiliation of slavery will be its own punishment for him. That said, he can also help clean up this mess he made. Rebuild the city. He'll help us dismantle Mage Hall, find the slaves new homes, livelihoods, food. It's going to be a lot of work."

"Good thing you have some unpaid labor on hand to make up for it." Jaena's eyes twinkled.

"What about Lord Sven?" asked Miara. "What's to become of him?"

"I've sent Dyon and a regiment to drag him out of his hole. He'll answer for his crimes. I thought perhaps Niat could take over his Assemblyship for him."

Jaena gaped. "The priestess who voted against you? His daughter?"

"Thel has had some... very positive things to say about her."

Miara suppressed a giggle.

"There's the Devoted too," he added. "We'll rout them out of Akaria, and Kavanar too. Then we'll see what we can do about their monastery in Takar."

Jaena's eyes widened. "The work will never end. Miara, wasn't there someone else you ran into? Some evil noble or something?"

"A petty constable. Paid him a visit while you were busy negotiating the Reilins out of our harbor." She smiled. "He won't be pushing people around again anytime soon. Being turned into a rat will do that to you."

"A rat?" Aven raised his eyebrows.

"Just temporarily. To make an example." Miara grinned.

"What a wicked queen," Jaena said, laughing. "Fear your rat-transforming wrath."

Now Miara really did giggle. "Gods, it really is over, isn't it?"

Aven reached out, slipped his arm around her waist, and pulled her close. "It sure is, my love. It sure is."

When they rode over the crest of the last mountain pass, Niat caught her breath, slowing her horse. It had been a long, slow ride—she wasn't used to riding horses, and her companions hadn't pushed her. She was as eager to arrive at their destination as anyone, except maybe Thel.

But as the pale stone bridge stretched out before her, her memory swirled, and she found herself dismounting.

"Niat?" The clink of metal and leather told her he was dismounting too, as of course he would. He already had. She already knew he would. "Is everything all right?"

She took a few stiff steps forward. The gray fortress was nestled into the mountain before her, a fearsome combination of sternness and safety, and the broad doors were just slowly heaving open. The watch towers had signaled their arrival.

Something in her stirred, danced, laughed, a whirlpool of visions twisting just below the surface of her mind. Much waited for her here. And whoever or whatever granted her the visions didn't quite want to spoil it. For now, the future didn't intrude.

He stepped up beside her, and she turned, smiling radiantly. "Everything is fine."

Thel smiled back, a little uneasily, his eyes searching her face. Then he held out a palm. "Estun. My home."

A home that was nothing like a temple, that was a lifetime away from the sea. A home where rock and earth surrounded all. There would be books, too, that he wanted to show her, and roaring fires and long talks and swords and brandy and laughter and children and—

The whirlpool swelled almost to overflowing—giddy, almost drunk. She fought the future and leapt into the present, throwing her arms around his neck and pressing her lips to his.

She was still smiling when the kiss faded, and the whirlpool with it.

"And now my home as well," she said, turning to face it.

The horses shifted impatiently behind them. He slipped an arm around her waist and squeezed her briefly against him. "I hope you like it as much as you think you will."

Fat snowflakes started to fall, dancing and swirling around them as she surveyed the bridge, the fortress, the glorious mountains around them, and the few cheery blue patches of sky. All things she had seen before in her mind, now before her for real this time. Things she hoped to see many, many times.

"I'm quite positive I'll be happy here." She slipped her arm around his waist too.

"I'm told it's a little... cold. Drafty."

She squeezed him back, just as he had. "With you around? I'm not worried."

Warm wind caressed Jaena's cheeks. It meandered across her neck, swept her collarbone, cooled her in the hot southern sun. She forced a breath. In her nose, out her mouth, in her nose, out her mouth. The water lapped against the side of the boat, deceptively peaceful, stirred by the persistent dipping and dragging of the oars in Ro's hands.

"Almost there," he said gently.

Maybe she'd get through the rest of the trip without throwing up. Or, maybe only one more time. Gods help her.

The glorious crystal blue of the water sparkled more brightly as they went over a particularly high wave, and she squinted her eyes shut, glad he wasn't as seasick as she was. Or perhaps it wasn't just the motion, maybe the earth was just too far away. She reached down for it, so very far down, almost dizzyingly beyond reach.

But that was just why they'd picked this very spot.

Keeping her eyes closed and breathing carefully through her nose, she tried to focus on the fortifying heat of the sun. "This is worth it," she told herself. "This is worth it."

He laughed softly. "This is probably far enough. Feel how deep it is?"

"Yes," she breathed.

"Think this is good?" He'd stopped rowing, not that that stabilized the small rowboat much.

She nodded. "You know, if the wrong wave comes by, we're done for out here." The rowboat was much too small for how far they were from shore. But they couldn't have operated anything else alone. Neither of them were seafarers. She risked a glance at the beauty of the coastline beyond, her eyes widening at how distant it appeared to be.

"We have ways of protecting ourselves," he said with a knowing smile. "Don't we?"

She nodded. She might be too panicked if such "ways" were needed, but she doubted he would be. He brushed a hand over his hair, tucking back a stray strand of white that had escaped, and he smiled at her.

"Ready?"

She nodded.

He twisted and reached behind him, pulling open the pack, opening the pack inside that, and unhooking the case inside that one.

And then there it was. The long, nondescript metal pole, so seemingly banal, even harmless. Any passing ship would have thought them insane to stare at it with such consequence. And on her part, such hate.

He raised it up. "You do the honors."

She reached out and took it by its middle. She wasn't anyone who would wield this as a weapon by the handle, and she damn sure wasn't touching the circular knot at the end that had so welted and scarred her, inside and out. Her and hundreds of others. Maybe thousands, over the years. Maybe even that wasn't enough.

"For you, Dekana," she said, raising her face up to the few clouds ambling through the perfect blue sky. "I'd rather have you back, but this is the best I can do."

Lifting it from his hands, she cast the evil thing into the water, throwing it like a harpoon, wanting it away from her as quickly as her muscles would allow.

The ocean swallowed it with an insignificant splash. She followed the metal as it drifted down, traced it with her mind. Ro's eyes closed, working, following it too.

As it neared the sand, she parted the earth, aching at the disturbance as she sensed creatures flitting away from inside the wet ocean floor. But they would find other homes. And hopefully, the brand wouldn't.

She parted the sand further and further until she found deeper earth, shoving wet soil aside and hitting rock and shearing a crack straight through that too.

Into it the brand tumbled, and then it settled, quiet and still in the dark, gentle water.

As fitting a tomb as she could devise.

Together, they filled the rock and earth and sand back in, burying it as deeply as they could manage. And then, realizing she'd closed her eyes, she opened them and met Ro's gaze.

"It's over," he said, his eyes warm and intent on her.

"I hope so," she said warily. "At least for now."

"Either way, we've done our best. And that's all we ever can do."

She smiled grudgingly. "You're right."

"Dekana would be proud of you."

Now her smile grew truer, more sincere if tinged with sadness. "I hope so."

"So, want to take this little boat back to Evrical? I've

heard it's a scenic journey along the cost." He grinned.

She snorted. "Get me out of here, will you? Haven't you seen me throw up enough?"

He chuckled as he took up the oars again. "As I intend to stick around for a lifetime, I'm pretty sure this is a small fraction of what I plan to endure."

She ducked her head, hiding her pleasure at his words. It felt dangerous, too optimistic to be effervescently happy at a moment like this, even though the feeling was stubbornly bubbling up inside her. "Ugh, damn you and your clever quips, *you* don't have to come up with clever comebacks while nauseated."

"That depends on what we eat tonight. You might get lucky and get your revenge."

She caught his eyes with a look of concern that melted to shaking her head. "I've had enough revenge for one lifetime, Tharomar. All I want to do now is fall asleep on the beach with you."

"That, my dear wife, can be arranged."

She flushed at the term, still fresh and strange in her ears. "And maybe have some shrimp later."

"I believe we can make that happen."

"And see if we can peddle any of our wares to those friendly villagers. Or that trader with the cart we saw by the road. Or—"

He laughed. "You will never be satisfied, my love. Don't forget we've already acquired enough vanilla to drown an army—and to fulfill our promises to our great queen and king."

"But I'm still looking for these fabled sugared violets. Someone has to have some."

"We can go into the city tomorrow, now that this work is done. Maybe they'll even have sugared rose petals or lilies."

"Hey, my merchant empire has to start somewhere."

"It already has, my dear, it already has."

The trees stood like pillars of a cathedral, tall and black and reaching their graceful arms up into a blue sky already streaked with purple and orange. Miara hugged her arms around her, gripping her shoulders tightly and raising her face into the late-day sunlight. The cloak was smooth under her fingers, silk lined, with layers upon layers that left her warm in spite of the crisp chill in the air.

A thin snow blanketed the earth, hiding just for one day all the imperfections of the world. It reached out like an interminable plane, dotted only with the tall trees, until it reached the water's edge.

Lake Senokin.

They'd finally made it.

The water looked dark, almost black from here, and she could see no one. Indeed, who would be here this time of year, save people as crazy as them? The priestess's small hut huddled near the water's edge and puffed warm, welcoming smoke from its chimney. Had it been another day, she'd have longed to head inside. Take shelter. Drink some warm wine, close her eyes, sleep the day away. She could do that, now that she wasn't a slave. She didn't, but technically she could. No amount of sleep seemed enough just yet, though, after the days in her crystal prison. Someday she'd get her fill. Might not be anytime soon.

Winter wind danced the hair across her face and up toward the sky as it sent small ripples along the water. She smiled at its caress. It was not just the wind of the gods that swirled across her skin. It was him. Beckoning her.

It was time.

She followed the path the priestess had shown her the day before. Her feet were the first to trod across this snow, leaving fresh tracks that her cloak swirled and dusted into a wide trail behind her. The trail was marked by stones, now only small white rises by a tree trunk or two, but she didn't miss them. She remembered the way. She might never forget it.

The cave awaited her at the end, the pool inside a strangely vivid blue, the air humid and wet and close all of a sudden. A slight crack in the cavern roof let in dying sunlight, but she took the flint and steel waiting and lit the torches solemnly placed there the day before.

She removed the cloak, removed the robe underneath. Removed everything and shivered in the frigid air, slipping quickly into the water. Warmth enveloped her, seeping slowly into her very core, and steam rose in a foggy mist around her face. She leaned against the far wall of the pool and closed her eyes.

It was time to wait now, for the sun to dip its final

path below the horizon.

Akarians and their strange customs. Kalan—who it turned out had been hiding in the Ranok kitchens and then her home for quite some time in the chaos—had wanted to attend her, but Miara had held true to the most traditional path of coming alone. They were her customs now too, weren't they? To some degree. There had been a day they were so foreign to her, when she'd dipped into Aven's mind and seen them for the first time, from his perspective, over the awkward jolting of that wagon. The memory brought a flush to her cheeks even now.

It'd seemed like they'd never make it out of there. How much more had they endured, overcome, since then?

She let the quiet of the forest smooth her thoughts, let the heat of the water permeate her body, to every strained muscle, to her bloodied hands, to bruises that were gone but not forgotten, to the ache of seeing so much of Panar crushed to dust by Daes's hand.

They'd stopped him, though. They'd stopped it all. It was over.

Mage Hall had been torn apart, first by the arriving Akarians and next by the unbranded slaves freed from the dungeons, from the drugs, from even a nearby mine. Teron had been lucky to find his mother in the chaos. Seulka—the Mistress—had been caught by some of the unbranded slaves, who'd been close to killing her before Akarian soldiers had intervened and thrown her in Mage Hall's own dungeons. The Fat Master, once they'd broken through his many locks and separated him from a hideous mound of gold coin and brass trinkets, had joined her there. Now Dom was overseeing bringing them back to Panar to face their crimes.

Seeing Mage Hall crumble made her sad in some small way. It had been a horrible place, but the place of her childhood too. Where her father had tucked her in at night. Where she'd taught Luha to ride a horse. Was Kres roaming free in the Kavanarian countryside, since the stables had been burned to ashes and torn asunder?

But most of her was simply relieved. Like smoke vanishing into the blue sky above, its mark upon the world was over now. The mages it'd held were free, or they soon would be. Aven, Derk, and Wunik had been nearly killing themselves undoing it all, bathing that one dark corner of Kavanar in starlight.

And thank the gods for that. For all of it.

Sometime later, she opened her eyes. Was that the splash of the priestess in the water? Darkness had nearly fallen, and Miara jumped to alert, her heart racing faster, those almost-relaxed muscles tensing once again.

But from the other side of the pool, she just barely made out the priestess's dark hair, her bronze skin, the white ghost of her robe swirling like a wildflower in the waters and clinging to her wet shoulders.

"Miara?" she called in a rich, low voice. Miara thought the priestess might have been Takaran once upon a time. How funny that she hailed from a people who loved such large weddings but now officiated over the quiet-est, smallest way in the world for two people to become husband and wife.

"I'm here," she responded, moving toward the voice. Away from the torches. Further into the darkness.

The rumble of the small waterfall grew louder as she followed the priestess through the waters. Here these pools tumbled into the lake, fog rising up on all sides, hiding anything but the barest glimpse of the form ahead of her as she slipped out of the water that'd grown almost too hot now. She followed the priestess quietly down the stone steps, no different at the moment than the day she was born.

She heard rather than saw the priestess splash into the lake, and then she was at the last step, the cold waters of Senokin lapping at her feet.

Taking a deep breath, she stepped out, and cold water swallowed her, slid across her skin, not nearly as frigid as she'd expected but instead almost refreshing. Exciting. Invigorating. Her body felt intensely and desperately alive.

"This way, Miara," called the priestess.

She swam toward the sound of her voice, leaving the cave and emerging into the night. She paused, staring up at the canopy of the heavens overhead. The sun had given up its fight, and the moon rose now, high and glorious in the sky.

Stars sparkled above her, exquisite and delicate as diamonds in a gown, bitterly powerful for all their winking and twinkling against the darkness.

When she lowered her eyes, she could see him now, a dozen yards off, the priestess waiting patiently by his side. She had waited for this moment. Longed for it. And she would have waited a thousand lifetimes more. But she was glad it had finally come.

Heart pounding, she swam toward them. For no reason she could discern, her stomach twisted, anxious, nervous, tense.

But not afraid.

She reached out, and his hand found hers under the frigid water, rough calluses from long days and hard fights scraping her skin, making her feel alive. As he always did.

They turned to face the priestess together, side by side in the silver light, his arm brushing hers with warmth and reassurance.

It was all over now, and something else—something better—was just beginning.

About the Author

R. K. Thorne is an independent fantasy author whose addiction to notebooks, role-playing games, coffee, and red wine have resulted in this book.

She has read speculative fiction since before she was probably much too young to be doing so and encourages you to do the same.

She lives in the green hills of Pennsylvania with her family and two gray cats that may or may not pull her chariot in their spare time. If you hadn't noticed, fall is her favorite season.

For more information:
Web: rkthorne.com
Facebook: facebook.com/ThorneBooks
Pinterest: pinterest.com/rk_thorne
Twitter: @rk_thorne

Printed in Poland
by Amazon Fulfillment
Poland Sp. z o.o., Wrocław